The Harvard Bride

STORY RIVER BOOKS

Pat Conroy, Editor at Large

The Harvard Bride

∼ A MOUNTAIN BROOK NOVEL ∼

KATHERINE CLARK

The University of South Carolina Press

© 2016 University of South Carolina

Published by the University of South Carolina Press
Columbia, South Carolina 29208

www.sc.edu/uscpress

Manufactured in the United States of America

24 23 22 21 20 19 18 17 16
10 9 8 7 6 5 4 3 2 1

Library of Congress Cataloging-in-Publication Data
can be found at http://catalog.loc.gov/.

ISBN 978-1-61117-720-6 (cloth)
ISBN 978-1-61117-721-3 (ebook)

This book was printed on recycled paper with
30 percent postconsumer waste content.

Alabama
1985

Prologue

THE WEDDING

"Wasn't that the most beautiful wedding, Mother?" asked Norman Laney, hoping to divert her attention as he tried to steer the Buick away from the curb, where an infuriating little orange Karmann Ghia had pinned him in from behind, while a fat-assed white Mercedes was still taking up more than its fair share of space in front of him. Of course it was a metaphor: People in Mountain Brook thought they owned—if not the whole world—at least whatever part of it they required at any given moment. Hence the Mercedes felt entitled to make one comfortable parking place for itself where two were intended, and the Karmann Ghia felt entitled to go where no one was supposed to, just like its owner. The message to him was equally clear: He did not fit in. But he had spent almost thirty years ignoring that message, and he wasn't about to start letting it affect him now. However, he did wonder if he should go in search of the automobiles' owners.

The white Mercedes could have belonged to any number of his acquaintances, but only one person in town drove an absurd orange Karmann Ghia. Everybody knew who *that* was. And the way it was parked—jutting out over the yellow line on the corner at a cavalier thirty degree angle from the curb—was a perfect illustration of the driver's personality. Obviously he had simply veered over and hopped out without the slightest regard for the necessities or niceties of parking properly (or legally). He had dashed into the church just seconds before the bride herself had entered. This kind of behavior was apparently part of his charm, among those who found him charming. Nobody expected him to attend the wedding in the first place, and he hadn't even bothered to put his pre-addressed, pre-stamped reply card in the mail. The bride had told her mother it was just a "courtesy invitation," sent for old time's sake, and he needn't be included in the head count for the reception, because he'd never show. He rarely went to weddings and she didn't expect him to attend hers when she hadn't seen him in years. He could be crossed off the list. Then at the last minute, they'd all heard the squealing of his tires as he swerved toward an inch of (illegal) parking space, (steps away from the church), followed by the screeching of his brakes as he just barely avoided crashing into the curb or the car in front of him (which was Norman's), then the slamming of the door as he hurtled out of his car, and finally his breathless arrival just in the nick of time. The dashing entrance into the church set off ripples of amusement and murmurs of pleasantly surprised satisfaction, as if some wayward god had crash-landed in their midst after a last minute impulse to grace the occasion with his presence after all. It was maddening. Norman Laney was not among those who found either Nick Scully or his orange Karmann Ghia at all endearing. And he thought he would be well within his rights to ram the backside of his Buick into the smirk on the nose of that confounded little car.

For the sake of his mother, he tried to restrain himself, and again attempted small talk. "Wasn't that a beautiful wedding?" he repeated. But again she didn't reply. Her gaze was trained out the passenger window, where she could see the streams of well-dressed wedding guests headed to their cars, which would be whisking them away to the festivities without the delay she was being subjected to.

Well! he thought with rising fury. If she was so concerned about getting to the reception in a timely fashion, she should have skipped the ceremony altogether and remained at the country club with Delores Waters, whom they had dropped off on their way to the church. He had actually urged her to get out with Delores, and the valet under the porte cochere at the club had opened the door to help her out.

"The bride will never know the difference," Delores had helpfully reassured Norma as they drove her to the club. "You're going to say the exact same things, whether you see it for yourself or not. The church was beautiful, the ceremony was beautiful, her dress was beautiful, and she was beautiful. It won't be a lie. Because we know it all *will* be beautiful. So just come sit with me in the foyer, and we'll be the first to arrive at the reception!" Delores had giggled at her own little joke.

But his mother was as stubborn as he was and insisted on attending the ceremony. Indeed, it *had* been beautiful, and Norman was forced to concede that the Elmores had known what they were doing when they joined Independent Presbyterian instead of St. Luke's all those years ago. If church was strictly for getting married and getting buried, then Midge had shrewdly chosen on the basis of which one provided the most impressive venue. Independent Presbyterian was easily the most gorgeous church in town even without any flowers; naturally Midge had spent thousands on the florist anyway, just in case.

Norman sighed as he resumed the stop/start maneuvers and the sharp turns of the steering wheel that were supposed to deliver him from a parallel parking jam. Of course it didn't work. He was an English teacher! A guidance counselor! The headmaster of a prestigious private school! He was not a professional driver! But just when Norman decided to go in search of the disreputable young man whose vehicle had put him in such an unforgivable predicament, Nick Scully came running up out of nowhere—tie flapping behind him—hopped into the front seat of his car, and peeled off.

Gratefully Norman put his car in reverse and followed in the wake of the exhaust pouring from the Karmann Ghia's sputtering muffler.

"Nick Scully," his mother observed.

Norman grunted. As if it could be anyone else.

"I'm surprised he came to the wedding," she said.

What not only surprised but still shocked Norman was that any two parents had ever allowed their daughter to date Nick Scully in the first place. Especially in this case, since he was a full *ten years older* than that particular daughter. Nick had been twenty-six, whereas Caroline Elmore was sixteen and a junior in high school when they had met at her cousin Lena's wedding to little Julian Petsinger six years ago. Julian and Nick had been best friends in high school until the Scullys realized that their position in society could be destroyed if they allowed their son to maintain his position in society. So he was shipped off to boarding school and then somehow managed to get into Princeton, where he got a degree not only with ease, but with honors. Unfortunately, he did have brains, which made him at least seem different from the usual ne'er-do-well with a trust fund. Even more unfortunately, he also had looks, which even Norman could not deny, much as he wanted to. But wit and charm? Norman had never seen a shred of either. And there was nothing nice about his reputation.

"You know my friend Nick Scully has a date with your valedictorian tonight," little Julian had told him when he arrived at Libba's for a dinner party one night. Five years ago this was, but the imprint on his memory was indelible, so great was the shock.

Actually, at first Norman thought it was a joke. As soon as he realized it wasn't, he had put his drink down on the nearest table, left the house without a word of explanation, and walked right next door, where he could see Perry sipping a martini while he read the paper in the sunroom. When Perry spied him through the glass doors, he leaped up to invite Norman inside.

"Can't," Norman told him. "Technically I'm at a dinner party next door."

So Perry had stepped outside. Norman barely had time to ask "Is it true?" before they both heard the chugging sounds of that wretched automobile as it struggled to make its way up the long, winding driveway.

"What a beauty!" Perry had exclaimed.

Norman could not understand it. Everyone but himself was as bewitched by the damn car as by the man who drove it. Norman simply could not see it. But Perry was drawn instinctively to the scraps of orange metal, which remained shuddering at the top of the driveway as Nick hopped out.

"I can't turn the engine off," he explained with a grin. "Because I might not get it re-started. I hope Caroline is ready. I told her we wouldn't have long with the car in park."

As if on cue, Caroline emerged from the house, with her mother trailing close behind.

Norman was disgusted. And flabbergasted. He had grown up in Pratt City, where a girl Caroline's age might already have two children, without benefit of either husband or high school diploma. And yet if Caroline had been *his* daughter, he would have insisted that any young man whose car couldn't wait while he rang the doorbell wasn't good enough for that daughter, who better remain upstairs for FIVE SOLID MINUTES after the doorbell rang before walking SLOWLY down the stairs, not rushing outside right into the guy's lap. What on earth were Midge and Perry thinking?

Midge was obviously not thinking, just beaming with pride. She appeared prouder of her daughter than he'd ever seen her before. The girl was a valedictorian, headed for Harvard, so Midge had every reason to be concerned about her future, having been brought up to believe that the one thing men most despised, deplored and feared in a woman was intelligence. Whatever intelligence Midge may have possessed herself had clearly either been squashed or atrophied from disuse. And as with any Southern woman of a certain generation, there was always the possibility that decades of playing dumb had in fact made her dumb. At any rate, this evidence of her daughter's desirability and marriageability was thrilling to Midge. Meanwhile Perry was busy peering into the car.

"What's that on the dashboard?"

"Oh!" Nick exclaimed. "Thanks for reminding me!"

Leaning through an open window, he struck a match and lit what turned out to be a candle affixed with wax to a teacup saucer balanced precariously on the dashboard near the steering wheel.

"My headlight!" he proclaimed.

The laugh he gave reminded Norman of the kind of cackle you might hear in a state insane asylum. Just then a violent spasm seized the car, which jerked and rattled as if in its death throes. Quickly Nick opened the driver's side door and slid inside in one seamless move which appeared to be a practiced maneuver.

"Hop in!" he called out cheerfully to Caroline, who obeyed with alacrity.

"I don't think your seatbelt works," Norman could hear him telling her as he pumped the pedal in a futile effort to calm the car's engine.

Somebody had to say something, and since Midge and Perry both appeared bereft of any brain matter whatsoever, Norman stepped forward.

"This young woman better be safe in your care!" he declared. "She's giving a speech to her graduating class in two weeks!"

"Don't worry," Nick called out as the car shot suddenly forward. "I'll have her back by then!"

"We'll be lucky if she's just pregnant and drug-addicted, rather than dead," Norman told her parents as the car sputtered down the driveway. "*If we ever see her again at all, dead or alive.*"

"It's her very first date," Midge offered by way of explanation.

"Let's hope it's not her last," Norman retorted.

"He's a Scully," Midge noted, as if the family's wealth and social prominence would insulate them and anyone in their sphere from danger or harm.

This was what Norman privately called "The Mind of Mountain Brook," his own variation on W.J. Cash's "Mind of the South." In The Mind of Mountain Brook, money and status were magical forces which conferred complete protection on those who possessed them. There was a large body of evidence contradicting this mindset, including smashed mailboxes, broken bones, wrecked BMWs that were otherwise brand-new, along with lives that were prematurely crippled, ruined or even terminated. But The Mind of Mountain Brook was not equipped to process information that challenged its foundation, so it never budged from the conviction that it was on top of the world—as it was on top of Red Mountain and Shades Mountain—where nothing from the valley of evil—where the black people lived and the steel mills rose in the distance—could ever reach it and knock it off its perch.

However, Norman would have thought that at least Perry, with his functioning intelligence, might have objected to his daughter's date with such an accomplished good-for-nothing as Nick Scully. But Perry only winked and said, "In my day, I was much worse." So in his own way, Perry had The Mind of Mountain Brook as well. Norman had simply stood there, appalled. Perry no doubt intended to reassure him when he added, "Don't worry. He takes her out all the time in that car."

"All the time?" Norman echoed, stricken.

"Since last summer." Perry started back toward the house.

Norman remained rooted to his spot, unable to move or process the information he'd just received. "How did I not know? Why did no one tell me?"

Perry stopped, turned around to look at Norman's frozen bulk of several hundred pounds, and shrugged with amusement. "This is the first time he's taken her out at night, so Midge wants to call it a date. But it's just friendship, Norman. I wouldn't have allowed it otherwise. From what I hear, Nick Scully has plenty of girlfriends his own age."

"This town is full of Nick Scully's ex-girlfriends, his current girlfriends, and his future girlfriends!" Norman boomed.

"My daughter doesn't belong in any of those categories." Perry winked at him.

"She doesn't belong in that car with him no matter what you want to call it!"

Norman could only shake his head as he walked back next door, wondering how on earth a candle in a teacup saucer could serve as a headlight or be mistaken for charm. Halfway back, an image of that teacup saucer popped into his head and stopped him dead in his tracks. That wasn't just any saucer. It was a piece of the family's heirloom china, a pre-Civil War blue on white Davenport pattern from Staffordshire, England, manufactured for W. & E. Smith importers in Mobile in the 1840s. It belonged in a museum, all twelve place settings, down to *the very last teacup saucer.* He had begged and pleaded with the Scullys to donate the whole collection. They had agreed to look into it. They never did. So Norman had looked into it for them. Just as he suspected, the Smithsonian jumped at the chance for such a valuable acquisition. But when they contacted the Scullys, it was like the Civil War all over again. From the way Evelyn Scully went on about it all over town, you'd have thought the Yankees were coming down to steal Confederate silver and china, just like a hundred years ago. At least she did have the decency to apologize, next time she saw him, and tell him she'd changed her mind. She had promised to keep all the china safe. And yet there was one of the saucers on the dashboard of her disgraceful son's disgraceful automobile. That's not what Norman called keeping anything safe. Nothing was safe around Nick Scully.

The teacup saucer didn't belong in that car with Nick any more than the girl did. Both were priceless and irreplaceable, and if anything happened to either one, there were several people who would not survive Norman Laney's fury.

As Norman drove his mother to the wedding reception, the memory of that evening five years ago, along with the mere thought of Nick Scully, had the surprising effect of calming him down instead of irritating him as it usually did. If Caroline *had* to get married, at least she had ended up with the complete opposite of an idle rich bum like Nick Scully. Her groom was an ambitious young man of purpose and determination who had come out of nowhere all on his own steam to take the world by storm: Class Day speaker for the Harvard Class of 1982; first in his class at Alabama Law School. He had a fine head of dark, wavy hair, with flashing dark eyes and strong dark brows, and he liked shaking your hand and looking you firmly in the eye. He had already shown what he was made of by working for the candidate who'd come within a hair's breadth of defeating George Wallace in the last gubernatorial election. Recently he had joined a top Birmingham law firm. Clearly, the world would hear more from this young man. Still, Norman did not believe yet in this marriage, coming so soon, just a month after the bride's graduation. Norman wanted to see *her* accomplishments, and had fully expected to see a glimmer of these before she even dreamed of getting married. His mother had warned him to keep his big mouth shut since everyone else thought it such a beautiful love story: two Alabamians finding each other at Harvard, falling in love, staying in love despite three years apart while she finished college and he went to law school back home. A golden couple, they seemed fated for each other and a bright, happy future together.

As a devotee of gossip and soap operas, Norman did not believe in golden couples or bright, happy futures. But he did believe that a young woman who had just become a Harvard graduate could have taken a little more time before becoming a bride. She had arrived late into an unlooked-for beauty which had blossomed miraculously during her stressful freshman year a thousand miles away from home. Before meeting the man she married today, she had never dated anyone, not counting Nick Scully, whom Norman didn't want to count and didn't think he had to, as everyone had always assured him Nick was not dating this little bookworm who was ten years younger and not much to look at. Going about with a teenage girl was just one of the many irresponsible, eccentric, unaccountable diversions that he pursued as much to shock others as to amuse himself. And since he was the only guy who'd ever shown any interest in her whatsoever, her parents had taken leave of their senses and let him take her places in that car of his. Then in college, out of her cocoon, an unexpected butterfly, she went for the first guy who ever looked at her as a woman.

"What's wrong with that, if they love each other?" his mother demanded.

Unaware that he had spoken his thoughts, he was startled by her voice.

"She has to marry someone eventually," his mother went on.

"Eventually is the point, Mother. It just seems too soon."

"They've known each other for years."

"But she's only twenty-one!"

His mother sighed. "We've been over this a hundred times. I know how you feel about her. But she is not your daughter, and it would behoove you to stop acting like the father who can't bear to give her up. You'll only make a fool of yourself, as usual."

No matter what she said, it was still too soon. And too easy. Life was not so easy, and love certainly wasn't either. There were no beautiful love stories, only messy ones. And besides, this bride had gone away to make a different life for herself from the one she was born into, yet here she was, of her own free will, coming back to the world she had deliberately left behind, stepping right into that life she had wanted to escape. He had tried to be happy about it, but he didn't understand it. Sex, he supposed, was the answer to the riddle. Sex got everyone in the end, except for him. As far as he could tell, he was much better for it.

* * *

When the bride entered the entrance hall of the country club, she was surprised to see Mrs. Delores Waters deeply ensconced in one of the large armchairs as if she'd been sitting there for hours. Caroline had hoped to be the first one to arrive at her own wedding reception, if only so she could go use the bathroom before the party really started. She had certainly been the first one out of the church after the ceremony, and the limousine had been waiting at the curb to whisk her and the groom straight to the club as planned. But here was Mrs. Waters, who'd beaten the bride by such a margin she'd even had time to *fall asleep* while waiting. How had Mrs. Waters—old, fat, slow and half-crippled by a bad hip—managed to be the first to arrive? It was almost as if—*she had not even attended the wedding.* But of course. Why would she, poor old dear?

"Mrs. Waters?"

The old lady's eyes popped open.

"You were so beautiful," she said. "Just radiant as you walked down the aisle. And the flowers were like nothing I've ever seen before. The church was so pretty and your dress was lovely. It was the most gorgeous wedding I've ever been to."

The bride had been prepared to receive all sorts of perfunctory congratulations. But she had not been expecting outright lies from someone who had once been her social studies teacher, and until her retirement two years ago, had been in charge of the Honor Council which adjudicated all Honor Code violations, such as students lying to teachers. What was she to make of a teacher now lying to a student? With a sudden jolt, the bride remembered she was no longer a student, and Mrs. Waters was not her teacher or anybody's teacher now. They were both just two adults interacting in the grown-up world, where people lied to each other all the time, and there was no Honor Council.

"Thank you," said the bride, with the uncomfortable knowledge that she was an accessory to a lie, perhaps even an accomplice.

Why didn't Mrs. Waters just tell the truth? the bride wondered. Especially because it was so much more compelling than those empty compliments. "My eyesight is so bad, I could not have appreciated the ceremony." Or "Sitting in a hard church pew hurts my hip." "I can't stand the heat of July even for five minutes. But I didn't want to miss seeing you on your wedding day." The truth would have been so much better than those stupid lies otherwise known as good manners. But perhaps, the bride thought sadly, it wasn't true that Mrs. Waters wanted to see her on her wedding day. Maybe she just wanted to see all her friends and former colleagues, and enjoy a good party. What made this all the more sad was that Caroline had always liked Mrs. Waters and had been genuinely glad—if surprised—to see her sitting in the entrance hall. It was disturbing to suspect now that all the affirmation and praise she'd received from Mrs. Waters in the classrooms and corridors of school had merely been another form of routine and hollow courtesy.

"Honey, can you help me up?" The old lady extended her arms from the depths of the chair which enveloped her.

The bride looked around for her groom, who was not standing by her side ready to offer his assistance. Where was he? She peered behind her, but there was no sign of him under the porte cochere, where they'd been dropped off by the limousine driver. No doubt he was talking to someone—anyone—he had never met before. He never met a stranger he didn't want to convert into a friend, and he wouldn't stop trying—or talking—until some point of mutual connection had been established. This was one of his most appealing characteristics. It was also one of his most annoying characteristics.

Sometimes—like on their wedding day—she just wanted him to be with her, by her side. But unfortunately, strangers were usually more interesting to him than loved ones. As unconquered territory, strangers were conquests just waiting to be made and enjoyed. Caroline loved this about him, except on her wedding day. His need to connect with everyone he encountered came from a powerful desire to people his life with multitudes, as if he were nothing but the sum of his friends and acquaintances. Everybody loved him for this, not just his bride. In contrast, Caroline herself was a hopeless introvert, headed for life as a recluse, as defined by Emily Dickinson. *The Soul selects her own Society, then Shuts the Door.* Aloof, stuck-up and haughty is what this was usually called, although it was not a fair description of her response to other people. A lifetime of failing to connect with others, starting with her mother, had taught her to hold herself back and keep herself apart, lest she be hurt or rejected by those like her mother, who were prepared to let her know in the most cruel ways that they didn't like her any better than they understood her. Besides her four-hundred-pound high school English teacher, Norman Laney, the only one who'd ever truly prized her was the one she'd married today.

Caroline managed to pull Mrs. Waters out of her chair, and after handing the old lady her cane, excused herself and hurried down the corridor lined with portraits of past club presidents, whose august masculine countenances seemed to be frowning at her lack of bridal decorum as she rushed by. Waving breezily to a cloakroom attendant she didn't recognize, she pushed through the heavy door of the ladies room and prayed for a few moments of solitude. It was never easy to know if you were alone in this particular restroom, because each of the three cubicles was like a padded cell, with foam filling underneath the silky fabric on the walls, within which an equally luxurious toilet was enthroned on a platform. The doors had louvered slats letting in a little light, but you couldn't really see in or out. Once inside, you felt like a queen of your own little world.

Growing up, the bride used to think that the entire town where she lived was like one of the padded cells in the ladies room at the Birmingham Country Club. It could even be said that she had not grown up in a city or town at all, but at this country club. It was one of the two poles of her seasonal existence. In autumn and winter, she went to school, while in spring and summer, she went to the club, where she spent her days splashing in the pool, playing tennis on the courts, and eating lunch on the covered terrace. It appeared that this was supposed to be not only her entire world, but also her entire life, first as a child, then as a grown woman with children of her own.

Even as a young girl, she had instinctively known that there had to be more to life than that, and she'd been determined to find out what it was.

Yet she had fond memories of the peaceful sanctuary to be found in this particular ladies room. On one occasion soon after obtaining her driver's license, she had driven herself over to the club just to go to this ladies room. In the privacy and silken silence of one of the padded stalls, she was going to figure out a better way than the one her mother had given her to deal with the curse of womanhood. In her mother's method of feminine hygiene, the belt, straps and clips that secured a thick absorbency pad resembled a chastity belt or torture instrument and comprised a serious bandage suggesting a crippling wound afflicting womankind. If the original condition did not incapacitate its victim, then this system designed to treat it certainly would. She knew there had to be a better way.

Thanks again to her car and driver's license, she had finally been able to procure a box of the product she had studied for three long years in the *Seventeen* magazine advertisements. But after two hours spent in that stall, scrutinizing the diagram, she could not figure out where she was supposed to place this product. Although she understood the pictures of the female anatomy perfectly well, and the arrows were quite explicit, she could not believe that she was supposed to put her fingers or place any item *there*. That just could not be. Nothing was supposed to go near there. Certainly not a foreign object or anyone's hands, including her own.

The written instructions were equally baffling. Insert? Insert where? For long, agonizing minutes which turned into hours, she pored over the little instruction pamphlet until it was torn and frayed. She wished she could go ask that plump black woman who was the cloakroom attendant during the weekdays. No doubt she could help her interpret the otherwise inscrutable diagram and directions. Her own mother was of course useless. Either she wouldn't know or wouldn't tell her. The list of things for which her mother had failed to provide guidance or assistance was long.

When her watch showed it was 5:30 and time to be home, she became desperate. She also became angry at the mother she would go home to, but could not go to for help. Why had that little voice inside warned that her mother would not approve of the product she now held in her hand? It was then she had her earth-shattering epiphany: the product *was* supposed to go THERE. But did she dare? It would be an act of courage and defiance such as she'd never yet performed. But she knew she had to do it. This is why she had come, and time was running out.

Hurriedly she tore the wrapping off the product and positioned it just as the diagram indicated. Summoning all that anger and desperation she'd experienced a moment before, along with her reservoir of courage and defiance, she plunged the product THERE. It didn't go in. And it hurt. But as she withdrew her hand, the product remained behind. She knew she was on the right track. Instead of plunging this next time, she twisted and wriggled it until finally, it went where she knew her mother did not want anything to go. When she emerged from the padded cubicle, she felt like a changed and different person. Certainly she was no longer a virgin. And this was just the beginning, she promised herself.

Now, a mere five years later, she was emerging from one of those cubicles as a bride. Although this was exactly what her mother had always wanted her to become, Caroline was certain this was her own self-determined step on her own individual path. She was doing this for herself, not for her mother. And marriage didn't have to be the trap she had always feared from observing her parents and their friends, who had all grown up together, attended Bama together, pledged sororities and fraternities together, then married each other as the grand finale in the script they had all been handed and done their best to follow. But the real ending had not been happy ever after for many of them, try as they did to pretend otherwise.

As a girl she had declared that she was never getting married, confident that this renunciation would spare her the same fate as the women who spent their lives watching children in the country club pool. If this was a boring way to spend summer as a child, what would it be as a *life* for a grownup? She vowed this would never be *her* life. But over the years, of course, she came to understand that marriage itself wasn't the problem. The problem was the groupthink of a provincial Southern society that believed it could shape human destinies to follow a simple, uncomplicated and straightforward narrative that could have come from a child's storyboard picture book, circa 1950, in which the girls all looked like girls were supposed to look, with bows in their hair and on their dresses; the boys all looked like little gentlemen, with carefully parted hair; everyone did what was expected of them and lived happily ever after. Those who couldn't keep their failures to conform to this approved plotline to themselves were either pitied or scorned, depending on the severity and notoriety of their transgressions. Although Caroline's mother had been raised on this picture book and imposed it on her children, over time the cardboard pages had become battered and frayed; Magic Marker scrawls defaced many of the boys and girls. In the meantime, better narratives had surfaced that presented a more honest reflection of life's complex realities.

Different faces and radically altered storylines had gained acceptance as it became clear that no one could truly conform to the rose-colored scenario depicted in that picture book from a naïve era.

The young man Caroline had married today was one of those refreshingly different faces, though his was as handsome as any she'd ever seen. He had grown up poor, in a small town, where he had not spent his summers on the tennis courts of a country club, but bagging groceries at the Winn-Dixie. The hardships of his background had either lit a fire inside him, or failed to quench what was already burning brightly within. The young man she'd met in college harbored a flame of nobility that had nothing to do with social class and everything to do with the ideals that animated his being and made his eyes flash like beacons. He was headed for great deeds whose value would be measured by what they did for others, not for himself. Although he came from a different background, they had embarked on the same journey that first led away from Alabama, then back. They had come together because they shared the same drives and goals which had put them on the same path of exile and return. The storyline of their life together would earn its happy ending, she thought, because they had chosen each other wisely and well; and by surviving a three year separation, their love had proven itself already. With a happy heart, if not with her groom, who was still nowhere to be seen, she headed for the reception, ready to receive all congratulations, perfunctory or otherwise.

* * *

The little old lady hobbling unsteadily with her cane toward the men's grill looked vaguely familiar.

"Mrs. Waters?" he ventured.

She stopped in her tracks, turned around and peered at him through the film of rheumy eyes.

"I remember you," she said accusingly.

"You couldn't possibly," he challenged.

"You're that wicked Scully boy," she said.

"So you do remember!" he beamed proudly.

"How could I forget?" she said, merriment crinkling the corners of her eyes. "Every time my back was turned, the erasers started flying across the room. *And you started it every time!*" She wagged a finger playfully in the direction of his bellybutton.

"Oh, come on," he cajoled. "I wasn't all that bad."

"You turned out about like we all predicted," she told him. "It's a mercy you weren't the one at the altar today."

15

Hooting with laughter, he slipped his arm through hers and steered her away from the men's grill. "So what's your opinion of the one who *was* at the altar today? Is he good enough?"

"I haven't seen him," she replied.

"What?" he cried, in mock astonishment. "Weren't you at the wedding like everybody else?"

"I mean I haven't met him," she corrected herself. "Have you?"

"Not yet," he said. "And we seem to be the only ones here, so we can't introduce ourselves now. Meanwhile, where can I take you?" He bent down to hear her reply.

"Usually by this hour," she said primly, "I have acquired a bit of a thirst."

He hooted again with laughter.

"Same with me," he said, as they approached a bar set up in one of the card rooms. "What can I get you, Mrs. Waters? A Coke? Perrier?" He winked at the bartender.

"Wicked boy," she said. "I'll have a gin and tonic with Bombay gin and a twist of lemon," she told the bartender.

As the first wave of guests entered the country club, they could hear Nick Scully's full-throated laughter rippling through every room.

* * *

The bride's grandmother was positive that the limousine hired to take her, her husband and daughter Shirley to the club was not at the place on the curb where Midge had assured her it would be. They had walked almost an entire block from the church in the stifling July heat before they found it. The whole point of a limousine, it seemed to her, was to be spared the walk, the heat, the confusion and uncertainty. The limousine should be *right there,* where she could step right into it, with her dignity and freshly fixed hair intact. The driver should have been standing by the curb, waiting to greet them and open the door. Instead, they'd had to tap on the window to rouse him: a white boy, a teenager by the looks of him, who didn't know his manners any better than he knew his job. She'd been expecting a proper chauffeur, an older black man full of deference and politeness. This is what she thought she'd paid for. But the world wasn't what it used to be, and the way her life had turned out, she rarely got anything she was paying for, and very little of what she wanted. The blast of the limousine's air-conditioner ruined what was left of her hair; she was sure of it.

"Mama, this isn't right," her daughter muttered as they settled into their seats. "We'll call on Monday and ask for a refund."

Mrs. Lambert nodded. Her daughter was right. Her husband, on the other hand, was useless as always. Instead of demanding what he'd paid for, he seemed to think his job was to make friends with the driver, who was young enough to be his grandson, had a face full of pimples and wires hanging out of his ears, which were plugged and couldn't hear a word Jim was saying. It was hard to believe Jim had ever worked for the FBI, because he couldn't even see what was right in front of him, plain as day.

"It was a beautiful ceremony," Shirley observed to her mother, as Jim continued to make one-sided small talk with the driver, who so far had not said a word. "But what did you think of the *dress?*"

Mrs. Lambert didn't know what to say. The dress had been a surprise; she wasn't yet sure it was a disappointment. But it had come from a fancy shop in Boston and cost more than her son-in-law wanted to pay. Midge had asked her mother for half, and Mrs. Lambert had obliged with a check. So she had expected something other than what looked like a lacy white nightgown. Usually, Birmingham brides looked like old-fashioned Southern belles in hoopskirted gowns. Obviously Boston would have different ideas from Birmingham, but still Mrs. Lambert had expected a full skirt, a long train, netting and seed pearls, maybe. At any rate, yards and yards of material. More money should buy more, not less, shouldn't it? However, Mrs. Lambert had never been able to refuse or quarrel with anything her granddaughter wanted. And if this is the dress she wanted, then Mrs. Lambert could not find it in herself to object. After her granddaughter went away to college like that, Mrs. Lambert had never expected to see much of her again, and certainly not at the church door. After thinking they'd lost her for good, she was simply grateful that her granddaughter had returned, in whatever dress she wanted.

The sun had been setting just as she appeared at the church door on her father's arm. The golden aura surrounding them had played optical tricks with Mrs. Lambert's vision, and for a moment she thought she was seeing the little girl who used to spend the night at her house in her little white nightgown. It was her beautiful little granddaughter standing there. Who could find any fault with that? Not Mrs. Lambert. She'd almost choked from the lump in her throat, and her eyes watered with tears that couldn't all be squeezed back.

Shirley leaned over and patted her hand. "Caroline was just beautiful, Mama," she said. "And the dress was *unique*. I'll bet they write it up in the newspaper."

Mrs. Lambert nodded; she had not thought of that. Perhaps in a way then, more money would end up buying more after all. But she was beginning to suspect that her daughter had deliberately misled her about the location of the limousine, which had been parked so much farther away than expected *because Midge wanted to delay their arrival at the country club.* Her

17

married daughter had done so well for herself that she turned up her nose at her own mother, who was always treated as if she was not good enough, though her money worked as well as anybody else's.

The fact that she didn't have as much as others was not her own fault. When she had first met her husband decades ago, everybody told her how lucky she was to be the object of his attentions. Jim had just graduated from law school when she was introduced to him during her debutante season. He was the tallest, most handsome of all the escorts, and an excellent dancer. Everybody said how distinguished he was. She was the prettiest girl of her year, so it only seemed right for him to seek her company above all others. It was considered a perfect match, and when he proposed that fall after her debut, she accepted him with delight.

But she thought she was marrying an attorney. How was she to know he was planning to join the FBI? Later he claimed he'd always told her he wanted to join the force. That's not what she'd heard. The firm, he had said. He wanted to join the firm. The *law firm*. Why did he think she'd marry an attorney if he wasn't going to join the firm? "What firm?" he had said. "I never mentioned any firm," he claimed. "I said *the force*." This quarrel had started early and lasted their entire married life. It had never been resolved, and she had never forgiven him for the way he'd deceived her and robbed her of the chance to live the life she expected and deserved.

Instead, he had dragged her off to New Orleans, of all places, where they did things different and she didn't know a single soul. She didn't see why people made such a fuss over New Orleans, and hated every minute of it. As if that weren't bad enough, Jim didn't even have a proper office job. He was a *field agent*. Besides the embarrassment, he was gone all the time, leaving her alone in a foreign city she didn't know and didn't like. What was she supposed to do all day by herself in a town where most people didn't even know she was there, and *nobody* knew who she was? It was clear to her they had no future there; she couldn't see any possible way they would ever acquire a position in that strange society. In New Orleans, she was nobody; in Birmingham, she would have been somebody.

But Jim loved his work a lot more than he ever loved her. She didn't understand it. He'd be gone for months on cases, and instead of making him angry or upset, it made him happy. The worst case took him into the bayou country outside Lafayette, where he had to live in a fishing camp like a swamp rat. The FBI believed that some lowlife named Frankie Jonfreau, one of their ten most wanted criminals, had returned to hide out in his native territory.

For six months, Jim, the hero, had posed as a humble, uneducated fisherman in a camp right next to the one where the suspect was living. For one whole month he did nothing but fish all day and wave every once in a while to his neighbor, who might or might not be one of the FBI's ten most wanted criminals. After six weeks of being next door, he went to go ask for some help with his skiff one day. He let another two weeks go by before he returned with a bottle of whiskey as thanks. Then a few days later, the neighbor suggested they go out together. They took to fishing side by side sitting on the banks of the bayou, sipping whiskey. Jim started wearing a wire then, which he was always afraid would show up under his clothes if he sweated too much.

He never asked any questions. They talked about fishing. They told stories. Jim had made up a whole different past for himself, growing up Cajun in Louisiana, learning how to make a living from fishing as soon as he could help on the boat with his father and uncles. He let this come out a little at a time. And gradually, over the course of another month, Jim learned bits and pieces from his neighbor that all fit what he knew of Frankie Jonfreau. One day he heard something that made him sure the man next door was Jonfreau. He waited three whole days before he went into town to telephone his report. Now they needed the evidence linking the man to his crimes. So about a week later, Jim confessed to his neighbor that he was in trouble with the law and there was a warrant out for him. His neighbor gave advice on how to avoid the authorities. Jim began to pretend that he admired his neighbor, and looked up to him for guidance and wisdom. Eventually his neighbor bragged that he was in trouble with the law himself, and told Jim what he'd done.

The FBI had what they wanted. Before dawn one morning, they encircled the fishing camp with agents. But it was Jim who took the handcuffs over and quietly arrested his neighbor.

As much as Jim loved living like a swamp rat and catching one of the FBI's most wanted criminals, she'd been miserable, all alone with no friends and no life in a strange city. When their first child was born, she'd insisted he take the job that opened up in the Birmingham office.

By the time they got back, however, it was too late. The world seemed to have passed her by. The circles that had formed in her absence—the Garden Club and the bridge groups—treated her more like a newcomer and out-of-towner than someone they had known all their lives. But the main trouble was—Jim didn't make enough money. They couldn't keep up. The husbands of her friends were all doctors, lawyers, or insurance executives. They could afford to join the country club. The Lamberts couldn't. Not only were they left out of a lot that went on, since much of it happened at the country club, but their inability to join marked them permanently as social inferiors. At first Barbara Lambert tried to overcome these handicaps by being the most superlative hostess in her set, the one who always offered to entertain, and produced the most impressive displays of silver, crystal and china, along with the most lavish spreads of food and drink. But soon her house itself became the problem. They couldn't afford to sell the small place they had for one bigger and better, as all her friends were doing, nor could they afford the latest appliances and new furnishings in all the latest styles. Barbara Lambert realized she couldn't be a hostess any longer, and eventually dropped out of her Garden Club and bridge group altogether. She couldn't bear for her friends to realize that she never even got a dishwasher.

Then later, all that trouble started with the blacks in Birmingham and the Jews coming down from the North. The FBI was involved, which meant Jim was too. Although it was the FBI's job to stop all the trouble being caused by the blacks and the Jews, people just didn't want to have to think about the things that went on downtown. It was her bad luck to be associated with all that in any way. She felt tainted by it, and knew her friends regarded her with distaste. Barbara got to the point she didn't even want to go out to the grocery store. In every way her husband had failed her. His perverse choice of career had provided neither the income nor the social status she needed in order to make a success of her own life.

Her daughter Midge's success, along with the four beautiful grandchildren, somewhat redeemed her sense of failure. But then Midge started treating her like her friends had: as if her house was some kind of disgrace, and it was a real shame they didn't belong to the country club. Midge had the husband, the house and the social life she'd always wanted. Instead of being thanked or respected for helping her daughter achieve this success, Mrs. Lambert was disdained and kept under wraps as an embarrassment.

This business with the limousine was just the latest in a long list of humiliations she had suffered from her daughter over the years. Not only had she been forced to walk in the heat of July and ruin her hair, but by the time she arrived at the club for the reception, she was swallowed by the growing crowd. She was not given a priority arrival because Midge *didn't want her to be noticed.* Her daughter would have been happier for her mother not to be there at all, to completely eliminate the risk that anyone would see her and know that was Midge's mother. There was no one to welcome them, no one to escort them through the throngs of people and guide them to a bar or help them get a drink.

"Get me a bourbon and water," she told her husband. To her daughter Shirley, she said, "Let's go out on the terrace and have a cigarette."

* * *

Ina pointed to the line of automobiles where her daughter's car now formed the tail end.

"Rusty," she said. "I think we're supposed to go up there. Shaye said for us to follow her."

"Nah," he said, as he pulled into the first parking spot he came to, right past the entrance.

"Look," she said, pointing. "Everybody's waiting in that line. Maybe we need to show our invitation and get a ticket to get in."

Rusty didn't reply as he took the keys out of the ignition and got out of the car. Ina remained seated as panic began fluttering in her chest. The only people walking through the parking lot were young men, all wearing black pants and white shirts. There were no wedding guests in sight, except for way up yonder where they were all getting out under what looked to her like the biggest carport she'd ever seen. Rusty seemed so sure of himself, but Ina did not think they were where they were supposed to be or doing what they were supposed to do. They were supposed to be in their car, behind Shaye and Bobby's car, waiting in that line of cars. Ina's determination to do the right thing, to follow her daughter's explicit instructions, kept her rooted to her seat in the car.

"Come on, Hon," Rusty said, shutting his door.

How could he be so sure of himself? He'd never been to Birmingham before any more than she had. Neither one of them had been farther north than Montgomery in their entire lives until now. They didn't know what they were doing, and for Shaye's sake, she did not want to make any mistakes. She did not want to be the cause of embarrassment to Shaye, her grandson, or the family her grandson was marrying into.

"Come on, Ina," Rusty urged. He was opening her door and reaching in to pull her out.

"Hon, I got a feeling this ain't right," she said.

"Nah," he said, grasping her firmly by the forearm. "Ain't a crime to park your own car."

Standing up, Ina gazed in shock over the rows and rows of parked cars toward the line of automobiles which contained her daughter and son-in-law.

"You reckon that's all it is, Rusty? All them cars waiting all this time just for somebody else to park for 'em?" She shook her head. "That can't be right,

Rusty. I don't think you know what you're talking about. That's the craziest thing I ever heard."

"Let's go, Ina." He tugged on her elbow and set off without her.

She followed reluctantly. She'd already made one mistake—with her dress—and was determined not to make another. The trouble was, she didn't know enough to understand right from wrong in this situation. Shaye had told her it was going to be a formal wedding. So her daughter Peg had taken her to Gayfer's Department Store in Mobile to get a formal. It was the first time in her life she'd ever needed a long dress, but she wanted to do things right for Shaye and this fancy wedding. The rental wear shop had not had a powder blue suit for Rusty that would match the color of her new dress, so they'd had to settle for navy. She was afraid that would not sit right with Shaye, but it was the dress that made Shaye purse her lips.

"It's all right, isn't it?" she had asked her daughter anxiously in the Birmingham motel room.

"It'll have to do," her daughter said. "It's too late, now, anyway."

It turned out Ina was the only one at the wedding wearing a long dress. She was certain Shaye had said formal, and didn't see how she'd made her mistake, unless she'd misheard somehow.

Hurrying to catch up with Rusty, she almost bumped right into one of those young men as he emerged from the front seat of a car. He peered at her closely, and for a second she thought she might faint. Then she remembered that their invitation was in her pocketbook, so if he asked she could produce it to prove they were entitled to be there.

"You all right, ma'am?" he asked, smiling, real friendly.

"Fine, thank you." She managed a smile of her own, and hoped her dentures didn't click too loud.

"Hurry up, Hon," Rusty called back.

But then she noticed her daughter waving at her and felt compelled to walk over to their car. Her son-in-law Bobby rolled down the window, and she could see Shaye gesticulating in the seat beside him, but couldn't make out what she was saying over the noise of the air conditioner going at full blast. The trembling in her chest started up again. Nothing in her life had made her so nervous as this wedding, not even her breast cancer ten years ago. She wished it was over and she was back at the motel. Actually, she wished she was back home. She hadn't wanted to come, had offered not to come and then almost refused to come. But Shaye had insisted.

"Wait for us right outside that door." Bobby pointed toward the large covered walkway, where two palatial doors led into the building beyond. "We'll go in together."

She nodded as he rolled up the window. Now where was Rusty? When she reached the spot where Bobby had pointed, there was no sign of her husband. She had to find him right quick, before Shaye and Bobby got out of their car. But he wasn't anywhere to be seen along the entire length of the walkway, which came to a stop at a little enclosure where all the young men sprang from whenever a new vehicle reached the front of the line. What in the world had become of her husband?

"Can I help you, ma'am?" One of the young men popped suddenly in front of her, startling her so badly he nearly knocked her down from the fright.

"No, thank you," she said. "I'm just trying to find where my husband has got to."

"A wandering husband." He smiled at her.

Not knowing what to say, she stood there politely, waiting for him to move on so she could continue her search. The panicky feeling returned; time was running out.

The young man didn't leave. "Could your husband be that gentleman over there, on the putting green?" He pointed.

Putting green? What did he mean by that? She didn't see anything.

"Come with me." The young man took her arm. "I'll show you."

Glancing behind her, where she saw no sign of Bobby or Shaye, she allowed the young man to lead her away.

"You don't need me at all," he observed admiringly. "You're very steady on your feet. Most of the ladies cling to me like a crutch."

Steady? If he could have seen her insides, he would have known that her nerves were anything but steady.

"Is that your husband?" He pointed.

Yes, that was Rusty, standing on a little patch of lawn studded with brightly colored flags.

"Is he supposed to be standing there?" she asked in alarm.

"It's fine when no one is practicing," he assured her. "Everybody stands there to enjoy the view." He let go of her arm. "Have a nice evening," he said as he turned and left.

When she reached him, Rusty was gazing down at the sweep of gently rolling hills that dipped and rose on into the distance, as far as they could see.

"Don't get a sight like this every day," he remarked. "Not where we live anyway, flat as it is."

"Shaye and Bobby will be waiting," she said. "They pointed out where we was to meet."

"I never seen this much green grass that wasn't pasture," he observed.

"Ain't it pretty," she said.

"Ain't it a waste," he said. "Who you reckon keeps it cut like this?"

"Mamaw!" Shaye was upon them, breathless and reproachful, using the grandchildren's name for her like she always did whenever her mother was guilty of being a stupid old woman.

"I was just coming to get him," Ina explained to her daughter.

"Why didn't you follow me in the car like I told y'all to?"

"I tried, Shaye. I tried telling him. But you know how he gets. You can't tell him nothing when he takes a notion in his head to do things his own way. I hope we didn't embarrass you none."

"Embarrass me? You didn't embarrass me. I'm just sorry Papaw made you walk through that whole parking lot in all that heat."

Ina stared at her daughter. Sometimes she thought they were speaking two different languages. First, there was the mistake about the formal; now Shaye was saying something about being out in the heat, which is how Ina spent most of her days back home, tending to her vegetable garden. Ina didn't understand it.

"Lot hotter back home," she said. "This ain't no heat."

"Well, anyway," said Shaye. "Let's get inside where it's cool and the party's starting."

Personally, Ina preferred being outdoors, even back home where it was hotter. Folks in Birmingham put the air on way too high for her liking, and she didn't even want to imagine the cost. But they had come here for the wedding reception, so they might as well go in and get it over with. This was the last night they needed to get through. They'd be on the road back home tomorrow before dawn.

But when Ina and her daughter reached the covered entranceway leading to the front doors of the club, they realized the men had stayed behind.

"Rusty can't get over all that grass," she told her daughter. "Mighty big front lawn they got."

"Mama!" her daughter clutched her arm and whispered fiercely. "*That's not a lawn!*"

"It ain't a lawn? What is it, then?"

"*It's a golf course!*" Shaye hissed.

"A golf course?"

"Sh! Mama!" Shaye looked around to see if any of the guests emerging from cars or milling before the entrance had overheard her mother.

Ina sighed. Try as she had, she had somehow made another mistake and embarrassed her daughter again, though she wasn't sure what was wrong with what she'd said. The best thing to do from here on out, she decided, was stick by her daughter's side the whole evening and keep her mouth shut.

* * *

Like everybody else, Hunter DuPont had heard all his life about Southern belles. It was the main reason he'd wanted to come down for this wedding to a part of the country he'd otherwise never have any reason to see. He was curious. Did they really have something that the girls he'd grown up with didn't have? Other than the accent, of course, which didn't do as much for him as it did for others. There were Southerners at Harvard—several had lived in Eliot House when he was there—and whenever he heard that accent it just grated on him, made him wonder what those people were doing here where they clearly didn't belong or fit in. The Southern women he'd known at Harvard, like his roommate's bride, had, in fact, been prettier than most other women on campus. Yet these women had not been what he would call *belles*. Ironically, they had been even more studious and hardworking than the average Harvard female, as if determined to call attention to their brains instead of their looks. In this, they succeeded. For example: what he'd always noticed about Caroline Elmore was her pensive, sober-minded personality rather than her appearance. And anyway, she spent most of the short time he'd known her in the library. Hunter suspected that the whole thing about Southern belles was mostly a myth, and that if he ever met any real belles, they would prove to be as overrated as the Southern accent. Still, he didn't mind the chance to find out for himself.

He'd found out as soon as he stepped off the plane. In the waiting area, a group of pretty girls broke into smiles when they caught sight of him as he emerged from the gateway. Waving enthusiastically, they practically performed the word "Hi!" in a chorus of sweet, sing-song voices. Although he was certain he'd never seen any of these people before in his life, their manner was as intimate and familiar as if they'd known him forever, and the exuberance of their greeting suggested he was among their dearest and most cherished—like a favorite out-of-town cousin. Flummoxed, he stopped in his tracks, unsure how to respond. Was it possible he did know one of these girls? Or could this be a welcoming committee? In either case, he was at a loss for the appropriate response, and wasn't used to this feeling of ignorance and uncertainty. Should he return their greeting or introduce himself? He didn't like not knowing what to do, especially when it was a matter of an entire group of very pretty girls. Then there was his roomie Daniel coming toward him to lead the way to the baggage claim.

"Wait a minute," Hunter said, craning his neck behind him. "Those girls back there. Do you know them? Are they part of the wedding?"

As they both looked back in the direction of the girls, they watched as great fanfare was made at the arrival of another girl—just as beautiful, Hunter noticed—as she entered the waiting area.

Daniel shook his head. "Never seen them before." A smile played at the corner of his mouth.

Hunter began to suspect that he'd been the butt of some joke or trick he still didn't understand. He tried to retain his composure. "Is that some kind of hospitality committee? The airport hires them to do that?"

Daniel laughed so loud people turned to stare.

Hunter didn't appreciate being laughed at, especially after asking a legitimate question. "No, really," he said. "I don't get it. What's with that?"

Daniel must have picked up on the edge creeping into Hunter's voice, because the smile disappeared from his lips.

"Look," he pointed. "That's the girl they came to meet. Now they're leaving, just like we are. I have no idea who they are, I promise you. Why would you think I did?"

Hunter shrugged and tried to regain his accustomed nonchalance. "They all smiled at me," he said. "They waved. Some even said hello."

Daniel couldn't stop himself from laughing again. Hunter forced a good-natured chuckle as they stepped on the escalator down to the baggage claim, but he still didn't understand. Had he been made fun of in some way? Were those girls *mocking* him?

"Why did they smile at me like that?" He forced a smile himself, to repress the anger trying to break back through.

Daniel turned toward him. "They smiled at you because you are a fellow human being," he said.

What kind of bullshit answer was that? "Come on," Hunter said, annoyed.

"Welcome to Alabama," said Daniel, as they stepped off the escalator.

Coincidentally, they could just see some of Alabama straight ahead beyond the glass walls of the airport. It didn't look any different from any other part of the country Hunter had ever visited. "Really," he said, not bothering to conceal his irritation and impatience.

"Yes," said Daniel. "Perfect strangers smile and wave and say hello to each other down here." Daniel did just that as he forged a path through the crowd to the baggage carousel. "Despite our ignorance," he continued, "we realize we are all fellow human beings, and it makes life more pleasant if we treat each other that way. But then again, we are backward down here." His eyes crinkled with amusement.

This insight revolved in Hunter's head as he observed his luggage revolving on the carousel toward him. The idea that people would smile and wave at each other simply because they were fellow human beings was not one that had occurred to him, any more than this experience had ever occurred to him in his own life thus far, until today. It certainly did help explain why the Southerners he'd met all seemed so incapable of being players in the real world. How smart could it be to treat other people like fellow human beings? Usually, other people were rivals or competitors. Or they were needy parasites trying to wheedle something out of you. At best they were just an annoying presence. The only intelligent thing was to stick strictly to those people who had something to offer you, and scrupulously avoid everybody else. It wasn't rude to observe proper boundaries between yourself and the rest of humanity; it was a necessity. Although there was something cute, even quaint, about the way those girls had greeted him so eagerly, their gesture had been largely lost on him and succeeded only in throwing him off balance. On the whole, he felt sorry for these Southerners, with their exaggerated concept of manners and misguided forms of politeness. It was obvious why they'd never made anything much out of themselves or their part of the country.

So far his entire experience had been like the one in the airport, at party after party leading up to the wedding: complete strangers—beautiful girls his own age—treating him like they'd known and loved him his whole life. At home, if any girl had been so effusive or familiar as all these girls were, he would have scorned such an obvious play to get his attention, his money, his family name. He would have distrusted her immediately. So the girls didn't behave like that back East. Everyone was guarded and suspicious of each other's motives. But down here, no one appeared to know who he was or what his name meant. The girls made a fuss over him simply because they made a fuss over everybody. It was the way they were: friendly, open, fun-loving and sweet, without ulterior motives or hidden agendas. Their only agenda seemed to be to make sure everyone had a good time, themselves included. Once he got used to the Southern way, he found himself reversing his original opinion. Thoroughly charmed—as he had the best time he could remember in ages— he was forced to admit that there *was* something special about Southern girls, although it was much more than their looks.

There was one girl in particular. Her beauty had taken him unaware, because what he first saw of her was her back, as she stood talking to someone else at one of the parties. Extremely petite—barely over five feet, he guessed—she possessed the kind of girlish, doll-like figure that made him expect someone cute. When she had turned around with the most dazzling smile, he had choked on his swallow of Scotch. Never in his life would he forget the first sight of those enormous blue eyes, fringed with long, dark lashes and slightly slanted into almond shapes, although that may have been because of the radiant smile on her face. Everything about her was perfect: the blonde of her hair, the tan of her smooth skin next to the white silk sundress. Even her feet were adorable in simple flat sandals with slender straps. He forgot his Scotch and drank her in instead, vaguely aware that he might not be making the best impression as he was being introduced. The next shock was the sweetness of her manner as she stood chatting with him. He would have expected a girl this beautiful to be remote, haughty or cold—in some way intimidating. But she chattered happily away, all innocence and openness like the little girl she would have seemed to be but for the generous swell of her breasts rising softly under the silk of her dress. Despite the power of her beauty, she appeared so fragile and delicate he wanted to take her immediately into his arms, plunge into her silken sweetness and softness and join himself to her forever as her protector and lover. No other woman had ever had this kind of effect on him.

She wasn't a bridesmaid, but she'd been at all the parties. He'd met her that first night of his arrival, after the party when everybody went to some dive where an old black blues musician was performing. What part of town that was, he couldn't say for sure, only that it was definitely a different part of town from where the party had been. To tell the truth, he was a little shocked, because, come to think of it, he'd never been in such a dive before. Considering himself a fairly worldly guy, he was surprised that this crowd of mostly Southerners had something up on him. He supposed he was more a veteran of the club scene. Although they were all recently out of college or graduate school, the Southerners seemed younger, and definitely more innocent. He wouldn't have thought they'd even know about a bar like this, let alone choose to go in their fine clothes to such a hole in the wall in some abandoned strip near an interstate overpass and what looked like it could be a housing project, though he didn't believe that's what it was. But apparently everybody went regularly to this place.

The other thing that threw him was the blues musician, an old black man from Mississippi. After all he'd heard all his life about Birmingham, he wouldn't have expected a bunch of pretty white girls and preppy white guys to go to a bar featuring a black musician in what he guessed was not the white part of town. No one seemed to be slumming, rebelling, posturing or trying to impress the Yankees, either. These people weren't like that—they didn't have enough self-consciousness to put on that kind of act. It had all been so spontaneous and natural. After the party, someone had said—Where should we all go? What should we do? Someone else had said: the Plaza. Yes, they all agreed, let's go to the Plaza, like it was a regular hang-out. With a name like that, he'd expected something different. But the upside down Plaza sign said it all, and the place seemed almost *dangerous*. Yet all these well-to-do white people appeared entirely comfortable. He supposed it was their innocence, their simple-minded belief that the world was their playground.

"Actually, we all started coming here because they never checked i.d.," the doll-baby who turned out to be Lily explained to him. "We could come here when we were fifteen and get a beer. Didn't you all have a place you went to get a beer when you were fifteen without i.d.?"

"Indeed we did," he chuckled, thinking these Southerners weren't so different after all. And yet they were. It was confusing. Nothing was as he expected, or as he'd been told. Above all, he hadn't expected to *like it,* to have this much fun at the same time he was constantly caught off guard and unsure of his footing.

Lily was the best surprise of all. She had a lilting, high-pitched voice completely in keeping with her appearance. He pegged her for a nursery school teacher, or something to do with children. She was bound to be good with children, he figured, as she seemed barely more than a child herself. When he inquired politely, he received yet another surprise when he learned she was a real estate agent, and a positive shock when she giggled and confided that if she kept up her current pace, she was headed for something called "the million dollar club." On reflection, he supposed he could easily understand her success: she was like an adorable Girl Scout selling cookies. How could anyone refuse to buy at least one box of cookies from this precious little girl?

Although he'd been very circumspect with everyone else he met, he found himself telling Lily that he had just graduated from business school. This information did not impress her; in fact, she seemed a little bored by the notion of business school. *Harvard* Business School, he told her, when she didn't ask. He would be starting his training at Lehman Brothers in a few weeks. He was immediately angry with himself, as if he'd spilled a personal secret that would render him vulnerable in all sorts of potential ways: to predatory females, to damn-Yankee Southern sentiment, to bitter envy or provincial resentment. But something had compelled him to reveal himself to this fetching pipsqueak of a Southern girl, lest she not have the right idea of who and what he was. He wasn't sure he'd accomplished his goal, however, because she didn't seem the slightest bit interested in what he told her about himself. She just seemed interested in him. Everything about her body language suggested

29

she was responding to his body as it stood there talking to her. He could have sworn that she didn't even hear the word "Harvard" because she was too busy sizing him up and deciding she liked what she saw. She couldn't care less what his last name was, where he'd gone to school or what job he was about to start. This was such a heady new experience that he felt he'd already captured her heart, and was equally ready to give her his own.

But as he inched along in the crush of people trying to enter the country club at the reception, he realized with rising panic that after this evening, he had no way to see her again. Given the huge crowd, he might not even be able to see her tonight. His plane left in the morning, at something like 9:23 A.M. Why had he booked the earliest available flight out of Birmingham? At the time, he'd had an excellent reason, but he couldn't remember what it was now. If possible, he could re-schedule, or even cancel. It wasn't as if he couldn't afford to pay extra, or lose the price of the ticket altogether. The important thing was to find this girl and make a definite plan to see her again. If he had to spend Sunday morning doing just that instead of getting on his scheduled flight, then he would do just that. But why had he left this till the last minute? All those conversations they'd had, and he'd never once mentioned the prospect of her visiting New York. He supposed he was expecting her to bring it up. Didn't everybody want to visit New York? At any rate, all his female classmates from Harvard who weren't working in the city were always bringing it up. Those who'd gone to D.C. or thought First Boston was better than New York—big mistake, he thought. But he was constantly fending off people who tried to invite themselves into his apartment for the weekend, and possibly, into his life for the future. He had assumed Lily would ultimately be no different, especially after the way she kept looking at him. At the very least he expected her to express curiosity and a desire to visit. He didn't realize how much he'd been counting on this to happen until it had failed to happen. What was even worse, if he didn't do something about it immediately, he might never see her again, because he had forgotten her last name and didn't even have her *phone number.* Of course any number of people would be able to give him this information and help him locate her later, but the impossible throng of people filling the country club made him feel that she was lost to him, at the same time he realized he'd never wanted any woman so much in his life.

* * *

It was time for the cutting of the cake, and Midge knew her mother would never forgive her if she missed this part of the reception, when the sterling silver pedestal and cake knife that were family heirlooms from her grandmother would be put on display. In Mrs. Lambert's world view, a true lady

30

was known and judged by her sterling silver, and the beautifully embossed cake stand with its matching knife qualified Mrs. Lambert for the highest ranks. Not many families possessed such special pieces, nor could you rent their equal. The club's own furnishings were only the most basic; on top of which they were silver plate, not sterling. Using that would have been the equivalent of printed rather than engraved invitations. And *that* was like proclaiming defeat, admitting failure, settling for second rate without even trying, and announcing to all the world that you didn't have enough money.

The previous Thursday, which was Pearl's day off from the Elmore's, Mrs. Lambert had hired Pearl for half a day just to polish these two items. The job had required an entire jar of silver polish, two sponges, four rags and a box of Q-tips for scrubbing the grooves, along with all of Pearl's usual forbearance as Mrs. Lambert hovered over her to supervise, criticize and complain. Naturally the job was not performed to Mrs. Lambert's satisfaction. (Nothing had been done to Mrs. Lambert's satisfaction in decades.) Her husband's remark that not all tarnish could be eradicated only agitated Mrs. Lambert further. It was exactly like him, to insist on the best for himself—as in marrying herself, for instance—and then not even trying to do the best by her and give her what she wanted. As far as she was concerned, he might as well not have retired, because she didn't appreciate having him in the den all day making one useless remark after another. Only when Shirley pointed out that a little bit of tarnish was actually *desirable* did Mrs. Lambert calm down.

"I read that, Mama, in *Southern Living Magazine*," Shirley soothed her. "They even said *not to try* to clean all the tarnish off, because a *little bit* makes the silver look *antique*. That's *the proof* that it is antique."

There was nothing like a quote from this particular bible to reassure a Southern lady like Mrs. Lambert. Grudgingly, she agreed that Pearl could go on home after carefully wrapping the pieces in their tarnish-proof cloth.

Throughout Pearl's half-day at the Lambert's, Midge had received regular updates from her sister Shirley. As soon as Pearl had left the Lambert residence, Midge began receiving the phone calls from her mother. When was she coming to pick the silver up to take to the club? After Midge had done this, it was: Had she kept the silver completely covered by the tarnish-proof cloth? Then: Where were they storing the pieces at the club? Was the manager making sure the cloth fully covered all the silver? When would they bring the pieces out for the reception? Who was responsible if the silver was lost, stolen, dented or scratched?

Now this long-awaited event was well under way. For several moments Midge stood on the threshold of the terrace regarding her mother's immobile profile trained toward the railing and the swimming pool beyond. To all appearances, Mrs. Lambert was every inch the Southern lady of a certain vintage. Her hair was still thick and luxurious, raven-black and rippling with waves that had been set that afternoon. One hand trailed down with casual elegance, holding a long cigarette burning between two blood-red tipped fingernails. The food lay untouched on the plate Shirley had brought her. But the glass of bourbon in front of her was only a quarter full. Midge knew her mother had been sitting there on the terrace and drinking since she arrived at the reception. And no matter how much she might seem like the quintessential Southern lady, the more she drank, the less human she became. Her eyes turned into the unblinking slits of a lizard's sleepy gaze, and the movement of her head from one person to another was the slow, incremental motion of a reptile. The loose flap of skin hanging from her chin moved up and down as she swallowed her bourbon, while her tongue flicked out to catch any traces left on her lips. But the worst was interrupting this creature as it basked in its bourbon element and risking its wrath, which completed the process of reverse evolution. The sound that lashed out was not Mrs. Lambert's voice, or the voice of any homo sapiens, female or male. It was the guttural noise of a primitive organism dredged up from the primordial murk. The point wasn't language, but inchoate fury. This was difficult enough to manage in the privacy of home, but here and now at the wedding, Midge didn't know what to do. It was impossible to predict how long it would take her mother to remember who she was and where she was: that she was a human being living in the civilized world; that she was a female in an advanced culture and in fact a lady in the best society, not to mention a grandmother at her granddaughter's wedding. Midge was afraid the transformation back into Southern womanhood could not happen fast enough to prevent a scene from occurring on the terrace in front of the other wedding guests gathered there. Her sister and father would be no better at preventing this than she herself would be. Something about their very existence was a provocation in and of itself.

"I'm told she was the most beautiful debutante of her year!" the voice boomed behind her.

Startled, Midge turned around to find Norman Laney peering over her shoulder.

"The fairest of them all, so the story goes," he continued.

"Yes," Midge confirmed warily, knowing this story did not have a particularly happy ending.

"That's what they say about Lula Petsinger too," said Norman.

"Yes." Midge concurred with greater pride. The Petsingers were one of the wealthiest and most prominent families in town. To be compared with them in any way was an honor she was only too happy to accept.

"What a shame the most beautiful girls are the ones who end up like this," he said, shaking his head. "Something is wrong with a world that uses up its great ladies this way. I do believe I'm here to help fix it, too."

"Oh, Norman," Midge said, clasping his arm and whispering, "What can you do?"

As Midge had a mind incapable of anything beyond the strictly literal and completely personal, it never occurred to her that Norman might be referring to anything other than her own immediate problem. She had especially seized on his declaration of being there to fix it. Well aware of the limitations of Midge's mind, he quickly adjusted his remarks. "Well," he said. "She looks fairly content to me. Why disturb her?"

"But it's time to cut the cake!" Midge almost wailed.

"I don't think it's cake she wants," said Norman.

"It's my great grandmother's cake knife and pedestal," explained Midge, now near tears. "I'll never hear the end of it if she's not there to see it!"

"And you may never hear the end of it if we try to get her up to go see it," Norman flatly stated the problem. He himself had never witnessed an episode, as the family did its best to prevent any public scenes by keeping Mrs. Lambert away from public places. However, Norman had heard the stories from her grandchildren. In her present condition, Mrs. Lambert was likely to respond to any intrusion like a sleeping crocodile who'd been stepped on or poked in the belly. The offender's head would be snapped off and blood would splatter far and wide. Everyone would be covered in it. There was only one person who did not provoke the monster.

"Midge," he said. "What could be more appropriate than the bride herself coming to fetch her grandmother to witness the cutting of the cake with the family heirlooms?"

If Norman could have bottled and sold the relief that came over Midge's face, he would have become a rich man.

"I'll go get her myself!" he offered. "Oh, and Midge," he turned back around. "It's a huge success," he whispered.

Delight transformed her countenance, which had been so desperate just a moment ago.

"Norman I think you're right!" she whispered back, excited as a child. "Would you believe: even Nick Scully is here tonight!"

The delight drained out of Norman's own countenance, and he turned quickly away to fulfill his mission before saying something he might regret later.

As she watched him go, Midge resolved never to doubt Norman's judgment ever again. Although there were many who still wondered why Norman was ever let into Mountain Brook society, she now knew the answer. It was precisely because he *had* come from nowhere. For that very reason, he understood that no one was perfect and life wasn't either. There was no need to pretend with him, you could take him your problems, and he would fix them. There was no shame in it, either. Everyone did it, and the ones who criticized him the worst often turned out to be the ones who needed him the most.

* * *

The grand ballroom where the band played, the guests danced, and the cake waited on its pedestal was the same place where the bride had attended many debut parties and even been presented as a debutante herself not so many years ago. Mr. Laney suggested that the bride pose with her grandmother next to the cake and the heirloom serving pieces, while he went in search of the groom so the cake could actually be cut and served. As the bride turned obediently this way and that at the photographer's suggestion, she remembered one particular debutante party where she had been humiliated in this very ballroom. As was customary, she had been randomly paired for the evening with a young man she didn't know. This custom was part of the very rationale of the entire debut tradition, which was designed—decades ago—to introduce marriageable young women to as many available and eligible young men as possible, *especially* those they had never had occasion to meet before. This young man turned out to be a Sewanee student, who called her promptly to arrange a dinner date prior to the evening's party. But three hours before he was due to pick her up, he called with the news that dinner had been "scrubbed." Several of his fraternity brothers had turned up in town unexpectedly, and he needed to "get with" them. At the party, he suggested she wait in line for the hot air balloon ride on the putting green while he went inside to fetch drinks. After twenty minutes, he had not returned with drinks and the line had not progressed because one of the ropes on the balloon needed replacing. Peering toward the ballroom, she glimpsed her escort laughing and talking to a group of friends, with *one* drink—his—in hand. Only then did she realize she had been *parked*. Being ditched was bad enough, even worse that it had taken so long to realize it, horrible to know she could have prevented it by declining to stand in line for a hot air balloon ride she did not even want to take. But the worst mistake was going inside to confront him as he stood there with the group of friends she guessed were the fraternity brothers he'd met earlier in the evening. The aura of alcohol encircling these Sewanee boys was so thick it was clear they had established this milieu long before the party and had brought it with them. When her date introduced her, one of these so-called Southern gentlemen from the so-called academy for Southern gentlemen said with drunken candor:

"She's not as bad-looking as we heard!"

Another said, "She doesn't look at all like she goes to Harvard!"

Back then she had been devastated; now the memory amused her so much the photographer complimented her on the best smile yet. Just then Mr. Laney arrived with her groom, whom he'd found deep in conversation with a black bartender from Tuskegee, not far from Opelika, where the groom had grown up. The image of her husband in an animated tête-à-tête with the bartender banished the specter of those pseudo Southern gentlemen. She had found the real thing, a rare individual for whom no one was beneath his notice or courtesy, including black men and unattractive women, which is what she was when they first met. Others might call him a "born politician," but it was so much more than that. He was the soul of democracy, which she had come to realize was the basis for all true gentility. When he reached her side at last, the bride's smile grew even wider, and the photographer's flashbulb erupted as if in appreciation. Now she could even feel sorry for those Sewanee boys, who wouldn't know how to treat a black bartender like an equal any more than they knew how to treat a Harvard woman—or perhaps any woman—with genuine respect. Once this had been her problem: she had despaired of ever finding respect or appreciation for the individual she was. Growing up in Alabama, she had not been the usual Southern girl. But up at Harvard, she had not been the usual Ivy Leaguer. In one place, she could not be a true Southerner; in the other, she could never be anything but a Southerner. Meeting this fellow Alabamian at Harvard had somehow solved the conundrum of her existence. Or at least, it made the problem posed by the Sewanee boys all theirs.

* * *

On the way home, Norman felt as proud and satisfied as if he was the one responsible for the splendid affair the reception had turned out to be; and in a way, he was. Although it was not his money that had paid for it, he was the one who had fielded Midge's constant phone calls and held her hand through months of planning and preparation. Many of the best ideas had been his, like the pink satin sacks of real rose petals handed out to each guest in lieu of confetti as the bride and groom left the reception. Midge was the typical

Mountain Brook woman who wanted to do exactly what everyone else did—only perhaps a tiny bit better. At the last wedding Norman had attended, white wicker baskets had been passed around for the guests to seize a handful of rose petals to throw as the bride and groom passed by. The little pink satin pouches Norman had suggested were a perfect improvement and perfectly in keeping with the formula for success in Mountain Brook, of doing exactly what everyone else did, only that little bit better. People counted on him for these ideas, and it was gratifying to see them translated into action with someone else's money. Midge would give him the credit, and give her husband the bills. His favorite moment would have to be when Virginia Cooley came up to ask if that dignified older couple standing slightly aloof from the crowd in the ballroom could be the DuPonts. Someone had told her the DuPonts were down for the wedding. "That beautiful long dress probably cost a fortune in Boston," Virginia said. Norman had concurred, without bothering to inform her that the couple in question was the groom's Mamaw and Papaw from somewhere between Vinegar Bend and Citronelle, Alabama, where they lived on a soybean farm. He laughed out loud at the memory.

"You drank too much, like always." His mother's blunt remark jabbed like a needle into his ballooning euphoria. He decided to ignore it.

"Wasn't it simply glorious, Mother?"

"It will never last," she grunted.

"What are you talking about?" He whipped his head around angrily.

"What we both know," she replied, staring straight ahead. "That marriage will never last."

The screeching of his brakes had less to do with the red light at Montclair Road than the wrath which had caused him to stomp his feet. "How can you say such a thing? Now? Of all times?"

His mother looked over. "He's not right for her," she told him.

Norman simply stared at her, speechless and oblivious of the green light. The car remained as motionless as he was. "Why on earth are you just now telling me this?"

A horn honked impatiently behind them and muffled his mother's reply. Slowly Norman eased his foot off the brake and let the car creep forward, as if distrustful of the green signal. His mother's bombshell had caused him to lose his bearings.

"Now what did you say?" he demanded sharply as he turned onto Montclair Road.

"Nothing you didn't already know," she told him. "Nothing you haven't already said yourself."

"Holy Mother of God!" he exploded. The car may have strayed over the center line as he focused a furious gaze on his mother rather than the road ahead.

"That's a cop car right up there," his mother pointed. "Slow down and stay in your own lane. If you get pulled over, we might as well start packing tonight for Pratt City. The Brook-Haven School does not want a drunk for a headmaster."

In deference to his inability to afford a DUI, a speeding ticket, a rise in his automobile insurance premium or the loss of his job, Norman concentrated on driving and said nothing more until he'd turned safely into the driveway of the apartment they shared. At least his mother had the decency to remain in the car so he could have this out with her then and there.

"Why didn't you tell me?" he shouted at her.

"I didn't need to tell you," she said quietly. "And lower your voice, Norman, or we'll have the neighbors all over us. You knew it already."

"But you tried to talk me out of it!" he cried. "Told me to keep my mouth shut! Not to make a fool of myself! Not to ruin the wedding!"

His mother rummaged calmly through the purse on her lap as he regarded her with fury. Plucking a cigarette from her pack of Virginia Slims with one hand, she pushed in the lighter on the dashboard with the other. He watched through narrowed eyes as she rolled down the window before putting the lighter to the cigarette between her lips.

"Well?" he demanded, as she took a deep drag.

"Of course I told you not to ruin the wedding," she said. "Would you really want to do such a thing?" She turned to blow smoke out the open window.

"I would have ruined that wedding every which way I could think of if it saved her from ruining her life!" he declared.

His mother had a way of scoffing at him that sounded like a cross between the croaking of a frog and the grunting of a hog. "Do you really think you can save people from themselves, Norman?"

"Of course I can, Mother," he replied without hesitation. "That's exactly what I do. I'm an English teacher and the headmaster of the best school in the state. My job is to save young people from themselves. From their parents and from the state of Alabama too."

His mother only shook her head sadly and blew more smoke out the window. This infuriated him further until, unexpectedly, his anger dissolved and seemed to settle in his throat, where it caused him to begin coughing. Only after his mother stubbed out her cigarette in the ashtray did he realize it wasn't his anger or her smoke that was causing him to cough. He was choking on his sobs. She reached over and patted his arm.

"You did save her, Norman," she said. "As much as you could. You got her away from her mother and out of Alabama. All the way to Harvard. That's more than anyone else could have done."

He couldn't speak for the tears drowning his voice. For several moments they sat in silence as the cars whizzed past on Montclair Road directly behind them.

"But she's throwing it all away," he said finally, his voice now quiet and calm. "Coming back home, getting married like this. I don't think I got her away at all. Those things Midge used to tell her: that she'd never get married, never be happy, never have a life. It got her."

"Naturally." His mother yawned and rolled up the window. "I never believed all that crap you were so fond of, anyway." She pulled hard on the door handle, more to haul herself up than to open the car door.

"What crap?" he said, not moving to help.

"That writer you were so crazy about." She struggled to rise, while he took extreme satisfaction in watching her fail.

"Thomas Wolfe?" His voice was icy. Of all the writers he dearly loved, Thomas Wolfe was the one who had saved his improbable life.

"That's it," she said. "All that can't-go-home-again crap." She turned awkwardly toward him. "You're a bigger fool than I thought if you really believe anybody can leave home in the first place. Look at us. We may live in Mountain Brook now, but we're still Pratt City through and through. Come on, Norman. Let's go inside. I'm tired."

He heaved a huge sigh and then heaved his even huger body up out of the car seat. He ignored his mother until they reached the front door, where he couldn't restrain himself as he fumbled for the house key in the dim porch light.

"I still think you could have told me sooner," he reproached her.

"Told you what?"

"That he isn't right! That you agreed with me!" He pushed the door open.

"What good would that have done?"

"We might have saved her from making this mistake!"

He watched in exasperation as his mother turned her back on him and plopped herself gratefully into the indentation on the living room sofa that had refashioned itself into a permanent state of readiness to receive her ample rear end. Norman heard the popping sounds that he believed meant his mother had released certain snaps, or straps, on the old-fashioned girdle she sometimes still tried to wear. Then she leaned back and released a protracted exhalation of pure relief. His stare turned into an angry frown as he watched her light another cigarette and take several contented puffs. He was startled when she spoke.

"She needs to make this mistake, Norman." His mother gestured with her cigarette for emphasis. "She needs to go all the way through with it until she sees it for herself. That will be how she figures out the kind of husband she needs."

Norman relented and went to join his mother in the living room, in his accustomed arm chair facing the sofa where she sat. "I'd rather she figure out she doesn't need a husband at all," he said. "What she needs most of all right now is her graduate degree. So she can have the career she's always wanted. If she'd just waited until *then*. . . ." He rocked his foot violently back and forth in agitation. "Of all the people I never expected to move back home. . . . Of all the girls I thought would be the last to get married . . . she was at the top of the list." He shook his head as if in disgust at the deliberate failure of a once-star student.

"Oh, I don't know, Norman," his mother said before inhaling deeply. "Remember what happened to Andy Upchurch?"

"What happened to Andy Upchurch?" said Norman sharply, rocking his foot with even more violence. "Has he left his research job at NBC?"

"No, no," said his mother, pointing at him with the glowing tip of her cigarette. "But he left his Ph.D. program in history at Yale because *it was just too lonely,* he told you. Remember? Not that it was *too hard*—" She jabbed in his direction again, "but *it was too lonely.*"

"What does this have to do with Caroline?" He fanned angrily at the smoke his mother's cigarette had left in its wake.

"Then there was Alexandra Sanders," his mother went on, unperturbed. "A prodigy on the cello. A girl so quiet—so shy—she could go through the school day without saying a word. Just nodding or shaking her head if anyone had something to say to her. Music was her voice, you used to say. And *she* is the only one you know of to get pregnant as a student at the Brook-Haven School."

"It wasn't a fellow student," Norman leaned forward to impress this point upon her. "I'm certain it was another musician in the Birmingham Symphony." He'd known he'd regret one day having told his mother this story. Now that day had come. "Why are you bringing this up?" he asked her. "Is this supposed to help me feel better about Caroline somehow?"

"It's the quiet ones, Norman. The serious ones, the dedicated ones, the brilliant ones. Who don't have a lot of people in their lives." As she paused to take another several puffs of her cigarette, her son became impatient.

"What about them?" he said impatiently. "What's your point?"

His mother exhaled slowly in her own sweet time. Finally she said, "Just that it's the extraordinary ones. Who don't have crowds of friends or dates or piles of party invitations. *They* are the ones who surprise us by getting married or getting pregnant. Maybe this is something you can't understand. How could *you* know what it means to be lonely when you've always had *thousands* of friends?"

"So you're telling me—"

"Caroline needs a husband, Norman."

"Needs a husband?!" he cried indignantly. "Mother, you might as well tell me I'm a complete failure, and then run a sword through my bowels."

His mother stabbed her cigarette into the ashtray on the table beside the sofa. "What does this have to do with *you*, Norman? Why do you think everything is about you?" She looked back toward him and pierced him with her gaze. "I thought we were talking about *Caroline*."

"I know very well what we're talking about," he retorted, trying hard not to rise to the bait while leaning forward in his armchair to cut the distance between them by half. "We are talking about how *generations* of our women have not lived the lives they could have, or should have, because they were told the only thing they *needed* was a husband. And the way they were raised and educated, or not really educated . . . unfortunately, they *did* need a husband." Leaning back, he drew himself up for his final pronouncement. "One of my goals in life, Mother, was to make sure that no girl who graduated from *my* school would ever *need* a husband."

"Oh, please, Norman," she scoffed, as if he were speaking utter nonsense. A fresh cigarette bobbed up and down from her lips with every word, making further mockery of his little speech.

"You don't believe in change? Or progress?" His fingers drummed in agitation on the arms of his chair.

His mother batted the air in front of her to clear it of the acrid trail left by a newly struck match. She seemed also to be waving away his attempt to provoke her. "Now you're just being stupid," she said, inhaling deeply.

"Okay, then," he snapped. "Explain it to me, Mother. Why does an intelligent, independent, individual young woman with a Harvard degree need a husband?"

"Because she's a woman, Norman."

He exploded. "You're impossible! I know you're not this prehistoric! You're just trying to get my goat for some obscure reason known only to yourself!"

"Norman," she rasped, her voice turning into the croak it usually became after a day of chain-smoking. "I know you think you can help change this town. Maybe you can. But you sure as hell aren't going to change human nature. Most women need a husband like most men need a wife. So what's wrong with that? Pretending that marriage is unimportant or unnecessary is not progress. It's just plain stupid, if you ask me. If progress is what you want, you're not going to get there by looking down your nose at one of the main things that has allowed human civilization to get where it is, and that is: HOLY MATRIMONY." She punched the air with the fiery tip of her cigarette to emphasize the last two words. Taking a deep drag, she added, "Pair bonding is what the evolutionary biologists call it."

Norman stared at her in disbelief. "Mother, what on earth?"

"It was on a PBS special," she explained as she exhaled. "Just the other day. Scientists believe that males and females pairing off helped the apes become human and the humans become the strongest race on earth. So you can kiss goodbye to progress if you think marriage is something you can make light of."

Norman knew better than to inquire more deeply into his mother's television viewing of either soap operas or the PBS specials she watched when her other programs were over. "Try this for progress, Mother," he said. "Caroline finishes her graduate program. Lands her first job. Launches her career. *Then* she becomes a bride. Instead of getting married right out of the box. Just like her mother. Her grandmother."

The image rose before him of Barbara Lambert sitting silent and still in her drunken stupor on the terrace of the country club. After graduating from high school, Barbara had married the young man who asked her for the most dances during her debutante season. Next rose the image of her daughter Midge, who had completed two years at Bama, where she went to keep an eye on Perry Elmore. When he proposed, her mission at the University of Alabama was complete. She dropped out and got married. This traditional pattern had done nothing but create unhappiness for everyone: men, women and children. Norman had wanted to break the cycle for once and for all. Of all the girls he'd fussed over, Caroline was the least of his concerns. Next thing he knew, Midge was crowing with delight over her daughter's engagement.

"You were so right to get her into Harvard, Norman," Midge had graciously conceded, magnanimous in her maternal triumph. "That was *exactly* the place where a girl like her was most likely to find a husband."

A girl like her, Norman thought wearily. So different. . . . "I thought Caroline was my true rebel, Mother," he said with resignation.

"Who says she isn't?"

He stared at her in surprise.

"That's probably why she needed someone sooner than most. If you're at odds with everyone around you, then you need at least that one other person."

"If she's going to try to make herself happy in this town, she's going to need more than just that one other person. She needs a career."

"Yes, she does," his mother agreed.

Norman did a double-take. His mother was the most infuriating person he knew. Even when she fully agreed with him all along, she loved playing the contrarian until she had him on his knees.

"Caroline needs a career just like she needs that one other person who can help her achieve it."

Norman yawned in reply. The conversation was beginning to tire him out in more ways than one.

"Don't you remember what you used to tell the boys in the sixties?"

Alarm cut Norman's second yawn short. His mother had always been queen of the non sequitur, but lately he'd begun to wonder if he was witnessing the onset of senility. "What in the world does this have to do with Caroline?" He peered at her curiously to see where she could possibly be going with this.

"You told those boys that sex, drugs, and rock 'n' roll were not going to make them free. That dressing like hippies was a silly way to set themselves apart."

Norman winced. His mother had a lifelong habit of reducing the grandeur of his accumulated wisdom to the most embarrassing clichés. "I believe what I said, Mother, was that true individuals had no need to broadcast their nonconformity. They simply went their own way. Sometimes they did what no one else was doing, while other times they did what everyone else was doing. Either way, they didn't care, because their sights were set on loftier goals."

"There!" declared his mother with extreme satisfaction, as if they'd finally struck an accord. "That's what I was trying to tell you about Caroline. But you've said it yourself."

Norman shook his head sadly. "But this marriage—"

"He's not the one who can help her get where she needs to go," his mother interrupted. "That's my whole point. He's not the right one for her." Norma pulled on the arm of the couch to begin the arduous process of rising.

"At least you didn't need to treat me like such an idiot when I was fretting so over this marriage." Norman screwed up his face as he began mimicking his mother's rasping voice. "It's a beautiful love story. A charmed couple. Everybody says so. Just shut up, Norman." He paused and resumed his own voice. "Why, Mother?"

His mother thrust herself forward. "It was the only way you were going to make it through the wedding," she said.

* * *

Alone in his room, as he undressed and prepared for bed, Norman reflected that if Caroline *were* to recognize what his mother called her mistake, then perhaps all was not lost, especially if this marriage came to an end sooner rather than later. Terrible turn for his thoughts to take on her wedding night, he knew; yet if it *did* run aground, he must be prepared to help her recover and reclaim her destiny. Truly, his job—like that of parents—was never over. The good thing about her coming home, he realized, is that he would be in the best position to help her. And here, she was least likely to repeat her mistake. As her own mother had pointed out, Alabama was not a good place for a girl like her to find a husband.

~ PART ONE ~

~ 1 ~

On the last night of their honeymoon in New Orleans, the newlywed couple sat down to chicken paprika, rice pilaf, and a vegetable medley in the banquet room of a Marriott that could have been in Akron, Ohio, or Topeka, Kansas. The bride did not blame her groom. She blamed herself. He had given her the choice: Do we combine our honeymoon trip with the International Key Club Convention, which had asked Daniel, as a former president, to be its keynote speaker, or do we tell them maybe next year? He had not pressured her or even hinted that he wanted to accept. The only reason he even considered the idea, he explained, was because of the honorarium, which would enable them to enjoy two nights at the splendid new Windsor Court Hotel. While planning their trip, they had pored over the brochure for this expensive palace of luxury, which boasted a 4½ star restaurant with an award-winning chef, a Polo Lounge with one of the best jazz trios in the city, and full-scale suites with living rooms and kitchenettes. Why not? she had thought. Daniel didn't have to attend the convention itself, just the Saturday night banquet. In return for one brief appearance, they could enjoy two days of luxury and a grand finale to their honeymoon.

But actual experience never did turn out to be as perfect as the glossy images in any brochure, Caroline reflected as she handed her uneaten salad back to the server at the Marriott. The iceberg lettuce, carrot strips, cucumbers, and tomato wedge had been assembled too long ago and had been sitting too long in some too cold refrigerator. Chilled past the point of return, or consumption, it was only a gesture toward the idea of salad, not a real salad that could actually be enjoyed.

In a way, the whole honeymoon had turned out like that, but it wasn't Daniel's fault. He had done the best he could with no money and no help from his parents. With the new car, new furniture for the apartment and his student loans coming due, they had only the bare minimum to put toward a

47

honeymoon. And without a job herself, Caroline had nothing to contribute except her willingness to forgo a honeymoon altogether, or else spend it at her parents' beach house in Florida. It would be a while before she could start earning money, especially because she was postponing graduate school for a year. Until she finished her degree and got a job of her own, Caroline would be living on whatever her husband made as an associate attorney. The least she could do was to expect little and demand less when it came to unnecessary spending. The honeymoon was an easy sacrifice, especially since they could always take a nice trip in a few months, after they'd saved some money.

Daniel had been tempted to agree until her mother recoiled with horror. No honeymoon?! What bad luck! Not to mention: What would people think?! And Florida wouldn't do either, Caroline's mother insisted. Everybody in Alabama went to Florida for spring breaks and summer vacations. Honeymoons were supposed to be special. It was she who had urged Daniel to accept the invitation to speak at the convention. This way, she explained, she could tell people the newlyweds were spending their honeymoon at the Windsor Court Hotel in New Orleans.

For most of the week, however, they had free use of a condo on St. Charles Avenue, with its own wrought-iron balcony where they could sit outside and watch the streetcars go by. The branches of the huge live oaks came so close to their perch it was like sitting in the tree itself. After a bottle of champagne on the afternoon of their arrival, they had hopped one of those streetcars to get to a nearby restaurant. It was as lovely and exotic to two Alabamians as if they'd flown halfway across the world to some famous European destination. They agreed they had made the right decision not to forgo or postpone the honeymoon.

* * *

The next morning, however, they had woken up to find Daniel's brand-new BMW had been broken into. During their two hour wait for the police to arrive, the Monday morning bustled to life with pedestrians passing to and fro on the sidewalk past their violated automobile. No one had a word of sympathy or even a glance of curiosity to spare on what was obviously a commonplace occurrence in their city. Likewise, neither of the cops was at all sympathetic about either their delay or the break-in itself. In fact, they regarded the young couple as the perpetrators of their own misfortune and the guilty party for wasting valuable NOPD time. Slow getting out of the car, they emerged only reluctantly, with accusatory expressions on their hardened faces. Nevertheless, Daniel thanked them warmly for coming out, and started to offer his hand until even he was momentarily cowed by their implacable hostility.

One of the cops, a thick-set Hispanic officer with dark, slicked-back hair, ran his fingers down his face in a weary gesture that pulled the corners of his mouth even further into a frown. "Car parked here," he said accusingly. "You're asking for trouble." He shook his head as he wrote down the license plate number.

Daniel apologized for being the victim of a crime and taking up their valuable time. "I'm sorry, Officer," he said. "I thought I was doing the right thing. Parking on a side street, instead of St. Charles Avenue."

"Registration?" said the cop.

As Daniel reached into the glove box through the jimmied passenger door, it was the black cop who deigned to clue them in.

"This is the Garden District," he told them, with a surly matter-of-factness that did little to conceal his disdain for their stupidity.

"Driver's license?" said the first cop, handing back the registration.

Pulling out his wallet, Daniel explained to the black cop. "That's why I didn't think something like this would happen, Officer. In the Garden District."

The black policeman scowled. "St. Thomas Housing Project is a few blocks that-a-way." He gestured beyond the condominium toward the heart of the historic New Orleans Garden District.

Daniel and Caroline had exchanged looks of amazement. Although Birmingham also had housing projects and a criminal element, neither of these could be found within miles of any location near them. This was part of the legacy of their segregated city and its enclave of Mountain Brook.

"Officer," Daniel addressed the black cop. "Are you seriously telling me there's a housing project next to all these beautiful mansions in the Garden District?" His voice now had a shade more of his South Alabama accent than it did when the cops first pulled up.

The black cop did not reply as the other officer motioned for his partner to join him in inspecting the car.

Daniel followed right behind them. "Should I have parked on St. Charles Avenue? Is that safer?"

"Shoulda parked in there." The black cop pointed to the gated parking garage underneath the condo building.

As the two policemen examined the car's interior, Daniel explained that the condo's owners kept a car parked in their spot for use whenever they were in town. The use of the condo unit itself, he went on, was a gift from one of his best friends, whose girlfriend's parents were the actual owners. Daniel had never met them himself, and had only met his friend's girlfriend once, so had not felt comfortable pressing the issue of a parking space. When the backs of both policemen proved utterly impervious and indifferent to this information, Daniel added that he'd just gotten married, but he and his wife could only afford a budget honeymoon, which was why they weren't staying in a hotel. His Alabama accent was now so thick he sounded like a complete rube.

Wishing she could go inside, Caroline settled for sitting down on the curb at some distance from the car and her husband's desperate efforts with the two cops. She had no doubt that by the time this ordeal was over, Daniel would have those two policemen right where he wanted them. Although she was proud of this special magic he had for dealing with people, sometimes it was painful and embarrassing to witness. This was one of those times, when Daniel felt called upon to bare his soul and all the personal details of his predicament and generally abase himself as the dumb, ignorant, powerless and penniless redneck the situation revealed him to be. He made sure it was Yes, sir; No, sir; Officer this; Officer that, like at least his mama raised him right, even if he had nothing else going for him. If his Alabama accent did not command respect, it could at times evoke pity, which was a definite improvement over contempt. Daniel could work with pity. Pity was in the same family as compassion, and this was one of the best things you could hope to get from another person.

Sure enough, as the police were wrapping up, the black officer told Daniel of a BMW dealership in Metairie, and advised them to find a way to park in the gated garage.

"Good luck," he said as they left.

It was the first hint of warmth either cop had shown. But it was enough. It was this Daniel needed, more than the information about the dealership or the advice about parking. He needed for these two cops to respond to him as a fellow human being, and with his persistent politeness, he had succeeded in making this happen by treating them as such despite their own initial lack of humanity. Caroline had seen him win similar battles with difficult professors, demanding law partners, as well as her own hard-to-please father. Daniel had to make it through to everyone he met; he had to connect with every stranger who crossed his path. He wanted everyone to like him, to be as nice to him as he was to them. This was the compulsion that drove his personality.

Afterwards, the newlyweds had stood silently for a moment, at a loss as to how to reclaim the day, along with their car. The police had discovered damage to the side-view mirror, and possible damage to the gearbox. If the thieves had known how to operate a stick-shift, the car would have been stolen. The passenger door no longer closed completely flush. Daniel looked stricken.

"Now we can finally get some breakfast." Smiling, she reached for his hand.

"Honey, I can't think about food at a time like this. I've got to get the car checked out and fixed."

"Why don't I bring us back some coffee and croissants?"

He shook his head. "I don't want to wait here at the gate. We've only got one key."

She decided not to argue. It was clear he had exhausted all his patience, politeness and charm on the two policemen and had only his anger and distress left over for her.

* * *

When the dinner concluded in the banquet room of the Marriott, a breathless excitement rippled through the audience as the climactic event of the Key Club convention got underway with Daniel's speech. The newlywed's honeymoon achieved an unexpected climax as well after seeming to collapse during the week with the break-in, the car repairs, the phone calls with the insurance company, the writing of the speech and the surprise appearance on Thursday, a day early, of two former Key Club associates and law school roommates whose claim on the condo could not be denied because one was accompanied by the girlfriend whose parents owned the place. This girlfriend had also claimed the sole bedroom for herself and her boyfriend, and then insisted that Will Hill leave on Friday for the Windsor Court with the newlyweds because she'd anticipated a more romantic weekend with her boyfriend. Daniel's friend Scott McMillan had sheepishly apologized for her rudeness, explaining he had long planned to break up with her after this weekend's use of her parents' condo. Will Hill offered to drive back to Mobile rather than crash the honeymoon couple's hotel suite, but because he owned an automobile that never really worked, he'd come over with the others in a car that wasn't his. Then his gallant attempt to decline the invitation to join them for dinner had backfired. After taking one look at the menu for the hotel's acclaimed restaurant, he declared that he couldn't afford those prices, and even if he could, he wouldn't want to participate in the rich man's ritual of throwing money away on outrageously expensive food. To Caroline's dismay, Daniel felt obliged to cancel their reservation for Friday night rather than let Will Hill go his own way for dinner. But she stifled the protest that formed on her lips because despite his good intentions, Will Hill had spoiled the outrageously expensive meal they would otherwise have enjoyed without him. And since the idea of a honeymoon was now so far gone, Caroline figured she might as well enjoy the trip on different terms. She really did like both Will

51

Hill and Scott McMillan, and their arrival had lifted the gloom caused by the break-in. Her husband's mood had improved tremendously.

All of these setbacks were overcome when Daniel stood proudly erect before his audience and began to speak. Daniel was one of those people who possessed the gift of public speaking even when he wasn't really saying anything, because it wasn't what he said so much as how he said it, with the warmth of his tone, the urgency of his delivery and the sparkle in his eyes. Although he had notes in front of him, he never once took those sparkling eyes off the audience to look at these notes. Even Caroline, who had helped him prepare, succumbed to the illusion that there was no prepared speech. Instead there was this spontaneous outpouring of free-flowing passion from someone who was opening his heart to them right there on the spot. More than once he made sustained eye contact with her and her alone, and she guessed from the rapt faces of all around her that everyone had a similar sensation, that he was connecting with them individually on a deep and personal level. In return, all the rapt gazes trained on him showered him with the admiration that made him seem to inflate in stature right before her eyes. The penniless, powerless small-town boy whose car got broken into because he couldn't afford a hotel was transformed into this exceptional personage who radiated power and importance.

It was clear that he would "go far." Unfortunately, in Alabama, going far in politics usually meant going to Montgomery. Caroline shuddered at the thought of living in the overgrown country town of their state capital, where Daniel would already be working in Aaron Osgood's administration if Osgood had defeated George Wallace for governor three years ago. As sorry as she was for Wallace's victory, she could hardly be sorry to be spared Montgomery while Daniel pursued a legal career as the path back into politics. How would she ever tolerate Montgomery if it came to that? Pushing the question out of her mind, she joined in the thunderous applause greeting the conclusion of her husband's speech.

* * *

The crown jewel of the Polo Lounge at the Windsor Court Hotel was a massive oil painting depicting a fox hunt in progress in the British countryside. It had been acquired at auction at Sotheby's of London for several million dollars, and appeared even more impressive in reality than it had in the brochure. To the left of it was the piano where the jazz trio played on Friday and Saturday nights. In addition to the pianist, there was a drummer and saxophonist, all clad in spiffy tuxedos which set a certain tone in keeping with the fox-hunting British gentlemen in the painting. Although the entire lounge was liberally sprinkled with plush sofas and armchairs, the choice seating was the grouping of furniture underneath the painting and next to the musicians. Usually this focal point was occupied by the kind of clientele envisioned by the management: affluent hotel guests, diners stopping in after their meal in the restaurant, stunning women provided by a high-end escort service for wealthy executives on business trips. The rich aroma from expensive cigars, the popping of corks, the rattle of the cocktail shaker and the up-tempo jazz completed this effect of big-city glamour and sophistication.

This ambience was not designed for the Alabama delegation from a Key Club convention trouping in en masse with a golly-gee-whizz hullabaloo that would have been better catered to by the packaged sleaze of Bourbon Street, which was primarily designed to give provincial sensibilities something outrageous to remember about their trip to the Big Easy when they went back home. Indeed, after the banquet broke up at the Marriott, the general plan had been to "hit" the French Quarter and "check out" Bourbon Street.

Caroline wasn't sure who had told the Alabama group that she and Daniel were headed back to their hotel for a drink at the Polo Lounge. But when it came to people, Daniel always thought more was better, and usually managed to gather a crowd. Somehow the honeymoon had become a communal event, like the wedding, where others were welcomed to witness the couple's union. For Daniel, public events were always more compelling than private ones, which lacked the validation found in widely shared experience. So when they set out, it wasn't just the two of them. It wasn't just Scott McMillan and Will Hill either. It was also Manley Hellman, principal of Cullman High and director of the Alabama Key Club chapter, along with his assistant principal and director, Irwin Dyce. Fortunately, only one of the high school delegation was with them: a boy named Randy Flowers who had grown up on a peanut farm and was president of the Alabama chapter. Unfortunately, they were also accompanied by a tall, ungainly man from New Jersey named Matt Nowak, who, like Irwin Dyce, was assistant director of his state's Key Club chapter. Also like Mr. Dyce, Matt Nowak had never married and lived with his mother. There was an excellent reason why both men had never married. Although this fundamental truth had been repressed by the men themselves, it was obvious to any perceptive observer. Nowak still looked like a boy who'd been bullied in school for wearing pants that were several inches too short and wedged firmly in the crack of his rear end, because even as a grown man, his pants were several inches too short and wedged firmly in the crack of his rear end. He carried himself with his shoulders slumped and his head canted slightly downward and to the side, as if signaling his submission to a cruel world which had already beaten him and didn't need to whip him again. Several years ago, Matt had adopted, or been adopted by, the Alabama chapter which treated him like a stray dog they'd rescued rather than an embarrassing loser or "re-tard." The money he didn't need to spend on wife, family or even rent and utilities he spent on trips to Alabama Key Club functions. The bond that existed between him and Irwin Dyce was understood by everyone except the two men themselves, who would never speak of it and did not know how it was to be acted upon except through attending these Key Club functions together.

Unhappily for Nowak, and the patrons in the Polo Lounge, Matt always called unwanted attention to himself because his voice was not as subdued as his body language. It boomed and grated with the kind of New Jersey accent for which the state was infamous. The rural Alabama accent of Randy Flowers was no better, and he spoke in the loud voice often found in those raised in the country or large open spaces like Texas, where you wouldn't be heard over the distance or the din of machinery and equipment unless you hollered. Though he was a polite, well-meaning boy eager to do the right thing in all circumstances, he possessed neither an "inside voice" nor "inside manners."

Mr. Hellman instructed his Key Club charges on the proper etiquette requiring each of them to order at least one drink along with a dessert. But they failed to endear themselves to the cocktail waitress by ordering four Cokes with chocolate mousse on four separate checks. Mr. Dyce had wanted iced tea, which the Lounge could not provide at this hour, and Randy had not known that mousse was a fancy kind of pudding, or that a single serving of it could cost ten dollars. By the time the waitress had taken their orders, the jazz trio decided it was time for their break. Other patrons decided they did not need another round of drinks after all. The sofa and chairs beneath the painting became vacant.

It was Matt Nowak who urged the group to take possession of the prime location while he excused himself for a minute. When he returned beaming proudly, he was trailed by a waitress bearing a bottle of champagne and a tray of flutes. Before anyone could recover from their surprise, Matt was standing knock-kneed before them in his ill-fitting pants proposing a toast to the newly married couple and thanking them for sharing their honeymoon with others who loved them.

For Caroline, it was one of those electrifying instants when the unknown beauty of another person and the unrecognized grace of the occasion crashed through incomprehension and rearranged consciousness. The disappointment of reality was not only redeemed but transformed into a moment of transcendence. Looking over at her husband, she lifted her glass until it connected with his. It was Daniel who made lovely moments like this possible. And it was he, more than Mr. Laney or Harvard University, which had liberated her from the remoteness of Mountain Brook and put her in touch with the world. This was why she loved him. This was why she'd married him. This was why her honeymoon included more than two people.

Will Hill stood up from his place on the sofa and held his glass aloft. "Here's to my best friend and his beautiful Harvard bride!" he proclaimed.

Not to be outdone, Scott McMillan jumped up immediately. "Here's to the former International Key Club president, and the woman who puts up with that!"

Amidst laughter, clapping and the clinking of glasses, Irwin Dyce rose laboriously from a large armchair and waited with primly pursed lips for the ruckus to subside. Anyone who'd ever been in a classroom when he arrived to make an announcement would have recognized the officious demeanor he wore when trying to summon seriousness from giggling students. Finally, when a sufficient level of solemnity had been achieved, Mr. Dyce flatly stated his important business. "Here's to the future governor of Alabama and his lovely first lady."

This toast caused even more of a clamor until all eyes focused on young Randy Flowers, sitting next in the circle. He stood up nervously and regarded the group in front of him with the mild panic that a year ago had forced Manley Hellmann to acknowledge the limits of Randy's prospects. His fear of standing before an audience and his inability to seize that opportunity would prevent him from becoming anything like the star that his hero Daniel Dobbs had been. Whatever wits Randy possessed deserted him immediately when he faced the smallest gathering, leaving him alone and defenseless on the battlefield of friendly fire. As he searched the countenances of his mentors for clues about what to say, he spied the (empty) glass he'd set down when he stood up. Hoisting it high above his head, he cried out, "Here's to champagne!"

Hysterics ensued. Until this evening, Randy had never before imbibed a drop of alcohol, and had looked askance when handed a glass of champagne, because it looked like ginger ale, and he hated ginger ale. He much preferred Coke. But after his first tentative sip, he had gulped it down in a few large swallows as if swigging a soft drink, and pronounced it "even better than Coke!"

Caroline found herself laughing, enjoying the champagne, the jazz, and the company of friends till well past midnight. Anyone who observed the happy group sitting beneath the large oil painting in the Polo Lounge of the Windsor Court would have thought it looked exactly like the glossy picture in the hotel brochure.

~ 2 ~

A month after the wedding, Midge Elmore told her daughter how lucky she was to have Daniel Dobbs for a husband. As a first-year associate attorney, he was already making a name for himself in a town he couldn't yet even call his own. "One of the first in, one of the last to leave, and always available whenever we need him, even on weekends," were the exact words a very pleased partner had said to Midge at a recent party.

Midge herself had never been so pleased with her daughter, even on the day she was born, because Midge had wanted a son, and her own father had said, "Too bad it's not a boy." Daughters were well and good, but it was hard to enjoy a girl as the firstborn, since it was men who inherited the earth, and a wife's main duty was to produce such men. Plus, Midge's infant daughter had a bright red strawberry birthmark right there on her neck for all the world to see. The doctor who delivered her said it would be years before anything could be done about it, and by then it would probably fade. Since beauty was the only coin women had in a realm ruled by men, Midge had been worried about Caroline's chances from Day One. The years only added to her worries, as Caroline turned out to be a perversely contrary child: a bookworm and a tomboy who cared nothing about looks, friends, or dates, of which she had none. Try as she might, day after day, Midge could not get her daughter to care about such things. She had feared this daughter would never get married. Then when Harvard took her, Midge *knew* Caroline would never get married. But here she was, the very first of her high school class to get married, and to a man who was already rising in the world. It was a triumph Midge had never expected to enjoy with this child, and the victory was sweet. Still, when other mothers asked how she'd done it, Midge was appropriately modest, and gave Norman Laney all the credit.

But for Caroline, the great surprise of her married life was that it wasn't so different from her unmarried life. In the drive to establish his career, her husband was not much more of a presence in her life than he had been when they were still students a thousand miles apart. During the week, he usually left before she was fully awake and often didn't return until after dinner. Oddly, it wasn't these long hours that made him seem so absent. It was when he was home that they felt farthest apart, because he wasn't really home, he was never really with her. He was not a husband or an individual so much as he was whatever case he was working on at the moment. In the grip of any case, he became a walking, talking legal brief, which expanded exponentially as he continued to work on it until there was no space for anything else. He woke up talking about the case; if he called her from the office it was to talk about the case; and if he came home in time for dinner, they still talked about the case. She was needed as judge and jury, a silent audience listening carefully to every word. As his work progressed, their apartment took on more and more the solipsism of the courtroom, devoted solely to this one all-important case and nothing else. No other subject, no other focus, no other topic of discussion could be introduced. Distractions and interruptions did not make it through the front door. Hurricanes could strike, wars could break out, a modern-day plague could threaten an entire population, but none of this news penetrated because it was not relevant to the case. The case was everything; nothing else mattered. The latest was undeniably important—millions at stake, legal precedents involved—so she could understand if this case had consumed him. But it was more that he had consumed the case. It had not taken him over so much as he had fed on it until he ballooned with a sense of his own importance. This balloon crowded the apartment so completely that nothing else had room to grow or even exist. It was actually a relief when he left for work in the mornings, because then she could begin to breathe.

In theory, the twelve hours of solitude she had to work with each day should have been exactly what she needed to get her own career going. But for her, the words would not come. Did not come. Had not come. Day after day, the blank notebook remained blank. She had known it was going to be hard, but had not expected it to be impossible. After all, she had spent her whole life preparing for this moment. She had an Ivy League degree. For the papers and exams necessary to earn that degree, the words had come easily. But now, nothing came. When she sat down at her desk, it was becoming harder and harder to face the blank notebook pages. Her eyes strayed out the window and her mind became lost in thoughts that did not lead to filling up the empty space on the page.

Indeed, these thoughts made it harder to focus on the path she had chosen because they led to doubts about the path she'd chosen. Just a few months ago, she had been a Harvard student, and as such, she had reached a pinnacle of achievement universally recognized by the whole world. She could have stayed at this pinnacle; perhaps she should have stayed to continue her efforts there. Because there she had been something. And nothing was like being there, at the top, at Harvard, to make anything you did seem like success. When Harvard was added to your identity, it was the ultimate validation. Subtracting this was not easy, and when you did, you needed a good substitute. Too late had she come to understand why most Harvard students either delayed departure as long as possible, or moved on to something equally great in the eyes of the world. For good reason, nobody did what she had done in deliberately stripping all supports to her identity so she could arrive at herself and herself alone. She had wanted to build her own sense of self from the ground up, without any pre-fabricated pieces, such as "Harvard." Like Thoreau, she had sought to place herself outside the reach of any society, system, establishment or institution. She had thought this was the only way to become a true artist of any kind. But she was not becoming the writer she'd always wanted to be. She was not becoming anything except the "housewife" she'd sworn she'd never be. The grand gesture of rejecting the Northeastern "establishment" was proving to be an empty one, which had impressed nobody but herself for a short period of time that had since come to an end. She had arrived only at rock bottom again, in Alabama, nowhere. She still believed, like Isabel Archer, that you couldn't live forever at the top of the mountain with all your choices laid out before you. You had to pick a corner of the universe and cultivate that. But she was beginning to fear she'd picked the most difficult corner to cultivate. A war zone would have been easier in many ways: she would have had the world's respect and a ready-made subject, along with the potential for both publication and payment.

There was nothing like the stubborn blankness of the page to inspire the most melodramatic sense of failure.

It didn't help that the only writing anyone wanted from her was in the form of thank-you notes for wedding gifts. She still had hundreds left to finish. Every day her mother called to check on her progress, report who had mentioned receiving a "beautiful note," and request certain individuals be moved to the top of the to-do list, usually because she expected to see them soon at an upcoming event. Caroline had set herself the task of twenty per day, and for someone who had no job or other duties, this should not have been an overwhelming daily chore. Nevertheless, it killed her day. If she did it first thing, she was demoralized by the banality of it. If she postponed it, she was demoralized by guilt and dread. Either way, her mind remained blank and stagnant, as if stubbornly refusing to stray from the one small job the world had given her to do.

It wasn't that she didn't have anything she wanted to put into words. There was so much inside of her begging for expression. But it was a confused muddle that so far defied formulation. Still, she had the box. This should have been enough. If she had been given this treasure trove of material in one of her college courses, she could have done what needed doing by the end of the semester and earned a good grade along with the professor's praise. Now a lifetime stretched before her like an eternity, and she didn't see how she would ever make anything out of it. The aged newspaper clippings inside the box were dry as dust; the power to conjure them to life was beyond her.

Perhaps the first thing to do, she thought, was list every item in the box and give it a brief description. Item number one, the most valuable, was the letter from General Joseph Wheeler to Jesse Edward Brown's widow, dated August 23rd, 1905.

> *My dear Mrs. Brown,*
>
> *I arrived in New York this morning and was deeply pained to read of your husband's death. Col Brown was a gallant and good soldier, a valuable citizen and a noble man. His loss will be felt by our state but the example of his life will be of very great value to the young men of Alabama. I beg to join my sympathies to that of Col Brown's many friends and admirers.*
>
> *Faithfully yours,*
> *Joseph Wheeler*

What had always intrigued her most was the reference to *Colonel* Brown. Her great-great great-grandfather had been a private when he enlisted in the Confederate Army at age seventeen. He was still a private when he lost his leg in battle and was captured by the Union Army. He had spent the remainder of the war in prison. His honorary "promotion" to the rank of colonel had come long after the war, in recognition of his many illustrious deeds as a citizen rather than a soldier. There was a story here about how the past became "transmogrified," how truth grew larger in the telling. A private soldier became a colonel; four years in prison became a bravely fought war. The only problem with this story was that William Faulkner had already written it.

And she didn't know how to begin writing her own version. She knew there was something she wanted to say about it; she just didn't know what it was.

She had only been to Scottsboro once, to visit the last living relative in a nursing home, and had never seen Brownwood. Rifling through the contents in the box, she came up with the photograph of Brownwood, reprinted on thick cardstock and sent out one Christmas as holiday greetings from the Browns. A huge Victorian pile, it was more monstrous than beautiful, a statement of power and wealth from a distinguished citizen who was once just a poor farm boy from the outskirts of what was first called Scott's Mill, in the northeast corner of Alabama. His father had a small subsistence hill farm, with only a few slaves to help work it; nothing like the big cotton plantations in the rich, fertile Black Belt of south central Alabama.

The war might have been the best thing that could have happened to the young Jesse Edward Brown. With his leg shot off at the Battle of Chickamauga, he came back a "hero," but unfit for farm labor. To enter a new life in a new world remade by the war, he armed himself with a law degree. With that and his wooden leg, he won himself a seat in the Alabama Legislature. Political power brought clients; clients brought money. With this money he bought up land in Scott's Mill which became valuable downtown property as well as outlying farmland. He became a landlord to tenant farmers and shopkeepers as well as a lawyer. Not too long after Lee's Surrender, the renamed town of Scottsboro was incorporated by the Alabama Legislature, and also became the county seat. Jesse Edward Brown became a rich man. He had literally helped put Scottsboro on the map. It was only appropriate to build a house in keeping with his stature in the community; it was named after himself and his wife, whose maiden name was Wood. The horse races held on the racetrack of his Brownwood estate were attended every Sunday by hundreds from miles around, including the nearby corners of Georgia and Tennessee.

The fortune made by Jesse Edward Brown along with the property he owned enabled his descendants to leave the small town of Scottsboro and prosper in the big city of Birmingham. Now Brownwood existed only in the stories told by her father and his sister, who had been sent as children to spend summers on the estate. There they could run as wild as they wanted, without any of the trouble this could lead to in the big city. Earl and Boo Gee, two black children of Brownwood's live-in servants, were under orders to follow the white city kids wherever they went and keep them from harm. "You better don't!" was what Boo Gee said to warn them off prohibited areas or forbidden activities. Their great aunt Eleanor, nominally in charge of them, supervised from the window seat on the second story of Brownwood, where she could survey the area for miles around while reclining against the cushions, reading murder mysteries and chain-smoking Pall Malls.

Besides the stories, all that was left was this box of memorabilia—letters, photographs, and newspaper articles charting the illustrious career of Jesse Edward Brown—given to her aunt when the family property was torn down to make way for more prosperous developments. Her aunt hadn't known what to do with it, so she'd given it to her niece in case she could make something out of it. Why had she been so sure that she could? Over the years, the contents of this box had come to seem like her own family inheritance, the legacy that had been given to her, the capital that she could put in the bank to help launch her own future. The vault of her imagination had stored it; the deposit had multiplied in her mind, occupying more and more of her thoughts. But now that she had returned to draw from the interest, it all seemed as useless as Confederate dollars.

* * *

One afternoon, as she was going downstairs to collect the mail after another day's failed encounter with the blank notebook, she almost collided with a stranger's lowered head as it charged like a bull up the steps, two at a time, until it nearly plowed into her.

"Sorry," he panted, grabbing the railing to stop his momentum.

Even two steps below, he towered over her. His body poured with perspiration. The tee-shirt clung to him like an older skin preparing to shed. His jogging shorts dripped. The stairs might have been the last leg of his exercise course, because instead of making way for her, he just stood there, heaving with exertion until she moved aside. At the top of the stairs, he lowered his forehead again to wipe it with the hem of his sweat-soaked shirt. Then he introduced himself as her neighbor, the occupant of the other unit on their floor. She was glad he hadn't tried to shake hands.

"I met your husband when he left for work this morning," he told her.

"We were beginning to wonder if anyone really lived in your apartment."

He nodded. "I'm away a lot."

When he opened his door, the corridor filled suddenly with the strong smell of roasting meat, which reached her halfway down the stairs. On her way back up, mail in hand, she saw his face emerging from behind his door.

"Why don't you and your husband have dinner with me tonight?" he said.

Startled, she was glad for a ready-made excuse. "He has to work late to-night," she smiled. "Some other time, we'd love to."

"That's too bad," he said. "I just learned I'm being stood up this evening."

"That *is* too bad," she agreed. "Someone will miss a good meal."

"But what about you?" he asked. "Couldn't you come? Think about it, at least. Say about seven o'clock."

She did not intend to accept this invitation. An excuse, an apology, a thank-you, a some-other-time was what she intended when she knocked on her neighbor's door a few hours later. But when he opened the door, so full of welcome, none of those words came. Candles flickered on tables, music played in a distant room, and gardenias floated in silver bowls. Charmed, she lost her chance to do anything other than come in, exactly as he was urging. Most surprising was her neighbor himself, who a short while ago had resembled nothing so much as a big wet brute of a dog returning from a muddy romp through the park. Now he was quite transformed, and dressed as if going out to a party or fine restaurant. She felt sorry for the woman who had been unable to enjoy the evening planned for her. She felt sorry for her neighbor, whose efforts would be given away to a stranger who didn't even remember his name from when she met him in the hallway a short while ago.

Handing her a glass of wine on a crisp square of white linen, he ushered her into a room crowded with massive mahogany furniture. Dark, heavy drapes hung from every window and puddled on the floor; rugs covered every inch of the blond hardwood. It was so different from her own identical south-facing unit, always flooded with sunlight and not yet fully furnished.

"It's my grandmother's stuff," he apologized, gesturing for her to sit down. "From Wilcox County."

"I'm not sure where that is."

"The sticks," he said.

"That doesn't really narrow it down in the state of Alabama."

He threw back his head and laughed at the ceiling. "Somewhere between Montgomery and Mobile," he said. "In the Black Belt."

She knew what that meant. "This came from a plantation?"

He nodded. "It doesn't belong in this apartment, but I don't know what else to do with it. I figure when I get married and move into a house, I'll let my wife decide whether it stays or goes."

Most certainly, the grandmother's furniture did not belong in a modern two bedroom apartment, and yet, as she sipped the wine and tried to make herself comfortable in a scallop-backed settee covered in faded velvet, she began to feel its appeal nonetheless. It was like stepping into a time capsule. Looking around the room, she could see that everything in it must have come from the plantation house: two bayonets hanging criss-crossed on the wall, oil lamps in floral patterned porcelain on the side tables, a stack of disintegrating cloth-bound books topped by a rusty dagger on the tea-tray in front of her. In broad daylight it might have been hideous or ridiculous, but in the glow of candles and the lull of wine, it possessed a certain magic.

"Did you grow up on the plantation with all this furniture?"

"Sort of," he said. "My parents lived in town on a nice paved road where the mailman came every day. But when my grandfather died, my grandmother didn't want to live alone in 'the big house.' So I lived with her during the week. All four years of high school."

The house wasn't even on a road, he told her, but on a crest above the Alabama River, accessible only by ferry, with mail delivery once a week at best. Every morning he took the ferry across the river to catch the school bus. Before and after the war, his family had owned a landing on the river where the barges stopped on the Alabama River to load more cotton on the way to Mobile. Fees collected from barge owners and cotton planters made them wealthy for a time. But the world changed: children of sharecroppers left to find factory work in the cities, became soldiers in world wars. Cotton ceased to be king. Barge traffic on the river diminished. Over the years, land was sold off or turned to pasture. The house became a forlorn relic of a way of life that was no more.

In his grandmother's final years, there was barely enough to maintain the house and family cemetery next to it. The last remaining tract of land, the back field, had to be sold off. If not for his mother's older brother, who chose to retire back home on the family property, the house itself might have been sold off too. His mother had never wanted to go back and live in what to her was just a big tumbledown farmhouse, with no central air or heat, and a kitchen lacking any of the latest appliances or conveniences. Electricity and phone service were unreliable; repair crews rarely came out. In his mother's view, it wasn't even a safe place to live, let alone desirable. She saw absolutely no romance or glamour of a bygone era in it at all, just a big white elephant of an old farmhouse. The place didn't even have an address, just a route number. There was nothing more embarrassing than that; it meant rural; rural meant the farm.

"My mother didn't even want the furniture," he said. "That's why it came to me when my aunt moved in with her La-Z-Boy recliners and Naugahyde sofas."

When he excused himself to check on the dinner and declined her help, Caroline sat in a daze as the wine buzzed in her ear and the summer evening turned dark. A vague disquiet crept up on her with the gathering darkness, which heightened the surreal quality of the candlelit room full of relics where she had chattered happily with a total stranger as if he were an old friend. A few hours ago she had been unaware of this man's existence; in a few minutes he would be serving her dinner. Something seemed wrong as well as weird about this, not because she wasn't enjoying the experience, but because she was. Usually, Caroline did not seek the company of others any more than she enjoyed it. Four years of high school and four years of college had given her one deep and lasting relationship, which was her marriage. It was not enough to say she didn't make friends easily; she rarely made friends at all. Never had she taken such an instant liking to someone as to her neighbor, and she didn't even know what he did for a living. She was fascinated by his connection to an antebellum South she had never come as close to as he had. Like the rest of the world, she'd once been seduced by the romance of the Old South, although there was nothing truly romantic about what was essentially farm life, especially when it was sustained by human exploitation, first with slaves, then with sharecroppers. And she certainly did not wish that she'd grown up in the middle of nowhere, in the Black Belt, or the small town of Scottsboro where her own family came from. Still, she envied her neighbor's direct link to the Alabama past.

The dining room in his apartment had the same antique furniture, illuminated by two silver candelabra. Once they were seated, he said, "Now it's your turn to tell me where you come from."

She wished she could be as interesting as he was, but what was there to say about Birmingham that he didn't already know, especially after living there for almost a year? The opposite of where he'd grown up, it was a post-war city that became a center of industry for the entire Southeast, second only to Atlanta. The concentration of businesses had led to a concentration of wealth, with most of the wealthy living in the pastoral seclusion of Mountain Brook, where she had grown up and attended school with scions of the founding families or current owners of U.S. Steel, Sloss Furnaces, Vulcan Materials, Barber's Dairy, the Golden Flake Potato Chip Company, Buffalo Rock, Coca-Cola Bottling, Cooley Construction, Hammond Coal, American Cast Iron Pipe, and way too many more to remember. Her cousins were Dixie Pies & Pastries; her aunt Libba had married the grandson of the founder. But the factories, furnaces, plants, and mills were nowhere near Mountain Brook.

"Surely you must have seen some of these places."

Just two field trips in elementary school, she explained, to Barber's Dairy in second grade and the Golden Flake Potato Chip factory in fourth grade. These were the family businesses of two of her classmates. But both excursions had been so excruciatingly boring that she felt deeply sorry for the children whose lives were tied to those dismal places. In their different ways, both the dairy and the potato chip factory had been thoroughly off-putting, with their cavernous structures, imposing machinery, strange odors and sometimes deafening noise. The worst was the workers, who all looked miserable, and did not speak or acknowledge the schoolchildren trouping through, as if they couldn't even see them. When Brett Boyd's father had informed the group that one day, Brett would take over the factory, Caroline could not fathom the pride with which he'd made this announcement. The glances she and many others had cast quickly at Brett had been looks of pure pity. Although no one really liked Brett very much, no one thought he deserved the fate of spending his whole life in a place that looked and felt like a prison. Everyone had agreed that a day in school was preferable to that field trip.

Afterwards, when assigned to write about what they had learned from the tour, Caroline realized that she had learned why Brett walked around in a daze all the time from which he never roused himself to make friends or good grades. He must have been so appalled by the prospect of his future that it had taken the heart completely out of him. Her cousins were not in the least concerned when Dixie Pies & Pastries had been sold to Nabisco. They were glad, they said, they weren't expected to have anything to do with it. On the whole, Caroline didn't envy the trust funds or family businesses that many children of her world inherited. There was something about money already made, as well as businesses already established, that oppressed rather than liberated. Expectations that were hard to escape came attached. The recipients of this good fortune often lost the chance to make their own lives, or failed to insist on having that chance. They stepped into a role when they stepped into their money or their place in the company. Caroline was grateful to have had a somewhat easier time avoiding the pressures of her society.

"Your husband. He's not from here, I take it?"

She shook her head with something akin to pride that her husband was a poor South Alabama boy unlike anyone she'd known in Mountain Brook. Having grown up around young people with trust funds, family businesses and inherited wealth, she had known money and rich people all her life. So poverty was exotic to her. She couldn't see that it had harmed her husband, either. On the contrary, it had instilled him with purpose, ambition and a drive to succeed that she often found lacking in the young people she'd known from Mountain Brook, like her old friend Nick Scully. Instead of a trust fund and a family business, her husband had been given a blank slate along with a free hand to write on it, and seemed infinitely better off.

"I look forward to getting to know him," he said as they cleared the last of the dishes.

"We'll have you over to our place soon."

On her way out, he grabbed a magazine off the table in the tiny entrance hall and thrust it at her as she turned to thank him for dinner. "I'd like your opinion," he said to her startled gaze.

Back in her apartment alone, she was besieged by the guilt that had been creeping up on her throughout the evening while her husband was still hard at work. It was more than a good time she'd had without him; it felt like she'd been on a date with another man. Of course it was intended to be a date, she reassured herself, a date prepared for another woman. She had simply stepped in at the last minute so it wouldn't go to waste: the lovely meal, the flowers, the candles. The problem was that she had enjoyed this date, and wanted another one.

Although she'd been married for a month to a man she'd known for over three years, what had happened tonight seemed almost like the first date she'd ever had. When she went out with her husband for the first time in college, it was to attend five o'clock church services on Easter Sunday, followed by sherry at the rectory. Afterwards, he had taken her back to her dorm room, not out to dinner. A penniless student, he couldn't even afford a café. The one time he'd invited her for coffee, he'd fumbled with the tab—credit cards cancelled, not enough cash—and she'd paid more than half the bill while feeling as if she'd imposed on him in some way. During college they had eaten together in the dining halls. During the summers when he was in Birmingham, they usually ate with her family. Until now, she hadn't known she'd missed anything, either. And it wasn't the food, the flowers, or the candles. It was the way Daniel had simply seized hold of her and taken possession right from the start, like some bird of prey zeroing in with hawk's eyes, swooping down, plucking her from the depths and bearing her aloft. At the time, it was thrilling, like being carried away on the wings of passion. And after all, he didn't have time for anything else. He was going places. But sometimes she got the feeling that she'd already been consumed by him, and all that remained of her were the indigestible parts, after he spit them out.

* * *

In bed as she waited for her husband's return, she flipped through the magazine her neighbor had pressed upon her as she left his apartment. For the life of her, she couldn't figure why he thought she'd be interested in a men's magazine like *Esquire,* or why he would want her opinion about it. Just as she was about to toss it back to the bedside table, the name Ken Newsome jumped out at her from one of the pages. Her neighbor's name. Rifling through again, she failed to find it and regretted all that wine making her see things that weren't there. Why would her neighbor's name be in *Esquire* magazine? She flipped to the table of contents and discovered that Ken Newsome was the author of one of the articles. Dropping the magazine in her lap, she stared into space.

* * *

Early the next morning, Caroline and her husband were woken abruptly by loud, persistent banging that echoed through the corridor of the apartment building. The alarm clock showed five A.M. It sounded like construction noise, but when she stuck her head out into the hall, what she saw was a highly distraught woman pounding on the door of the other unit. If not for her swollen and tear-stained face, the woman would have been beautiful: tall, with Titian red hair and a complexion of cream instead of the freckled or dead-white skin normally found on a redhead. She said something, but in a voice so strangled with emotion it was incoherent. It seemed best just to nod and withdraw without further ado. The woman gave her a rueful smile. "I'm sorry," she said before continuing to knock in more subdued fashion.

"His girlfriend, I guess," her husband had yawned, sitting up in bed. "The one who stood him up last night. Must be a lover's quarrel." He pulled on the sash of her robe. "Let's pretend we just had a lover's quarrel and now we're making up."

But when they did, the face that looked down at her through her own closed eyes was that of her neighbor.

~ 3 ~

Cobb Lane Restaurant was everyone's favorite little lunch place, hidden behind an old brick alleyway in Five Points. Its Southside location drew the ladies from Mountain Brook as well as the business crowd from downtown. Although there was a charming indoor dining area with painted wall murals and tinkling water fountains, most patrons preferred sitting on the cobblestone courtyard shaded by huge oaks and brightly colored umbrellas sprouting from every table. August was normally one of the least popular months, but this particular August day had been so overcast from the start that the usual heat and humidity had been chased away by the storm clouds and an unheard of breeze for this time of year. With the tree canopy and a fan blowing from every corner, the patio today felt like late fall or early spring, and it was packed with people.

Lily Templeton waited at a tiny round table for two near the entrance and a row of potted palms that partially obscured the brick alley on the other side. She was not used to being stood up or sitting alone. Usually, she was the one who didn't show or kept somebody waiting. She wished now that she'd insisted on picking up Caroline, or had not quit smoking. Was it possible she still had a cigarette or two at the bottom of her purse? Rummaging, she managed to produce a somewhat crumpled Winston Lite at the same time she spied a fresh pack of matches in the ashtray on her table. Winston had never been her brand, but she was always finding mysterious objects of unknown origin in her handbag, the little legacies of nights on the town. Looking around, she noticed a few others smoking at the patio tables. So no one could argue. And she wasn't going to *smoke*. She was just going to light up and press the cigarette to her lips every so often. It was only a way to be doing something instead of sitting still as a statue, which she could never do for more than half a minute. Plus, she wouldn't look *alone* with a cigarette in her hand. She would be part of a happy, attractive couple: Girl with a Cigarette.

Sure enough, as soon as she and Winston got going, she drew the gaze of a good-looking guy at the corner table. An attorney, she guessed, like the rest of the guys at the table, with their ties loosened and jackets slung across the backs of their chairs. The women sitting with them were not silly enough to be secretaries, but seemed less serious than wives. Paralegals, probably. Turning slightly away as if she hadn't seen them, she caught a glimpse through the palms of a car coming up the alley. Couldn't be, she thought, afraid it was. She pushed her sunglasses up to get a better view of the driver. *Dear God,* she prayed, *please don't let that be Caroline. I know I just asked you to get her here, but not in that car, dear God.* Stealing a glance at the group of lawyers, Lily was relieved to see their backs turned to the parking lot, where they could not see her lunch date getting out of the most embarrassing automobile ever made. Even brand-new it would have been a no-no.

She stood up and flung her arms around Caroline as if they hadn't seen each other in ages. In fact, they had run across each other in the grocery store two days ago. No doubt this explained why Caroline was taken aback by the effusiveness of her friend's greeting. Caroline didn't know that this was all an act, or that she was supposed to play a part to make it work, because this wasn't a form of knowledge she even recognized. She thought it was just two friends having lunch, and would never understand the game anymore than she could ever be a player in it. But here is what Lily knew: You could be the most beautiful girl in the room, which Lily usually was, but if you weren't in anyone's line of vision, your beauty wasn't going to do you a damn bit of good. First, you had to attract attention, to get people's eyes focused on you. Then you could put your beauty to work. For all Caroline's supposed brilliance, there was so much she didn't know. Actually, she could be downright dumb. For example: that stupid car. If half of success was showing up, then at least half of showing up was showing up in the right car. Also, once you had attracted attention, you had to keep smiling. Instead, Caroline was frowning as she sat down.

"I thought you quit smoking," she said.

"I have," said Lily, cheerfully ignoring the evidence to the contrary in the ashtray lying between them on the tiny wrought iron table.

Wrinkling her nose in a way that was anything but cute, Caroline picked up the ashtray and placed it among the debris at the just vacated table next to them. All wrong, Lily thought. All wrong. After you have started the show, you do not frown, you do not wrinkle up your face in any way, and you don't transfer attention to the pile of dirty dishes at an empty table. That just makes people turn away. Who wants to see frowns, wrinkles or dirty dishes? People like to be entertained; they want to see a fun show, with beautiful people. Best to behave always as if you're a star on camera, filming a movie being viewed in real time by everyone around you. That's the way to be a star in your own life. If you act as if the camera is always on you, everyone's eyes will always be on you as well. Lily realized she was lucky to have been born with this instinctive knowledge; she was always torn between feeling superior to others and feeling sorry for those without her instincts.

"Did you have to borrow the maid's car or something?" She turned slightly sideways in her chair and crossed her bare legs.

"Sorry I'm late," said Caroline, missing the point completely.

Lily leaned across the table as if to whisper a scandalous morsel of unspeakable gossip. Just a little bit of cleavage, not too much.

"Don't look now," she warned. "But I want you to tell me if those guys at the table in the corner are lawyers. Maybe your husband knows them."

Clueless, Caroline turned to stare right straight at them, but the waitress saved the situation by arriving with menus and a tray of iced water. Next, Caroline proceeded to study the menu as if it were a book. Frowning in concentration, utterly absorbed in the printed pages, Caroline was lost to everything around her, while everything and everyone were equally lost on her. She had gone through all four years of high school in the exact same way, Lily well remembered. In the classroom, in the lunchroom, in the library, during study hall, during free period—basically whenever she could—Caroline would be so submerged in the open book in front of her it was as if she lived there, in that foreign underworld, which gave her the oxygen and sustenance she required for her own peculiar existence. She certainly didn't inhabit the same world that everyone else around her lived in. She could be teased, joked about, mocked and ridiculed, and it made no difference, because she couldn't even *hear*. Caroline's powers of concentration were so strong that she heard or saw nothing of the real world when she was focusing on the printed page. Despite what everybody said about the value of reading, Lily simply did not place any value whatsoever in the failure to see and hear what went on around you. And to Lily, the only thing more boring than reading was watching someone else reading. If those handsome young professionals were still looking, they wouldn't be for long. People wanted to see action, beautiful girls in motion. They liked faces brought to life by animation, bodies made exciting by movement. This was the age of movies, not still life. Caroline had missed every single cue, and the performance Lily always strived for was not getting off the ground. If she'd been here with some of her Kappas, they would have created a different scene entirely, but today she needed Caroline for other matters.

Resigned, she leaned back in her chair to scrutinize her friend, who continued to scrutinize the menu. Thanks to her dyslexia, the study of the printed page had never been for Lily. What she studied was women: in person, in magazines, on the screen. Hair, clothes, makeup, jewelry—yes—but mainly style, which for Lily meant a woman's way of being in the world. What did other women get right? What did they do wrong? What effects could Lily duplicate? What did she need to make sure to avoid? There were no greater lessons to learn than these.

As for her friend, Caroline's appearance had changed dramatically in the four years since they'd graduated from the Brook-Haven School. Almost unattractive then, she was almost beautiful now. Her hair was growing out nicely from that super-short cut she used to wear, but it still needed to be re-styled. Although it was blonde enough, it could have been blonder. There *was* such a thing as too blonde, Lily knew. A good colorist was essential for achieving that fine line between looking like Hollywood and looking like trailer trash. Overdoing the blonde just the slightest bit resulted in lower rather than higher-class looks. But Caroline needed just a subtle highlight or two more than she naturally had. Her hair was pretty enough, but didn't have that WOW effect possible with blonde. Same for her face, which was devoid of makeup. If Lily had not known Caroline as well as she did, she would have been insulted. Was Lily so insignificant that Caroline didn't need to make an effort? She could just throw on any old clothes and drag herself out of the house at the last minute? At their age, lack of makeup was no virtue. It was either ignorance or arrogance, or both. Of course Caroline was plenty attractive, or Lily would never have invited her to lunch, because she would never allow herself to be seen in the company of an unattractive or overweight female. Associating with a loser would not send the right signal, create the right image, or attract the right kind of attention, if any. Everything connected to you reflected on you, including the car you drove and the other person or people with you. Everything was your accessory—not just your handbag or your jewelry. Whatever—and especially whoever—shared the stage with you had to be chosen with care because it became part of how you presented yourself to the watching world. For Lily, good-looking friends were not so much rivals as assets to be used when going out in public. This is one of the many things belonging to a top sorority had taught her. Whatever Caroline had learned at the place she went to college, it wasn't showing. But Lily had a soft spot for her old classmate, who so clearly needed Lily's help, like she had in high school, with learning how to shave her legs, how to purchase tampons, how to adjust her bra and so many other essential matters. Since she was such a bookworm, Caroline had no other friends, and Lily always felt sorry for her.

Finally Caroline looked up from the menu and smiled beautifully like she should have done from the first.

"There's really only one thing to order, isn't there?"

"She-crab soup," Lily confirmed.

After giving this order to the waitress, she leaned across the table again.

"Tell me everything you can about Nick Scully," she said.

Taken aback, Caroline only shrugged. "I haven't seen him in a long time," she said. "Do you know him?"

"I met him at your wedding."

Out of the corner of her eye, Lily noticed the group of young professionals rising from their table. She wasn't sure, but she believed the good-looking one had stared blatantly in her direction before heading out.

"We were all surprised he showed up," her friend was saying.

"Why?" Lily said, more eagerly than she intended. Curiosity was getting the better of her. "Was there a bad breakup between you?"

"There was no breakup," Caroline said. "We weren't dating."

The group of lawyers and their paralegals was gathering in the alley just on the other side of the palms from where the two friends sat. Lighters clicked and the smell of cigarette smoke drifted over. Lily shrieked with gaiety.

"Don't be so modest!" she cried. "Of *course* you were dating him! One of the most eligible bachelors that heaps of women have tried to get their hands on!" Lowering her voice, she instructed her friend: "He picked you up in his car and took you out. I think you can call that dating."

Caroline shrugged. "What does it matter now what we call it?"

"Your dating history is who you *are*," Lily hissed, annoyed at her friend's obtuseness.

Caroline made no reply as she accepted a steaming bowl of soup from the waitress.

"Whatever you want to call it," she said after they were both served. "We were just friends when I was in high school. Then I went to college and haven't seen him since. Except briefly at the wedding."

Lily poured sherry in her soup and stirred absently. One question at least was answered: They never slept together. Lily had always wondered. Everyone had. Given his reputation with women and the amount of time they spent together, it was hard for anyone to believe he had not spent some of that time in bed with her. On the other hand, given Caroline's youth, innocence, wallflower looks and librarian's personality, it was equally hard to believe that he would have wanted her for something he was easily getting elsewhere, from much better looking women his own age. So what was he getting from Caroline? Why had he spent all that time with her? These were the crucial questions. Lily knew she'd have to work carefully toward getting the answers.

"What was he like?" She brought a spoonful of soup up to her mouth and nibbled a piece of crabmeat.

"Nick is one of the most interesting people I've ever known," said Caroline, smiling as if at the memory. "Also, one of the smartest. It's just, he's—" She stopped to test her own spoonful of hot soup.

"He's what?" Lily prodded, impatient. "Wild?"

Caroline swallowed and wiped her mouth. "Not wild, exactly," she said. "More like he's bored. So he does these crazy things out of boredom."

Boredom, thought Lily, was a problem she often solved for people. Just then the handsome young attorney in the alleyway leaned over to stub out his cigarette in the soil of the potted palm. Along with the butt, he left a business card.

"What kind of crazy things?" Lily took a deliberate swallow of soup and kept her eyes away from the card.

Caroline considered. "Once he took me twenty-five minutes away to a barbecue shack in North Birmingham," she said. "Out near where our maid lives—where everyone's maid lives. We were the only white people for miles around. Another time he took me to the last drive-in movie theater, out in Pell City. We ate Chinese food out of cartons in his Karmann Ghia."

Lily was shocked. This was far worse than she had heard or anticipated. She was actually at a loss for words.

"It wasn't really that crazy," Caroline went on. "Just different from what anyone else would do."

Lily nodded as she chose her words carefully. "Why do you think he wanted to spend time with someone so much younger?" she said.

"I don't know," Caroline hunched her shoulders in a graceless gesture. "It could be because he's the youngest in his family and liked having me along as a little sister. That's what it felt like, anyway."

Lily bit her lip. She was not meant to be any man's kid sister. That was not a role she ever wanted to play. And she would have died before going on a date to the black part of town or a redneck drive-in movie theater. She would never have allowed the insult of being taken to such places. Her reputation would have been ruined. Nick Scully was going to be more difficult than she thought.

Caroline squeezed a wedge of lemon in her iced tea and took a sip. "Why all this interest in Nick Scully?"

All nonchalance, Lily gave the merest hint of a shrug. "We went out for a drink after your reception. I liked him; I wouldn't mind getting to know him better. That's all."

Actually, Nick had taken her straight to his apartment. A month had gone by since then, and with each day that passed without a phone call, she blamed herself more and more. Not that she had anything against sex, especially when the guy knew what he was doing, like Nick, and she didn't have to do any work. It's just that wasn't how she normally played it, for reasons that were demonstrating their validity in this very situation with Nick Scully. Blow jobs were as far as she usually went; she'd gotten through high school and even college mostly on blow jobs. Guys worshipped you for it, and what's more, they tended to keep quiet about it too, like you were their little secret, to be carefully guarded. Quite unlike how they bragged about getting laid, so proud of their conquest, for being able to do something to a girl, for whom they afterwards lost all respect, as if she'd been a fool to let them get away with it. With a blow job, you were doing something to them, for them. And you could script it to fulfill their fondest dreams and desires, which was to experience the sex of a porn film. If they didn't get all they wanted, they got enough of what they needed to remain smitten, devoted and grateful, working toward the day when you would feel the time was right to go all the way. Meanwhile, you kept the upper hand, you kept your reputation, and you could keep your freedom too. It was almost too easy, the way a girl could absolutely enslave a guy through something as simple as a blow job. Although it might be true that the way to a man's heart was through his stomach, in Lily's experience, the best and fastest way to a man's heart was through his penis. Satisfy the hunger that came from *that* part of a man's anatomy, and he was all yours. With just a little bit of discretion along with careful planning, you could go out with a bunch of guys, make them all want you more, keep them all sweet and keep your options wide open. At least that's how things had worked out for her at Bama.

Nick Scully was not like any other guy she'd ever met, and that had thrown her off balance. At the wedding reception, she had flirted up a storm with him like she did with everyone. If it was shameless, it was also harmless. This was just her personality. It didn't mean anything; it was just fun. What threw her was the way Nick flirted back with a kind of verbal ping pong that was soon hard for her to keep up with. In her experience, most guys were not that verbal. They were too busy looking at her cleavage and devising schemes to get their hands on her. Naturally, she'd been intrigued by Nick, although she suspected he was mocking her in some way. This was more of a challenge than she was used to, but she liked the challenge of it, especially because he had more money and better looks than any other guy she'd ever met. It was thrilling to feel she was playing for higher stakes than ever before. The ten year age difference only added to the effect that he was beyond her reach or out of her league, which made it all the more exciting. That night at the reception, she'd thought she'd lost him when he failed to come back with the drinks he promised. Then out of nowhere he'd grabbed her by the hand.

"Impossible," he told her. "Let's get out of here."

That unexpected touch of his hand had actually sent an electric charge through her body which she'd never felt with anyone before. She still got goose bumps when she thought of that moment. It was like the unexpected promise of victory after the fear of defeat.

When he took her not to a bar but his apartment, she decided to gamble and play it differently, since he himself was so different. She could tell he was a man who wanted more from a woman than sex. She had no idea what that might be, but she thought her only chance of finding out and landing him was to go ahead and give up the sex, as if she was no prick tease who played those silly games with men. So far her gamble had not paid off. She'd been hoping her friend could tell her what else a man like Nick wanted in a woman, but figured she wasn't going to get any more help from Caroline, who had not gone as far with Nick as Lily had, despite all that time they'd spent together.

The lunch crowd was clearing out at Cobb Lane and the patio took on a defeated air, with mostly empty chairs and tables piled with clutter. This was no longer the place to be; the scene had moved on, and Lily always felt the pull of the tide. She pushed away her half-eaten bowl of soup.

"I have found the perfect house for you and your husband," she announced. "What's his name again?"

Caroline looked up from her soup in surprise. "We don't want a house," she said.

"Of course you do," Lily told her. "Your very own mother is the one who put the bug in my ear. Now remind me: your husband's name."

"Daniel."

"The last name?"

"Dobbs."

That was it. Dobbs. Lily knew it was unfortunate as well as forgettable, as most common names were. One of her mottoes was: always trade up. If you were going to give up your own good name, make sure you were getting a better one in return. For example: Scully. A name that was neither ordinary nor outlandish, a name that meant something where she lived. That was the ideal. She liked the sound of Lily Scully. It had a nice, high class ring to it. Lily figured Caroline had gone for the first man who'd ever been interested in her, as if he'd also be the last. Shame it had to be some Dobbs from Sticksville, Alabama. Plus he was way too short. Cute, but short.

"Caroline Dobbs." Lily tried the name out loud.

"I kept my own name."

"Oh, that was smart," Lily told her. "I would have too, honey." She giggled. "Where did you say he's from?"

Caroline was scraping the last of her crabmeat from the bottom of her soup bowl. "Opelika," she said without looking up.

Lily giggled again. "It's funny, isn't it?" she said. "You go all that way to college, only to marry a guy from a hick town back home. You would've done better if you'd gone to Bama. Then you could have found someone from Mountain Brook." She signaled the waitress for the check.

Caroline bristled. "I don't know about you, but *I* went to college to get an education, not a husband," she declared.

"I went to college to have a good time," Lily laughed. "Anyway, *I'm* not the one who just got married," she added slyly.

When Caroline turned red and didn't reply, Lily realized she needed to steer the conversation back to safer ground. "Honey, all I meant was, I thought the whole point of going so far off to school was to stay up there. If you were going to marry someone from Alabama and move back home, why go all that way in the first place?" Lily reached across the table to squeeze her friend's hand. "But I'm so glad you're back and I've got three houses I want to show you today."

Caroline stared at her. "I told you. Please listen to me, not my mother. We Don't Want A House," she repeated emphatically.

"Of Course You Do," Lily countered, with equal insistence. "You just got married."

"What does that have to do with it?" Caroline looked at her as if Lily were speaking a foreign language.

"Silly," said Lily, stifling impatience. "The next step is buying your first house. If you don't take me as your agent, you'll just be pestered by everybody else who wants your business. Trust me. We fight over the newlyweds."

"Why would real estate agents fight over newlyweds?"

Lily ticked off the reasons on her fingers. "Starter house, house for the new baby, house with yard for two kids, house when your husband makes partner. You need to pick an agent now so all the others will leave you alone."

"We're not ready for all that," Caroline protested, shaking her head. "And we just signed a lease."

Lily waved away that objection as if swatting a mosquito. "That lease is nothing," she said. "Those apartments have a waiting list that goes on for *miles*. Besides, I know the manager." She pulled a credit card out of her wallet. "That reminds me," she said, shaking her head at Caroline's twenty dollar bill. "Somebody told me about a guy in your building—I can't remember his name. But they said he's tall, dark and handsome, like a movie star."

"He's my next door neighbor," said Caroline. "Why don't I leave the tip?"

"Lucky," said Lily. "He sounds unbelievable. He played football at Bama, you know."

"No," said Caroline, frowning and shaking her head. "That must be someone else." She put a five dollar bill down on the table. "My neighbor is a journalist. He writes for a magazine."

"Yes! That's the one. That's what I heard." Lily handed the credit card folder to the waitress.

"It can't be the same guy."

"But it is," Lily insisted. "He played football in college and afterwards became a sportswriter for some newspaper somewhere. Now he writes for a magazine and moved to Birmingham. *Sports Illustrated* is what I heard." She bent her head down and scrawled her name on the credit card slip.

"Thanks, hon," said the waitress. "Y'all have a nice day."

Caroline looked all shook up. The signs were unmistakable.

"You've met him," Lily said. "Did he make a pass at you? Have you slept with him?"

Caroline burst out laughing. "I just got married!" she exclaimed.

Lily shrugged. "What does that have to do with anything?"

Caroline couldn't help herself. They laughed hysterically, like silly schoolgirls. Lily was glad to see her friend *enjoying* herself for a change; the girl had never known how to have fun. Never. Not once in the years Lily had known her at that dratted high school had she known Caroline to have fun. She was always reading or studying. Didn't go out at night, didn't come to parties.

"If you're not interested in him, see if you can set me up, would you? Tell him you have the most fabulous friend. Make it all up. Make me gorgeous, vivacious, charming—everything."

Caroline smiled and sipped her iced tea. "I think he has a girlfriend."

"Of course he does, honey! All the good ones either have girlfriends or wives, or they wouldn't be good ones! Don't tell me *your* man didn't have anyone when he met you." Lily pulled a lipstick and makeup mirror out of her purse and worked openly to repair the damage from lunch since there was no one on the patio but the two of them.

Caroline blushed and said nothing. Lily feared this time she'd finally gone too far for her friend's limited sense of humor until Caroline said, almost teasing, "I thought you were interested in Nick Scully."

"Honey," she said, snapping her compact shut as if for emphasis. "I'm interested in *all* good-looking men. And the world is so full of good-looking guys. It's one of the things that makes life worth living. All those possibilities out there. And don't forget what our mothers used to tell us." She wagged her finger at Caroline as she adopted her mother's voice. "Even if you don't like *him,* go out with him anyway. He may have a friend you do like."

Instead of nodding in corroboration, Caroline gave her a sour look.

Lily cocked her head. "Don't tell me your mother didn't tell you the same thing."

"You never know how one person you don't care about will lead you to another person you do care about." Caroline's mimicry was less than playful.

Arching her eyebrows, Lily said, "Well, what's wrong with it? Don't you agree?"

"Using people is wrong. That's what's wrong with it," said Caroline.

Lily sighed. Caroline could be so tiresome. As they pushed back from the table, Lily waited until her friend had turned to go before palming the business card from the potted plant. As usual, Caroline didn't notice a thing. Not for the first time, Lily pondered the definition of intelligence. According to what the world called smart, Caroline was and Lily wasn't. This seemed backwards. No one she'd ever met was slower on the uptake and more unaware of what went on around her than Caroline Elmore. So what if she'd made all those good grades and earned a fancy degree? None of that had done her a bit of good, as far as Lily could tell. At lunch she had seemed even quieter than usual, and not particularly happy. If that's what smart was, then Caroline could have it. Lily would much rather be happy.

Caroline turned toward her on the way to the parking lot. "What about my husband's roommate from college?" she said. "Are you interested in him? He certainly seemed interested in you at the wedding."

"He calls me all the time," Lily acknowledged, stifling a yawn.

"Well?" Caroline smiled.

"I guess I might go up there to visit, when he's finished that training program."

A sudden gust of wind whipped their hair around and spattered a few large raindrops. Both girls stopped to look up at the sky.

"You know who he is, don't you?" said Caroline.

"Who?" said Lily, yawning outright. For some reason, lunch always made her sleepy, no matter how little she ate. She really needed a Diet Coke, and wished she could have a cigarette for real.

"My husband's roommate."

"What about him?" Lily took her friend by the elbow and steered her over to where her own car was parked in the lot.

"He's a DuPont."

Lily fished for her keys. "So what's a DuPont? I don't know any DuPonts," she said. "That's not a name from around here."

"No," Caroline smiled. "But it's a name from up there."

Lily shrugged and unlocked her front door. "Who cares? What use to me is a guy who lives so far away? And who would want to live up there? I always thought New York was more trouble than it's worth. Don't you? Go ahead and get in before we get rained on."

Mule-headed, Caroline declined to get in the car and insisted that she and her husband weren't interested in a house, didn't want to buy, didn't have the money. Same things they all said, until Lily found the perfect house. And she always found the perfect house. She may not have been a great reader of books—not with her dyslexia—but she sure could read people. Once she knew who a person was, she could go out the next day and find their dream home. In the case of a couple, you had to know them both, see them together, spend some time with them.

As another gust of wind unleashed more raindrops, Caroline gave in with a sigh. "Okay," she said. "I'll follow you in my car."

"You will not come anywhere near me in that car," Lily stated emphatically. "Now get in before the rain ruins us both."

At first Caroline sat in a stubborn silence that Lily was used to from clients who didn't yet realize they were clients.

"Have me over next week, why don't you?" she suggested to her friend. "Just for a drink. I want to know your husband better. I'd like to get to know your neighbor better, too. Invite him over while you're at it." She laughed at her own joke.

"I don't know him that well."

"Perfect reason for inviting him over. Why wait for things to happen when you can make things happen? Why go slow when you can go fast? That's always been my philosophy."

Caroline stared out the window and didn't answer.

Undaunted, Lily said, "I could always just knock on his door and introduce myself."

"Are you serious?"

"Sure. Why not? I have the perfect excuse. It's my job."

"Your job?"

"I sell houses, dummy. I can call up perfect strangers or knock on their door with a sales pitch. I do it all the time. It's very exciting. You never know what it will lead to." Lily smiled to herself as she thought of the business card containing a phone number she would be dialing soon—not today, but tomorrow, or maybe even the day after, when the guy had stopped wondering if he would hear from her and started hoping he would. "How did you know I was a real estate agent?" she would ask him. "How can I help you? What are you in the market for?"

~ 4 ~

The offer from Caroline's mother to host a small family dinner party to celebrate her daughter's birthday had been extended confidentially to Daniel.

"I don't know what you have planned," his mother-in-law had said to him. "But if you'd like, I'd be happy to have Caroline's birthday dinner here at our house."

Believing there was only the one polite thing to do, Daniel had accepted with gratitude. Obviously he should have been developing his own plans for the occasion, but since he had not, he was fortunate his wife's mother was such a foresighted and generous ally rather than the adversary she could have been. Instead of looking down her nose at his no-account background or scoffing at his ambitions, she did everything she could to help his career, his marriage and his life in Mountain Brook become a success. It did not even occur to him to decline her kind offer. Also, as much as he tried to hush the internalized voices of his parents, he could still hear them pointing out that this birthday dinner would be free, and it would take place at one of the most exclusive addresses in Mountain Brook. As far as he could see, there was nothing not to like about the whole idea. Caroline's dismay took him completely aback.

"She went to you because she knew I'd say no! You let her play you!"

"Your mother's just being sweet," he had protested in defense of both himself and his mother-in-law.

"No, she's not," Caroline had retorted. "Being sweet is the camouflage she's perfected over the years."

"Camouflage?! For what?"

"Manipulation."

First, he was astounded. Then, he burst out laughing. "Why would your mother need to manipulate anyone?"

"It's the way Southern women like her were raised. Not to demand what they want. Or pursue it directly. That's not lady-like. So they have to use strictly underhanded means while appearing to be nothing but *sweet.*" The scorn with which she uttered this word made sweetness sound like some kind of crime.

"You're over-analyzing this," he said, not for the first time in their relationship. "It's just a dinner invitation. Your mother is offering to do something *for you.*"

Caroline only shook her head. "She always uses other people to get what she wants for herself. That's part of the cover too."

"Cover for what? What could she possibly be getting out of this?"

"We'll find out only when it's too late."

Then it was Daniel who shook his head, partly in amusement, partly in bafflement at the strange dynamics between mothers and daughters. These dynamics were even more mysterious than the ones between husbands and wives, which he was still trying to figure out. However, one thing Caroline made sure he did learn from this incident is that a married man presented with a proposition of any kind should first check with his wife before making a decision.

When Mrs. Elmore later asked, "Is five too early?" Daniel now knew to say, "Let me check with my wife."

Indeed, five was a bit early, but they agreed anyway. When they drove toward the Elmore's house, it was the most beautiful time of day on that early fall afternoon. The blaze and glare of the Indian summer sun had subsided into an incandescence which cast precisely that rosy glow the original developer of Mountain Brook had in mind in the 1920s when this special enclave was carved out of the thickly wooded Appalachian foothills of Red Mountain and Shades Mountain. In the sunset shimmer of this luminescence, it didn't matter that Mountain Brook's New South replicas of Old South plantation houses looked like a South that never was. The sloping neighborhoods and winding roads studded with trees and white-columned mansions nestled in lush estate-sized lots looked like the South as it should be. Here the plantation South was not gone with the wind, but right up on the mountain above the industrial, post-Civil War steel city. Mansions that looked like Tara competed grandly with others that re-created the baronial splendor of England and Scotland. The captains of industry made so much money in the valley that the mountainside enclave where they lived in such splendid isolation was one of the ten wealthiest communities in the country, despite its location in one of the poorest of all the states. Enveloped by the intact original canopy of

trees, it was also one of the most beautiful. In short, Mountain Brook embod-
ied a perfect union between Mother Nature and the almighty dollar. It was,
in fact, the best of all possible worlds, the Tiny Kingdom, a fairytale universe
of beauty and riches which had nothing to do with that "other Alabama" of
poverty and ignorance, and as little to do with "the real world" as possible.
The grimy downtown of Birmingham in the valley below, with its inferno of
soot, smog, and smokestacks, inhabited another universe. The glaring contra-
dictions of antebellum and feudal grandeur in a city of blast furnaces, of so
much wealth amidst so much poverty, did not bother anyone who resided in
Mountain Brook.

Instead of going directly inside the house with her husband when they
arrived, Caroline went first for a stroll through the rose garden. When she
was a child, her job had been to "freshen the flowers" every day, which meant
removing the faded roses from their vases in all rooms of the house and replacing them with new ones just gathered from the garden, which always had
some flowers in bloom most times of the year. Next to the four plots of rose
bushes was her father's tremendous vegetable garden, now planted for a late
autumn yield. A still-verdant wisteria vine overwhelmed the wrought iron
fence at the edge of the backyard. For a moment she lingered there to watch
the lights of the "Magic City" begin twinkling in the distance.

There was no denying the beauty of the place where she had grown up.
During her four years away at college, she had appreciated this beauty like she
never had when she lived with it every day, although she'd always been told
how lucky she was to live where she did. Unfortunately, she'd never felt lucky.
She had only felt tricked. And trapped. With a child's unadulterated instincts,
she had known something was missing from the world where she lived; something was wrong with this too-perfect picture. It was all a sham: an artificial,
parallel universe manufactured by parents and foisted on hapless children to
prevent them from having any fun. Somewhere out there was the real world,
she knew, hidden from children by the grownups. Somewhere people were
living what could be called life. Where she lived, nothing ever happened. She
knew that couldn't be right. But whenever she and her siblings had expressed
discontent with their days, especially during the eternal summers, they were
chastised for not being thankful for all they'd been given, because they had
been given EVERYTHING. Perhaps from an adult's perspective, it was everything: beauty, luxury, safety, peace and serenity. But to a child, all this was
nothing. Little did she even know then that the world had its own reasons
for hating her hometown; hers were the reasons of a child. To her, the town
was guilty of the worst of all possible sins: it was BORING. Children don't want

peace and serenity, the calm of the dead. Children want excitement, activity and adventure. But all she had was just the swimming pool at the country club, along with the house where she lived and the yard she was forbidden to play in when it was too hot outside.

And it was usually too hot outside. Mothers raised their children as they had been raised, when the threat of infantile paralysis, which thrived on heat, forced children indoors during the hot summer days. Advancements in medical science that eradicated the scourge of childhood brought no immediate advancement in the mentality of Southern motherhood. Although the danger lurking outdoors was obsolete, it was now tradition to keep children sequestered and sheltered indoors during the hottest summer months. This is what was done by parents who knew better and raised their children right, unlike white trash that let theirs run around outside all day like "hooligans" because they didn't know any better. Progress might be able to wipe out things like polio, but it had a hard time changing customs in the South.

In any case, the circumscribed confines of her small world were not enough. Although there was everything to delight the senses, there was nothing for the mind to feed on or the soul to live on. This world was as beautiful and empty-headed as the Southern belle it was raising her to be. So she could not comprehend the good fortune of her circumstances; what she knew was the existential despair of an undernourished soul and an un-stimulated mind. Out of this despair she had discovered books, which became her salvation, although she had to read in defiance of her mother, who feared that books would ruin her chances in life. Every time she saw Caroline, her nose was stuck in the pages of "some book," her eyes were crossed in concentration, and her brow wrinkled with mental exertion. "Don't squint so!" her mother always scolded. "You'll end up wearing glasses." Her mother was afraid Caroline was already turning into an old maid. Boys would not go on dates with girls who wore eyeglasses and were smarter than they, she warned. And if Caroline never had any dates . . . she would never have a life.

But nothing had stopped her from reading. The words filled all the blank spaces of her life and the vacancy of the world she lived in. Literature gave her a way to go inside herself and grapple with her desperate soul; likewise it gave her a way to go outside herself and her own circumscribed place and time, and grapple with the world beyond her ken. Books transported her out of the Tiny Kingdom and into the real world which she knew was out there, hidden from the children by the grown-ups' conspiracy.

The parents were only doing what they thought they were supposed to do. She understood that now. Except for a brief four-year interlude of fraternity and sorority parties at the University of Alabama, located in Tuscaloosa, forty-five minutes away, these parents had lived all their lives in Mountain Brook. The purpose of their so-called college years was to have fun before settling down back home with someone they'd probably dated in high school. This was deemed success. To be a further success as parents, they needed to make this good life possible for their children, which meant keeping them safe and sheltered from all the harmful influences lurking outside Mountain Brook. A child who left to pursue "success" in that outer world often brought shame and even suspicion on the parents, who must have failed in their duty to groom their child for the best of all possible worlds, which could only be found in Mountain Brook. First and foremost, success was defined by living in Mountain Brook. No matter what their achievements, those who lived anywhere else—be it New York, D.C., L.A., or Chicago—had failed in the most important respect: they did not occupy the Garden of Eden which was the Tiny Kingdom. When someone from Birmingham held a position on the outside—like, say, editor-in-chief of the New York *Times*—this was probably because that unfortunate person had not grown up in Mountain Brook. Few who occupied a position in Mountain Brook would seek one elsewhere.

However, she had known from an early age that she could not live in a place where nothing ever happened. If anyone had tried to tell her as a child that Birmingham was the battleground for a revolution that had changed her city, her state, and even her country, she would not have believed it. Throughout her childhood, she had yearned and searched in vain for such meaningful excitement. No way, she would have said, could they keep *that much* from us. But they had. Although she'd grown up in Birmingham in the 1960s, she'd known nothing of the Civil Rights Movement until she encountered it in a high school textbook a decade and a half after it had happened in her own native city and state. But her backyard stopped at the wisteria-laden wrought iron fence. That was as close as she usually came to the actual city of downtown Birmingham. In this way Mountain Brook had continued to serve its original purpose of shielding the wealthy and privileged from unpleasant realities. Designed to be an idyllic refuge from the noise, pollution and hordes of steel mill workers in the industrial city, it later shielded its residents from the racial convulsions that occurred on the streets of downtown Birmingham. These convulsions may have rocked the nation and even the world, but they were not able to penetrate the tree canopy that kept Mountain Brook cloistered.

Mr. Laney had gotten her out. He'd gotten them all out. He rescued all souls in despair, be it the soul of the black girl born to racism and segregation, or the soul of the white girl born to wealth and privilege. Because of him, both the white child and the black child could attend the best school together in Birmingham, and no graduate of this school would ever be conscripted into the life of a maid or a belle. From the moment she'd first met him, Caroline had loved all several hundred pounds of him; the power of his individual force outmatched the power of an entire society that had marshaled all its strength to preventing anything from happening and to denying anything had happened, even when one of the most important events in American history occurred on its doorstep. This society was fiercely protective of its fairytale paradise, where girls like Caroline were supposed to become princesses —or at least debutantes—who married a prince—or at least a man like their fathers, who could provide the good life in a big, beautiful house like the ones where they'd grown up in the best of all possible worlds, the Tiny Kingdom of Mountain Brook. But Mr. Laney had punctured the hermetically sealed cocoon where they were kept sheltered, and released them into the open air, where they were free to seek their own destinies instead of those allotted for them in the butterfly hothouse of Mountain Brook, where they would have led captive, if pampered, lives. He pierced the veil, showed them the way out, and convinced their parents to stand aside as they all accomplished their exodus.

And Caroline had chosen to return for reasons that were becoming less clear to her by the day. She had made her escape, she was free and clear, yet she had chosen to come back to the place that had kept her in thrall. Why had she done this to herself? Why had she deliberately put herself in this difficult position?

* * *

Inside the house, the TV blaring from the library broadcast not only the pregame show but the reason her mother had schemed for company on this particular evening. And why she'd set such an early hour. An Alabama football game kicked off at six.

Like most other Alabama residents and former Bama students, Midge Elmore thought a Crimson Tide football game was party time. But over the years, her husband had become one of those fans who refused to leave his own house when Alabama was playing a game. Midge loved game-day brunches and backyard barbecues. But her husband believed the games were too important to be co-opted by a social occasion, and several years ago placed a moratorium on football parties. At these events, he missed half the action because he never got a good enough view of the TV screen, and he missed half of what the announcers said because there was always too much chatter in the room. The primary annoyance came from those few guests who were not even Alabama fans and had no business being at the party, such as the insufferable Ed Blankenship. Besides the unacceptable fact that he was a plaintiff's attorney, he also came from somewhere in the Midwest. In addition to his obnoxious laugh, he lacked any appreciation for football, which resulted in derisive remarks calling into question the seriousness of football in general and the supremacy, significance and social purpose of the Alabama Crimson Tide in particular. Even in the best of circumstances, her father could not abide Ed Blankenship, and preferred to encounter him in a courtroom setting, where he could—and had—beat the man in front of judge and jury. This kind of conquest was not possible at a Saturday morning brunch or evening barbecue where women and children were present. When Perry Elmore watched the games alone with his wife, he could shout at the television and/or his wife as much as he liked when Alabama played badly, just as he used to shout at the children whenever they made bad grades. Fortunately, Alabama rarely played badly, just as the children had learned never to bring home a bad grade. Still, the experience of watching games with her husband was less than festive. So Midge had used the excuse of her daughter's birthday to orchestrate the kind of football-watching party her husband normally refused to allow or attend.

But when she secured her husband's agreement to the birthday dinner, Midge omitted any mention of the scheduled game. By the time he found out, it was too late to cancel the party. When Caroline entered the library where Daniel and her mother were enjoying the pregame show in the conspicuous absence of her father, Midge shot her daughter a look of concerned commiseration. It was, after all, *Caroline's* birthday that had imposed on the game day. Midge bore no responsibility for this unfortunate accident of timing.

"Your father's in the sunroom," Midge confided ominously to her daughter, while making an exaggerated frown suggestive of her husband's mood. "He didn't realize your birthday dinner was the same night as the game."

Midge had not failed to inform; her husband had failed to realize.

"Maybe you could talk to him," her mother urged.

This was coded language to convey that Caroline's father would only blow up at Midge and create a scene in front of company; whereas the birthday girl might be able to nudge her father into the party spirit.

Sighing, Caroline left the room. Once again, her mother was getting everything she wanted while everyone else had to pay the costs and grin and bear it. There was certainly something to be said for manipulation. You didn't have to fight for what you wanted, or negotiate its terms. You just had to set your trap well and watch the others walk right into it. And it wasn't just one night, a birthday celebration or a football game. It would be your whole life if you didn't watch out.

In the sunroom, her father shot her only a baleful glance before returning to the newspaper in his lap, as if to suggest that twenty-two-year-old married daughters should not require their parents' help in celebrating birthdays during Alabama football games.

"I think I'll go next door," she said when her father failed to greet her. "See if Lena and Julian are ready to come over," she continued, referring to her cousin and her husband, who were the only other guests and had stopped at her aunt's house to say hello first.

Her father looked up and flapped his newspaper shut, signaling his readiness to acknowledge her presence. Then he took a sip of what she knew was a very dry martini, which caused his lips to curl with tart pleasure.

"So!" he addressed her, as he always had, like a military commander calling on one of his troops to give an account of herself.

No matter how well prepared she was, these moments had always jolted her into panic. Afterward, she always vowed to herself that next time, she would report the most extraordinary accomplishment that would finally elicit actual praise, rather than the mere nod of approval that was all he normally gave. As for her father's love as well as his praise, there was no question of love. Of course he loved her; she was his child. How could he not love this piece of himself? Love wasn't the issue. This piece of him shouldn't require a pat on the back any more than he did. But this piece of him did need to prove worthy of being a chip off his block.

"How is the writing going?" Her father took another sip of his martini, and the pursed lips and narrowed eyes this gave him were aimed directly at her, as if she were responsible rather than the drink.

Her heart began racing in its familiar reaction to one of her father's interrogations. Growing up and getting married had not, after all, released her from the old patterns of her existence. Indeed, now it was worse. Now she had nothing tangible to produce: no grades, no test scores, no teacher comments, no report cards. Just the mere fact of her existence was all she had to offer. This was not enough; it had never been enough for her father. She must *do* something with this existence that proved her worthy of his regard, worthy of being his daughter. Simply to be an ordinary individual who lived an ordinary life: this was a C in a teacher's grade book, and according to her father's standards, a C was the same as an F. It was failure. To be average or ordinary was to fail to be extraordinary. Such was her father's scorn for a life or individual that failed to stand out, she might as well have been in prison, or drug rehab. Her immediate presence was no more compelling than her mere existence. On the contrary, now that she had been to Harvard, now that Mr. Laney had introduced them all to the idea of success in the larger world and her father had enjoyed an intoxicating taste of it through her Ivy League education, he would rather his daughter be in some far-flung location performing remarkable and noteworthy deeds than living an ordinary life back home. The fact that he was living an ordinary life was all the more reason that she should not, especially as he had submitted to the ordinary precisely so that these various pieces of himself he had produced would have their chance to be extraordinary, and in the process, demonstrate to the world how extraordinary their progenitor was. She owed the both of them nothing less.

"The writing is going well," she told her father, although so far, this "writing" consisted of hours spent looking out the window and a few scribbled pages that were already in a landfill somewhere.

"Great!" he said. "What's the next step? What do you do when it's finished?"

He gave her no choice but to overlook the fact that "it" was not even begun, and therefore, far from finished.

"Two classmates of mine took jobs in publishing houses in New York," she said.

Her father nodded slightly as he sipped on his martini. This was rather thin, she knew he was thinking, and she wasn't even telling him that one of these publishing jobs was in graphic design, and the other was with a cookbook imprint. He would have preferred to hear of a lucrative contract with an imminent publication date. This was the kind of achievement he expected, and had every right to demand, given the money he had spent on private schools and an Ivy League education. Anything less would prove a waste of thousands upon thousands of dollars he had lavished on her advancement.

"Well, keep us posted," he said, taking another sip of his martini before looking back down at his newspaper.

And so she was dismissed; the interrogation was over. It was clear she had given a disappointing report, and "keep us posted" did not mean she was to share with him the difficulties and struggles involved in the writing process, or the steep learning curve confronting any would-be author seeking publication. He was not interested in process, only in successful results. What was Harvard for, if not to confer upon her the means to produce stupendous and instantaneous results? Let others of lesser intelligence and ability, with lesser degrees, labor in those mundane ways of daily endeavor. It was time for her to step out on stage, unleash her voice, or otherwise show the world what she was made of. Her father didn't want a daughter; he wanted a star.

* * *

"Twenty-two years ago today," her mother started off. "I was sitting in those stands at Denny Stadium in Tuscaloosa, during Alabama's homecoming game against Miami. Nine months pregnant. Joe Namath was quarterback."

"Twenty-two years minus one day ago," her father interrupted. "Caroline was born the day after you went into labor. Just like I predicted twenty-two years minus one day ago."

"Well, whatever," continued her mother. "I went into labor in the third quarter. Alabama was ahead by only three points, and Miami was about to score."

"The stadium was packed," said her father. "Shoulder to shoulder, and the crowd was going wild. I had to pry myself out of my seat so I could get to the top of the stands and see if there was any way out."

"No," said her mother, laughing and shaking her head. "First you told me that you weren't about to leave the game in the middle of the third quarter, with Alabama ahead by only three points and Miami about to score."

"Would I say a thing like that?" asked her father in mock disbelief.

Everyone laughed.

"But I do go to the top of the stands," he continued. "What I see tells me there is no way out of that stadium except by helicopter. In those days, you had as much chance of getting a space ship. But that's what it would have taken to get us out. There was nothing but cars for miles and miles. The entire town of Tuscaloosa had turned into a parking lot for Denny Stadium. No way for an ambulance to get in. No way for any car to get out. We would have had to walk to the hospital."

"No emergency planning in those days," observed Julian. "Back in the dark ages."

"No emergency planning whatsoever," her father concurred. "I don't know about the dark ages. I was in law school. This was only twenty years ago."

"Twenty-two years minus one day ago," corrected Julian.

"So I go up to this nice older couple sitting next to us," said her father. "Told them my wife was in labor, but there was no way out. Could they make a little room for her? And I'm telling you: It was like the parting of the waters, Moses and the Red Sea. Midge lies down, the baby holds off, and Alabama wins the game."

"We even got to have the party we planned afterward," said her mother.

"First thing you did right, before you were even born," Julian said to Caroline. "You didn't interfere with the Alabama game. That's the first lesson everybody needs to learn if they're born in this state."

"You are so right, Julian," Midge concurred. "In Tuscaloosa, the sorority houses are only a block away from the stadium," she noted. "We could see Denny Stadium from the Kappa house. I knew if I was going to have a life, I'd have to learn football. It was all anyone cared about."

* * *

Back home, when her husband fell asleep, Caroline crept quietly out of the bedroom and tiptoed to the couch in her study to take stock of her twenty-two-year-old self. It was not a pretty picture. Here she was, a college graduate and a married woman who was somehow still stuck in her childhood existence: the invisible webs her mother wove to make husband and children unwitting pawns who did her bidding; the overt terror tactics her father employed as his male prerogative to impose his will. Although neither parent succeeded completely, they did not fall far enough short of their mark to leave each other or their children unharmed. In going to college and even getting married, Caroline had failed to escape the flawed dynamics of her family life. Her father still put the screws to her as if she were some do-nothing who'd never once made him proud or glad to have her as a daughter. Her mother was still spinning webs to steer her daughter's course toward her own aims and desires: the big wedding, the honeymoon "at the Windsor Court," the young couple's first house. Caroline had thought that her marriage would fulfill all her mother's hopes and dreams, and that with this main goal in life achieved, her mother would be satisfied and leave her alone. This wasn't the reason she'd married so young. She'd married because she was lonely and in love, but it would have been more practical to finish graduate school first. However, she would never have heard the end of it if she'd "embarrassed" the family by staying with Daniel on weekends home from Tuscaloosa. Marriage would secure her privacy as well as the man she loved, she believed, and delaying graduate school for a year would give her a chance to write while she established her marriage. But the book was not writing itself, and the marriage had only increased her mother's desire for Caroline to shine in society. The daughter would not be left alone. Marriage had made her more public, not less. Now she was a wife, she needed the right house, the Junior League, and soon enough, there would be hints about children. The only way to avoid her mother's manipulations was to avoid her altogether. And the only way to avoid her altogether was to live somewhere else. Especially because Caroline's husband had become such a willing pawn. He wanted her mother to tell him what to do. He wanted to shine in this society.

In the kitchen, she hunted for an herbal teabag while waiting for water to boil. The recitation of the birthday story, her origin myth, had not helped any, she reflected as she searched through cabinets. Her parents were still not prepared for her birth as a separate individual, any more than they had been twenty-two years *minus one day* ago in the third quarter of the Homecoming game when Alabama was ahead by only three points and Miami was about to score. Then there was the specter of the sorority house, located in the shadow of the stadium where the Alabama game was played out, the game that in turn cast its shadow over the population of an entire state, which believed, as her mother had, that if you don't play this game, or can't, you wouldn't have a life worth living. It was the game played everywhere, exacerbated by the culture and heritage of Alabama, in which those with the most power trampled those without. Her mother had submitted to this because it was the only game in town, although she came out the loser, a woman who depended entirely on a man who didn't respect her and didn't much like her either.

Caroline blew on her cup of hot tea as she made her way back to the study. She had vowed to escape the shadow, and refused to play the game. Yet here she was, back in Alabama, dependent on a man. At least he respected and loved her, but she was beginning to fear that she hadn't escaped either the shadow or the game. A "writer" who couldn't write and didn't earn any money had no power in this world, especially as a woman. Worst of all was the sensation of being trapped until the game was over, of having no exit, no way out of the stadium once you had entered and become part of the game. Years ago she had promised herself she would go far away and never come back, never get trapped. Why had she taken the risk of returning? What had she come back for? It wasn't just her husband's political ambitions. And it wasn't just Mr. Laney, who had told them all they had to do more than get out. They also had to come back. He hadn't meant they needed to come back either literally or permanently. Yet this was what she had chosen of her own free will for cryptic reasons of her own she couldn't even explain to herself.

One reason might be her reaction to Harvard. In her high school years when she was struggling for escape from the closed world of her home, she had projected all her hopes onto "the North," which she envisioned as a promised land of enlightenment and progress. Yet when she gained coveted admittance and finally arrived there, these hopes were betrayed. Harvard seemed just another closed, cocksure world, smug in its conviction that it knew everything, had everything, had nothing to learn or gain from anyone or anyplace outside itself, and was therefore justified in keeping to its elite self. In its arrogant solipsism, it was not fundamentally different from Mountain Brook: a self-satisfied society believing itself the best of all possible worlds and the ultimate arbiter of the good life. The fact that Harvard was a pinnacle of education while Mountain Brook was on top of nothing more than a few inconsequential Appalachian foothills only made Harvard worse. All those smart, well-educated people should have known better than to succumb to hubris and humorless self-importance. Whatever else Harvard had given them, it had failed to confer the true wisdom of knowing you knew nothing, which theoretically led to modesty and humility.

And she had not really escaped the South. On the contrary, the South had come to claim her when she first arrived on the campus of the great Northeastern university. For a girl raised in the green womb-world of the South, the harsh urban landscape of the North was a rude shock. If the South had everything to please the senses and nothing to stimulate the mind, the Northeast was the reverse, with everything to overstimulate the mind and torture the senses. She knew right away she had not come to the place where she could put herself or her life together. There was too much wrong with this world also, too much missing. From the very beginning she had missed the beauty, warmth and softness of the natural world of her homeland and the people who lived there. Crossing Harvard Yard, fellow students and acquaintances would lower their eyes as they passed her, to avoid the encounter. At first she thought this was a personal rejection of her inadequate and Southern self, which wasn't good enough and didn't belong there. Later she realized that only the Southerners and Californians smiled and waved at people they knew. The Southerners smiled and waved at people they didn't know too. The Northerners wouldn't even look at you. They weren't intentionally rude, perhaps, just intense, driven, ambitious and single-minded. These preoccupied minds did not notice or care when someone else passed by. As for the professors, they regarded all undergraduate students only as the necessary evil of their academic existence. After all, these famous professors had their own important work to do, conducting research, applying for grants, writing books and articles. The two or three times a week they lectured for college courses was really the most they could do for the undergraduates.

Stricken with acute homesickness, Caroline had suffered as if from an actual disease. She lost weight, she stopped menstruating, and her face broke out in a rash so alarming she was tested for lupus and other autoimmune illnesses. When the tests were negative, the doctors told her the cause must be stress.

She had been so miserable, she was sure she was failing. She *was* failing: she hated it. Surely it was failure to be so unhappy at this most ultimate destination, Harvard University. Out of habit and pride she completed her work, certain it would be branded the failure she knew herself to be. To her astonishment, she had somehow managed to make all A's in the midst of her personal despair. But instead of calming her, that first report card only inflamed her further. She had come a thousand miles away from home to a cold, bitter climate to live amongst cold, unfriendly people in order to participate in a charade which seemed never to have been exposed before simply because those who got to take part in it benefited so greatly from the cachet attached to it. The hardest part about it—and it was truly hard—was simply being there. The work itself was—if not nothing—far easier to master than those on the outside would have supposed. The formula for success was quite simple: do your work, go to class, and expect nothing from your professors. Instead, attend all (optional) section meetings, because the overburdened, underpaid graduate student section leaders who had their own course work and dissertations to complete were also the ones who graded the undergraduates' work. Those who were known to their section leaders through faithful attendance were the ones who did the best, especially because there were so many geniuses and high IQs who didn't "need" section meetings and thus remained complete strangers to those who would determine their final grade. Once this basic fact of life about big research institutions was understood, it was not hard to succeed, even at Harvard. Far more people would do perfectly well there than would ever have the chance to do so. After all, if a desperately lonely and unhappy girl from Alabama could do it, then who couldn't? The key was becoming one of the chosen few who *got in*. It was not much different from being accepted by a sorority or a country club. She had thought Harvard would be different, and would take her away from that shallow world of unearned and arbitrary supremacy, where those who ruled were merely the lucky ones who *got in*.

The prospect of using her Harvard diploma to *get in* to other closed worlds of power and prestige in places she didn't want to live was untenable. After four years of Harvard, it had not been hard to say "No thanks!" to all that. In fact, it had seemed the only viable thing to do. The only course of action for someone who hoped to create herself rather than become a product of any society's creation. And if that place wasn't as good as she had imagined it would be, then maybe her own wasn't as bad. She had overvalued one place; it could be she had undervalued another. In any case, she had never truly escaped the South at all, so perhaps that was why she'd been compelled to come back and wrestle more conclusively with the place of her birth. Instinct told her that only through the struggle to live there as an adult and an individual on her own terms could she become the person and the writer she wanted to be. It wasn't easy, and it was much harder than Harvard.

~ 5 ~

Adelaide Whitmire had been put in charge of the grand opening gala for the new wing of the Birmingham Museum of Art, which meant Norman Laney was doing all the work. One Saturday afternoon in October, as he was passing through the lobby on his way to the offices, he caught sight of Nick Scully eating lunch in the new museum café with a young woman Norman didn't recognize from her back. Unfortunately, he was sure Nick had caught sight of him as well. This was one of the many disadvantages of being several hundred pounds heavier than the normal person: Norman was never inconspicuous. And Nick had donated generous sums for both the gala and the new wing itself. Norman tried to put on his best smile, and forced himself into the café to offer his thanks.

To his surprise, the young woman turned out to be Lily Templeton, another of his former students, who hopped up and hugged his neck with cries of delight as soon as he approached their table. A mere four years ago, she would have ducked for cover and run in the opposite direction if she spied him either in a public place or in the hallways of school. Technically, she still belonged in the hallways of that school, because several term papers for several of her senior classes had yet to be turned in. She had been allowed to graduate only because she would have destroyed the school's 100% graduation rate if she hadn't walked across the stage with her classmates.

Nick rose and shook hands so vigorously a forelock of blond hair tumbled down on his forehead, which he pushed back into place just as vigorously after releasing Norman's hand. "Sit down!" he urged. "Have some lunch with us. The food is actually not bad."

Norman was on the verge of politely declining when his stomach issued a huge rumble that would have put to the lie any excuse that he'd already eaten. Nick laughed that crazy laugh of his and dashed over to the salad bar, where he called out for all to hear: "You can't say you're not hungry!"

Fortunately only two other tables were occupied in far corners of the room near the window. For a moment Norman watched helplessly as Nick loaded a plate with large scoops from the bins on the salad bar. Realizing he was actually hungry as well as tired of standing, Norman decided to sit down, just for a moment, if only to stop Lily from fussing at him to do just that. When he'd managed to settle as comfortably as possible in a chair half the span he needed, Nick arrived with a plate piled high with food and served it with a proud flourish, as if he'd prepared it himself. Then he disappeared again to press a twenty dollar bill on the cashier. By the time she rang it up and handed over the change, there was no one to hand it to. Nick was already seated back at the table. This cashier was female, not unattractive, and closer to Nick's age than the girl he was with, and she deemed it necessary to make a special delivery of the change. Nick waved it off and told her to keep it, which caused her to smile.

Norman sighed as he wondered if this was what people meant when they referred to the so-called charm of Nick Scully. If so, it confirmed many of his worst suspicions about charm, which often seemed to correlate with the material wealth of the supposedly charming individual. In any case, the food was certainly charming, he had to admit: a chicken salad studded with apples and walnuts; a shrimp salad sprinkled with dill; black olives; artichoke hearts. Not only was it irresistible, it was there, in front of him; it was already bought and paid for, and he was even hungrier than he'd thought. He decided to let himself enjoy it.

"Beautiful food!" he cried, his mouth full. "I had no idea!"

"Isn't it delicious?" Lily agreed. "I would never have known about this place if Nick hadn't dragged me down here." She looked over at him as if he'd accomplished a Nobel prize-worthy piece of work.

Norman tried to make himself agreeable in return for the unexpectedly good meal he was unexpectedly consuming for free. This was easy to do with someone like Lily, who had a talent for chatting happily about nothing. Norman traded news and gossip with her while taking the opportunity to observe Nick out of the corner of his eye. It had been years since he'd had a chance to scrutinize him this closely. He didn't appear much changed since he'd been a student in the all-male school where Norman had taught before it became Brook-Haven. Nick's hair was still the yellow-blond of a tow-headed boy, un-darkened by time or age, retaining all the dazzle of youth and inno-cence. Long on top, where he ran his hands through it constantly, it tousled and tangled into an unruly mop which partly accounted for his boyish ap-peal. He didn't smile, he grinned, revealing two front teeth slightly at odds with each other, one of them chipped. This grin put a wicked gleam in eyes that sparkled like blue diamonds. With that blond hair and those blue eyes, Norman reflected, he had the best of his mother's very good looks. Also like his mother, he was an avid tennis player, had been on the tennis team both at prep school and Princeton, and kept a year-round suntan that was all the more striking for the blond of his hair and the crystal blue of his eyes. He had his mother's long, lean body as well, which might have been too slight for a man if not for the strength and conditioning that came from the sport he still played every day, according to what Norman heard.

There had been a photograph of him in the paper recently, from Caroline Elmore's wedding reception, that had not done him justice because even a detractor like Norman had to admit it was his personality that made his appearance come to life: his wild cackles of glee, his supposedly quick wit, his insouciant, devil-may-care attitude of being ready to do or say anything that came to mind, regardless of public opinion, propriety, or even, perhaps, the law. Norman was certain it was this contrast between the innocence of his features and the naughtiness in his manner that attracted all the girls, and just as readily alarmed their fathers. Norman was even more certain that what really made his looks stand out was the social prominence of his name, and the fortune behind it. Take away the money and status, and he wouldn't be nearly so good-looking. But with it, he could get away with anything, and did. For example, the chipped front tooth, which might have been a flaw in someone else, was apparently part of his roguish charm, or so Norman had been told. If an event was black tie, Nick would be wearing a tuxedo like every other guy, except his might be missing one or two studs. The imperfections that others needed to correct were part of his allure, and a thrilling demonstration of his power to thumb his nose. Still, the hint of danger in his nature had always created a cloud over his reputation. Here was someone who didn't follow the rules. He was always rumored to have done many scandalous things; it was unclear even to Norman, who heard all the gossip in town, what it was he'd actually done.

In the present situation, Norman's well-honed headmaster's radar sensed developments he needed to know about. Assuming his most avuncular manner, he ceased his banter with Lily and addressed them both. "Now what are you two young people doing besides having lunch?" he said.

Giggling, Lily looked over at Nick. "Should we tell him?" she said.

"Tell me what?" Norman said quickly, bracing himself for developments far beyond what he'd anticipated. Had this idiot child already entangled herself with Nick Scully?

"I think Nick needs a house," said Lily proudly, as if this were an original and unusual idea, completely unrelated to her own self-interest. "And I'm going to sell him one," she proclaimed.

"Do you think what I need is a house, Norman?" Nick winked at him.

Drat the boy, Norman scowled to himself while struggling to retain his outward good humor. Everything he couldn't stand about Nick Scully was rising up at him: the taunting, the mocking, the winking, the familiar use of his first name when Nick was neither friend nor former protégé, but had been one of those few students Norman could never reach. His relief when Nick left for Andover in tenth grade was overshadowed only by his sense of failure, which persisted to this day, especially because the Scullys had been cool to him ever since, as if Norman were nothing but one big fat fraud. Usually it was a pothead or a jock Norman couldn't get through to; a student of Nick's brilliance was supposed to be Norman's whole reason for being. Most galling of all, Nick had become so many things Norman believed in passionately— an Ivy League graduate, a lover of art, a patron of the museum—and Norman could not lay claim to one iota of credit for any of it.

Lily pushed her plate of half-eaten food toward him. "Here, Mr. Laney," she said. "Have mine."

Ignoring her barely suppressed mirth, Norman stared down at his own plate, shocked to find it empty. While thinking he couldn't possibly eat half of what was on the plate, he'd somehow consumed it all.

"No need for him to eat leftovers." Nick frowned and started to rise.

"I'll go get him a fresh plate!" Lily jumped up from her seat before Norman could protest.

Alone with Nick, Norman used the opportunity to inquire after his parents and thank him for his substantial donations. Nick only shrugged, and looked down in embarrassment. At this, Norman's estimation of him rose just the slightest, since he didn't know Nick had the decency to feel embarrassment. But to Norman, there was nothing more embarrassing than vast inherited wealth in someone who wasn't even trying to be worthy of it. Mountain Brook had many such specimens of shame, but most had not set foot in any classroom led by Norman Laney.

Wickedly, Norman could not resist the impulse to put the young man in his proper place. "Now tell me what you're up to these days, dear boy," he said.

Was it just his imagination, or did Nick redden ever so slightly?

"The usual," Nick replied, as Lily returned with a new plate of food.

"Thank you, darling," Norman told her, stabbing his fork under a mound of potato salad. "What's the usual?" he asked Nick.

"Nothing," he laughed wildly.

"The usual nothing," said Norman, happy to let the phrase remain suspended in space, where it spoke for itself.

Lily looked from one man to the other, trying to determine if this was a joke or an argument, where she fit in or how she could inject herself.

"I loafe and invite my soul," Nick grinned.

Norman was stricken. Could Nick possibly remember this was one of Norman's favorite poems? Even worse: Could this possibly be one of Nick's favorite poems? This thought was unbearable to contemplate, and in any case, Norman realized he was not going to win against Nick's grin, his money, or his ability to quote great poetry to justify his derelict behavior. Not ready to give up entirely, Norman decided to try another tack.

"Where have you been hiding yourself all this time? I hadn't seen you in years before Caroline's wedding."

"He's still in that same crummy apartment he's had forever!" Lily announced. "I've got to get him out of there."

"I spent a lot of time in Europe," said Nick, running a hand through his hair in characteristic fashion. "Travelling."

Norman's eyes moved from Nick to Lily. "So now you're back," he stated flatly. "Ready to settle down?" he challenged.

"That place of his won't do *at all.*"

Lily appeared to be voicing not only her professional appraisal but her own personal experience of these living quarters. Nick gave her a look of amusement, as if indulging the nonsense of a small child. Shuddering inwardly at the thought of the intimacy of Lily's experience, Norman wondered whether she was hoping to put herself in whatever house she found for Nick.

"Now what about you?" he turned on her abruptly. "I didn't see your name on the list of recent graduates the University of Alabama sends us every fall."

A schoolgirl blush suffused her face and she looked down, wordless, at the table. Mr. Laney had found her out; she hadn't gotten away with anything after all. When she raised her big blue eyes, they were moist beneath the long dark fringe of her lashes. "I'm still working on my degree." It was almost a whisper, delivered so softly, with bewitching shyness.

"In Birmingham?" Norman decided to remain ruthless, and feigned much more amazement than he really felt. "How can you work on your degree in Tuscaloosa when you're in Birmingham? What's your major?"

"That's just it," said Lily, seizing the new topic with more confidence. "I've decided to change majors, so it's going to take me longer to graduate."

"I see," said Norman in a tone of contempt, suggesting he wasn't fooled for a minute.

"Meanwhile," said Lily, gaining even more boldness, "I've discovered I'm very good at real estate. You may not want to believe this, but I'm actually supporting myself, Mr. Laney. I really am! I don't even need any help from my father."

"But your degree?" Norman persisted. "That's quite important, you know."

"She can always finish her coursework at UAB," Nick observed, winking covertly at Norman out of a perfectly straight face.

"Exactly!" she agreed, looking at Nick with more than gratitude.

What in the world, Norman wondered, was Nick Scully doing with this slip of a girl whose brain wasn't big enough to power a bug through a twenty-four-hour lifespan? Actually, Norman knew just what he was doing, and it disgusted him. Not that sex disgusted him—he realized people had to do it—but this particular coupling was so completely wrong it turned his stomach. Although Lily was as beautiful a girl as you'd find anywhere, he'd given Nick credit for more discernment, higher standards: the desire for a woman's mind as well as her body. The waste of it all he deplored as much as anything. Nick continued to drift through life in his usual haphazard, nihilistic fashion, with no purpose or moral compass, as if nothing mattered that much or meant anything, taking advantage of one girl after another who threw herself at him until she gave up and he moved on to the next, committed to nothing but throwing away his mind, his money and his life on a completely rudderless existence.

Norman suddenly slapped his wrist and clutched at his watch. "My God!" he groaned dramatically. "They expected me in the office an hour ago!" He pushed back from the table, his overburdened chair screeching against the tile floor. "Don't get up," he told the other two, but Nick rose anyway to shake hands in farewell. Once again his tangled blond hair tumbled down on his forehead.

"What do I owe you?" Norman said politely.

"You don't owe me anything," Nick said, his words somehow weighted with a significance far beyond the routine exchange of formalities. It seemed to Norman that Nick had spoken with a deliberate seriousness.

For a moment he stood transfixed, staring at the young man. This was the crux of his own personal problem with Nick Scully: Norman still felt he owed him something he should have been able to deliver a long time ago. Nick had just told him he didn't. But he did. A wild hope flared up in Norman's heart:

perhaps it was not too late to save this boy after all; perhaps there was still a chance Norman could reach him and turn his life around.

"Why don't you come see me up at school on Monday morning?" he suggested casually, as Nick resumed his seat. "You obviously take an active interest in our museum, and I could use your help on this gala."

Nick grinned and shook his head, as if Norman had just made some kind of joke. "Put me down for a table, though," he said.

"A table?" Norman was confused.

"For the grand opening."

So it wasn't a total loss, Norman reflected, as he squeezed through the glass door of the café. And anyway, trying to save Nick Scully's soul would lead only to heartache. Norman had been down that road before.

~ 6 ~

Lily knew he didn't like the house because he gnawed his cheek. This was the way he processed disturbing thoughts or emotions. She'd always been good at reading people, but after going into real estate, she became expert at it. For one reason or another, clients often didn't express all their thoughts verbally, and it was essential to have other ways of perceiving what was going through their minds. When his wife stepped into the backyard, she detained him in the kitchen.

"I don't like it either," she told him.

At first he was startled, then broke into a smile of relief. "It's just so . . . small," he said.

"The kitchen alone is a disaster," she concurred, nodding while she stored away the fact that he'd been afraid of hurting her feelings by questioning her taste. "Nothing's been updated in years. But come, let me show you the other issues." Taking him briefly by the hand, she led him back into the living room. She looked up and pointed. "Eight-foot ceilings. Too low. No molding."

"I know I can't have what my in-laws have in Mountain Brook for quite some time," he acknowledged ruefully. "But still, I was hoping for more than this. I mean, the carpet," he gestured toward it in dismay. "I didn't expect wall-to-wall carpet."

"Hardwood floors underneath," she said, consulting the listing description. "Protected by the wall-to-wall. But." She gave him a look of commiseration. "You'd still have to get them re-finished after all these years. That's trouble and expense." Crooking a finger, she beckoned him into the hall, where she stuck her head into the powder room and turned on the light. "These little bitty tiles are from the 1950s," she noted. "When the house was built. Now some people would keep them. Some people like that retro look, but personally, I . . ." Shaking her head, she let the unfinished sentence complete her point.

"Are you sure you don't remember me?" he said.

Lily acted ever so slightly taken aback by the abrupt switch from the professional to the personal. "Let me think again," she said, pulling out of the bathroom. "I remember Bethany Ball coming around the Kappa house with a guy named Bill Hagerty."

"He was right after me," he said eagerly. "She brought me by before football games two or three times. Our first year of law school."

"And you say she *introduced* us?" Lily stood stock still in the tiny foyer, as if her whole body was concentrated in the effort to recall.

"Yes," he nodded even more eagerly in his own effort to help her recall.

"I'm sorry," she said, shaking her head slowly as he gave a sigh of resignation. "So many people were always coming by the sorority house. *Especially* before football games. We met *everybody*. And . . ." She allowed herself a brief fit of giggles. "I may have already been . . . well . . . you know . . . if it was before a football game."

"Drunk?" he said.

She nodded sheepishly.

"Not at all," he declared gallantly. "I promise you."

"Well, that's good to hear," she said, suddenly clutching his arm as they both heard his wife re-entering through the kitchen door. "I only wish I *had* met you back then," she confided in a playful whisper. "I mean, to remember. Back then, I was so silly. I thought a guy was a guy. You know? If I only knew then what I know now, I'd have done *a lot* of things differently." She rolled her eyes at her own youthful folly.

Just then Caroline found them in the foyer. "Except for the yard," she said, "this place is not much bigger than our apartment. And not nearly as nice."

"We all agree then," said Lily. "Let's get out of here."

They waited for her politely on the front steps as she secured the lock box. "You need more house," Lily said leading the way toward her car.

"No," Caroline protested emphatically, stopping in her tracks on the walkway. "We don't need a house at all. Our apartment suits us perfectly."

"Of course you need a house!" Lily cried. "Everybody knows that. A young couple, just married, must be in need of a house!"

Giving her an odd look, Caroline muttered something about having heard that line before.

"See?" said Lily triumphantly. "I know your mother's telling you the same thing!"

"Look," said Caroline. "No matter what anybody's telling me, an apartment is the best thing for us right now. And it's what we can *afford*."

"Oh, don't be so stubborn," said Lily, pulling gaily on her friend's arm. "We're just getting started. I have lots and lots to show you. This dog of a house would never have been on my list, but you *insisted* on seeing something in that price range." Opening the front passenger door, she gestured for Caroline to get in, while turning around and giving her husband a conspiratorial wink.

"I don't want to waste your time," Caroline said as they drove off. "There's no way we could afford anything more expensive."

"Of course you can," Lily assured her breezily. "I've sold much more expensive houses to guys who don't make as much as your husband. And I don't even know what *you're* making." At the stop sign, she turned to look at her friend, whose face was suddenly full of chagrin. "Don't be embarrassed," Lily told her sweetly. "I know writers don't make much. Just tell me what it is."

Caroline mumbled something and looked out the window. In the rearview mirror, Lily could see Daniel chuckling to himself in the backseat. Since no cars were coming up behind her, she remained at the stop sign, genuinely puzzled. "No need to be shy with me, honey," she told her friend. "We go *way* back. The things girls have to help each other with in high school?" She lowered her voice. "Tampons and panty liners and busted bra straps? We should be able to tell each other *everything* by now."

Caroline turned toward her. "I'm not making anything," she said.

"I understand," said Lily, rapidly recovering from her surprise. "You get paid when it's done."

"No!" Caroline exclaimed. "You *don't* understand. I don't have a contract. I don't have a publisher. I may never make anything out of this. I may never . . ." Her voice trailed off sadly.

"Oh, I do understand," Lily reassured her as she eased the car past the stop sign. "I understand completely. It's just like me. We're in the same boat exactly. *I* never know if I'll make anything either. I do all this work, run myself ragged showing houses all over town without any guarantee that I'll make a penny from any of my efforts." She patted her friend's hand.

Lily busied herself locating the next address on her list. Although she knew precisely where she was headed, just a few blocks away, she deliberately made a couple of wrong turns just to give Caroline time to calm down. Then when she finally turned on the correct street, she pretended to need the husband's help in spotting the house number.

"Now this place," Lily told them, pulling up to the curb. "Same nice Crestline neighborhood. Same basic starter house. But wait till you see the inside. It has been perfectly redone. Fabulous upgrades." Grabbing her purse and clipboard, she hopped out of the car.

"Starter house?" asked Caroline, not moving from the front seat.

Lily leaned back in and looked from husband to wife. "As far as I'm concerned," she told them, "we can skip right over the whole starter house category. You can afford it," she informed Daniel proudly. "If you can get a loan, you can afford it, and trust me, with your salary, you will get a loan." Once Lily had entered the real estate business, it had not taken her long to learn that complimenting the size of a man's salary had the same effect as if she'd complimented the size of his penis.

Caroline still didn't budge, and her husband was trapped in motion, half rooted to his seat, half poised to get out, with his hand on the door handle.

"Fine with me if we skip the starter houses," repeated Lily, making to get back in the car.

Caroline sighed and opened her door. "Let's go ahead and take a look at this," she said.

Inside, Lily decided to shake things up a bit. Instead of taking them to the kitchen first, she led them straight down the hallway to the bedrooms. "You've got to see this." Flinging open one of the doors, she indicated for them to enter with a triumphant flourish. "Have you ever seen anything so cute in your entire life? This house won't be on the market for long. I can guarantee you that."

Although her husband seemed suitably impressed, Caroline didn't seem to know what to make of the canary yellow walls covered with a lively assortment of Disney and Dr. Seuss characters, painted larger than life in bold colors that made the room seem positively occupied by everyone's childhood favorites: the Cat in the Hat, Snow White and the Seven Dwarves, Horton the Elephant, Sleeping Beauty amidst her animals. The listing sheet did not disclose the name of the artist who had done the murals, and Lily was told she could not find out unless she had buyers considering a serious offer. The sellers wanted to keep the painter's name as their own little secret; otherwise *everyone* would hire her to do the same murals in their house.

"Have you ever seen a more *adorable* nursery?" Lily cried.

"Nursery?" said Caroline.

"Or children's room. Either one. Both! Start off using it as a nursery, then change out the furniture as the child gets older. This will work for a boy or a girl's room. See?" Lily pointed to the various characters. "There are just as many boy figures as girl ones." When she looked back at her clients, she was dismayed to find them gripped with tension. Dropping her purse and clipboard on the beanbag chair, she plopped down on the child's bed and folded her arms across her chest. "Okay, you two," she said. "Out with it. Tell me what's wrong. Caroline, honey, are you *infertile*? Because if you are, I can give you the names of two doctors at UAB who have made more babies than you would *believe*."

"Infertile?" said Caroline, taken aback. "Whatever gave you that idea?"

Lily made a great show of relief. "Most people just fall in love with this room," she explained. "But!" She hopped up off the bed and gathered her belongings. "Okay. Moving right along." She led the way out of the room.

"We won't be needing a nursery for quite a while," Caroline told her.

Shrugging, Lily turned to look at her. "So what? It will be here when you need it. And you *will* need it, eventually. You *do* plan to have children, don't you?"

"Of course we do," said the husband.

"But not for a long while," said the wife.

"You never know," said Lily, moving down the hall. "Once the other couples you're friends with starting having children? You'd be surprised how *contagious* pregnancy can be." She giggled. "No matter what you think of it. If it looks like they're enjoying parenthood, you'll want to join the fun. If they look miserable, you'll want to go ahead and get it over with, just like they are. From what I hear, it's a lot of both. But believe me, it may all happen sooner than you think. It's best to be prepared and not be desperately house-hunting when you're pregnant."

Caroline came to a stop when they reached the front door. "I won't be getting pregnant soon," she stated flatly.

"You will some day, honey," said Lily. "Now come let me show you the kitchen. It's a dream come true."

Not moving from the foyer, Caroline gave her husband a meaningful look which probably signaled her desire to leave, Lily guessed. Meanwhile, her husband was once again torn between the momentum of the two different women. The dutiful part of him wanted to please his wife; the rest of him wanted to please Lily, who was quite familiar with this split-screen scenario.

Ignoring Lily, Caroline addressed her husband. "I may not even be here in the fall," she said. "Remember?"

Wisely, Lily took a moment or two to craft her response as the husband merely shrugged. Although she had sensed this husband and wife were not on the same page, she would not have predicted open discord so soon. Surely Caroline had not just announced a possible marital split? Looking from one to the other, Lily decided to play dumb. "So you all may move away from

Birmingham, then?" she said, heaving a big sigh. "I just knew we couldn't hold onto you. Two Harvard graduates."

"No, no," said the husband quickly, looking briefly at his wife. "All she means is that she may be starting a graduate program in the fall. At the University of Alabama. Depending on her course schedule, and teaching duties, she may end up renting an apartment in Tuscaloosa."

"If I'm only here on the weekends," Caroline added, "it wouldn't make sense for us to buy more of a house than we can afford, or need."

"But of course it does!" Lily cried. "Surely I don't need to explain to two Ivy Leaguers that the worst thing you can do with your money is throw it down the drain in rent. It's *always* better to buy *anything,* especially in Mountain Brook, where you're building equity and have something to show for the money you spend on your place of residence. That's Economics 101. Now come see this kitchen." Without waiting for a response, she turned quickly on her heels and led the way.

Despite Caroline's exasperated sigh, they both followed. In the kitchen, Lily realized she had lost half her audience. The husband still gave her his close attention, while his wife tuned her out and made only a polite pretense of listening. This was no problem; Lily knew exactly what to do with a husband's attention. First, husbands liked looking at Lily as she moved about. Next, they liked the numbers, the mathematics of their money multiplying through ever-rising property values. Since property values were ever rising in Mountain Brook, it was not hard to make a husband happy. Often Lily felt this part of her job was like playing Vanna White on *Wheel of Fortune,* except Lily was better looking than Vanna White, and when she spun the wheel on Mountain Brook property values, it always landed on a very high number. It was a piece of cake. The combination of Lily's looks with the big number she could always deliver turned husbands into Play-Doh in her hands. If this husband had been a single guy, he'd be putting in an offer on one of the houses she was showing today before the afternoon was over.

There were three others on her list. If Caroline didn't object to seeing them, she didn't bother to take an interest in them either. This was fine with Lily, to have unfettered access to the husband. Lily could always get a husband to do what she wanted him to do. Once again, Caroline was clueless. It was worse than refusing to play the game; she didn't even realize a game was being played.

As Lily gave the tour and recited the numbers on the remaining houses, Caroline tended to linger alone in a room or wander off by herself. She was preoccupied with her own thoughts, and Lily believed she knew exactly what those were about. When she had arrived at their apartment earlier in the afternoon, she'd been delighted to discover their next door neighbor had already dropped by and was chatting like this was habit with him. He was even better looking than described, much more movie star than football player, although he did have the build of an athlete, with his height and broad shoulders. But he had dark, brooding eyes between a prominent brow and prominent cheekbones. His hair flowed back in dark, rippling waves from his forehead, and his eyebrows went on for *miles*. He was so striking looking it was a real shame he spent his life behind a desk instead of in front of a camera. He should have been an actor or at least a model, with those eyes and that chiseled face. As soon as she saw him, Lily felt her heart hopping around like a cricket at the prospect of meeting him and getting her hands on this client.

But then the weirdest thing happened. Only once or twice in the bluest moon had Lily experienced this before when first meeting a good-looking guy. Although his manners were perfectly polite, he was so uninterested in her *it was as if he did not even see her.* Whereas most guys could not take their eyes off her, this guy's eyes didn't even seem to notice her although they looked straight at her. The reason soon became clear: he had eyes only for Caroline. When the introductions and greetings were over, he and Caroline bent their heads over whatever newspaper or magazine article they had been discussing when she arrived. The husband was different, with eyes only for Lily. This was what she was used to. But the weirdest thing about this neighbor of theirs, this Ken Newsome, was that Lily felt none of her usual drive to make this man her own. Perhaps she realized it was a hopeless cause. He was smart in the way Caroline was smart, interested in the same boring things. A man like that was not the right material for Lily. She decided to write him off entirely then and there. Handsome though he was, he was still just a writer of some kind, from a small town she'd never heard of, and probably made no money to speak of either. Not worth it. Meanwhile, the husband was all over her. Caroline didn't notice this any more than she noticed the peculiar dynamic in the room among the two couples, with the married people happily pairing off with the unmarried people. Not that this was strange in and of itself, since Lily dreaded the finality of marriage and didn't know how she would ever submit to the tedium of being with just one guy she didn't need to flirt with anymore because she was married to him.

As Lily made her way through the houses on her list, Caroline remained in such a trance-like state that Lily suspected she wasn't entirely insensible to what was happening. Once again, Lily felt sorry for her friend. If she found herself attracted to a man other than her husband, Caroline wouldn't even know how to *recognize* it for what it was, let alone know what to do about it. As always, she would need Lily's help.

So at the last house she made a point of seeking out Caroline, who had tarried, predictably, in the den amongst the bookshelves. Some girl talk was in order.

"I wanted to let you know," Lily whispered excitedly. "I've been seeing a good bit of your friend."

"My friend?" Caroline turned reluctantly from the books.

"You know," said Lily. "Nick Scully."

"Oh. Nick," said Caroline, already bored with the conversation.

"I thought I should tell you. I hope you're not jealous."

"Jealous?" said Caroline, surprised. "Why would I be jealous?"

Lily shrugged. "Sometimes girls can be very possessive about their old flames."

"I told you," Caroline said with impatience. "I never thought of him that way."

This gave Lily a perfect opening. She was on the verge of asking if Caroline had ever thought of any man that way besides the one she married. But Caroline spoke first. "Does this mean you don't want to be set up with my neighbor?"

The nervousness and anxiety in her voice told Lily everything. "Oh, no, honey," she said. "I'm not interested in your neighbor now." Caroline's relief spoke another volume.

On the drive back to their apartment, Lily opted for a change of subject. "What are you going to do about the Junior League?" she asked her friend.

"What do you think I'm going to do about it?"

"But isn't your mother bugging you to death? Mine sure is."

"My mother has been bugging me to death most of my life to be something I'm not. The Junior League is just the latest."

"Is it already time for the Junior League?" the husband piped up from the back seat.

"'Fraid so," said Lily. "I think I'll do it just because it will be good for business. Being a Kappa alum, I get a lot of referrals through that, but as my mother pointed out, I'll get even more through the Junior League."

Caroline's jaw was set in defiance. Lily was amused and curious. "What argument did your mother make with you?" she asked.

Caroline pretended not to hear the question.

"Come on," Lily coaxed. "Tell me."

"Is that what your mother said would be good for *my* business?" came the husband's voice from the backseat.

"Well, that *is* something to consider," Lily mused, observing him in the rearview mirror. "Does your firm expect you to bring in clients?"

"Of course they do," he said. "Once I make partner. If I can do it before then, we can be sure I *will* make partner."

"See?" said Lily, looking over at her friend. "Your husband's not from around here. He'll need your help meeting the right people so he can bring business to his firm. Let's do it together. It won't be so bad. It'll be like a sorority for grownups."

"She's got a point," said the husband.

"I don't need it for *my* business," said his wife.

Caroline stared out the window and Lily could see the husband gnawing his cheek when she checked surreptitiously in her rearview mirror. She pulled into the parking lot just a few moments later. Caroline thanked her sweetly if not sincerely, while the husband thanked her most sincerely. He lingered behind to let Lily know that he would discuss the houses she'd shown them with his wife and would love to see more possibilities whenever Lily found something she thought they'd like.

Driving off, Lily knew for a fact that she would never find a house to suit this particular couple, because no such house existed. They wanted completely different things in life, and no dwelling on earth offered a good house for that. Lily figured the best way to help her friend in this situation was to go through the husband. In general, Lily always had the best results with the man.

~ 7 ~

When Caroline invited her neighbor for the promised dinner, the meal she served was a simple one of pasta with tomato sauce, but the tomatoes and basil were fresh, grown in her father's backyard garden.

"If I were your husband, I would not have missed this meal," Ken joked after his second helping. "Is your husband having an *affair*?"

The boldness of this gibe, along with the effects of the wine which he had brought, unleashed a bitterness she hadn't known she harbored. "I think he *is* having an affair," Caroline replied. "With himself."

This sent him reeling in his chair, where he leaned his head back and sent gales of baritone laughter up to the ceiling. "Explain, please," he said.

Feeling guilty already, she was glad for the chance to reverse course and disavow her too-clever remark and the laughter they had shared behind the back and at the expense of her absent, hardworking husband. In all seriousness now, she explained how anxious her husband was to succeed in his new job, at one of the best law firms in town, where he'd been assigned to work on one of the biggest cases they'd had in years. It was an honor, but a terrible burden too, with enormous pressure. She was proud of him, happy for him. He had become so committed, so dedicated to doing well. In law school he had really buckled down to the task at hand, as if knowing this was his main chance, and he couldn't afford not to make the most of it. Coming from a small town, with parents who had grown up on farms, he had made it so far in the world all by his own efforts, but still didn't seem to think his achievements were real, or solid. He still seemed to fear that the life he'd built would disappear in a few puffs of smoke as if it had all been a magician's illusion. His need to spend every waking hour at work was more about his own peace of mind, she guessed, than the needs of the big case or the demands of his partners.

What she loved about talking to her neighbor was that she *could* talk, and he would listen. Her husband was too preoccupied nowadays to register anything she said, and nothing she had to say seemed worth the effort of trying to get through to him, since *she* didn't have a job or a livelihood at stake. At first, this was why she welcomed Ken's presence in their apartment, invited him frequently to share their dinner and encouraged him to drop by on weekends. With a third person in the room, her husband allowed himself to forget about his work, the law firm, his billable hours and partnership prospects. The third person didn't just bring himself, he brought the rest of the world with him into the apartment, simply because he was a piece of the rest of that world, a reminder that The Case was not everything and there were other subjects of interest and importance. They both enjoyed talking with their neighbor, getting to know him and hearing about his experiences as a second-string wide receiver for the Crimson Tide, then a sportswriter for the Boston *Globe,* now a staff writer for *Sports Illustrated.* His small-town Alabama background, his four years in Tuscaloosa, his six years in Boston, and his writing career gave him much in common with both of them.

When she and her husband went out to dinner or a movie, they got in the habit of calling or knocking on Ken's door to see if he wanted to join them. Quite often, when he was in town, he did. Grateful for the invitations, he explained that he'd just endured a painful breakup, which is what they assumed, since they'd seen or heard no more of the redhead who'd pounded on his door that morning. He was still somewhat new to Birmingham, didn't know many people in town, and traveling so regularly for his job, didn't have many chances to make friends. When he hesitated about being a third wheel, they assured him they preferred having a third wheel. Although they all treated this like a joke, it wasn't really. Their marriage needed this third person to help it come truly alive. She felt more like a couple, and she guessed her husband did too, when this other person was with them. Whenever she was alone with her husband, she became invisible to him as his preoccupations took over. Instead of his wife, she felt more like a mother or sister, part of the given background of his household. But with a guest along who warranted attention, her husband gave her his attention as well. She wondered what it meant, that her marriage required a third party in order to function at its best. It simply could not be that she would suffer the same fate as her parents, who needed people besides each other if they wanted to have a good time. She had worked too hard to avoid their fate.

* * *

One Saturday afternoon, her neighbor dropped by while her husband was putting in a few hours at the office. There was a book he wanted to borrow, if she had it. *Stars Fell on Alabama,* by Carl Carmer. Published in the 1930s, it was written by a "damn-Yankee" who had taught at the University of Alabama for a few years, and wanted to share his outsider's perspective on the Southern culture he'd encountered. Ken's editor had mentioned he might be able to pull some fun quotes out of the book to use for an upcoming article he was writing about the Alabama football program. After fetching the book from her study, she sat down with him and thumbed through it to show how she marked certain passages. Perhaps he could start with those to see if they would serve his purposes, in case he didn't have time to read the whole thing.

"For example," she said, pointing to one of the lines she had flagged. "Listen to this: 'Tuscaloosa lives a life of its own—an enchanted life in an age other than ours.'"

Frowning, he reached for the book. "When did you say this was published?"

Turning back to the copyright page, she handed the book over.

"1934." He shook his head in wonder.

"The statement is as true today as it was fifty years ago," she said.

"Uncanny," he agreed.

"Do you think that line will work in your piece?"

"It's perfect," he told her. "That line will fit in anywhere, and I haven't even written the piece yet."

They both burst out laughing.

"I doubt Mr. Carmer intended his observation as a compliment," Ken noted. "That Tuscaloosa exists in its own enchanted world."

"No," she concurred. "But any Southerner would interpret that as a compliment."

"It's the entire cultural divide in a nutshell."

"Exactly," she said. "Southerners pride themselves on having their own separate, fantastical world. The rest of the U.S. prides itself on its place in the real world."

Nodding, Ken made to rise. "Thanks a million," he said. "You don't mind if I borrow this, then?"

"All yours," she smiled.

* * *

A few days later, on Wednesday afternoon, he tapped on her door with the book in hand. He'd finished reading, but wondered if he could hang onto the book a while longer.

"Of course," she said. "Keep it as long as you need to."

"If you have a minute," he said tentatively. "If I'm not interrupting . . ."

"Come in," she said.

Soon it became routine for him to knock on her door around four in the afternoon to chat for an hour before he went for his jog.

"After a day at my desk, my mind is emptied out," he told her one day. "I need human interaction, someone I can exchange ideas with, to put some fresh thoughts in my head and get my brain going again. Does that happen to you?" he asked. "After a day of writing?"

"Absolutely," she agreed, although there was still no writing to speak of despite the hours she spent trying to produce it.

Once when she confessed her difficulties, he confided that his apartment in Boston had been littered with his futile attempts at writing fiction. Wishing to move on from the daily grind of his job at the newspaper, he had hoped to finish a novel, get a book contract and take his career in a different direction. It hadn't worked out that way. When he had no luck with a novel, he jumped at the offer from *Sports Illustrated*. It wasn't the ultimate job, but it was more interesting, paid better, and removed him from the daily pressure of a newspaper. Meanwhile, he still scribbled notes for a novel when he had the chance.

"But it is *hard*," he stated emphatically. "No one even understands how hard it is unless they try to do it themselves. I think it's the hardest thing of all to write, except for maybe poetry. Nonfiction is a cakewalk in comparison. Journalists like me have to learn that the hard way. We—" Stopping suddenly in mid-sentence, he looked at her sheepishly. "Am I boring you?"

"Of course not!" she protested. "Please go on. What were you about to say?"

"Well," he continued shyly. "Only that we journalists tend to think novelists have it so easy, that nothing could be easier than writing a novel. No facts to get right, no sources to track down, nobody to interview, no quotes to verify, no events to cover, no phone calls, no running around, no editor standing right over your shoulder and breathing down your neck at deadline. Nothing except yourself and whatever you want to throw on the page. How hard could it be, with the skills we've developed through the *real* writing we've done for the world to read on the front page of the morning paper?" He gave her a knowing glance and shook his head. "I was sure I could toss off a good first draft of a novel after three or four months. But I fell flat on my face," he admitted. "I couldn't do it. Pulling stuff out of yourself is so much harder than writing about what happened yesterday, or last week. And there *are* facts to get right as well." Laughing softly at himself, he shook his head again.

Reassured, encouraged, delighted to hear of his efforts, she confided more and more about her own. Unfortunately, talking about these problems did not solve them. All of her work continued to be in vain, at least in terms of producing any pages that might one day comprise a manuscript. Some days she didn't even try to write, but spent her time reading instead. This gave her an idea, and she made a trip to the library to check out all sorts of books about Alabama history. For a day or two afterwards, the impressive stack she brought home to her study gave a shape to her project, made it seem more solid. But the reading proved dull; the facts and dates did not give a shape to her narrative or impart the inspiration she needed. Even worse, she began to feel she shouldn't be reading anything else, strictly for pleasure. But after a few minutes with the history books, her mind lost focus and became distracted by errant thoughts having nothing to do with her work. What work? There was no work. Days went by when she read nothing at all, made no attempt at the blank notebook, and wandered through the apartment in utter despair. She began to question both her existence and her identity in the most fundamental ways. Who was she and what was she doing? *Nothing* was the only answer that ever came back to her from the void she now inhabited.

With nothing to give structure to her days or sense of self, she lost the will to do anything other than the most essential domestic duties. Fortunately the small apartment was easily taken care of. But the thank-you notes, still unfinished, began to seem like a herculean task. Even one was now too many. *Dear Mrs. Newcomb,* she would begin. *Thank you so much for the lovely crystal vase.* So far, so good. But then she was unable to go on with the expected platitudes as her imagination wickedly produced unacceptable truths. *Unfortunately, the vase you chose is way too big for the apartment I live in. Beautiful as it is, I tried to make use of it, but I had to spend $35 on a bouquet big enough to fill it, and then it looked absurd on our breakfast room table. Since we don't have people over very often, no one besides me even saw it except my husband, who had to keep moving it off the table for our meals. Clearly this vase was meant to grace a much larger home where a great deal of entertaining takes place. It's really a shame that I don't ever want that kind of house or social life, or I might one day be able to enjoy this vase as it deserves. I kept it only because my mother begged me not to exchange it for store credit. She said you'd find out since your granddaughter has a summer job at the Dandé Lion Shoppe. She also said this vase would be a godsend to me one day, but she's never understood me. I'm so sorry you had to spend money on something I'll never use, especially since we hardly know each other.*

Although the truth could write itself, Caroline could no more dash off a note filled with pabulum than she could live the life those wedding gifts were designed to foster. The act of writing was as sacred as her own existence; it was the reason for her own existence, despite her inability to write anything at all at the moment. In any case, she had never been good at going through empty motions. But now she couldn't do anything else either. Sensing trouble, her mother called even more frequently to spur her daughter into action. Fewer and fewer people were remarking on notes they'd received. To her mother's mortification, Adelaide Whitmire made a point of traversing aisles and aisles in the grocery store to inform her that she had *not* received a note. Every afternoon her mother called with a list of names that Caroline *had* to send notes to immediately if she wanted her mother to be able to hold her head up in town. This list became the only goal Caroline aspired to, the sum total of her ambition. Some days she even achieved it.

The focal point of her day became the time she spent with her neighbor in the afternoons, if he was in town. She became acutely aware of his schedule, intimately familiar with how he spent every hour of his day. She watched for his car in the parking lot, listened as he came and went in his apartment, and above all, waited for the knock on her door, which heralded an hour of happiness and made the rest of her life an exquisite misery. It was when she faced two weeks without his visits that she put a name to her embarrassing condition.

She was in love with her next-door neighbor.

Her first reaction was that she must now avoid him at all costs; at the same time, she would have done anything to be in his presence. The joy she experienced in his company was so intense it felt illicit. But she did not want to have an affair, for crying out loud, although part of her felt she was already in the middle of one. To save herself, to save her marriage, she needed to get away. She also needed to get more of a life, for heaven's sake; perhaps this "love" was simply something to fill the emptiness of her existence. And if she had her own job, maybe she wouldn't be so bothered by her husband's absorption in his. But where could she go to sort out the situation? What could she do?

* * *

On the Monday after Thanksgiving, Ken knocked at nine-thirty that morning to collect his mail. She didn't trust herself to say much of anything or look at him too directly. Instead, she offered him a cup of coffee and busied herself in the preparation.

"Is anything wrong?" he said, peering at her curiously as he sat down on the sofa.

"Visits to my in-laws always put me in a bad mood," she told him. Although this was true, it was no true answer.

He laughed. "As bad as you feared?"

She nodded. Unable to resist the temptation, she launched into details of the Thanksgiving visit. His laughter was a tonic. If only her husband could have laughed that way. Of course he loved his parents, but he couldn't stand visiting them any more than she could. They wreaked a havoc on him that he could not avoid precisely because he couldn't laugh about it. Whenever he saw them, they managed to wind him up as tightly as they wound themselves, and for weeks afterward he was even more frenetic about his work.

For the first time, she was beginning to understand the price he was paying for his own Southern heritage. The poverty his parents had endured had not empowered them any more than it had ennobled them. She'd been a fool to think it had ever empowered their son. Yes, he possessed drive, purpose and ambition—but only to achieve what her peers in Mountain Brook had been born into. And no, this didn't have to be the case, but he was his parents' child, and precisely because he had not inherited money or social standing, he had inherited their need to acquire both. As far as she could tell, this desperate need to obtain what they didn't have had ruined his parents' lives. In escaping the enslavement of poverty, they had managed only to enslave themselves to a daily grind which offered little hope of joy or pleasure.

She knew it didn't have to be this way, because his grandparents, at least on his mother's side, were quite content with their lives on the farm, and this contentment gave them a grace of spirit that could never come from a mere fortune or pedigree. Their distinction came from not wanting or needing anything other than what they now had. They had emerged from the Depression with the rare ability to be happy with what was right in front of them. Although they had less money than Shaye and Bobby, they seemed far richer, because they were happy, and never talked about money, debt, bills, loans, or mortgages.

The Thanksgiving trip had opened her eyes to the terrible truth that her husband was headed down the same grim path as his parents, where everything was put in service to the struggle to get ahead. In college she had applauded Daniel's relentless work ethic as he completed his senior thesis about the role of religion in Alabama politics, then drafted and rehearsed the Class Day speech for graduation. In law school he had similarly devoted himself to an Alabama Law Review article denouncing the state's regressive tax code, which burdened its citizens, some of the poorest in the nation, with a high sales tax while favoring businesses even as they strip-mined the environment and inflicted permanent ecological damage. But with this same single-minded focus now trained on his legal work, he seemed to have lost any sense of a larger focus or purpose. This current work was not about anything beyond itself. The causes being served were those of the law firm and the corporations that hired it. And these causes were important mainly to those who made money from them.

When she'd first fallen in love with him, he'd been headed on a different road, working for the candidate opposing George Wallace in the last gubernatorial campaign. But his parents had been adamantly opposed to any extension of this job beyond the summer before law school started. They had hectored and nagged him endlessly about it. As soon as he walked through their front door, they were on him. They went after him at the dinner table. In between visits, they persecuted him on the telephone. Their behavior during that summer was so extreme she used to laugh it off. She was sure they would lose this fight for their son's soul just as they'd already lost him.

But for some reason she still didn't understand, he'd resigned from the campaign before it was over. Then Wallace had won again, and any questions she'd had about her husband's choice disappeared along with his former candidate. But during the three subsequent years he had spent in law school, he had changed in ways she was only now becoming aware of. She wasn't entirely sorry that he'd resigned from what turned out to be a losing campaign in order to start law school, but it did bother her that he'd lost any semblance of higher ideals beyond his own self-advancement. He used to believe in something, and had committed himself to something besides his own career path. He'd had a vital spark that drove him toward goals that had nothing to do with material success. But the idealistic young man she'd known had discarded those ideals as if they'd been no more than props or parts of a costume for an unsuccessful role he was tired of trying to play. If he did go into politics as he'd always planned, she was afraid it would be to further his own cause, because the larger ones that used to motivate him seemed to have fizzled out. That vital flame was being extinguished.

Now it appeared that he had no more escaped his parents' clutches than she had escaped from hers. They had his soul in their hands and were steering it towards their own stunted values. If she tried, she could have wrestled for control and gained possession. She could have steered him away from the big law firm, toward a good cause he could serve with his degree. A cause that would, in turn, ignite that divine spark that used to animate his whole being. He could stop worrying about making partner and start finding satisfaction in doing a good job that needed doing. After all, they didn't need a big house, or any house at all at the moment.

But she recoiled at the prospect of taking calculated control of someone else's psyche. Partly it seemed like the worst sort of sacrilege, "a violation of the sanctity of a human heart," as Hawthorne called it. Also, she didn't think it would work anyway. A true individual gained possession of himself no matter who tried to get their hands on him. There was no way to make him the best man he could be. Only he could do that. If she were to try, she would be guilty of the same disservice as his parents, the same manipulations as her mother. It didn't matter that it would be for his own good. That's how her mother justified her own machinations. Sadly, his parents also had his best interests at heart, even as they posed a great danger to his well-being.

For her neighbor's benefit as well as her own, she tried her best to portray the family dynamics as a comic spectacle to be laughed at, as she had once been able to do.

"I missed having these conversations with you," he told her. "Twice I almost called you from the road to get advice about this stupid story I had to file. Now—"

"Oh, you should have called," she said, seizing immediately on this chance to change the subject. "The closest I come to writing is when we talk about yours."

"It's getting you down," he said.

"This can't go on," she said. "I've got to do something about it. I've even thought about calling the English Department at the University of Alabama, to see if I can start the graduate program next semester. Or if for some reason they need a teacher in the middle of the year."

She wasn't sure where this idea had come from; certainly she hadn't been consciously thinking about it. It had popped out unbidden, more a desperate ploy to keep the conversation focused on impersonal subjects.

He put his empty cup down on the coffee table, leaned back and looked at her so long she was sure he was seeing through her subterfuge.

"I think that's a good idea," he said finally, with what sounded like reluctance. "I'd miss you, but it's probably for the best that you do this. Writing can be very hard to do in a vacuum. Even if you have less time, doing something else that stimulates your mind can be better for writing than focusing on it all day."

"I have no idea if I can start midyear," she said. "And I doubt they need any teachers at this point."

"Worth a try," he said. "It's just a phone call. Do you know who to talk to?"

She nodded. "I visited the department when Daniel was in law school. Met the chairman and discussed the program. She knows I'm applying for next year. My transcript and recommendations have already been sent to her office."

"Well, there you go," he said, slapping his thighs and preparing to rise. "I'd miss you, but I go to Tuscaloosa quite a bit for my job. I could see you there." Gathering his mail, he said, "Good luck with the phone call. Let me know how it goes."

If only because she knew he would ask, she forced herself to place the phone call later that morning. She didn't relish making such a cold call, and didn't expect anything but an awkward moment to come out of it. In all likelihood, the chairman would not even remember her. After overcoming that awkwardness, they would move on to the awkwardness of Caroline's inquiry, until they managed the awkwardness of ending the pointless call. Still, a few moments of stilted conversation with the chairman of the English Department at the University of Alabama would at least give her a safe subject to discuss if she needed one next time she saw her neighbor.

But to her surprise, the chairman remembered her perfectly. To her shock, the chairman offered her a job on the spot. One of the English Department professors, who was slated to teach two courses, two seminars and direct two undergraduate thesis students in the spring, had just suffered a stroke over the Thanksgiving holiday. In an emergency, the chairman had the authority to make a temporary appointment. She even hoped for someone who could take over *now*, and finish out the fall semester, but they would make do until after the new year and the start of the new semester if Caroline couldn't begin immediately.

"But . . ." Caroline protested, astounded by the direction the conversation had taken. She was also beginning to suspect that the chairman had her confused with someone else. "You do realize," she began tentatively. "I only just graduated . . . from *college*," she admitted.

"Harvard," the chairman said. "Senior thesis on William Faulkner. I've got your file open right here on my desk. I was planning to call you later this morning."

"You were?"

"Dr. Brinkley, who had the stroke, is our professor of Southern literature. You're a perfect candidate to replace him for the semester. I'm going to fudge just the slightest and put you down as a graduate student of the university. Since you *will* be entering our graduate program next fall?"

"Ah, yes," said Caroline, both thrilled and unnerved by the speed of these developments.

"All we need is your completed application. We'll go ahead and accept you into the program. I'll let you know if you'll need to enroll in a graduate course in order to make this all official. You could do that, couldn't you? Take just one course along with the teaching load?"

"Ah, yes," said Caroline.

"Any chance at all that you could begin next week?"

"I'm afraid that's too short notice."

The chairman sighed. "Of course," she said. "But we'll see you before the Christmas holidays. You'll need to come over to get oriented and make arrangements."

"Of course," Caroline agreed absently, her head spinning.

"Good. Just get me that application as soon as possible. I've got everything else I need in this file."

The conversation continued for several more minutes while the chairman droned on about various logistics that Caroline could not process with her overwhelmed brain. Only after the call concluded did Caroline realize she had a dozen questions. Nothing had been said about salary, or the specific courses she would be taking over, whether she needed to devise a syllabus and reading list for each one, if she needed to order books. And she also had at least a dozen things she needed to do immediately.

After languishing in despair and dormancy for months, this sudden demand for her abilities felt like a rebirth. In a few seconds she had been transformed from a nonentity into one of those underpaid, overburdened graduate student section leaders such as she'd known in college. She was determined to be a good one. The failed novel now seemed silly and frivolous, a bit of child's play before she became immersed in adult responsibilities. And there was something else . . . What was it? Oh, yes! She almost laughed in relief when she remembered Ken Newsome. Just this quickly, that whole . . . thing . . . whatever it was . . . seemed simply a quirk of fate designed to catapult her out of her funk and onto the path where her future lay.

~ PART TWO ~

~ 8 ~

Shaye Dobbs had scheduled her husband's appointment with the cardiologist at UAB for the Monday of Martin Luther King Day, when neither she nor her husband had to go in for their jobs with the Opelika City School System. Daniel made sure to get home in plenty of time to greet his parents and little sister when they arrived on the Friday afternoon beforehand. They had not been to visit since the wedding in July, and had never seen the apartment after he and Caroline moved in. He was proud of what they had done with it, and was glad they were finally going to see it, especially if he ended up buying a house sometime soon. His parents would be impressed enough with the apartment, and then even more impressed when he showed them some of the house possibilities which Lily Templeton had arranged for them to tour over the weekend. He could give them what they'd always wanted: the sense that he was headed for great things.

He had his father's bourbon, his mother's wine coolers, the soft drinks for his sister, the cheese, Carr's Table Wafers. All was ready. When he spied their car pulling into the lot, he went down to help with the bags and show them the way to his unit. His mother exclaimed just like he thought she would when she entered the apartment for the first time.

"How beautiful!" she cried. "Caroline did such a good job." His mother looked around, not so much at the furnishings, as to see where his wife was. Naturally, she expected her daughter-in-law to be on hand to greet them.

"Caroline will be here soon," he told his mother. "She's got a surprise for you."

He saw his parents exchange glances, while his father's eyebrows shot up. Then his father abruptly sat down on the sofa in the living room, drummed his fingers on a side table, and tried to conceal his complete lack of interest in the apartment, along with his desperate desire for a cigarette. In the kitchen Daniel poured his father a drink and brought it out to him as compensation.

His mother pursed her lips in disapproval, but before she could object, Daniel picked up her luggage and showed her into Caroline's study, which was also the second bedroom and did have a fold-out couch, already made up. Without invitation, his sister Tanya had settled herself in the newlywed's master bedroom, where she had turned on the TV to a cartoon he would have thought much too juvenile for a fourteen-year-old girl. At least Caroline's absence had prevented her from witnessing that.

After giving his mother the full tour, he led her into the kitchen, where he got a beer for himself, a wine cooler for her, and the tray of cheese and crackers. When he and his mother sat down in the living room, his father seized his bourbon glass with an entire palm placed around it, no doubt to disguise the amount he'd already consumed. Shaye gave him a quick look which indicated she was not the least bit fooled, while Bobby assumed the pained expression of a much misunderstood man. Now would be the perfect time for Caroline to arrive, Daniel thought.

"Well," said his mother, straightening her posture and smoothing her skirt. "What's this about Caroline, Son?" But it was her husband she looked at.

"What do you mean?" said Daniel.

"You said she had a surprise for us. Is she pregnant, Son?"

Daniel looked at her in astonishment. Then he had to laugh at the expression of serious concern on both his parents' faces. "No, no," he assured them. "It's nothing like that."

His father exhaled a deep sigh of relief.

"You had us worried there for a minute, Son," his mother told him, before taking a first sip of her wine cooler, apparently in celebration of the fact that her son and his wife were *not* expecting their first baby.

"There's no reason not to wait on something like that," his father said. "With your student loan debt."

"Plus Caroline is so young," his mother pointed out. "She's got all the time in the world. Better to wait until you're sure this job will work out, maybe even until you've made partner. What's the partnership track at this law firm you're working for, Son? Joab Tucker was asking me just the other day, and I had to tell him I didn't know."

Daniel decided to ignore the topics of his student loan debt and the partnership track at his law firm. That wasn't what he wanted to discuss as he tried to relax on Friday afternoon after a week of work. The problem was, his parents had never known how to have a conversation about abstract subjects or issues that did not affect them directly and personally. They had both grown up on farms, the children of Depression survivors whose own parents had been sharecroppers. Talk was for discussing the weather, the animals, the corn, the soybeans, the next meal—whatever pertained to the moment's most immediate call for action. They did not know how to talk about nothing at all. Likewise, his mother did not know how to sit still and do nothing at all.

"Is there something I can do, Son, to help get dinner on the table? While we're waiting for Caroline?"

"No, Mother. Don't worry. Here. Have some cheese." He cut a slice of the Brie, placed it on a cracker and handed it to her.

She looked at it with distrust and only reluctantly accepted it. "Just one," she told him, as if she were doing him a favor by taking it. "Now that I'm over forty, the pounds are starting to add up, and I have to watch my calories just like I've always watched my pennies. It's a good thing I have that discipline. But your father could use a cheese cracker. With all he's had to drink already, he needs something on his stomach."

Without a word, her husband rose from the sofa and went into the kitchen. They could hear the sound of the bourbon as it splashed defiantly into his glass. His mother leaned over as if to whisper something extremely confidential. "If we don't get some real supper in him soon, I don't know what will happen."

"I heard that, Shaye," Bobby called from the kitchen. "You'd think after a full day of work and a two hour drive to Birmingham, you'd let me relax."

Daniel was relieved to see amusement on his father's face when he emerged from the kitchen. Undoubtedly his fully replenished glass of bourbon, which his wife would not have allowed him at home, contributed to his tolerance for her fussing. Daniel shot his father a surreptitious look of commiseration as he passed by on his way back to the couch in the living room.

"Yes! Let's relax!" said Shaye. "Although I'm happy to get dinner started. Just tell me the menu Caroline has planned, and I'll get to work."

Where she came from, dinner was just another chore that needed to be accomplished before bedtime. Daniel doubted whether she'd known any other form of relaxation besides the unconsciousness of sleep.

"Actually," he announced. "Caroline and I thought it would be fun to go out to eat tonight."

Instead of being delighted by this news, his parents exchanged their usual looks of consternation.

"Well, Son," his father began, before breaking off and looking to Shaye for confirmation. When she nodded vigorously, Bobby resumed. "We're not sure how much insurance is going to pay for the doctor's visit on Monday. . . ."

"My treat," Daniel offered quickly, hoping to interrupt any tale of financial woe that might be forthcoming. And there was always one ready and waiting to be told. "I might as well tell you," he said, playing his best card in a desperate bid to start a conversation they could all enjoy. "The reason Caroline isn't here yet is because she's got a job."

Jobs were something his parents heartily approved and fully appreciated. Their daughter-in-law's plan to "write" for a year without a job was no more than a pretense, they had suspected, to disguise her real plan for getting pregnant as soon as possible so she'd have a genuine excuse to remain unemployed. Why else would someone with the world's best ticket into the job market decide not to use it? Daniel knew it had taken all their self-restraint to keep quiet on the subject of that brand-new Harvard diploma going to waste. On hearing his news, they began to look cautiously optimistic. But since this was as happy as his parents ever got, Daniel was gratified. They all rewarded themselves with sips of their drinks.

"I'm glad she's not thinking of getting pregnant just yet," said his mother.

"What's this job?" his father asked.

"She's teaching English at the University of Alabama," Daniel told them proudly.

Frowning, his parents looked at each other.

"In Tuscaloosa?" his mother said, searching her son's face with alarm.

"In Tuscaloosa," he said, emphatically, although he didn't understand her concern.

"But, Son," his father objected. "What does the gas cost, there and back, every day, to Tuscaloosa?"

"Oh, she's living there," he said quickly.

"Living there!" his parents exclaimed in scandalized unison.

For a moment everyone was silent. Daniel realized that once again, he had badly miscalculated with his parents. In his imagination, he always attributed to them the normal reactions and responses of normal people. But his parents were not normal people. They were children of parents who had endured the Depression as sharecroppers, and they were permanently warped as a result, not so much by their lives on the farm as by their desperate attempt to put it so far behind them it would be as if it had never happened. He always forgot the extreme extent to which everything was a potential problem that might land a person back where he never wanted to be again. His debt was a problem. His wife's pregnancy would have been a problem. Life was a problem. He realized now that perhaps he should call Lily to cancel the showing of the houses this weekend. That would be a problem too for his parents. They did not know how to be happy about anything; they only knew how to worry about everything.

"I hope she's making good enough money to justify living over there," Shaye said.

Exasperated, he couldn't stop himself. "Mother," he said. "You're a teacher. Do you make good money? Have you ever known any teacher anywhere in this state who does make good money?"

No one spoke. His mother looked down at her lap and smoothed her unwrinkled skirt again. "Well, what's the point then, Son?" She looked up at him as if confronting a delinquent student in her business administration class, which was longhand for typing. Then she raised her hand so she could begin ticking items off with her fingers. "Rent, utilities, food, gas. You two are paying probably double the cost of living, and if there isn't that much of a return, I don't see the point."

"The point is her career, Mother," he said wearily. "If this is what she wants to do, then she's got to start somewhere."

"That's true, Shaye," said Bobby, inclining his head through the haze of bourbon beginning to accumulate in his personal sphere.

"She'll have to get a higher degree if she wants to advance," Shaye warned. "At least a master's."

"We talked about this before we got married," he informed her. "If she wanted to enter the graduate program, she'd either commute every day or take an apartment and come home on the weekends."

"Why did you even get married, then?" his mother cried wildly.

"Shaye!" boomed his father in his deepest baritone, the one he used when he was still a Southern Baptist preacher. "We commuted for years when we were married."

"That's right. We did," Shaye asserted. "Your father lived in Troy while he was getting his degrees. I stayed in Eight Mile for my job at the mini-mart. He came home on the weekends. I'm not going to lie to you, Son. It was not easy. It was hard. We're all lucky our marriage survived."

Daniel did not wish to reflect upon whether the survival of his parents' marriage was lucky or not. His father had passed that point with his bourbon where nothing anyone said could penetrate the thick haze surrounding him. But his mother was so nervous that she fixed herself a piece of Brie on a cracker and actually ate it.

"Let me ask you this, Daniel," she said. "Just how much money is Caroline making?"

"Shaye!" boomed his father's voice. "That's none of our business."

"It's a legitimate question," she argued.

"Your parents didn't ask me what I was making during all those years I preached for nothing but a rent-free apartment," he wagged his finger at her.

His father's intervention was so reassuring that Daniel was emboldened to tell his mother: "Money is not the point."

Immediately Daniel knew he had miscalculated again when his father sank back against his sofa cushion in disgust, with a shake of his head suggesting he wasn't sure if he'd raised his son right.

"Money is always the point, Son," said his mother, just like he should have known she would. "Commuting takes a huge toll on a marriage. I hope you and Caroline did a cost/benefit analysis before she started down this road. The career Caroline wants to have may not be worth the cost to your marriage, especially if the money isn't there. She can always get a job here in town teaching high school, or some other job. That may be a sacrifice she needs to make in order not to put her marriage at risk. If the money isn't there, I think she should put her marriage first."

Daniel sighed and excused himself to get another beer from the kitchen.

"While you're at it," called his father.

Shaye hissed fiercely. "You've had enough!"

When Daniel got back with the bourbon and the beer, the door of the apartment opened. Caroline walked into what felt like a funeral. Little did she even know that she was the dead person. Even he was more irritated than happy to see her, because if she'd been here when his parents arrived, he would have been spared the excruciating ordeal of being alone with them. Her absence had definitely cost him more than any benefit he'd received from her new job. Could his parents possibly have a point?

~ 9 ~

The party at the chairman's house took place on the Friday after midterm exams, one week before spring break. The chairman—who was actually a woman—lived on a leafy Tuscaloosa street in a sprawling Victorian house that had last been renovated at least a decade ago. The hardwood floors were worn and scuffed, the walls badly needed a fresh coat of paint, the kitchen cried out to be updated, and the plumbing hammered whenever any faucet was turned on. But this shabbiness was comfortable and inviting, so unlike the typical Mountain Brook residence Caroline was used to, with its immaculate perfection and expensive décor, places where people could pretend to live and pretend to have a good time, if they were careful. In the chairman's rambling Victorian, a chaotic jumble of overstuffed, mismatched sofas and chairs filled the front two rooms in what had once been a formal double parlor. When Caroline arrived at five, the front door was wide open, as were all the windows, bringing the early spring indoors along with all the guests. Bottles of beer sprouted from coolers filled with ice; trays of chips with bowls of salsa were on the tables.

In the dining room on her way back from the bathroom several hours into the party, a hand clapped heavily on her shoulder. Caroline turned around to find Alan Melrose, the R.W. Russell Distinguished Professor of American Literature, who also hosted a popular half-hour show on NPR every Wednesday afternoon called "Fun Facts about Fiction." Saying nothing, he bent his large frame until his face was level with hers, where he searched her countenance at length. As her eyes darted around the room, Caroline noticed it was empty except for all the boxes, folders, papers, magazines and old mail piled on the dining room table. For a nervous moment she wondered if Alan were going to make a pass at her like he had at the beginning of the semester. But when he opened his mouth to speak, his voice produced only a loud hiccup. Caroline smiled at this distinguished professor, her senior by at least thirty-five years. Undeterred by the hiccup, which he seemed not to have noticed, Alan Melrose moved his face even closer. It was whiskey, not beer, reeking from his breath and seeping from every pore of his body. The hand gripped her shoulder.

"Thank you so much," said the distinguished Dr. Melrose, in a surprisingly proper voice. "Thank you so, so much. I owe you a huge debt. Thank you so much." Squeezing her shoulder blade as if to emphasize his final thanks, he dropped his hand and then lurched backward on unsteady feet.

Caroline did not know what she was being thanked for, or if he was confusing her with someone else. "Oh, no need to thank me," she said breezily, hoping this reply would suffice for whatever circumstances applied.

Melrose looked at her as if she'd lost her mind. "Of *course* I need to thank you," he said, putting a fist to his mouth in an unsuccessful attempt to stifle a belch. "If not for you, they would have made *me* teach one of those classes. But you came. You're here. You're doing the job. I owe you a huge debt. Bathroom that way?" He looked longingly beyond her toward a greatly desired destination.

She shook her head. "Behind you. That door in the hall. On the left."

Either he had come from the kitchen and walked right past the bathroom, or he had looped in a circle downstairs, unaware that he'd missed the bathroom and was headed back toward the front rooms. Barely suppressing a giggle, she watched as he staggered around, then picked a precariously zigzag path through a dining room whose floor was as cluttered with boxes and stacks of papers as the table.

This was not the first time Alan Melrose had thanked her for taking on his ailing colleague's classes, nor was he the only one who'd expressed such gratitude. In fact, the entire faculty had welcomed and befriended her as if she were some prize scholar they'd lured from a top tier university instead of a temporary instructor filling in for the spring semester. This was less a credit to her than to the members of this English Department, which was an eclectic, freewheeling group of individuals who—despite the predictable ideological divisions—embraced everyone in every way. In general, they observed no distinctions between the tenured and the untenured, professors and students, young and older, married and unmarried. The only distinction that had been forced upon them in recent years was the one between female undergraduates and everyone else. The coeds were now officially off-limits. Otherwise, everyone behaved as if young and unmarried, especially those who were older and married, who also tended to be the tenured professors, some of whom held fancy endowed chairs, like Alan Melrose. The clumsy, unrequited passes they made publicly at parties seemed almost perfunctory, as if they were just doing their duty in upholding the obligatory lecherous reputation of entitled male academics. Failing as lechers, they succeeded in making fools of themselves, which appeared to be their true agenda, so they could place themselves on the same human level as everyone else. Before the end of January, Alan Melrose and another tenured, married professor with an endowed chair had made their clownish passes at her, and seemed enormously relieved when she gently deflected them. Now that the necessary compliment had been paid and this charade was out of the way, they felt free to behave as friends, and include her in invitations to all the parties, film festivals, author appearances and panel discussions that took place constantly on campus. She had thoroughly enjoyed every minute of social life in the small university town. She could have gone out every night to some interesting event; one week she did. In a few short months at the University of Alabama, she'd enjoyed herself more than in four years at Harvard. The irony was not lost on her.

Tonight's party, like none other she'd been to in Mountain Brook, was like all others she'd attended in Tuscaloosa. Really just an open house, it began whenever the first person had shown up, and would end whenever the last left, probably around midnight or two A.M. There was no other food besides the tortilla chips and store-bought salsa. At some point, a dozen pizza boxes were delivered, and everyone scrambled to produce enough dollars. It was more fun than any party she'd ever been to, including the wedding parties given in her honor. As for parties at Harvard, there hadn't been many that she was invited to, certainly not at the house of the English Department chairman, a man whose name she didn't even remember. In Tuscaloosa, the key element at all the gatherings was the thorough mixture of people, all ranks of professors and instructors, graduate students and undergraduates, talking and laughing freely without regard to rank. It hadn't taken her long to meet all the professors and graduate students in the program. Until now, she'd never known what it was like to belong to any group, or even to want to belong. She even began to think that perhaps she'd finally found her own place in the world. Again, the irony was not lost on her. She had once struggled so hard to avoid the fate of attending the University of Alabama; now she embraced it. However, this was possible only because she *had* rejected it first. After rejecting what was foisted on her, she was then free to choose it on her own terms.

She was also free from that silly infatuation with the next-door neighbor in Birmingham. Only during that one week before classes began did she think of him and wait for the phone to ring. When it never did, she had called him once and left a message giving her new phone number and confirming the date of his interview in Tuscaloosa. But then her life changed radically with the start of spring semester. Each day was a race to get prepared in time, the thrill of being in front of a class, an onslaught of papers to grade. In addition, there was the one graduate course she enrolled in so she could officially be a graduate student teacher. She had hardly noticed when the date of her neighbor's interview came and went without his phone call. Even better, she didn't care. It was a relief to learn he had no hold on her imagination, no claim on her heart. She was not in love with him, and never had been. The whole affair, such as it was, had taken place entirely in her unoccupied brain, a product only of her boredom and despair, not of any romantic feeling for him or lack of feeling for her husband. The affinity her neighbor had felt for her went no further than friendship. "I go to Tuscaloosa quite a bit for my job. I could see you there." This was not desire, just good manners. Fortunately, the one message she'd left on his answering machine was similarly innocuous.

She was incredibly lucky. The folly she was guilty of had been committed entirely within the realm of her own consciousness. No one else was aware of it, not her neighbor, not her husband. Nothing had been destroyed; her marriage was intact. The dissatisfaction with her husband and their marriage, she was now convinced, was displaced dissatisfaction with her own life. She was equally convinced that now she was getting her career underway, all discontent would vanish, and she would be able to see her husband as she had when she'd first fallen in love with him. It might even be possible, she had learned, to have a Tuesday/Thursday schedule next fall, making it feasible to commute from Birmingham twice a week rather than rent in Tuscaloosa and go back on weekends. Then she could really put all the pieces of her life together.

* * *

On Wednesday afternoon, two days before Good Friday and the beginning of spring break, her husband showed up unexpectedly at her apartment. Although feverishly trying to finish grading midterm exams, she was delighted to see him. But he did not want a conjugal visit. He wanted a divorce.

As she struggled to absorb her shock and pain, she realized that she'd been a bigger fool than she knew. Of course her folly had not escaped notice. Of course he had known, as a good husband would, when his wife's affections had strayed.

"It's all my fault," she said tearfully.

"No," he said, shaking his head. "It's no one's fault. It's for the best. You belong here. It's been good for you. This is what you're meant to do. But we need to be free to make our own lives."

"No!" she cried, pleading. "We also belong together! We're meant to be together!"

"How can we be together when we're apart?"

His coldness was frightening. When her hands automatically reached out toward him, he gave nothing back to her, no embrace, no touch, no movement that could result in the slightest contact between them, as if connection were no longer possible or desirable.

"We stayed together for three years when we were a thousand miles apart!" she cried. "Now we're just forty-five minutes away from each other. I could have a Tuesday/Thursday schedule next year. I could commute. We'd be together every night." She was beseeching, groveling even.

"It won't help. It won't work."

"What are you saying? That you don't want me to go to graduate school?"

"No. I'm saying I want a divorce."

"But why? What's happened? I don't understand. Tell me. What's going on?"

For a long while he looked at her without answering. They were both still standing in the middle of her tiny living room. When she'd tried to take him by the hand and lead him to the couch, he'd only shaken his head and shaken off her hand.

"Do you doubt my commitment to our marriage?" she asked him. "Is that it?"

"No," he said. "I just think it's better if we end our commitment. We want different things."

"How can you say that? We just got married."

"Sometimes you don't realize something isn't right until you go ahead and do it."

"What's not right? Is there something I've done, or said, that made you think I didn't love you anymore?"

"Of course not. I know you love me. And I'll always love you. But it takes more than love to make a marriage work. Two people have to want to create the same life together. Not lead two separate lives. So it's best we do this now."

This made her cry. "I don't want two separate lives!" she sobbed. "Yes, I do want my own professional life, but not a personal life separate from you. I didn't mean to leave *you* when I came here."

"I know that," he said. "But when you did leave, it helped me realize that something was wrong. In a way, it's a good thing you left. We found out sooner what we would have found out later, when it might be much harder to do this."

"Counseling," she said through her tears. "We need to get marriage counseling. Or couples therapy. Whatever it's called."

"No," he said emphatically, with a harshness he'd never used in speaking with her before. "That will only drag it out, make it more painful, delay the inevitable."

"Just let me get back to Birmingham for spring break." She wiped her tears with the back of her hand. "We can talk this through. We can work it all out."

"No," he said again. "There's no need for you to come to Birmingham. A lawyer in my firm is preparing the document. In the state of Alabama, an uncontested divorce petition can be granted in three days. I'm going home this weekend for Easter, to tell my parents."

Sorrow turned suddenly into anger. "That's it?" she snapped at him. "Just like that? You want to throw our whole relationship away without even discussing it? I don't understand. *Why?*"

"I just want to make this as easy as possible on us."

"Divorce isn't supposed to be that easy! For a reason! Most couples," she gulped, swallowing words in her distress. "Even those that bicker and fight, like we never have," she managed. "Most try their hardest to *save* their marriage! They don't just casually throw it away!"

He moved away from her emotion, toward the door, done with talking. "I'll send you the document next week. It's very simple really. We don't have much, and we can each keep what's ours. All you have to do is sign it."

"I'm not signing anything." She followed him to the door.

He sighed. "You can get a lawyer to look it over if you like. I'll pay for it. But you don't need it."

"I'm talking about *counseling!*" she shouted at him. "I'm not signing anything until we have some *marriage counseling!*"

He started to open the door. "I hope you change your mind. Because no amount of counseling will change mine." Pushing through, he left without another word.

As she watched him go, she felt like she was looking at a total stranger. Part of her feared that divorce had already happened; he was no longer her husband in body or spirit. It was even as if he'd never been her husband in the first place, such was the complete absence of warmth or tenderness in his manner to her. She had never known him to treat anyone with the cool, forced civility he'd just used with her. Not once had he touched her, not even to wipe her tears or calm her distress. But she couldn't blame him any more than she could question his actions: He had behaved as a betrayed husband toward the wife who'd had an affair with another man. If only he would let her explain. If only it wasn't too late.

~ 10 ~

Wednesday night she did not sleep. The adrenaline of raging emotions and the turmoil of racing thoughts kept her up all night, like punishment for her misdeeds and mistakes. Thursday was a blur, sometimes literally, as her eyes frequently filled with tears even when she stood in front of her classes. When she got home that afternoon, she flung herself on the bed to vent all the same emotions that had kept her up the night before. A fitful sleep overtook her finally, but gave her no rest; instead it tossed her about further as it sent her nightmares filled with childhood monsters and terrors unleashed from the deep. When Friday arrived, she met her classes only to dismiss them. It was Good Friday, after all. More than half the students had already left for the spring vacation. Briefly she toyed with the idea of joining her family at the beach house in Florida, but her mother would only make matters worse, and besides, she was in no state to drive four hours, mostly on back roads. Help was what she needed, but she didn't know who to turn to or where to find it. Meanwhile, the telephone still did not ring. All the frantic voice mails she'd left on her husband's answering machine went unanswered; he did not call. If not for his planned visit home, she would have driven like a banshee over to Birmingham to talk with him, no matter what he said about not wanting to talk.

She didn't know how she was going to make it through Good Friday night, let alone Easter weekend and an entire week of nothing and no one but her own failed self in a dismal basement apartment that now looked out on the razed stump of what was once a glorious and ancient magnolia tree. This afternoon she'd come home to find her landlady dusting her hands in the barren backyard in good riddance to her only flowering plant, whose roots and leaves had gotten on her nerves. Thanks to the extra money she was getting in rent, she explained to her tenant, she had finally been able to get the detested tree cut down. In Caroline's agitated state of mind, there was no escaping the awful symbolism.

A knock on the door interrupted her thoughts and gave her a moment's wild hope followed quickly by a moment of dread. Her husband, she prayed fervently, come to explain and beg her forbearance; her landlady, she feared, come to complain.

"Nick Scully!" She could not have been more unprepared to see the person who stood behind the outer screen door.

"Forgive me," he grinned. "I would have gotten here sooner, but the dragon lady detained me at the castle gate."

"I am so glad to see you," she breathed. The sight of him brought so many emotions—surprise, relief, gratitude, delight—she didn't know which to act on, so she simply stood there, speechless, gazing at him in wonder.

"Well?" he demanded. "Are you going to let me in?"

"I'm sorry," she said, releasing the latch on the door. "Come in." She stepped aside as he entered.

He peered quickly around the room, then back at her. "This place is a dump," he said. "Are you all right?"

"Not really," she admitted.

"That's what I thought," he said.

For several awkward minutes they stood there looking at one another in silence. He was scrutinizing her face as if he could read her troubles from its expression. She only wished he could, to spare her the anguish of explaining her predicament.

"Well," he said finally. "I've come to get you out of here."

"Out of here?"

"For the week anyway. It *is* your spring break, isn't it? Let's do something!"

If she hadn't been trembling on the verge of tears, this would have made her laugh. This was his line, what he always used to say when they were pals during her high school days: "Let's do something!" It's what they would carve on his tombstone.

"How did you know?" It was little more than a whisper she managed.

"How did I know what?"

"My spring break. My—" she broke off, not knowing how to characterize the sudden disintegration of her life.

"I make it my business to know these things," he said.

If only he did know everything, she thought, putting her face in her hands. Maybe he could explain it to her.

"Come on!" he said, seizing her arm and ignoring her distress. "Let's get you packed."

She struggled to control her face, keep her tears in check. But she couldn't put one foot in front of the other any more than she could question the need to get packed.

"Just point me to the bedroom." He tugged unsuccessfully on her arm. "Okay. I'll find it myself. Shouldn't be hard. Process of elimination."

He moved behind her and pushed her playfully along until she had led him into her room. At the bed he shoved her gently down to the mattress. "Just sit there while I pack." He whirled around toward the closet. "Suitcase!" he cried, as if hoping to summon it forth. With the quickness of a cat, he pounced on the closet door, flung it open and squared his stance as if expecting imminent attack from a flying suitcase or the contents of the closet.

He hadn't changed a bit, she thought. Still the same old Nick, behaving in his usual antic fashion. It's what everyone else had called "immature," "eccentric," "wild," or even "crazy." She'd always been amused by his madcap behavior, which had something of Harpo Marx in it. It used to make her laugh, and would have had her laughing now if she had been capable of laughter. But she was incapable of anything except sitting silently as she observed this Marx Brothers comedy routine of a guy let loose through a girl's clothes drawers, scooping up panties like forbidden treasure, dangling a bra in front of his puzzled face as if trying to figure out what this was.

It was preposterous, but she was powerless to stop it. She didn't even know where he was planning to take her, but then again, he'd always liked leading her into the unknown. She had never been sure where he was planning to take her. He just came to get her, and off they went. Usually it was some place she'd never been before, where no one else would think to go, like the barbecue shack in North Birmingham, or the drive-in movie theater in Pell City. One Sunday he had picked her up at noon, and without telling her where they were going or what they were doing, he'd driven all the way to Montgomery, where he had tickets for the two o'clock matinee of *The Tempest* at the Alabama Shakespeare Festival. He liked to surprise her, but she had never felt unsafe or scared in his company. He treated her like the little sister he'd never had, while she found in him a big brother she'd never known. Four years later and here she was again, the kid sister he was leading by the hand. She followed him now like she'd followed him then, not only because she trusted him, but because what she needed most at that very moment was to get away, if only for a short while.

Suitcase in hand, he stopped at the threshold of the bedroom to grab the books on her bedside table. "You get what you need from the bathroom," he told her. "I'll put this in the car."

As he pulled out of the driveway, he asked "How about some dinner?"

"Fine," she agreed, although she didn't feel like either eating or talking. She wasn't even interested in getting to the bottom of what he knew or how he knew it. The suffering she'd endured since her husband's visit two days ago had so completely hollowed her out she was empty even of simple curiosity. Fortunately Nick said nothing and still seemed able to read her mind, like he had in the past, when they shared that silent communion of siblings who always knew what the other was thinking. The only thing she felt like mentioning was his new car.

"What happened to the Karmann Ghia?"

"I had to retire it," he grinned. "It was an antique, as you know, even when I drove you around in it years ago."

"Did you sell it?" The thought made her sad.

"Oh, no. I'll never do that, although it's worth more now than when I bought it. I still use it on special occasions."

"What is this you're driving now?"

"An Audi."

"Nice," she said mechanically, not really caring.

The restaurant he drove them to was also nice, a place she'd never been to overlooking the Tuscaloosa River, which under normal circumstances would have been delightful. The view gave her an excuse to look away from his gaze and pay little heed to the conversation he kept up with minimal contribution from her. It was early when they arrived, with sunlight still on the water. It was soothing to watch the day fade into darkness and the lights begin twinkling around them. She gave scant attention to what she ate or what he said as he chattered nonstop throughout the meal, in what she knew was a deliberate attempt to take her mind off her troubles. Still, the food and the company helped a great deal. She was grateful, and tried to rouse herself to make some kind of effort in return.

Pushing away her plate, she looked at him directly and made an attempt at a smile. "It's really good to see you again after all these years," she said.

"Likewise," he said, with his characteristic grin.

"How did we get out of touch?" She posed the question to herself as much as to him, trying to recall. He stared out the window at the lights on the river.

"I remember writing several letters my freshman year," she continued. "You never wrote back, and then I left some messages on your answering machine when I was home for the Christmas holidays."

"I was out of town most of that year," he said.

"That's what I figured. Didn't someone tell me you were traveling through Europe?" she smiled. "Sounds like you."

"Switzerland, mainly." He pulled away from the window.

"Switzerland?" This surprised her. "I'm not sure I see you in Switzerland. For you I'd think that might be too boring. I see you in the world capitals."

"I was in rehab."

"Rehab!" she exclaimed.

A ghost of his usual grin flickered briefly across his face. She looked for an explanation, but he said nothing more and resumed staring out the window, just as she had done previously.

"I'm sorry," she said eventually. "I didn't know."

When the waitress arrived to clear their table, her thoughts ran riot. Not only had she not heard anything about a stint in rehab, she had not known he'd had a drug or alcohol problem of any kind. Of course, those rumors were always swirling around his name; he was supposed to be thoroughly debauched, dabbling in all sorts of drugs and other illicit activities, just as he dabbled in everything else and generally dabbled his life away. But she herself had seen no grain of truth to any of the gossip. The summer before her senior year in high school, the summer afterwards, and the school year in between, she had spent a considerable amount of time with him, and not once had she known him to mention any drug use, let alone engage in it. As a result, she'd been inclined to discount all those rumors as the usual tall tales often told about young men who hadn't yet settled down like others their age were starting to do. She found herself shocked, not only that he'd had such problems, but that she'd never known or even suspected. Whenever she'd been with him, he'd always been like a happy-go-lucky kid bent on the day's adventure, which might make the grownups frown—North Birmingham, Pell City—but was essentially harmless. Now it struck her that this was probably the reason he had spent so much time with her: she had served as a shield from temptation, at least temporarily.

"I'm sorry," she said again, after the waitress left. "I really had no idea."

"I didn't want anyone to know. That was the reason for Switzerland."

"I see," she said. "Did it work?"

"It took a while. A long time. Most of one whole year. Parts of two others."

She struggled to maintain a neutral expression belying the shock she felt. Almost three years in rehab! "What was the . . . problem?" she said quietly.

"Mainly cocaine," he said. "The best way: with a needle."

Inwardly she shuddered at the image of him sticking his arm with a needle full of cocaine. "You never struck me as someone with a drug addiction," she said evenly, trying to hide her dismay.

"I was never an addict," he said. "I wasn't even a very heavy user. But—"

"I knew it!" she exhaled in relief. "All that time we spent together, I would have noticed *something*. Some indication, some evidence, if you were using drugs all the time. I never noticed anything of the kind. Not once. Ever." She smiled.

Surprisingly, he failed to return her smile. "No," he said, with a rueful shake of his head. "I didn't use drugs all the time. I used drugs some of the time. The problem was, I *thought* about using drugs all the time. Which is bad enough in and of itself."

Her heart sank again, and she looked at him sadly. "Not to mention that thinking about doing something all the time can easily lead to doing that something all the time," she said softly.

"Yes, not to mention that. I thought it was best to get help while my problem was still more of a psychological dependence than a chemical one. What I really needed was a good psychiatrist."

"Did you find one over there?"

"Yes."

Not wanting to pry, she waited for him to say more. Instead, he looked away and peered through the window at the lights along the river. So many moments passed in silence she expected him to change the subject. But when he turned back, he said with a grin, "I was diagnosed with an existential condition."

"What do you mean?"

"The gist of three years of sessions with excellent European psychiatrists: It wasn't the cocaine itself that was the biggest problem, but finding a reason for living."

"Have you?"

Again the shadow of a grin passed across his face. "I wouldn't go so far as to say that."

"But you said the rehab worked."

"I haven't done cocaine or any other drug in over three years. But rehab doesn't give you another reason for living."

"But you're okay?"

"I've put myself in—" he paused to find the words he wanted, and grinned outright as it came to him, apparently a phrase he was quoting: "'a healthy psychological position' where it's possible to find a reason for living. That's the best I can do at the moment, and I'm doing it."

* * *

In the dark she couldn't tell where he was driving, only that it was out of town. When he turned off the main road onto one that was narrow, poorly paved and even more poorly lit, it finally occurred to her to ask.

"My family has a house on the Black Warrior River," he told her.

She nodded.

The road came to an end at a sign she could read only because of the headlights on the car. "Private Property," it said. "Owners and Guests of River Cove Association Only." He turned onto a gravel drive.

"This is an inlet off the river," he explained. "There are houses all around the inlet in kind of a horseshoe."

All she could see in the pitch black were big trees. Gradually she was able to make out the tastefully modest houses tucked beneath these trees. There were no lights on in any of these residences, no cars in the driveways they passed by. She couldn't see any lights from the houses across the river either. The only illumination came from a few weak street lamps attached to some of the utility poles. He turned into one of the driveways. When they got out of his car, the earthy smell of the river hit her immediately.

"Here we are," he said, unlocking the front door and pushing it open in front of her.

She walked into a large room with a high vaulted ceiling.

"It's my favorite of all my family's vacation places," he said. "I even like it better than the beach house in Florida." He came in after her and switched on a lamp. "Tell me what you think."

She looked around. There was not much she could see in the dim light of one lamp. "It's beautiful," she said automatically, knowing it was expected of her, and knowing it would be beautiful with the Scully's money. At the moment, she was incapable of noticing or caring what the place looked like.

"Wait till tomorrow when you can see the view out that window." He pointed ahead to an expanse of glass that formed the rear wall of the room.

"Does your family come here often?" she asked, trying to make polite conversation.

"Not since they built the house on Logan Martin," he called over his shoulder. He disappeared with her suitcase through a door off the great room. "The house on the lake is bigger," he said as he emerged a moment later. "And for them it's better, because there's a social life at Logan Martin." He grinned and shook his head. "Nothing like going out to the lake to get away from it all, only to see the exact same people you would have seen at the country club if you'd stayed in town. But I'm thankful," he added. "They're all happy to let me have the run of this place. Come on," he motioned her forward. "Let's go outside, on the deck. I'll build a fire."

The deck had three levels, one right off the kitchen, with a table and chairs, one underneath that with ceiling fans and hammocks, and one right on the water, leading out to a pier. She followed him down a steep flight of stairs to the bottom deck. Under the covered portion, Nick peeled the wrap off a huge piece of furniture, custom-built by the looks of it. The seat cushion was as big as a queen-sized mattress, and a jumble of pillows in all colors and sizes filled in the backs and the sides. An entire extended family could lounge comfortably all together, which no doubt was the purpose. From a drawer built in at the bottom he pulled out two zippered plastic cases containing stacks of heavy wool blankets.

"Wrap yourself in some of these," he said, "while I make the fire."

First he switched on two heaters, tall as lampposts, on either side of the sofa. Then he moved over to a huge stone fireplace at the edge of the deck. In a closet next to it he turned on a light and found kindling and firewood.

"Remind me what your family's business is," she said, settling into the sofa with her blankets. "Where does all the money come from? I know you told me before, but I've forgotten."

"Palmdale Mills," he said, squatting down by the hearth with a handful of kindling.

"Oh, that's right. I remember now."

"Textiles," he said. "So fascinating I wonder how you could forget." He dusted his hands from the kindling sticks and began placing the firewood. "We make the cloth used for socks, underwear, tee shirts. I was supposed to grow up and manage the mill in Sylacauga. Of course I was going to get a fancier title than manager. Something like Vice President of Operations, but it boils down to manager. However, I refused to grow up, then I refused to move to Sylacauga, and finally I refused to manage a mill. The one in Sylacauga makes hosiery." He turned briefly to look at her. "You know what hosiery is? It's the stuff for panty hose. I ask you: Do you like panty hose? Do you wear panty hose?" With a snort of derision, he turned back to resume building the fire. "I hate panty hose, and no one even expects me to wear it. No woman should be expected to wear it either. I've been told many times it's extremely uncomfortable. It must be one of the worst inventions ever made. How could I spend my life managing the manufacture of something I don't believe in? I don't see how my parents could reasonably assume they were conceiving a child who would want to live in Sylacauga and manage a panty hose mill. I was definitely below the age of consent when they signed me up for that. They appear to have committed me to it when I was still in the womb. Is that fair? My brother and sister seemed to think it was, but they got to stay with the main plant in Birmingham. They've always been furious at me for not doing my duty, because they thought it meant one of them would have to move to Sylacauga. And not that I don't love them, but what hypocrites! 'Hire somebody!' I told them. 'Find someone who will be happy to live in Sylacauga, train this person, and hire this person.' Simple! 'That's money you won't be making,' they told me. 'That's money going out of the family.' 'What's wrong with that?' I said. I have more money from my trust than I'll ever know what to do with. I could support a harem of wives and a hundred children. 'Let somebody else make a good living managing that mill,' I told them. 'I don't need to.'"

She only half listened to his playful rant as she watched him build the fire and then coax it into a blaze. No comment was required from her, just like at the restaurant; he was only trying to amuse her and divert her attention. When he was satisfied that the fire had definitely caught, he moved into a corner of the big couch and pulled one of the blankets up with him. He seemed to have run out of words, and concentrated on observing the flames to make sure they grabbed a firm hold on the wood. She was grateful for the silence, and the pristine elements of water, fire, pure spring air and the earthy river smell which enveloped her. Nature, she remembered from the Chinese proverb, was one of the world's best physicians. If so, she hoped it could help heal her.

"Do you want to tell me what this is all about?" he said.

She did not welcome this interruption of the soothing silence, and wished she didn't have to respond to it. She still didn't know how he knew about "this," or how much; also, she didn't even want to find out, because she wasn't ready to talk about it with anyone. For some time she kept her silence and her gaze trained out on the water, even as he cast several surreptitious glances in her direction. She hoped he would get tired of waiting for a response and change the subject, or resume the idle banter that made serious subjects temporarily disappear. But when the silence only grew, she began to feel obligated to fill it. After what he had done for her today, she owed him some explanation.

"My husband drove over to see me this week," she told him. "Said he wanted a divorce." Just saying the word made her want to cry. It was the first time she'd said it aloud, and the first time she'd told anyone.

Nick only nodded as if this were old news to him.

"This came out of nowhere! We just got married!" She felt like shouting.

"Did he say *why* he wanted a divorce?" Nick tore his gaze from the fire and looked over at her.

"Not really. That's what I can't get over. Just that when I left for Tuscaloosa, he realized we weren't right for each other. We're too different, he said. Want different lives. But we had discussed this before, that I would probably start a graduate program at the university and commute to Tuscaloosa. Or from Tuscaloosa. I don't understand."

"He didn't give any other reason?"

"No!" She shook her head with vehemence. "And the worst is: He doesn't want to talk about it, doesn't want to get counseling, doesn't want to give it time. He just wants a divorce, and he wants it now. He even went so far as to tell me that in the state of Alabama, a divorce petition agreed on by both parties can be granted in as little as three days. Three days! We just got married!" she protested again. "I don't understand! He doesn't even want to help me understand. It's over for him, he said, and that's all I need to know." Her voice trembled on the edge of tears.

He fished her hand out from under the blanket, gave it a tight squeeze and then held onto it. "Listen, sweetie," he said. "Let ole brother Nick tell you what's really going on."

"What?" she said sharply, irritated by his manner of knowing more than she did about her own marriage.

"Your"—he paused, searching for the right word. "Husband," he said tentatively, as if it were not the right word. "Is . . ." He shook his head while his voice trailed off.

"Is what?" she demanded.

He squeezed her hand. "I'm afraid he's seeing another woman."

She wrenched her hand from his grasp, not in the mood for one of his jokes. With their usual telepathy, he knew what was going through her mind.

"I'm afraid I'm not joking," he said, reclaiming her hand and giving it another squeeze.

She couldn't believe it. "I don't know what you're talking about."

"Of course you don't. That's why I had to come tell you."

"What do you mean?"

"Who," he sighed. "'Who' is the question. And it's Lily Templeton."

Lily Templeton! This did not make sense. She still didn't understand. "I thought Lily Templeton was dating you!" she said.

"No," he shook his head. "Not really. I've taken her to lunch a few times. Listened patiently to her sales pitches. That's all."

"Are you sure? She seemed to think she was seeing you. I'm certain of it."

"I just didn't want to be a cad." He looked back at the fire.

"How could you be a cad? Did you sleep with her?"

"Once," he admitted, his gaze focused on the flames. "The night of your wedding."

For a moment she said nothing, looked absently at the water, then the fire, without really seeing either. Her thoughts raced around in circles of confusion. She could not make sense of what he was saying. There had to be some mistake, some miscommunication, some misinterpretation. He must have heard some tangled rumor or piece of gossip based on the times Lily had taken them to look at houses. People were always drawing guilty lines between innocent dots.

"How do you know for sure she's involved with my husband?"

He shrugged. "She told me."

"She told you?!"

He put his hand back between them on the couch, as if she might need it. "There's a house she wants him to buy. You know about this?"

"I know he's wanted to buy something. We looked together last fall. I told him it was too soon."

"Well he's found something," Nick said. "The closing is in a few weeks."

"What?!" she cried.

"And he wants her to move in with him. She told him she wouldn't dream of doing such a thing with a married man. Putting two and two together, I deduced some kind of involvement prior to discussions of moving in together. When I asked her about it, she admitted they had been seeing each other ever since you left for Tuscaloosa. From what she said, I gathered it was happening behind your back. I'm sorry," he added after a pause.

She shook her head in disbelief, as images from the past bombarded her imagination: their first date, in church, on Easter Sunday; their first kiss along the banks of the Charles River; their first time in bed together; their wedding day. These memories came roaring at her with hurricane force, deporting her back to the past. Alone in her freshman dorm room, as usual on Saturday night, she had been surprised by the ringing of the telephone. Except for her, the whole world was out on Saturday night. Perhaps it was her parents, calling with news. Perhaps it was someone wanting to know the whereabouts of her roommate. Perhaps it was a wrong number. But it was a young man she knew, a senior, a fellow Alabamian, calling to invite her to attend Easter Sunday services with him the following day. She couldn't remember what she said because she wasn't aware of whatever it was she said, only that she had agreed. Afterwards, she'd remained sitting on the window seat next to the telephone in a profound daze. His voice had been so hesitant, so unsure of himself, making nervous small talk—on Saturday night!—as if afraid to come to the point. When he finally did, it seemed to her that he held his breath, in fear of rejection, in anxious hope of a miracle, in full knowledge that he was a peon, a peasant, while she was the peerless princess.

But he was the prince. A senior! So handsome, so charming. A favored protégé of one of the most revered professors on campus. He hosted Sunday brunches once a month in the private dining room at Eliot House, for all Alabamians on the Harvard campus. Students from the law school, the medical school, the business school, the divinity school, as well as the college, all gathered at his invitation. He presided over these events with such perfect social grace that she was shocked to learn he was a financial aid student from a small town.

If he was a prince, his girlfriend was the true princess, a billionaire's only child. He was smitten with her. Although she came from Connecticut and went to Wellesley, she attended all the brunches. One Sunday in October, they'd had their Alabama brunch on picnic blankets spread on the banks of the Charles River, where they could watch the crew boats from all the Ivy League schools compete in the Head of the Charles. It was a singular experience, the one and only time her college days provided her with a tableau from an Evelyn Waugh novel or an Impressionist painting. The Cambridge weather, typically dull, dreary, gray and cold, had decided to smile on this day. The sun shone in all its brilliance, dazzling the water and the heads of all those who rowed on it. Only the most gentle breeze blew, barely strong enough to ruffle a girl's hair. The picnic food supplied by Eliot House was not the usual joyless cafeteria fare. Delicate, crust-less little triangle sandwiches, a bowl of strawberries—of all things in October—tiny chocolate éclairs delighted them all. Both sides of the river were completely populated with blankets and students lying lazy and indolent in the gorgeous warmth.

It was the first time she thought she might be able to make it through the year at that cold, forbidding place. Because on that day, it was not cold and forbidding. It was warm and inviting, beautiful and magical. The race itself, with all those graceful little boats skimming across the sparkling Charles River, was not a competitive event so much as a spectacle of sheer beauty designed to delight the eye.

And it was he who had made this day happen, this handsome boy from home. As she watched him sitting on his blanket, holding hands with his girlfriend, feeding her a strawberry, she found herself hoping that one day she would find someone like him, who would love her as much as he loved this girl whose hand he held. Meanwhile, she was grateful to him for that day, which she kept with her through all the bleak, cold days that followed, like a talisman that carried her through hard times and gave her a vision of a future happiness that might be possible.

Not only did she make it to Christmas, she made it all the way to spring, when it dawned on her that she had more or less made it through the year. And if she could make it through that first year, there was no reason she couldn't make it through the other years to come. The stirring of hope and pride fluttered within like the beginnings of spring which were gradually coming to life in the barren world around her.

Then one day she discovered that handsome Southern boy in line behind her at the Harvard Coop. She turned around to greet him, but he didn't seem to know who she was. Lately, she had not attended any of the Alabama brunches because she had not wanted to walk all the way down in the cold from Harvard Yard, where the freshmen lived in dorms, to the river houses, where the upperclassmen lived and it was even colder with the brutal winter wind coming off the Charles. Still, she had not thought he would ever forget a name or a face. Whenever she had gone to the brunches, he always greeted her like he'd known her forever, and introduced her to any new faces with perfect recall of everyone's names. Yet in the Coop he seemed not to know her. This puzzled her so deeply that she had to speak to him, to remind him who she was.

"Caroline!" he had exclaimed, in such astonishment it was clear he still did not recognize her. Although she had lost so much weight from the stress of that first year that her period had stopped for six months, she had not dreamed that her appearance had altered so radically. She knew it had changed somewhat, and obviously for the better, because she was aware of more glances in her direction than she'd ever attracted in her life. But surely she had not transformed so completely as to be unrecognizable. Yet the way he said her name, gasping it out as if someone had just socked him in the stomach, made her realize that what had just struck him was the sight of her. Either that, or Cupid's arrow. How could this be? And yet, it was.

She had known at the time that something had happened, that something had begun. On the deepest level, she had been expecting that telephone call, although it was still a shock when it came. But afterwards, when she sat there on the window seat in her empty dorm room, she had known she was going to do more than go to Easter services with this young man tomorrow. She was going to marry him.

Now, as she sat in darkness on a deck beside the Black Warrior River, the force of all those experiences and the emotions that accompanied them swept through her again with the same power as when they originally occurred. This force was real; it was true. It had not been a figment of imagination, and it was still strong. It wasn't over. It couldn't be. She still didn't understand how Lily Templeton was a part of any of this.

"It's just so sudden," was all she could say.

"Lily moves fast," said Nick. "Like all real estate agents. Like all sales-people. They can be a very destructive force, you know. Telling you what you already have isn't good enough. You need something more, something better."

"I really thought it was you she was after."

He got up to put another log on the fire. When he came back, he stood in front of her, waiting patiently as she stared ahead without seeing him, lost in her thoughts.

"Tell me what you want to do," he said finally. "I can drive you back to Birmingham right now, if you want. You can confront him, hash the whole thing out. Or you can stay here a day, a few days, the whole week if you need to. Think things through, figure out the next step."

It was then the devastation hit her: Her own folly which had triggered this destructive chain of events; her husband's betrayal; the treachery of one friend and the kindness of another who had taken such care in breaking bad news. She put her face in her hands to cover the sobs, but she couldn't stifle or hide them. He sat down on the sofa and pulled her, blankets and all, into his arms, where he rocked her back and forth. "It's all my fault," she sobbed uncontrollably. "It's all my fault." He brushed wet strands of hair out of her face and wiped tears from her cheeks. Nothing helped; nothing could make the crying stop. Wracking sobs continued to convulse her body until she couldn't breathe, she couldn't see, and she could barely hear whatever it was he kept repeating, something about everything going to be fine. She knew this couldn't be right, but it didn't matter; the mere sound of his voice seemed to be the point. Still she heaved, even when her sobs ran dry and her swollen face ached. Finally he settled deeper into the back of the couch and pulled her head onto a cushion he placed on his lap. It seemed appropriate somehow, this regression to an infantile state, a fate she had brought upon herself. She was lucky only in the witness to her degradation being someone she trusted.

He stroked her arm, smoothed her hair, and began to croon a lullaby she didn't recognize. Probably it was something silly he made up as he went along, which ordinarily would have had her laughing if laughter had been possible. Instead, she must have slept, because the next thing she knew, she was opening her eyes to feel his palm sliding down across her forehead and his fingers pausing to close her eyelids. He resumed his crooning, and she must have slept again. Several times he shushed her back to sleep like this until once he was yawning when her eyes opened. Her neck was stiff; her back sore. The fire had gone out and it was cold. She pulled her head up from his lap as best she could.

"Get back down," he said, his voice a dry husk. "I want you to sleep."

"I need to get in the bed," she told him.

"Will you be able to sleep?" He yawned again.

"Yes." She nodded.

"Okay, then."

With an arm around her blanketed waist, he led her in the pitch dark up the stairs and into the house, not stopping to turn on any lights even when he reached the bedroom. First he pulled down the bed covers, then peeled the heavy woolen blanket off while she stood there like an invalid, which is exactly how she felt. Before she could move toward the bed, he began undressing her with practiced skill; taking clothes off a woman was something he had obviously done many times. But this was different, like in a hospital, where he simply performed a necessary task with clinical efficiency. The sheets were cold to her bare skin.

"Sleep now," he whispered, drawing the covers up around her.

One of the layers was a thick wool like the blanket from outside. Soon the warmth grew around her while her eyes grew heavy. She heard him lower the blinds, creep out of the room and close the door before she fell back to sleep.

~ 11 ~

Daniel dreaded all visits to his family in Opelika, even when he wasn't bringing home bad news. But the Easter weekend went better than he ever hoped for right from the start. Arriving early on Saturday morning, around nine-thirty, he found his mother still in her robe drinking coffee. His father had just left on his round of errands. It was clear from the gratified shock on his mother's face that she hadn't expected him till much later in the day, and interpreted this early arrival as some sort of personal tribute to herself. Usually he arrived as late as possible and as near dinnertime as possible in order to minimize any blocks of unfilled time with his parents. Invariably, he arrived even later than planned, while the dinner burned and his parents went into full-blown panic mode, imagining him not dead on the highway, but loaded onto a stretcher without the penicillin alert tag around his neck they were no longer able to force him to wear after he left for college. This was their kind of bad luck: Their son not killed in the crash, but poisoned by the penicillin the paramedics administered in the ambulance. His parents were always so distraught by this scenario that when he finally walked through their front door, they had nothing but anger for this ghost of their son who'd killed himself by refusing to wear his penicillin tag.

"I didn't expect you till dinnertime!" his mother exclaimed, hopping up and hugging him fiercely. "Is there something wrong?" She pulled the sash of her robe tighter.

His parents always thought something was wrong. If he was late, something was wrong; if he was early, something was wrong. Still, it gave him an opening, but he hadn't planned on introducing the subject so soon. He hesitated, and sat down with a sigh at the kitchen table. His mother regarded him with concern. "Let me get you a cup of coffee," she offered, moving over to the counter. Although he hated his mother's coffee, a generic brand which tasted like the inside of the IGA store where it came from, he did not decline.

He knew his mother enjoyed fussing over him, that his absence had deprived her of perhaps the most enjoyable outlet for her anxious energies. He let her fuss, pour the dregs of the last scalded bit of liquid from the Mr. Coffee pot, and stir in the nondairy Coffee-Mate, which he also hated.

She was babbling away nervously but also happily, apologizing for sleeping late, still being in her robe, not having any breakfast for him. "But let me fix you something!" she cried. "It won't take ten minutes! Whatever you want, Son. Eggs, pancakes. Just tell me."

Actually, he had not had any food that morning, since he'd hit the road as soon as he showered and dressed after getting up. "Mother, I'd love some scrambled eggs," he admitted.

He could not have given her a greater gift. She literally began buzzing around the kitchen, talking so rapidly to herself as she pulled things out of cabinets, out of the refrigerator, that no words were formed, only this buzz which sounded like her motor kicking into overdrive.

"Bacon?" she asked, even as she placed several strips on the ribbed tray that went into the microwave. "And I've got some biscuits left over from the other day. I've forgotten what kind of jelly you like, though. Will grape do?" She produced the IGA jar of grape jelly and showed it to him.

"That's great," he said, gratifying her further.

As she stood at the stove, scrambling his eggs, she bombarded him with all the news from her domestic front: The round of errands his father was sent on; his sister Tanya's all-day fundraising mission at Wal-Mart for the Youth Fellowship trip; the new heart medication prescribed by the cardiologist at UAB; the possibility of promotion and a raise for her at the high school; the latest burden Cloyd Mullins, school superintendent, had placed on his father, assistant superintendent, for no extra pay. Daniel felt like a kid again, still living in his parents' household, sitting alone at the kitchen table, listening to his mother talk a mile a minute as she unburdened herself to him before placing a huge plate of food in front of him. Ever since he'd left for college, he'd spent little time back home: the minimum at Christmas, and only one summer because he always made sure to have a job lined up elsewhere. But this is how his mother wanted him: all to herself, a solitary captive in her kitchen, an appreciative audience to her herculean struggles along with her cooking. Of course, she also wanted him to go out into the wider world because that was where he would make a lot of money and do great things that would testify to her own improbable rise in the world. Yet somehow she still expected him to be sitting in her kitchen keeping her company as she toiled her way through the day and all her days. This was the essence of the conflict that had sprung up between them when he left home, and of the internal conflict that tore her apart. She wanted him to be two completely different people in two completely different places at once. But at this miraculous moment, those conflicts dissolved as she triumphantly placed *her* cooking in front of *her* son in *her* kitchen.

"Now you eat while I go make myself decent," she told him, already moving down the hall and muttering reminders to herself.

It surprised him how quickly she returned, fully dressed and made up. He'd barely sat back down from emptying his coffee in the sink. Naturally, this was the first thing she noticed.

"Son, should I make a fresh pot of coffee?"

"If you'll sit down and drink some with me, Mother," he said, spreading jelly on a biscuit.

She hopped back up and busied herself with the coffeemaker. "There is nothing I'd love better than to spend the rest of the morning sitting down and drinking coffee," she said, rinsing the pot. "Just relaxing, for a change."

Daniel expected now to hear a litany of reasons why relaxing was out of the question. Instead, he learned that one of his father's errands was to pick up the honey-baked Easter ham they were selling at First Baptist today; his mother had thought they could have ham sandwiches for lunch; warm ham slices garnished with canned pineapple rings for dinner tonight, and ham quiche for Easter brunch tomorrow. The only thing she really needed to *cook* was the quiche, but she couldn't do that until Bobby got home with the ham, which wouldn't be for a while. So she had plenty of time to drink another cup of coffee. She only hoped he liked ham. She couldn't remember, because it had been so *long* since he'd really been *home*.

Daniel loathed ham, honey-baked or otherwise, and the prospect of three ham-centered meals in a row filled him with a desperate urge to flee his parents' house and get back on the road to Birmingham. He didn't see how he would make it through the quiche at brunch tomorrow. What he hated even worse than the ham was the ironclad planning of it all. Somewhere in the kitchen his mother would have a meal planner, like she had a lesson planner at school, and these three ham-based menus would have been inked in days ago. Growing up, he often felt like his life was a pre-planned trudge through one calendar day in the meal planner after another. His parents allowed no room whatsoever for spontaneity in their meals or in anything else. Where they came from, spontaneous events usually spelled trouble or even disaster. A storm, a blight, a freeze, and a crop would fail, an animal would die, a valuable piece of equipment could be damaged. They did everything they could to keep spontaneity at bay, and would never have understood how for others, himself included, it was a tonic or even an elixir of life.

"I love ham, Mother."

"What's wrong, Son?" Concern creased her forehead. She sat down with the coffee pot, but forgot to pour.

He heaved a sigh, not sure how to begin or what tack to take.

"Is it Caroline? Is your marriage in trouble, Son?"

"How did you know?" He tried to look surprised.

"I only figured, Son, with you coming alone for Easter. I mean, I know Caroline doesn't *enjoy* visiting Opelika, but I didn't think she'd be *rude* enough to let you come alone, unless . . ."

"Mother," he said, "I'm sorry to have to tell you this, but I'm afraid you were right. You were right about everything. You're right that my marriage is in trouble. And you were right that Caroline's teaching job in Tuscaloosa would put our marriage at risk. It did. It has. And now I'm afraid it's over."

His mother needed only a moment of silence to absorb this bad news, cushioned by that life-affirming sensation that she had been so *right*, both to predict it in the first place, and then recognize it immediately now. Instead of coming undone with dismay, she snapped to with brisk efficiency, remembering the coffee, pouring their cups full, hopping up to replace the pot in the coffeemaker, returning with the Coffee-Mate and fresh spoons. He always forgot this about his parents: Adversity was their comfort zone. When crisis did strike, they were at their best, immediately at the ready to cope. It was the uneventfulness of daily life or even joyful tidings they couldn't handle well. To them, good news was just the precursor of bad news, or else it was bad news in disguise. But when that bad news arrived, his mother could fight like a tigress, although sometimes he wondered if she didn't pounce too quickly at the merest hint of blood, and move prematurely in for a kill which might be unnecessary or even counterproductive. In this instance, however, her everready wildcat instincts were operating in his favor.

"Okay, Son," she said, stirring her coffee rapidly and placing her spoon on the table. "I'm listening. Tell me what happened."

"I'm not sure what happened, Mother," he said with perfect sincerity. "Just that you were right. Something went wrong when she left for that job."

It wasn't his wife's fault, but he wasn't sure it was his fault either. As near as he could pinpoint, what happened had started that evening in late January when he first went out with his neighbor for a drink. After work one day, Ken had invited him in and offered him a beer. They stood chatting in the kitchen and decided to go out for the next drink. As they were leaving, Ken had paused in his entranceway to turn on the answering machine. By mistake, he pressed the replay button, and suddenly the sound of Caroline's voice filled the apartment. It wasn't what she said that affected him, because it was all perfectly innocent. Ken explained while they drove down to Highlands. He was doing an article for *Sports Illustrated* on the new athletic director at the University of Alabama. He had told Caroline before she left that he would take her to lunch on the day of the interview in Tuscaloosa. She had simply called to confirm the day, although in the end he had gone and come back without seeing her because he'd been kept waiting three hours for his interview. What was strange was the sudden realization that his wife was living another life now that did not include him. The only time he'd heard her voice that day was in someone else's apartment, on someone else's answering machine. She felt gone to him for the first time since she'd taken the job. It was as if she had left in more ways than one. He couldn't put his finger on why he felt this way, but he'd been overcome by the sensation of abandonment.

Then sitting at the bar in Highlands—Lily Templeton and two of her sorority sisters from college. As soon as she saw him enter with Ken, she had swiveled out of her chair and come right over to greet him as if he were the one person she most hoped to see. Draping herself around his shoulders, she had almost clung to him after giving him several long, slow embraces, during which she confided in a breathy, indiscreet voice that she was a little drunk and might need his help getting back to her seat at the bar. Putting his arm around her tiny waist had given him a thrill he hadn't felt in a long time. He couldn't deny it. Then at the bar, she had eagerly introduced him and Ken to her friends, and the girls had responded as if the two of them were Birmingham's biggest VIPs. With his height, his good looks, and his football player build, Ken might have been used to this kind of welcome from women, but Daniel was not, especially when the girls were as gorgeous as these were. Then, to his astonishment, Lily had proceeded to tell her friends exactly who he was: a graduate of the law school, where he'd been number one in his class, a member of the law review, *and Bethany Ball's boyfriend.* This last was obviously the most important bit, and she completely left out the bit about him now being married to someone else.

This moment may have been the crossroads for his marriage, the turning point where he could choose to remain on the straight and narrow, or light out again for larger vistas. At the time, he wasn't aware of making a choice. He simply forgot about his wedding ring, failed to mention his marital status and drank one beer after another until the impression was firmly established, at least in his own mind, that he and his neighbor Ken were two good-looking single guys enjoying the company of three good-looking single women. This sensation of being a young, single, eligible man totally available to young, single, beautiful girls perhaps affected him most powerfully of all. He liked this feeling of life opening back up from the confines of marriage to the infinite possibilities of the universe. He felt more alive than he had since . . . well . . . since before he was married. In all honesty, marriage had been a bit of a letdown. Of course the wedding and all those parties had been a blast. But afterwards, coming home night after night to dinner on the table had not been nearly as exciting as being out at Highlands, surrounded by pretty girls who hung on his every word, as well as on his shoulder.

Along with the beer, everything else about Highlands was an intoxicant. First, just the place itself was magical: a world-class establishment that would have been stunning by the standards of New York or Los Angeles. It made Birmingham seem less like Birmingham. It made his ordinary life as an ordinary attorney in an ordinary town somehow feel extraordinary. It was the beauty of the place, the beauty of the affluent, well-dressed patrons, the beauty of the food that passed by on its way to the diners in the other room. And the festive hum of a hundred excited conversations made him feel like he was at the center of an important hub of the universe.

Only vaguely aware that he himself was also talking nonstop, he was not at all aware of whatever it was he said, but completely aware that Lily Templeton was giving him her rapt attention. Ken was occupied with the two other girls. At the back of his mind, the knowledge that Lily Templeton had never forgotten him worked on his mind like the most intoxicating drug of all. Around Caroline, she must have feigned ignorance so as not to arouse suspicions or sow marital discord. Which was smart of her; he could see that now. But she obviously remembered him from three years ago, and if she hadn't been interested in him back then, she was extremely interested in him now. Her eyes remained fixated on him and him alone, as if the bar area were not full of other attractive young men, including his neighbor Ken, whom she'd barely glanced at. He calculated rapidly: Perhaps now that she was out of college and away from the sorority and fraternity party circuit, her social life wasn't quite as full as it had been back then, when she had repeatedly turned him down for a date. Maybe she was able to appreciate now that he was that little bit older, and becoming established in his professional career, not just preparing for it, as guys her age were busy doing.

When Ken caught his eye, tapped his watch and winked, he was shocked to see it was 11:15. He hadn't even noticed how much the crowd had thinned. They'd been at the bar over three hours, he hadn't had a bite of food, and had not wanted a bite of food, because Lily had not once removed her focus from him since he'd arrived. Only reluctantly did she accept their leave-taking. They all agreed it had been so much fun they should do it again next Monday night, when drinks were half price.

A week later, his neighbor was game, and Daniel had thought of little else for seven days, despite his wife's weekend visit. When he had sex with her, it was Lily he thought of. On Monday, his fears that his drunken imagination had exaggerated everything, that it wouldn't be the same, or that Lily wouldn't even be there were immediately put to rest. Not only was Lily already seated at the bar when they arrived, she seized on him instantly as if he were her *date*, coming to meet her at Highlands. Before he left that evening, she told him coyly: "You know the joke going around town about Highlands?" When he shook his head, she said, "If you're spotted at the bar twice without your wife, your marriage is in trouble."

Ever since, it had been no joke: his marriage was in trouble. Still, something kept telling him that it wasn't all his fault, because Caroline was just so *gone*. She had *left*. And when he started seeing Lily after that, it was seemingly innocent: he had simply renewed his search for a house. This led to lunches, progressed to dinners. On the first occasion she agreed to come inside his apartment after dinner, he was nervous as he sat down beside her on the couch his wife had picked out. Although all he'd been thinking of for weeks was putting his arms around Lily and kissing her, the reality of his marital state suddenly felt like an insuperable barrier. The next thing he knew, she was teasing his belt open with a hot pink fingernail, unzipping his pants, pulling him out and going down on him like this was what *she* had been thinking of for weeks. It was undoubtedly the most unexpected and exciting sexual encounter of his entire life, a mind-blowing thrill.

Afterwards, she had sprung up from the sofa as if embarrassed by what she'd done, gathered her purse, rushed to the door, whirled around to say "Call me!" and blow him a kiss, then she was off down the stairs before he had recovered his wits or his ability to move. He hadn't even kissed her, told her he loved her, sent her flowers, given her jewelry, taken her on vacation, or done any of the other things guys usually had to do, in his experience, to get a blow job.

Call her?! He did nothing but call her whenever he wasn't with her. The next time he took her out, two nights later, he was afraid she'd refuse to come inside again, then afraid she'd keep a demure distance to let him know that what happened the other night couldn't happen again. But no sooner had she sat on the sofa than she pulled him down with her, pushed him onto his back and attacked that part of his body that was more than ready for such an encounter. As before, she was so overwhelmed afterwards by modesty, shyness or embarrassment that she vanished from his apartment while he could only offer a feeble protest.

It was a week later that he first had sex with her. Her body was even more alluring than the pornographic fantasies of his teeming imagination, and he was afraid he wasn't going to be able to control himself long enough to make anything happen for her. Again she surprised him, by coming almost immediately. As soon as he entered, one hand was digging into his back, the other was stifling a scream, and her back was arching. She had come quicker and better than any woman he'd ever known, including his first girlfriend, Ricky Jill, who he'd always thought of as the Queen of Come. He didn't even know what he'd done to make it happen so well and so fast. Apparently it was just *him* entering *her* that had done the job. *He hadn't even had to do anything.* And she hadn't broken a sweat. This girl was amazing, one in a million. But again she'd left immediately, dressing with lightning speed and departing before he could rouse himself from that blissful dream state.

The next night she had told him shyly, barely able to look at him from underneath the long fringe of her eyelashes, that she couldn't have sex with a married man: it just wasn't right. This didn't stop the blow jobs. And it did start the process of divorce in his mind. How could he help it? With Caroline gone and Lily there *right where he most wanted her,* it began to seem reasonable as well as desirable to make this arrangement permanent. And after all, Caroline was the one who had chosen to leave her life with him to pursue a life without him. Now she had this other life that she herself had wanted, so it wouldn't be as if he were leaving her in the lurch. Perhaps she wanted out as much as he did. At any rate, it certainly wasn't fair to her to stay married when he enjoyed the attentions of another woman so much.

Meanwhile, Lily had found a house that she told him would be her own dream home if she had the means. The house was perfect, the price was manageable, and the signals were clear: If he weren't married, she would be in that house with him, having sex and spending the night. In due time, of course, they could get married. Not only would such a marriage be perfect for him, it was sure to please his parents. Unlike Caroline, Lily had already established a career, and hers actually brought in money. And unlike Caroline's profession, Lily's would complement and dovetail beautifully with his. If there were any people in town Lily didn't already know, she was sure to meet them through real estate. And through her he would meet everybody he needed to know. Like him, Lily loved being with others and having a good time, whereas Caroline preferred to live like a recluse. On the whole, he felt lucky that Caroline had left and Lily had come on the scene when she did.

At the moment, however, the only parts of this he could share with his mother were the ones involving his estrangement from his wife and the offer he had put in on this house, along with the earnest money. The problem was, he explained, if he and Caroline got divorced after the sale closed, then she would have a claim on half the value of the house. If he backed out of the deal, he stood to lose the thousands he'd put down as earnest. His mother's money-minded brain quickly grasped the solution: better to go ahead and get divorced sooner rather than later. He admitted this is what he'd been thinking too. But he had not realized the extent to which the horror of divorce would pale in his mother's mind next to the horror of a financial hit of any kind. When she inquired about Caroline, he told her quite honestly that his wife wanted to wait, give it time, perhaps go through counseling. His mother pointed out this could simply be a delaying tactic designed to give her a claim after the sale went through as joint marital property.

"You may be right, Mother," he sighed, omitting to mention that Caroline knew nothing about the purchase of this house.

When his father arrived with the dry-cleaning, the groceries, the stuffed animals and Easter candy for his sister's basket, along with the honey-baked ham, his mother suggested Daniel take his things downstairs to his room while she broke the news to his father. By the time he returned to the kitchen, both the ham sandwiches and his divorce had been prepared and were promptly served up on a plate with his mother's usual efficiency.

~ 12 ~

The morning was far advanced when Caroline finally woke. Looking around the room, she couldn't see a clock anywhere, but the way the sun hammered against the blinds and stormed around the edges told her it was late. She knew she needed to get up immediately, because what she wanted was to go back to sleep for years, until the mess she'd made of her life had resolved itself. She pulled a robe from the suitcase at the foot of the bed and stuck her head out the bedroom door. There was not a sound in the house, which had the absolute stillness of being empty. It was too good to be true. She wasn't ready to face the world with a single person in it, not even a true friend like Nick, who had been so kind. Venturing into the great room with its expansive view of the river, she stood gazing at the water as she listened for the faintest sounds of movement from anywhere in the house. After several minutes of hearing nothing, gathering her courage and piecing together enough inner equilibrium, she made her way into the kitchen. The digital display on the coffeemaker told her it was ten forty-five. There was hot coffee in the pot, also a note on the counter beside it. "Enjoy the day. See you later for dinner." She breathed a sigh of profound gratitude. As much as she appreciated everything Nick had done for her, nothing was as helpful as his being gone this morning.

There were English muffins in the freezer, and after putting one on low in the toaster oven, she poured a cup of coffee and stepped out onto the deck. The river water rippled with bright sunlight, which appeared to be winking at her. With the hot sun and the early-April chill still in the air, the temperature outside was perfect. It was a beautiful spot: trees all around and houses nestled among them. Her impression from last night appeared to be correct; no other property owners on the inlet were currently in residence. There were no sounds or sights of human habitation, no doors slamming, no car engines, no voices, no lawn mowers, no dogs barking. All this would come in a month

164

or so, when summer vacation began and families came for weekends or weeks at a time. But for now, all was silence and stillness except nature: the stirring of the breeze, the lapping of the water. There was no one to know or care who she was, what she had done, why she was there. No witnesses to her grief and torment, the sorrow of her soul. In such complete solitude, it was almost possible to believe that none of it had even happened, and that, if it had, it didn't matter so much. The sunlight winking at her from the water seemed to be sending her the same message, that all was well, although she knew it wasn't, couldn't possibly be after what she'd done. Still, she was cheered, and remained on the deck until it must have been high noon, with the sun right on top of her, when it became too hot in her thick bathrobe.

Inside, her English muffin was toasted to a brown crisp, but not burned. As she ate it she wandered around exploring the house, which she had not much noticed the night before. The house was really not as large as it seemed with the vaulted cathedral ceiling in the living room giving the whole place the feel of a palace. But other than the room where she'd slept last night, there was only one other bedroom downstairs, a small one, with a partial view of the river from a side window. The upstairs consisted solely of a large sleeping loft, with a double bed in the middle and built-in bunk beds on either side of the room.

She could tell this was the room where Nick slept, not just from the barely made bed, but from all the photographs lining the walls. Until that moment, she had completely forgotten about his passion for photography, which had been as much a part of all their outings years ago as anything else. Wherever they went, he brought his camera with them always: an expensive, complicated professional piece of equipment he had purchased for the courses he took at the International Center for Photography in New York. Although she'd never been to his apartment in Birmingham, she knew he had converted one of the bedrooms into a darkroom, and was forever in trouble with his landlord because of the chemicals.

She went over to the wall to inspect the images more closely. Some were of the city—downtown Birmingham—and some were from the country—rural Alabama, she supposed—barns and cotton fields. A few were taken here on the Black Warrior River, one with the heads of three children bobbing up in the water, his nephews and niece, she guessed. With a shock of recognition, she spied her own younger self in one of the frames, standing small and diminished as she gazed up at the smokestacks of a derelict steel mill on the outskirts of downtown. The day suddenly came back to her in a vivid rush, all the stronger because she hadn't thought about it once since it had happened. But this was one time she had not wanted to go: had not wanted to violate the NO TRESPASSING signs posted everywhere or step over the iron chain barring entry. The chain link fence, she'd pointed out to him, was going to prevent them from getting into the old ironworks anyway.

"I know a way in," he'd assured her. "I've been here many times. It's perfectly safe, I promise you. Totally abandoned. No one ever comes. Nobody will know. Come on. *Please.*"

The forbidding, rusting smokestacks looked menacing and dangerous. They made her think of wailing police sirens and the fury of her father. It was hot and the place was filthy dirty. She stepped over the iron chain only because Nick gave her no choice. He was going ahead, and if she didn't follow, she'd be standing exposed and alone while he was gone for who knew how long. He led her around the side, where there was a gap in the chain link fence she suspected he might have made himself on a previous occasion. It was just big enough for his body to squeeze through. She had to admit, there was something thrilling about his audacity, but frightening in this case as well. They were trespassing; they were breaking the law. Amazed and scared, she had not wanted to be a part of the photograph. She just wanted him to hurry up and get it over with, and she didn't see the point anyway. There was nothing here of beauty. What was left of the defunct steel mill was an ugly, sooty slag heap.

"That's the point of my photograph," he told her as he set up his tripod. "Beauty and the beast."

This had irritated her further, because she was no beauty. She wasn't wearing anything in particular, and didn't want to be photographed.

"This isn't a close-up," he explained. "You're going to look like a midget next to these monstrous erections." He laughed wildly at the pun. "That's part of the point too."

Stepping closer to the wall, she squinted hard at the matting, where she could make out a handwritten caption beneath the photograph. "Beauty and the Beast." It had turned out well, she acknowledged, and he'd been right, after all, to insist on taking that picture. What was left of those steel mills had since been demolished, and a part of Birmingham heritage was no more to be seen, except in photographs like the one he'd taken. She was glad now that she'd been part of it.

Suddenly she remembered another photograph that she'd been part of, and moved along the wall in search of it. She found it above one of the bedside tables. This one was not nearly as interesting as the other, mainly because it did focus on her, standing next to the plaque commemorating Tuxedo Junction, in Ensley. The building that had once housed the famous black jazz and blues club in the twenties and thirties was still standing, though unoccupied and unused. There wasn't much to see besides the plaque itself; still, he had wanted her to see it. On the drive out, he had played a tape he'd compiled himself, of the different versions made over the years of the "Tuxedo Junction" tune. He had Ella Fitzgerald, Duke Ellington, and all of them, probably.

Until now, she'd never seen the prints he'd made, and the memory of those particular days had submerged into a general impression of all her days with Nick, stored in the back of her mind. When she told others about what she did with him, they called it crazy, wild, strange, eccentric. Dates that girls went on with boys were supposed to take place on certain days, at certain times, and involve certain activities and locations. Nick was more likely to pick her up at one in the afternoon to take her someplace like the statue of Vulcan, which she had to admit she'd seen all her life but never once visited. These were not dates, she had tried to explain. Nick was ten years older; he had dates on Friday and Saturday nights just like everybody else, and did the usual things that he complained of later in hilarious detail to her: the dull parties he'd had to dress up for, the stupid movies he'd been forced to watch. They had laughed about his girlfriends: silly, impossible creatures who wanted to do the most boring things, like go on double-dates, to weddings, to cocktail parties at the country club. They wanted an escort; they wanted a husband. He wasn't cut out for that; he just wanted to have fun. What he did with her was fun; he took her along as a buddy, for company. His wildness was simply that he did what he wanted to do, went where he wanted to go, and refused to be anything other than himself. He wasn't afraid to go outside the lines, to venture into the black or redneck parts of town to do something other than the usual parties, pizza parlors, bars and hangout spots. In other words, he was his own person in a community that frowned on that, especially if he was supposed to be managing one of his family's textile mills instead of taking photographs.

As she left the room and went back down the stairs, she realized how good it felt to have him come back in her life, and not just because she needed a friend right now. She wished she'd never lost touch with him in the first place, and resolved to try to keep him a part of her life from now on, especially because he obviously needed a friend too. It was disturbing that she'd known nothing about his drug problem or rehab, that he'd had to go alone to such extremes: all the way to Switzerland, for years. She had simply given up on him when he disappeared, forgotten him and never looked back. She vowed to herself she'd make it up to him someday. But first she had to solve her own problems.

~ 13 ~

His choice of *The* Club surprised her, but then again, just about everything Nick Scully did or said surprised her, and *The* Club was the least oddball place of any he'd taken her to so far. The invitation itself, for a nice long lunch— today—had to be today—was the first surprise, although by now she should have been used to the way he did everything at the last minute.

"I already have plans," she told him.

"Of course you do. Can you change them?"

"What about some time next week?"

"Today," he insisted. "I want to see you today."

Lily flipped rapidly through her schedule book so he could hear the turning pages over the telephone. "I could do lunch on Tuesday," she offered. "Oh, no," she corrected herself quickly. "No, I'm afraid lunch is impossible on Tuesday, but I could do dinner that night."

"It's got to be today."

Lily breathed a long sigh into the mouthpiece. "If you say so," she gave in finally, with a perfect mixture of resignation, reluctance and annoyance in her voice.

"I'll pick you up quarter till twelve. Wear something decent. We're going to *The* Club."

"*The* Club?" she couldn't help herself. "I thought you belonged to the Mountain Brook. Or is it the Birmingham?"

"Both," he said. "*The* Club too."

She hadn't been there in years, not since grade school when somebody's grandparents had taken her for dinner on a spend-the-night with a friend whose family belonged. It was a place strictly for grandparents, and even more strictly for those grandparents who didn't belong to the Mountain Brook or the Birmingham country clubs. It *was* beautiful, she had to admit when she and Nick arrived at its aerie perch on top of Red Mountain. Much more beautiful than the Mountain Brook or the Birmingham, with its breath-taking panoramic view of the "Magic City" in the valley below. She agreed with him.

"But that's not the point," she told him. "Nobody goes here. What good is the view if no one comes here?"

He gestured at the tables in the main dining room as they passed through. "I see plenty of people here."

"No one we know. Nobody we'd want to know."

He shrugged as they followed the hostess through a door out onto an empty side terrace overlooking the city. At first, she thought this was even worse. At least in the main dining room inside, there was the possibility that she'd be seen with Nick Scully by someone who mattered. Not as good as being at the Mountain Brook or Birmingham clubs, but better than being alone with him on the terrace outside. Then it occurred to her that being alone might be the whole point of coming to *The* Club in the first place. *I want to see you today. It's got to be today.* A little thrill went through her, the surge of hope and excitement she always felt when she was closing in on a deal. It had not been easy to make arrangements at the eleventh hour on Easter weekend to get in to see the two houses he liked best, but it was a good thing she'd pulled it off.

"I'm glad we're out here," she told him. "Inside it's just as cheesy as I re-membered."

"At night it's even more cheesy," he said. "When they have the Lawrence Welk-like band and the old folks get out on the dance floor."

"I'm surprised you'd want to be associated with Lawrence Welk music or old folks dancing," she teased. "What would people think about you if they knew?"

He shrugged again. "What do I care what people think?"

Another little thrill went through her, as if she were in the presence of danger. Nick might be the only person she knew who would say he didn't care what people thought of him. And a person who didn't care what people thought was a person who might do anything.

When the waitress arrived with the menus, he waved them away and told her, "Just bring Welsh rarebit, for two, and a bottle of pinot grigio. The Es-tancia." He peered at Lily after the waitress left. "That's all right, isn't it? The Welsh rarebit? The cheesiest thing on the menu? What all the old folks order? We must go along with the spirit of the place, don't you think?" He grinned.

Giggling, Lily agreed with him, although she didn't know what Welsh rarebit was. But she loved it when a guy ordered for her, and she loved seeing

Nick in a jacket, which was required at *The* Club. He looked more handsome than ever, but seemed a little preoccupied, serious even, which was not like him. She hoped this meant she was getting to him, and wondered if it would have helped had she brought in the listing materials, to give them a natural way to jumpstart the conversation.

After the waitress had poured the wine, he lifted his glass in her direction. "Cheers," he said.

"Cheers," she agreed, smiling. The wine was a pleasant surprise. This was the first time he'd wanted wine with lunch, and she couldn't help but consider it a good sign. There was something celebratory about wine with lunch; she very much hoped there'd be something to celebrate later in the meal, or this afternoon.

"So tell me," he said, putting down his glass. "Are you really serious about another woman's husband?"

She looked askance at him, as if taken aback by such an abrupt and intrusive question. "You're the last person I'd expect to be judgmental," she said, smiling as she fumbled in her purse for sunglasses.

"Oh, I'm not judgmental. Just curious."

"If I tell you something, will you keep it to yourself? Promise not to tell anyone?"

"Other than the society columnist at the Birmingham *News*? I won't tell anyone."

She giggled and took a nervous gulp of wine. "I haven't told anyone this before," she began, then stopped to take another sip of wine.

"I'm listening." He sounded impatient.

"Well," she started again, lowering her voice, leaning across the table. She enjoyed how the breeze off the mountain blew her hair softly to and fro. "This so-called 'husband' has been trying to ask me out for years." She whispered dramatically, although there was no one to overhear.

He frowned. "What do you mean?"

"I'll tell you the whole story," she said, leaning back, wine glass in hand. She always felt more elegant with a wineglass in her hand. It added glamour and sophistication to anyone's appearance. "I was a co-ed at Bama when he was in the law school."

"You knew him then?" He looked at her sharply.

She shook her head. "Not really. But he dated a law school student. Bethany Ball. From *Montgomery*. But. She had been a cheerleader for the football team. Also a Kappa, like me."

"He *dated* her?"

She nodded emphatically, pleased at his reaction. "That's what I'm trying to tell you."

Frowning again, he said, "I understood he and Caroline were more or less engaged by the time he graduated from college."

"More in her mind and less in his, I guess," she said, sipping her wine and savoring the smirk her line had produced on his face.

"I see." He bit his lip thoughtfully.

"I met him when Bethany brought him by the sorority house before a football game," she explained. "That would have been three years ago, I guess. His first year in law school."

"Does Caroline know any of this?"

"What do you think?" She gave him a sardonic look. "Caroline didn't know anything. She was a thousand miles away, and you can bet her head was in a book."

"Ahem," he grinned and cleared his throat in a stagy way. "Caroline was in college. Pursuing her education. Sticking her head in a book was probably required for her studies. It usually is, so I'm told." He winked at her.

"I love her to pieces!" Lily cried. "And I know she's your friend. It's just she doesn't see what's going on around her. She misses everything that's important. It's kind of sweet: it's like she's so innocent. But I feel sorry for her."

He raised his eyebrows and leaned forward to pour more wine. "You feel sorry for her."

"Think about it," she said. "Caroline may have had a ring on her finger where she was, but she was nowhere around, and he didn't have a ring on his finger. Yet. So he was dating a former Bama cheerleader, and when Bethany started dating someone else, he asked me out."

"He asked you out," Nick repeated, staring out into the valley.

"He asked me out," she affirmed.

The waitress arrived with their food. Lily never ate breakfast and only a bite of lunch, with Diet Cokes throughout the day to take care of her appetite. If she had a date in the evening she ate before going to dinner so she wouldn't be too hungry. But today, the wine she'd consumed on an empty stomach had made her ravenous, and the Welsh rarebit was unexpectedly good, especially considering she didn't even know exactly what it was she was eating. Before she knew what she was doing, she'd consumed several mouthfuls. She glanced over at Nick in hopes he hadn't noticed. Fortunately, he was absorbed in his own thoughts, along with his meal.

"You've hardly touched your wine!" she exclaimed playfully. "What's going on here? You want *me* drunk, and yourself sober?"

"I remembered I've got a tennis match later this afternoon," he told her. "But that shouldn't stop you." He poured more wine in both glasses and took a sip. "So you were saying?"

"What was I saying?" She took one more bite and pushed her plate away. "You don't like it?"

"I love it," she assured him, delighted by the concern in his voice. "I'm just not that hungry."

"So, as you were saying. This husband asked you out when he was some-one else's fiancé."

"I wasn't interested." She forced herself to look away from the plate of food. "None of the Kappas would go out with him, so that's the last I saw of him. He dated a couple of Phi Mus that I knew of."

"A *couple* of *Phi Mus*?" Nick shook his head.

"I know. Really," she said. "But it was the best he could do. He badly wanted a Kappa, but seriously. No Kappa was going to go out with someone from Opelika. He didn't even belong to a fraternity in college."

"They don't have fraternities where he went to college." Nick grinned.

"Can you *imagine*?" Lily laughed. "What's the point of a college that doesn't have fraternities?"

"I wouldn't even want to speculate." He laughed in that wild way of his.

Although he winked at her too, as if she were in on the joke, Lily began to suspect he was mocking her as well, like he had on the first night she'd met him. She needed to steer the conversation back to safer ground, to subjects she knew something about. Education was not something she knew much about, but she was quite familiar with adultery.

"Here's what you're not going to believe," she told him. "When I saw him again last fall—at their apartment—he actually asked me right in front of Caroline if I remembered him. Trying to spare Caroline's feelings, I told him no. But he wouldn't let it go. He even mentioned Bethany, like he could jog my memory with that. *Right in front of his wife,* I tell you. So you see . . ." She looked down shyly at her lap. "He's always wanted to go out with me," she said softly.

The waitress arrived to take away their plates. They said nothing more until she left.

"What about you?" he asked then. "Why are you interested in him now? You weren't back then, and now you know what a sneaky little cheat he is. Plus, he's cheating on *your friend*. With *you*."

She shook her head adamantly in a way that tossed her hair around her face. "It's not like that," she protested firmly.

"It's not like what?" he said. "Are you telling me he's not cheating on Caroline? He's not sleeping with you?"

Lily blushed and looked away, unsure what the best thing to tell him would be.

"If that's too personal a question, I withdraw it," he said. "With my apologies." He leaned back in his chair, wineglass in hand. He took a few sips and regarded her thoughtfully.

Blushing again, she admitted, "I forgot myself with him once. But I was very clear with him afterwards that I couldn't do that with a married man."

"So you *are* interested in him?"

"It's not like you think," Lily insisted. "At first I went out with him just as friends, to keep him company after I showed him houses. If it turned into something else, it's because his marriage is *over*." She leaned toward him to place emphasis on this word. "I think he felt it right away. As soon as she left for that job. She was gone, and he realized they weren't right for each other. She's so serious and bookish. Quiet. A loner. He's not like that. He likes to go out. To parties. To bars. To have a good time. Same as me." Lily paused for dramatic effect and looked down at her lap as if abashed by Nick's penetrating gaze. Slowly lifting her lashes, she effected anguished eye contact. Then she whispered, "He wants to marry me."

Nick responded only with a fierce stare. Lily appeared utterly indifferent to his reaction. "And you?" he asked finally. "Do you want to marry him?"

Lily gave a slight toss of her head to indicate his probing questions had finally gone too far. "A girl has to get married sometime," she said lightly. "And a girl could do much worse than marry a guy who's always been madly in love with her, even after he married someone else." Lily kept her tone both playful and subdued, so he couldn't tell whether she was teasing or trying to hide serious personal truths.

Nick frowned at the waitress, who arrived to ask if they wanted coffee or dessert. He looked inquiringly at Lily, who shook her head.

"What about Caroline?" he asked her.

"Listen," she leaned across the table confidentially. "This is all going to work out just fine. I think Caroline has fallen for someone else herself."

"You're kidding me," he said. "Who?"

"Her next-door neighbor."

"Her next-door neighbor?"

Lily nodded.

"Isn't he that journalist? Who played football?"

"An absolute dreamboat," she told him. "Like something out of a movie. But he's quiet. Serious, like she is. Also a writer. I saw them talking together a few times, and from what I could tell, he definitely had something for her. I wouldn't be a bit surprised if she didn't up and leave Birmingham to get away and figure it out. So you see, this could be the best thing for everyone."

"Excuse me," Nick said abruptly, shoving back from the table. "I've got to make a phone call."

Lily took out her makeup mirror, checked her hair, reapplied lipstick, blotted it with her napkin.

"I've paid up," he said when he returned. "Are you ready?"

"I'm more than ready," she said gaily, springing up from her seat. "I'm prepared. In spite of your horrible habit of always calling me at the last minute, like the bad boy you are, I've arranged for us to get in both those houses you liked."

He took her by the elbow and helped her up the stairs leading off the terrace. A bad boy, but a gallant one. She liked that combination.

"I'm not in the mood to see houses anymore," he muttered.

Her heart sank. She was coming so close; she could feel it. All she needed was a little more time.

"I'm sorry," he added. "Some other time."

Nevertheless, she reflected after he dropped her off at her apartment, she'd accomplished a lot today. He had been uncharacteristically silent on the drive back, but graciously thanked her for changing her plans and wished her a happy Easter. She was getting there with him. She knew it.

~ 14 ~

Usually Hunter was unable to reach Lily on a Saturday night. But on this particular Saturday, he was at his parents' home in Connecticut for Easter weekend, and called a little early. The sound of her voice elated him as it always did, even more so on this occasion, since he hadn't really expected to hear it. Desperately wanting to know if she had plans for later on, he needed all his willpower to refrain from asking questions whose answers only caused him pain. Lily was always disarmingly frank in letting him know if she had a date. And when he'd asked her once if she was dating anyone in particular, she'd acknowledged that she was seeing several men on a regular basis. After much reflection, he'd concluded this was better news than he could hope for. If she was "seeing" several different men, she probably wasn't too serious about any one of them. Yet. And he doubted she'd be sleeping around with various people; she seemed too innocent and sweet for that kind of promiscuous behavior. Plus, he didn't think Southern girls were brought up that way. A few months ago he'd not been able to stop himself from asking if one of these men was the guy he'd seen her leaving with from the wedding reception last summer.

"You mean Nick Scully?" she asked.

Hunter had loathed that name from the very first time he heard it, when he'd seen her flying out of the reception with him, pointed him out to one of the locals, who told him the guy's name. The searing shock of finally spotting her at the party, only to watch as this guy came up out of nowhere, snatched her by the hand and practically ran out with her was a blow that had not diminished over time. In Hunter's mind, the mutual attraction that had formed between himself and Lily during those wedding festivities had evolved into the unspoken agreement that they would find each other and pair off at the next party. After all, this is what had happened at party after party, and he'd made the mistake of assuming it would happen at the reception as well. On the morning of the wedding, he'd been by her side throughout the wedding-day brunch, and when he gave a casual "See you at the reception" in farewell, he envisioned being by her side throughout that event as well. This was one of the most careless assumptions he'd ever made in his life, along with the equally witless assumption that he would soon find Lily by his side after the wedding was over. She would appear in New York, in his apartment, and they would pair off there just like they had when they met in Alabama. This is usually how it had worked for Hunter. If he showed the slightest interest in a girl, she did all the rest.

Even when he left Birmingham the day after the wedding, he still believed this is what would happen. Lily had been too interested in him not to follow up, and the Scully guy had been nowhere around at any of the parties. Hunter felt sure Lily would track him down through his old roommate Daniel and give him a call in New York before the week was out. It was when this phone call never came that Hunter was forced to realize his mistakes, and also humble himself, first by calling Daniel to procure Lily's phone number (along with her last name), and then by calling Lily herself. She had been just as he remembered: bubbly, cheerful, high-spirited, full of chatter—glad to hear from him, as she'd always been glad to see him at the parties. But when he'd asked if she'd like to visit New York, she'd demurred, pleading too many deals pending, an upcoming trip to the beach, a full social calendar.

"Maybe sometime?" he suggested.

"Maybe sometime," she echoed noncommittally.

After analyzing that unexpectedly disappointing conversation, he recognized more mistakes. First, he had asked if she wanted to visit New York. New York wasn't the point. That wasn't what he wanted her to visit. His pride had prevented him from asking if she wanted to see *him*. Worse, his pride had prevented *him* from telling *her* that *he wanted to see her.* That he would pay for her air fare, of course, and arrange for a hotel if she preferred, which he suspected she would. Lily had been entirely right to blow him off, he realized, instead of fawning all over him just because he'd picked up the phone to call her. The sense that she really was something special became an entrenched certainty in his mind. No woman he'd ever been interested in had ever forced him into this kind of self-examination, called for him to swallow his pride and lay himself on the line like this girl from Alabama, who was putting him to a bigger test than any woman he'd met on the Harvard campus in college or at Lehman Brothers in his training program. His desire for her only grew, and, encouraged by his insights, he could hardly wait to call her again, but forced himself to hold off for several days.

When he finally placed the next call, she wasn't home or didn't answer. Messages left on her answering machine were not returned. His imagination tortured him with possible scenarios, most of which revolved around the guy he'd seen leading her out of the reception. He was extremely blond and good-looking, taller than Hunter, also somewhat older. The boldness of the way he'd grabbed her and virtually run off with her met with no resistance from Lily, only unabashed delight. Who was he? As Hunter continued to place calls down to Alabama with no luck, he couldn't stop himself from trying to find out.

The name of Scully in Alabama quickly led him to an industry called Palmdale Mills; that much he easily found out at Lehman. But what he learned of Palmdale Mills did not allay his fears. A family owned, family-run textile business for almost a hundred years, it was still very much a going concern, with a main plant in Birmingham and a smaller mill in a nearby small town. It supplied cloth and hosiery to clothing manufacturers all over the U.S., such as Hanes, Vanity Fair, and Fruit of the Loom. He couldn't find a Nicholas Scully involved anywhere in the management, but perhaps this Nick character, just like Hunter, needed to prove himself outside the family business and wait his turn. In any case, he knew Palmdale Mills had to be Nick Scully's family, and that family would be rich. Not as rich as Hunter's family, of course, but rich enough.

Rich enough had never threatened Hunter before, because . . . well . . . because it had never occurred to him he couldn't have any girl he wanted. It wasn't that he was such an entitled jerk, but he always *had* gotten any girl he wanted, and over time, this lifelong pattern of getting whatever he wanted had developed into an assumption that he always would. What an arrogant prick he'd become! The world was full of guys who were taller and better-looking than Hunter, and plenty *rich enough*. Just such a guy had nabbed the girl he'd wanted most right out from under him. Hunter could only hope it was nothing more serious than a post-party drink or two.

When Lily finally picked up his call one night, he could scarcely contain his delight or train his voice into the casual, offhand tone he'd planned to use.

"I've been trying to catch up with you for a while," he told her.

"Oh!" she said. "I was at the beach with friends."

His spirits soared. Friends! Z-Z-Z-Z-Z-Z: the loveliest sound on earth, the sound of plural! He tried for a lighthearted chuckle. "Party time, eh?" he said. "You and your girlfriends at the beach?"

She yawned. "Yeah. One of my sorority sisters has a family house in Florida. A group of us went for the week."

Thrilled, he zeroed in on his target. "Listen," he said. "I'd really like to see you again."

"That would be fun," she said.

"Just tell me when," he said. "I'll make all the arrangements. Plane tickets, hotel room."

"You've got business in Birmingham, then?" she said, yawning again.

Birmingham? Why would she mention Birmingham? It took him a moment to realize she thought he might go down there. "I thought you could come up to New York," he said with impatience he couldn't conceal.

"New York?" she said, as if she'd never heard of the place. "I'm so worn out from my trip to Florida, I can't even dream of going anywhere else right now."

Her voice had sounded bored and sleepy. Hunter couldn't even remember how that call had ended. Perhaps rudely; certainly abruptly. What was worse than making a fool of himself was that she didn't even notice, or care. When he'd met her he'd been struck by her lack of haughtiness and reserve, but now he wondered if the conceitedness that usually came with supreme beauty just appeared in a different form with her. After all, she had as much beauty as his family had money. No doubt she was used to men flocking around her. Still! The idea that he would go to Birmingham! That was ridiculous. Why would she think he'd want to go to Birmingham?

Hunter was so irritated that he stopped calling and tried to write her off. He'd given her a chance; she'd failed to jump at it, so to hell with her. There were plenty of attractive women from his training class at Lehman. When he asked them out, *they* certainly jumped at the chance, and they slept with him too. It was good. He decided he'd been stupid to think he was ready to focus on one woman. He was still so young, New York was so much fun, and the women were willing.

But he couldn't get Lily out of his mind. Meanwhile, the women he went out with began to get possessive, jealous, hurt, angry, or demanding, at the same time they became less and less interesting. Once he was out of the training program, work also became more demanding. Often he was too exhausted to go out. Except for Wall Street, he might as well not have been in New York for all he saw of the city some days. It was then he understood yet another of his mistakes, in thinking that he was at the center of the universe in New York, so that all good things, or at least, those good things he desired, would naturally flow in his direction as if to the ultimate destination where all good things went. Now that he was in the throes of trying to master his new job, New York was not even the center of his own universe. It was the desk at his office and the walls of his apartment, or, rather, the walls of his bedroom where he collapsed after a long day of work and a late delivery of take-out food. What he found himself craving in the loneliness of his daily grind was not the nightlife or cultural attractions of his city, but the companionship of a beautiful Southern girl who lived almost a thousand miles away.

Once outrageous, the idea of going to Birmingham now struck him as absolutely imperative. What a fool he'd been! If he wanted this girl, he had to go get her. It was as simple and clear-cut as that. This is what guys did. This is especially what guys did with Southern girls, who were raised to be courted and pursued. This is what that Scully guy had done at the wedding reception. He had wanted her, so he had run up, grabbed her, and taken off with her. Jesus Christ, but Hunter felt like such an ass, who'd lost both his mind and his manhood, thinking that a goddess of womanhood was simply going to descend from the heavens into his lap, courtesy of Delta Airlines. HE HAD TO GO GET HER. This was a fundamental law of nature, and he'd been a blind, oblivious, stupid fool to think that he was exempt from such a law. Hunter picked up the phone to call Lily and tell her he'd like to come down and see her.

To his amazement, she suggested the following weekend. This was a bit short notice, but he was not about to argue. It turned out to be Alabama's homecoming weekend, and he had the time of his life. On Friday night they ate at a restaurant called Highlands Bar and Grill. He would never have suspected that Birmingham could have a restaurant as good as any in New York, but this one was. Then they drove over to Tuscaloosa first thing on Saturday morning—a warm day in November—and went from one fraternity party to another. It was like a huge block party up and down fraternity row, in perfect autumn weather, about sixty-five degrees, with a blue sky and blazing sun. Not only did he love football, he loved this taste of a college experience he'd never had. Harvard didn't have a Greek system, and wasn't a football school. Not like Bama. He'd had an absolute blast. The weather had been great, the girls were all gorgeous, and he was with the most beautiful one of all the whole weekend.

It had been like a trip back in time to the 1950s, and in keeping with that fifties feel, he and Lily had not come close to sleeping together. Truly, there had not been time, and staying in a hotel had not allowed for any opportunity. On both Friday and Saturday nights, she had dropped him off at the entrance to the hotel lobby before driving back to her apartment. Of course he'd invited her up for a drink, but she had declined on both occasions. If he was disappointed, he wasn't really surprised. He had not honestly expected that an innocent Southern girl like Lily would go to bed with a man after just a few dates anyway. For all he knew, she was a virgin saving herself for her wedding night. The idea that he could be the first and only one to possess her excited him like nothing else ever had. He arrived back in New York on Sunday night, happily hungover and exhausted.

Bitter cold and biting sleet awaited him at home. This was the least of the reasons he would gladly have returned to Alabama at the earliest opportunity. But when he told her he'd like to come back down, she suggested some time in the new year, as if it were all the same to her, whether she saw him again in two days or two months. He didn't get it. When he'd been with her for homecoming weekend, she'd clung to him as if she owned him and was never letting go, proudly introducing him and showing him off, as if they were "pinned," or whatever the 1950's phrase was. But afterwards, when he was back home, it was as if he were just another guy, and the weekend was in the past, which might as well have been dead and gone as far as she was concerned, although it was alive to him still. It was puzzling and maddening. However, when he took apart his anger, he had to admit she didn't owe him anything. He was mad only because he wasn't getting what he wanted. Along with love, his respect and admiration for this girl increased. No other woman had made him work so hard or shown him so much backbone. He hoped to get her to New York for New Year's Eve, but she was going skiing with her family.

February and March were not great months to visit New York, and he couldn't keep proposing trips to Birmingham when she kept saying it was "inconvenient just now." What this meant, he realized, was plenty of dates on her social calendar, and yes, one of them was the Scully guy, she admitted. Once again he cursed himself for a fool, believing that what he wanted was going to come to him, which had only allowed this other fellow to get the jump on him. His best hope now was to get her in New York and show her the time of her life. With April and spring in the air, he would at least be able to lay a New York she could enjoy at her feet. When he called her that Saturday night before Easter, she not only agreed to come visit, she proposed a date—not the following weekend, but the one after that. She was closing a deal on that Thursday, but would be able to leave on Friday.

He strove for nonchalance. "Any chance you could stay for more than a weekend?" he asked her. "If you were here for a week, we could see a show or two, have some real fun."

"A whole week?" she sounded dubious.

Painful experience had taught him not to presume too much. "I know you've got a lot going on," he said apologetically. "Just thought I'd put that out there."

"Actually, I'd love that," she said.

Trying not to pounce on her words like a dream come true, he couldn't trust himself to say anything for a moment. When he allowed himself to speak, it was to ask which hotel she preferred.

"Oh, you pick," she told him.

The Pierre, he thought.

For a long while after hanging up, he sat staring into space and thinking, even as his mother called up to let him know that his older brother and his family had arrived. But Hunter deserved a moment to savor his success and congratulate himself. He also wanted to clarify in his mind exactly how and why he had reached a goal with this girl almost *a year* after he'd first met her. During that time, he had been subjected to rejections, humiliations and disappointments unlike any he'd ever known, but he realized they were necessary and even deserved. He had been arrogant and presumptuous. He had assumed he could have this girl just because he wanted her. Worse, he'd assumed that she would want him without having to think about it or get to know him, and regardless of his behavior. Who had he thought he was? A DuPont, obviously. She had shown him how little that name counted for when it came to evaluating his character and deciding whether he was worthy of her life and love. The name DuPont meant nothing to her, and rightly so, because you didn't sit across the table from or go to bed with a *name*. It was only the person who mattered, and she'd been right to shy away from the person he'd been at the beginning, when he first met her. Since then, he had matured and evolved a great deal, and that's why he had finally succeeded tonight. He had made her an offer with no expectation of acceptance and without the attitude that it was any better than the countless offers she was receiving from other guys who might be better looking, taller, and *rich enough*. He had treated her as an equal, who didn't need him at all and might never want him. These were the lessons learned, the lessons he must continue to heed when she came to visit in two weeks. Just two weeks!

~ 15 ~

Caroline took a book and settled into one of the hammocks on the deck's middle level. Reading proved impossible, however; her eyes were drawn by the sparkling of the water and her thoughts drifted with its current. As the afternoon advanced and the sun lowered in the sky, she had to turn on the ceiling fans and change hammocks to avoid the sun's rays. When these no longer reached in on the deck and the breeze from the fans made her chilly, she realized the entire afternoon had almost slipped away. She hadn't read a single page of her book. To clear her mind, she went for a jog on the gravel road along the inlet. She had just showered and dressed when she heard Nick return. The day had passed miraculously without effort on her part.

She found him in the kitchen, unloading groceries. He was in tennis whites and looked like he'd come directly from the courts, with sweat bands on each wrist and damp strands of hair clinging to his forehead. "Let me help," she said, reaching for one of the bags.

"There you are," he said.

"You've got a lot of stuff here."

"In case you want to stay." He placed a carton of milk in the refrigerator. "It's up to you." With his head in the refrigerator to shift items around and make room for his groceries, his voice was muffled. "I can take you to Birmingham, to your apartment in Tuscaloosa, whatever you want. Right now if you need." He pulled his head out of the fridge and turned toward her.

She hesitated.

"How are you?" he asked, studying her face for the answer, as if he didn't expect her to tell him the truth.

"Better than last night." Embarrassed by the memory of the previous night's flood of tears, she stuck her head in one of the bags and began handing him the contents to place in the refrigerator.

"So you want to stay or go? I'm ready either way."

"I guess I'd like to stay a little longer, if it's okay."

"In that case." He rifled through the sacks until he produced a package wrapped in brown butchers' paper, along with a bottle of Dale's Steak Sauce. "I'll marinate these."

He placed two huge slabs of meat on a platter and covered them with the steak sauce. "I hope you're hungry."

"I am," she realized. Besides the English muffin, she'd eaten nothing all day.

"Good." He balled up the butchers' paper and threw it away. "I'll just go shower and then put these on the grill."

"Let me do something."

"You can make a salad if you want."

On his way toward the stairs, the phone rang for the first time since she'd been there. When he answered it in the living room, she couldn't help but overhear enough to understand that someone was giving him a hard time. A date, she speculated. Possibly his girlfriend. In any case, it was someone he'd had plans with for the evening. She dropped the bag of mixed greens on the counter.

"Nick," she said, moving into the living room when she heard him hang up. "I'm fine here by myself."

"Oh, that was nothing." He turned toward the stairs.

"I know that was a woman," she said to his back.

"So what?" he called over his shoulder.

"Nick, look at me," she said, waiting for him to pause on his way up the stairs. "You shouldn't change your plans on my account. Was that your girl-friend? Someone you're interested in?"

"No," he said, amused. "Permission granted to do what I want on my Saturday night?" Laughing, he didn't wait for a reply, but bounded up the stairs and into the bathroom, where the door rattled behind him.

So she made the salad, he grilled the steaks and they ate outside on the upper deck, with the warmth from two heaters in the corners.

"This is wonderful," she told him after her first bite of the steak. "I had no idea you could be so domestic."

"I like to cook," he protested.

"Really? I remember pizzas from Magic Mushroom, cartons of Chinese take-out, barbecue," she teased. "You never cooked with me."

"How could I, little girl? Cooking requires a kitchen. My kitchen happens to be located in my apartment. I didn't dare take your sixteen-year-old self anywhere near my apartment, for fear your parents would never let me take you out again. And do you think Mr. Laney would have believed I'd taken you to my apartment so we could *cook*?" He hooted with laughter and cut into his steak.

She laughed too as the image of a furious Mr. Laney popped into mind. She could imagine him confronting Nick: "Cook? You want me to believe you took her to your apartment so you could *cook*?" She laughed so hard she had to dab her eyes with a napkin.

"I finally did it," he said, toasting himself before taking a sip of wine.

"Did what?"

"Got you to laugh."

In unspoken agreement, they did not reopen the painful subjects of last night's discussion while they enjoyed the meal. Instead, he said, "Let's talk about tomorrow. Easter."

"I'm sure you have plans with your family."

He nodded, took a sip of wine. "There's always a big Easter egg hunt in my parents' backyard for the grandchildren. My nieces and nephews. I'm supposed to hide the eggs, and"—he grinned at her—"play the Easter bunny."

"You're kidding. You actually put on a bunny costume?"

"They're too old for it. And I'm definitely too old for it. But none of us wants to admit it. Besides, what is crazy ole Uncle Nick good for if not to put on the bunny suit?"

"Well, you're not going to break this tradition on my account."

"You could come with me."

"Thanks, Nick. But you know I can't."

"I hate leaving you all alone on Easter."

"Actually," she hesitated, looked out over the water, then at him. "Don't take this the wrong way. But I prefer being alone right now. Solitude is the best thing I could have. Today was perfect."

He poured more wine in her glass, which was somehow empty. "You seem better," he said.

She nodded. "Today was good for me. I'm glad you brought me here."

"What did you do?" He poured more wine in his own glass.

"Nothing. Stared at the water and thought about things."

"Did you arrive at any conclusions? Decisions?"

She toyed with the last bite of steak on her plate. "Not really."

He leaned back in his chair, wineglass in hand. "Last night you kept telling me it was all your fault." He waited for her to comment, drank his wine, gazed at the water, giving her time. When she said nothing in reply, he went on. "Surely you realized—" he began carefully—"after the shock wore off—that it's not your fault. Your husband . . . is having an affair."

She rose from the table and picked up her plate. "It's not that simple, Nick."

"It's not?" He rose too and picked up his own plate.

"No." She walked toward the kitchen.

"Well, tell me then."

He was right behind her. They placed their dirty dishes on the counter by the sink. He waited expectantly, deliberately putting her on the spot. "I"—she started to tell him, but couldn't go through with it. She looked through the window above the sink, although all she could see was darkness beyond. "This is too embarrassing," she told him.

He shrugged. "If you say so. But what could be more embarrassing than rehab? I told you about that, and I've hardly ever told anyone else. You're one of three people who know about it. Everybody else thinks I was just bumming around Europe all that time." He tugged on the sleeve of her sweater. "Let's go back outside, drink some more wine."

They sipped their wine in silence for what could have been half an hour. He waited patiently, saying nothing.

"I fell in love with my next door neighbor," she finally blurted in a rush, because there was no other way to get it out. She looked at him out of the corner of her eye, afraid to face his reaction. But there was no reaction. He only nodded absently, as if he'd known this already. Again she had that uncanny and irritating sensation that he knew more about her own life than she did. This was beginning to make her angry.

"Don't tell me you've heard anything about this," she said with annoyance. "I never told my husband, I never told my neighbor, I never told anyone. I just took the job at the university so I could sort out the situation. There's nothing you could have heard."

"I've heard a little about him." He looked at his glass as he swirled the wine around inside it.

"What have you heard?"

"Are you still in love with him?" He gave her a sudden, piercing look.

"I never was in love with him."

"I don't understand. What happened?"

"It was nothing but a foolish infatuation. I left town and started teaching to get away from it, and when I did, that was the end of it. It blew over as quickly as it started up, like the stupid schoolgirl crush it was. And just when

I thought my strategy had worked"—she shook her head and gave a short, bitter laugh—"just when I was congratulating myself for sorting out the situation without destroying my marriage, my husband comes over to ask for a divorce."

"It sounds to me like you did handle the situation well."

Another bitter laugh escaped her lips. Without wanting one, she took a sip of wine, as if she could swallow the bitterness that kept rising in her throat. "If my husband wants a divorce, then I didn't handle the situation very well. And no matter what, I can't get away from the truth that I left my husband for another man."

"Sweetie," he said soothingly in his big-brother voice. "There is no other man. You said that yourself. But there is another woman."

She turned around in her chair to confront him in frustration. "Don't you see?" she cried. "Not everything happens in words. I'm sure my husband could feel that I'd lost interest in him. So when Lily showed an interest in him, or he felt an interest in her, there was no reason not to pursue it. He was entitled to the attention his wife was giving to *another man*. So it *is* all my fault."

"Tell me this," he confronted her in turn. "Do you know how your husband and the neighbor got on after you left?"

She was startled by the question, failed to see what connection it had to her point. "I didn't tell my husband there was another man," she reminded him. "I said nothing about my neighbor. I'm just telling you I'm sure he could sense there was someone else."

"Answer my question."

The steel in his voice surprised her. What was the question he had asked? Her mind wasn't working so well anymore; wracked and wrung out by emotion, it couldn't think in a straight line, but went round and round in meaningless circles.

"After you left," he repeated patiently, "how did your husband get on with your neighbor? Do you know?"

"Fine," she said. "Fine. They even became friends."

"Figures," he muttered, and rose abruptly from the table.

She stared at him as he went into the kitchen, slamming the door behind him. He returned with another bottle of wine, which he opened with a few savage twists of the corkscrew. She shook her head at him.

"I don't want any more," she told him.

"Yes you do." Ignoring the hand she had placed over the top of her glass, he took it from her and poured a generous amount, which he thrust at her until reluctantly she accepted it. After filling his own glass, he sat down. "Do you know Dick Schofield?"

"I know who he is," she said, jolted by the abrupt change of subject. "Isn't he one of your friends?"

"I was in school with him until I left for Andover." He took a generous swallow of wine.

"Well?" she prodded.

"Well. Did you ever see his wife?"

She shook her head, becoming more annoyed at this change of subject and the strangeness of Nick's behavior.

"Beautiful girl. From Luverne, Alabama. Tall, redhead."

"She sounds vaguely familiar, but I can't think where I might have met her."

"You won't now," he said. "She's back in Luverne, recovering from what happened."

"What do you mean? What are we talking about anyway?"

"This next door neighbor of yours," he said grimly. "He met Dick Schofield and Patricia when he moved to Birmingham a year or so ago. He didn't know anybody; Patricia didn't know anybody. He came from a small town; so did she. It turned into quite a threesome. Patricia fell for him, and when the marriage was in trouble, Dick turned to his good friend Ken for advice and support. So there's Patricia, trembling on the verge of what she thinks is an affair; meanwhile this guy is already having an affair. With her husband."

She was confused. "What are you saying?"

"I'm saying your next door neighbor is gay."

The steel was gone from his voice; nevertheless, the shock of what he said was like the jab of a sharp needle injecting a flood of adrenaline into her system. There was the sudden stab of pain, followed by the racing of her heart, the pounding of blood in her ears. She gasped for breath, which resulted in a gulp of wine choking her throat and causing her to sputter and cough. Reaching for her napkin, she pressed it against her mouth while continuing to cough. Unbidden, the image of the tall, beautiful redhead she'd seen outside her neighbor's unit came to mind. Now she knew who it was. "What happened with your friends?" she managed to say, her voice weak from coughing.

"Divorce. Breakdown. Patricia was hospitalized for a while. I heard she was suicidal. Dick's having a rough time too. Coming out of the closet and getting divorced at the same time." Nick shook his head sadly. "Not easy, little girl."

"So it didn't last? Between him and my neighbor?"

"Dick couldn't handle it all at once. Having a relationship with a man, having people know. Not many do. He doesn't even know I know. *I* wasn't even sure I knew." He grinned at her. "I thought it all might be a crazy rumor behind the divorce. But I called Julian today and he told me the whole sad story." His voice changed. "Are you cold?"

She wasn't even aware of rubbing her arms until he said this. Without waiting for a reply, he went over to the heaters and turned them both on high so that the flame burned almost like a fire from the tops of each.

"It's just so"—she stopped, unable to find the right word. Incredible? Shocking? Sad? It was so many things, and she could neither assimilate them all nor process them through her addled brain.

"You didn't just fall for him," Nick said, slapping the table for emphasis. "He *made* you fall for him. Didn't he?"

A warmth that didn't come from the extra heat flushed from her neck up her face. "I thought he was interested in me," she confessed. "But when I left for Tuscaloosa and nothing happened, I began to believe I imagined the whole thing."

"You imagined nothing," he told her. "Neither did Patricia. And the consequences were certainly very real. For both of you."

She shook her head. "It doesn't matter. It's still all my fault. I even left a message on his answering machine once. What if my husband somehow heard the voice mail message and drew certain conclusions? Even if he didn't, it's still all my fault."

"Don't you see, sweetie? Your strings were pulled. Whether the guy consciously manipulated you, or acted unconsciously—I don't know—but he went after you to get to someone else. Not for the first time, and probably not for the second. You didn't just up and leave your husband. This guy got you to leave. He created your absence. Whether he knew what he was doing or not, it was all so he could have a shot at your husband. Instead, it gave your husband a shot at another woman. It gave another woman a shot at your husband, which he welcomed. If you want to find fault, there's plenty of blame to go around."

When she made no response, a long silence took hold. They drank more wine, looked at the water. From time to time he peered over at her for signs of distress or further comment, but she was numb and impervious to his presence. He rose and gathered the remains of the meal from the table, the bottle of salad dressing, the bread basket. She knew she should go inside to help when she heard the sounds of running water and the loading of the dishwasher, but she felt paralyzed. The temperature had dropped to a point the heaters couldn't reach. She was cold and tired, unable to acknowledge his return to the chair beside her or apologize for not helping wash the dishes. He allowed the silence to persist as he sipped his wine quietly.

"I really liked him," she said suddenly. "He seemed to like me too."

"I'm sure he did," said Nick, leaning forward to set his glass on the table. "I'm sure he liked Patricia. But he hides himself in these relationships with women, and the women get the wrong idea. Then he uses his bond with the woman to get in range of a guy. It's rotten. Even if it is subconscious."

"Why do you think he does it this way?" she said. "Go for married men, I mean? Through their wives?"

Nick shrugged. "We know it can't be easy being gay in Alabama. It's not easy being anything in Alabama. Even if you're a wealthy white male who's straight." He gave a shout of sardonic laughter.

"I guess if you're forced to live undercover, and make a secret of your true identity, it warps your relations with everyone."

Nodding, he said, "Who knows? Maybe this guy thinks he's supposed to act like he's attracted to the wives of his neighbors and friends, just like he imagines a straight guy would be."

"Still," she said. "The bottom line is I fell for him. I left. And I wouldn't have, if . . ."

"If what?" He stifled a yawn.

"That's what I need to figure out," she smiled sadly. "And you need to get to bed so you can be a good Easter bunny tomorrow. Bright-eyed and bushy tailed." She forced the smile to stay on her face, as if she were capable of enjoying the joke.

Yawning outright, he didn't argue. They both rose from the table with their glasses. She took the half-empty bottle of wine into the kitchen while he turned off the heaters. "Just put these in the sink," he said, looking at her glass when he joined her in the kitchen. Too worn out to protest, she did as he said. "Sure you'll be all right tomorrow?" he asked her.

"I have a lot to think about," she said ruefully. "This is the best place to do it. I'll be all right."

"Okay then." He leaned over and gave her a little peck on the cheek. "Happy Easter."

~ 16 ~

Norman Laney was thrilled with the turnout for the museum gala on the Saturday night before Easter Sunday. Although that had been the only viable date without major competing events on the spring social calendar, the gamble was entirely his, because he would shoulder all the blame if no one had shown up. Meanwhile, Adelaide Whitmire would take all the credit for any success. But this was their long-term, if unspoken contract: Adelaide proudly embraced a civic responsibility that would get her name and photograph in the paper; Norman Laney did any actual work involved; Adelaide enjoyed the honor and praise that came from a job well done; while Norman would receive all the blame for the slightest mistake. But tonight was already a glittering triumph. The Albrittons; the Petsingers; the Cooleys, with Virginia in a stunning new dress that looked like molten silver when she moved. Frank Keller with his new wife; Dirk Pendarvis with his wife Carla, whom Norman rarely saw; the Scullys. Norman did a double-take, but his eyes had not deceived him: that was Evelyn and Thomas Scully standing next to the Stedmans. Norman couldn't believe it. Their son Nick had purchased the table, but Norman had been told Mr. and Mrs. would not be attending. He wasn't surprised: Tom Scully cared nothing for the arts and never donated to the museum. Yet here they were; it was a triumph indeed.

Norman threaded his way over as quickly as a fat man could to make known his delight at the Scully's presence. "Evelyn, darling. You should never wear any other color but that exact shade of blue. It brings out your eyes from across a crowded room."

Those eyes of hers sparkled with mischief just like her younger son's often did. "I wore this dress just for you," she told him. "Because you've said that before about this color blue."

"Darling," he protested. "Certain truths bear repeating. And besides, if I could say the same thing in a clever new way every time, I'd have taken my talents elsewhere long ago." Assuming his most serious expression, Norman turned quickly to her husband. "Tom," he said soberly, shaking hands. "Wonderful of you to come."

Thomas Scully Sr. acknowledged the truth of this statement with a polite nod. Knowing this was the most he was likely to get from Tom, Norman turned back to his wife. "Now tell me where I can find that son of yours so I can thank him for buying the table and getting you here tonight."

"You won't find him here," said Tom curtly, and then turned around as if in disgust to resume a conversation with the Stedmans.

"What?!" Norman cried, looking in dismay at Evelyn, who winked at him.

"Who knows where Nick is?" she said playfully.

"But not here," Norman stated flatly.

Evelyn shrugged and held her palms up in a gesture both cavalier and elegant. "It's all my fault," she suggested in the same playful manner. "He's the one child who took after me."

This was no more than Norman had long suspected: that this tall, slim, blonde, blue-eyed beauty had a soft spot for the son who so closely resembled her. Her indulgence could well have been exactly what had ruined him, and Norman often had trouble refraining from telling her so. He saved himself this time by exclaiming: "But I'm certain I saw Nick's date! Over by the bar! With Tom Jr.! Getting a drink!"

Evelyn's manner suddenly became more serious, and she moved closer to Norman Laney to tell him something under her breath. "I do think Nick had every intention of coming here tonight," she said. "He wanted me to make sure to tell you. And he begged me to come in his place. That's why we're here."

"Oh," said Norman, instantly mollified. Given the choice between the parents and the wastrel son, the decision was easy. If he couldn't have it all—a lesson he should have learned a long time ago—he would infinitely prefer the senior Scullys, a much bigger score. He knew he needed to show his satisfaction with this trade-off immediately. "Now tell me, darling," he said in his best conspiratorial manner. "I know you have *some* idea why your son couldn't make it here tonight."

"Well," said Evelyn. Her voice remained low, but her mood had become playful and mischievous again as her eyes began twinkling. "I got a call today from the cleaning woman who does our place on the river." Evelyn moved even closer and bent slightly so she could whisper something directly into Norman's ear. "When she went there this morning, there was a girl out on the deck, drinking coffee. *In her robe.*"

"One of Nick's." Norman's voice flattened as he forgot to mirror Evelyn's mood.

Evelyn pulled back. "No sign of him, apparently, but of course."

Norman tried to keep his tone casual and upbeat. "I've always found it impossible to figure out Nick Scully's personal life," he said. "Obviously, he can't figure it out either."

Just then Adelaide Whitmire broke in without preamble or apology. "Norman, the caterer has a question. I sent the woman to the main office. You'll find her there."

Normally, Norman bristled when Adelaide ordered him about like a servant, but at the moment he was grateful for the rescue. He wasn't sure whether he had refrained from offending Evelyn or actually had offended her. One thing was for sure: if they continued to talk about her son, he *would* offend her. Earlier that afternoon, his mother had reported that her friend Phyllis had spotted Nick having lunch with Lily Templeton at *The* Club. So there was Lily, plus the girl in her robe at the river, as well as the date Nick had lined up for tonight, which made three different women that he knew of, *just in one day,* and who knew how many more in his life? As Norman made his way to the museum office, he wondered: Why did he have to *care*? If only he could be shallow, superficial and utterly frivolous. That would have been a much safer path to social success in Mountain Brook society.

Typically, the question from the caterer was one Adelaide could easily have answered herself, if she had cared to listen and were not in the habit of delegating even that slight exertion to someone else. Over at the bar afterward, Norman made a point of going directly to Tom Scully Jr., his wife, his sister and her husband, where they stood clumped in a family group that might or might not be open to approach, but was definitely not engaged in outreach. Norman was hoping to grab them and get them with the parents, because he had just noticed the arrival of the photographer for the Birmingham *News*. Just as Nick took after his mother, Tom Jr. and his sister Paula took after their father in both looks and personality. They all had stocky builds, somewhat on the short side, and brown hair, with matching personalities that were dull, all business, and humorless. That didn't matter. This wasn't a beauty contest; this was the society page. What mattered were the names and the physical evidence that these names had attended this event. Fortunately, little Julian Petsinger was standing nearby with Nick Scully's abandoned date. Norman included them all in the sweeping motion he made with his arms to shepherd them toward the museum's new wing and the supposed focal point of the evening's celebration. The Scullys and the Petsingers were two of the biggest names in the room. They were U.S. Steel and Palmdale Mills.

"Excuse me," he said, no nonsense and all business in a way he knew the junior Scullys would respond to. "The Birmingham *News* needs your picture. Come with me. Over here. Right this way. You too, Julian, and you, darling," he said to the jilted date.

Norman loved the way even the rich and the powerful became obedient at the behest of reporters and photographers from the newspaper. And for once he was grateful for the way Adelaide ignored anyone who looked the least bit menial, as did the photographer, who had a beard and wasn't wearing a tuxedo. If she had bothered to deduce from the camera around his neck the reason he was there, she would have cornered him herself. Norman snagged him on his way to the Scully parents, and dispatched little Julian to get the Petsingers. For his most important shot, he needed his most important people fanned out under the archway to the new wing. The flashbulbs attracted the attention of Adelaide Whitmire, who hurried over to take charge, as was only right, since she was in charge of the entire gala, and had worked ceaselessly to ensure its success.

"Oh, there you are!" Norman cried when she assailed him. "I looked all over for you darling. This young man is from the Birmingham *News,* and he needs help finding all the right people. You're the one to work with him on this."

Turning away quickly, he nearly collided with Nick Scully's date, a young woman known to him only through hearsay. She had divorced her husband a year ago after he had committed the unpardonable misdeed of accepting a promotion which required him to leave Birmingham and move two and a half hours away, to Nashville. Apparently she had not liked Nashville, because she knew no one there and no one there knew her. The only one who eagerly desired her presence in the city was her husband. But what good was this marital triumph if she had no audience to appreciate it? After just a few months, living in her hometown of Birmingham proved more important to her wellbeing than living in Nashville with her husband, and since they had not yet had children, divorce was the obvious solution. She was the sort of person who irritated Norman so much he would normally have avoided her, except he hoped he might startle some information out of her.

"Why didn't Nick come tonight?" he asked her abruptly.

She gave a slight, bored shrug. "Something came up, was all he said."

"It's not like he has a job," Norman boomed at her. "What does he have going on that could possibly come up on a Saturday night?"

"I have no idea," she replied wearily. "I'm about ready to give up on him completely."

"By far the best thing you could do!" Norman proclaimed. He pulled on the arm of little Julian's wife Lena and muttered in her ear. "Why don't you take this poor creature over to the Kellers," he suggested. "Frank's son is here with him tonight, the one who just moved back from Hong Kong. He might enjoy meeting an attractive female."

Lena's eyes grew wide and she clapped a hand on her mouth. "That's perfect!" she whispered.

"Now tell me where your friend is," he ordered her husband when Lena led the girl away.

"Beats me." Little Julian threw up his hands. "He asked us to pick up Natalie and bring her, because he couldn't come but she still wanted to."

Norman narrowed his eyes. This was the way he got most of his gossip from men, and sometimes from women. He didn't act like a gossip; instead, he was the inquisitor, whose difficult job was to ferret out the truth. Someone had to do it. "You know more than you're telling." He made his voice as accusatory as possible.

Two tell-tale spots appeared on little Julian's face. "You ought to get to know him better, Norman."

"I'd like to," Norman retorted icily. "But how can I when he's not here?"

"I promise you, he's changed."

"I see no evidence of that tonight." Norman's eyes swept the room as if to emphasize Nick's absence. "I see no evidence of a new Nick, since I see no Nick. Just another woman twisting in the wind, obligations willfully ignored, no explanation, parents stepping in to cover for their son . . . Looks like the same old Nick to me. As far as I can see." His eyes swept the room again.

Little Julian chuckled. "Give him another chance."

"I was intending to give him a little speech of thanks for all he's donated this past year," Norman said with a flourish, as if slapping down his trump card.

"Oho! So that's what this is about?" Little Julian chuckled again. "Well, if you want to thank him, why not give him another chance instead of the speech? He might surprise you."

"That's what I've always been afraid of with Nick Scully," said Norman, before stomping off in search of a well-earned drink.

~ 17 ~

On Sunday Caroline returned from a jog down the inlet road to find Nick's car in the driveway, gleaming in the early afternoon sun. It was too soon for him to be back. She'd expected him to spend the day with his family, and truthfully, she'd wanted him to. As the revelations from the previous night's conversation registered more and more deeply on her consciousness, they proved more and more humiliating rather than less. It was the farcical stuff of a comic opera: the bored, dissatisfied young wife, who falls in love with the handsome, mysterious man next door. She thinks he loves her too, but she doesn't know he's gay, so he wants her husband, not her. Meanwhile, the wife's girlhood friend has captured the forsaken affections of the abandoned husband. Two people wanted her husband; no one wanted her, especially not the abandoned husband. Who did she want now? Did she want to reclaim the husband she had wronged? Was her husband's wrongdoing merely a reaction to hers? Or did his transgression prove his character unworthy and their marriage empty? Her muddled brain produced no answers to these questions. It just raced around in circles of confusion without arriving at any conclusions. The one person who could have provided some answers did not want to talk to her; he only wanted to divorce her. She didn't know what to do or think, except that she'd set in motion a mortifying comedy of errors with the rare distinction of inducing no laughter, only tears.

She could hardly face herself, let alone another person, even a good friend. If she had to see Nick, she'd hoped it would be after dark, when the shame and folly of her actions wouldn't feel so exposed as in broad daylight. Yet here was his car in the driveway. Frowning, she wondered what had gone wrong, how he might have pissed off his parents this time. All too easily she could imagine what had happened, what often happened when he couldn't stop himself from saying the exact thing calculated to embarrass his parents

196

the most. Holidays, birthdays, and special occasions, especially if celebrated at the country club, brought out the worst of his mockery. It was the Fourth of July barbecue she'd attended with him at the club when he'd observed that Independence Day still didn't extend to black people, who were spending their holiday working like slaves to white people. The waiters who'd overheard looked down in shame, his mother had gasped as if in physical pain, and his father had asked him to leave if he couldn't mind his manners. Taking his father literally at his word, Nick had made such an eager exit she suspected he'd engineered the whole episode to achieve this result. "They never let me off the hook until I force them to," he acknowledged later.

The annoyance she'd felt then came over her now. Instead of going inside, she went around back to the pier and dangled her feet in the cool water. She was remembering now why she had told herself it was for the best he hadn't answered her letters or returned those phone messages, how she convinced herself that she shouldn't persist in trying to reach him or find out where he was. She should let him go and forget about him. Because if he didn't want to take a part in his family's business, live in Birmingham or join his parents at the country club, he didn't have to. Despite what he said, no one could make him. He was twenty-six, twenty-seven years old; he had his own money. What he didn't have was anything better to do, anyplace better to go. That was his problem, it was a big one, and he'd done nothing to solve it. He had rejected his parents' expectations, but that was all. Rebellion was not enough. He still needed to fill the void, and had never done so. Those scenes he staged with his parents were just charades, designed to make his parents look like the enemy. They weren't any worse than anyone else's parents. He was his own worst enemy. She'd seen that years ago without even knowing about the drug problem.

"You could have let me know where you were!" he yelled down from the upper deck.

"Sorry!" she called out, not turning around. She splashed her feet in the water.

He came and squatted beside her, panting from running down the steps. "Let's do something!" he said, like he always did.

"How was Easter?" she turned toward him, squinting in the sun. It was hotter than yesterday.

"The usual." He settled next to her on the pier.

"Does that mean you said something you shouldn't have?"

"How'd you guess?" he grinned.

"Nick." She shaded her eyes and regarded him with disappointment.

He laughed. "Just kidding. I didn't spoil anybody's Easter. Promise." He pointed to a structure she hadn't noticed before, half hidden by the trees next to the deck. "There's a boat in there," he said. "Let's go for a ride."

Without waiting for her to agree, he sprang up and pulled her with him. The prospect of a boat ride was too tempting to turn down, the exuberance of his personality too strong to allow anyone to remain in a permanent state of annoyance with him. This was how he got away with everything, she thought.

* * *

It was glorious out on the open river. The speed of the boat made conversation impossible, so she closed her eyes and gave in to the pleasure of the ride, the feel of the wind in her hair. Every so often he shouted out to call her attention to a barge or a particular bird he wanted her to see. Eventually he turned the boat into another inlet off the main waterway, only this one was perfectly unspoiled by development of any kind. He dropped an anchor and pointed ahead, above the trees.

"We'll see a nice sunset there, after a while. Now turn around and close your eyes for a minute. I want to surprise you."

Laughing to herself, she did as he said.

"Okay, turn back around now." He beckoned her to the rear of the boat, where he'd arranged a spread that covered the whole length of the bench seat. There were cheeses, fruit and an artichoke dip he must have remembered she liked. A bottle of wine stood sideways in an ice bucket next to two plastic wine glasses.

"I'm guessing you haven't had Easter brunch," he said, pleased with himself and the look on her face.

"This is exactly like the picnic you brought with us to Oak Mountain that time."

He chuckled. "You remember that?"

"How could I forget drinking wine like that? In the middle of the day? In the middle of the woods? At my age?"

"Speaking of wine," he said, pouring a glass and handing it over. He gestured for her to sit in the captain's chair, then poured his own wine and squeezed in next to the food on the bench seat opposite her. "Those were great times we had," he said, lifting his glass.

"They were," she agreed, tapping his glass with her own. "All the girls in my class were so jealous. They thought it was so exciting I was going out with a guy ten years older. I never could convince them we weren't dating. They thought I was just being modest."

"I never understood why the guys in your class weren't dating you. Why you were always available."

"Nick, really." She shook her head and shuddered inwardly.

"What?" he said, leaning over to select a strawberry. "I still don't get it."

She reached over and swiped at the dip with one of the crackers. "Don't you remember what I looked like? I was just about the ugliest duckling ever hatched. At least that's what my mother kept telling me. To boost my spirits, build up my self-confidence." She plucked fiercely at the grapes.

"The bad haircut," he nodded. "The glasses. I remember. You were a little chubby. I thought it was kind of cute."

"It would be cute in a kid sister, I suppose. But the guys in my class were interested in *girls.*" She sliced into the Brie. "What made *you* want to be with such a plain little Jane?"

Leaning back against the seat and looking up at the sky, he appeared not to have heard her. It was just as well. She thought she knew the answer to the question that had mystified everyone, herself included, and it would only embarrass Nick to spell it out honestly. Knowing what she did now about his problems back then, it was clear that he had used her as a diversion, an escape from boredom, the temptation of drugs, and the adult responsibilities he didn't want to take on. It didn't really matter. However it had started, it had turned into a true friendship.

Leaning back in the captain's chair, her thoughts wandered to the night she first met him, at the party her parents had given before Lena's wedding. It was a backyard barbecue, with twilight giving way to torches illuminating the patio, the lawn, the gardens of roses and vegetables. She remembered the fireflies that night, and the seventy-five miniature pecan pies she had baked in tribute to the heiress of Dixie Pies & Pastries. Julian Petsinger introduced one of his groomsmen, Nick Scully, as his best friend. Nick's date was the oldest St. John sister, Mooky, who had the same old-fashioned Southern-belle beauty as all the St. John girls. Wherever they went, their lush, pageant-length blonde hair and huge blue eyes attracted an immediate crowd, and when the crowd claimed Mooky, sixteen year-old Caroline was left alone with Nick, who failed to follow in Mooky's wake. He spent most of the evening talking to her, and ate three miniature pecan pies. Whenever Mooky came to check on her date, she found him deep in conversation with Lena Albritton's gawky, bespectacled cousin. Mooky didn't mind; the St. John sisters were as sweet as they were beautiful. Leaving the party, Nick told the host that his daughter was the most interesting woman he'd ever met. Then he asked for permission to take her out. Just so he could talk to her some more. Laughing, her father agreed.

But it seemed no more than an elaborate exchange of compliments between the two men. Nick Scully was a jokester and a prankster who took nothing seriously. The awkward adolescent girl was just a way to flout his duties, his beautiful date, the lovely party. Asking to take her out was an extravagant thank-you for the cover she'd provided. A week later she was stunned when he called.

"I don't think I'll be allowed . . ."

"I asked your father. You were there. You heard him say yes."

"But I'm not sure he meant it."

"Ask him again," he urged. "*Please.* . . ."

Sixteen year-old Caroline had no intention of asking her father if she could go out with a twenty-six year-old man. It was her mother who made it happen. It was her mother who had fielded Nick's phone call and heard the first male voice ever asking to speak with her daughter. After this conversation concluded, she went straightaway to her daughter's room to find out who he was and what he wanted. When Caroline told her, she shot straight into orbit, as if all her maternal prayers, hopes and dreams had been fulfilled beyond her wildest fantasies. She herself had been *married* at nineteen, just like her own mother, while Caroline at sixteen had never even had her first *date*. Even Shirley, now an old maid, had pledged A D Psi and never lacked for dates in high school.

Caroline's mother had done all she could to steer her daughter toward success, the definition of which was marriage. Failure was spinsterhood, and as her mother saw it, Caroline was headed for failure. She had no friends as well as no dates, did nothing to improve her appearance, and spent all her time alone reading one book after another. Who would ever be interested in such a peculiar creature? No one she knew. The failure would not just be her daughter's. Fingers always pointed at the mother, whose *job* it was to make the daughter turn out right. Disgrace lay in store if she could not make of her daughter the success she was herself. She seized on Nick Scully's phone call with rabid desperation.

"You've got a lot to learn," she scolded when told what Caroline had said to him. "With a man like that, you may only get one chance. He'll have plenty of other options. He may never call back. You should have said yes and figured it out from there."

She assured Caroline of her father's permission, but Caroline still had no intention of irritating her father's short temper with such a request. Behind her back, her mother did the asking, and surprised her a few days later with the news of her father's consent to a *friendship* with Nick Scully limited to daytime activities.

"You've got to start *somewhere*," her mother said. "This is better than nothing. And nothing is all you've gotten from the other boys you know. You just better hope he calls again."

But Caroline hoped he wouldn't. Informing him of her father's restrictions would be embarrassing enough, but this would lead to the even worse awkwardness of Nick's inevitable about-face. And then she'd have to tell her mother. Better if he didn't call again at all.

But he did, and immediately demanded to know what her father had said.

"I told you!" he gloated.

Caroline was silent.

"What's wrong?" he said. "You don't want to go out with me?"

"It's just . . . I can only go out during the day."

"That's great!" he had exclaimed. "I don't have nearly enough good things to do during the day!"

The memory made her smile.

"Look." Nick touched her arm and nodded toward the sky, where the sun was beginning to sink.

For a time they observed the sunset in silence, enjoyed all the food, drank the whole bottle of wine. It was nice to say nothing for a change, to have no serious conversation filled with devastating revelations. She badly wanted to discuss the news of her husband's affair with Lily Templeton, but not with Nick. After all, he had slept with Lily himself. What she needed was the advice and counsel of someone with no involvement whatsoever in any of the events. For that she would have to get back, figure out who she could talk to. Ideally she would drive to Birmingham to see Mr. Laney, if he was in town for spring break. In any case, if she was going to get to the bottom of what was really going on and what she wanted to do about it, she couldn't stay at the river. It had helped her get through the holiday weekend, but it was time to go. She sighed.

Nick began to gather the remnants of the picnic. She stood up to help. "I guess we better get going before it gets too dark," he said. "There are some jackets in that duffel bag." He pointed. She took one and handed him the other. "About tomorrow," he said, zipping up his windbreaker.

"I think it's time I got back to Tuscaloosa." She shivered and rubbed her arms for warmth.

"Get some blankets from the bag. You'll need them for the ride back." He leaned over the side of the boat to pull up the anchor.

The return trip was uncomfortable and cold. If the day had felt almost like summer, the night which fell all too fast felt almost like winter. Even with several layers of wool wrapped around her, the chill of the wind bit through

201

to her skin and froze her exposed face. Nick had to drive slowly while standing, the better to see in the dark. The lights at the bow of the boat provided only a little illumination. He navigated mainly by memory, which required total concentration and prevented any conversation. It was a relief when they finally pulled into the boathouse. He handed her the picnic basket and the duffel bag. "If you'll take these, I'll put up the boat. Then you go in and take a hot bath," he suggested.

She hesitated on the landing in the boathouse, not wanting to be unhelpful or unsociable. "I do feel like a bath," she admitted. "Then I think I'll just get in the bed. All that wine made me sleepy, and I'm definitely not hungry."

He nodded, absorbed in hooking the boat to the cables from the lift. "Fine," he said. "I'll take you back tomorrow, then."

"Thanks, Nick," she said. "For everything."

"Oh, my pleasure." He leaped off the boat and flipped a switch on one of the posts. Slowly the boat rose from the water, but in a lopsided fashion. Frowning, he pressed the switch down to lower the boat back to the water.

"What's wrong?"

"Oh, nothing. One of the cables. I can handle it. Don't stand here in the cold. Go run a hot bath."

"Well, okay," she said, but it was awkward. He was back in the boat, leaning over the far side, cursing under his breath. Realizing she could thank him again tomorrow when he drove her back, she said goodnight and turned to go.

"Say!" He looked up just as she reached the door of the boathouse. She turned around, picnic basket in one hand, duffel bag in the other. His hands were covered in rust from the cable.

"Nick, let me help."

"No," he said. "Only I was thinking. We never did go to Hale County."

"Hale County?"

"You haven't forgotten what that is?"

"No, of course not. But what . . . ?" She really wanted to take a bath and get in the bed.

"Maybe later in the week we could visit Hale County. Like we always talked about doing."

"Maybe," she said doubtfully.

"Okay then," he said, wiping his hands on a rag. "Good night."

"Good night."

The boathouse door banged softly behind her. As she went up the stairs, he called out "Happy Easter!" As these words echoed over the water, she suddenly remembered the Easter Sunday four years ago, when she had her first date with the man who was still her husband.

~ 18 ~

Sorority row was a block of antebellum-style mansions, one after another on both sides of a shaded street overhung with graceful trees set back behind wide sidewalks. Bryant-Denny Stadium rose in the distance just a few blocks away, where her mother had gone into labor with her during an Alabama homecoming game twenty-two years ago. Each of the houses was a little different. Some had façades of red brick, with wrought-iron scrollwork. Others had tall white columns. All of them looked like something from the plantation South. If not for the closeness of one house to another, it would have looked like one of the more exclusive neighborhoods in Mountain Brook. The house where she was expected had a classic colonial façade that reminded her of the home where she had grown up. In a way, she realized, a girl who grew up in Mountain Brook and then spent her college years in one of these sorority houses never really left home. Caroline's mother had been one of these girls who never left the bubble of Mountain Brook, and if she'd had her way, Caroline would never have left either.

The student who had invited her for lunch was the one who greeted her at the door like a hostess welcoming a guest. Stepping inside, she felt as if she were arriving at a party where she was the honoree. A chattering group of well-dressed girls rushed over eagerly to be introduced and make her acquaintance. They continued chattering away with her as if they had not just met but had known her forever. Indeed, they did know many people who had known her in high school. They rattled off names excitedly. The clicking of heels on the gleaming white marble of the foyer made them all look up to see a handsome older woman coming toward them.

"Girls," she said pleasantly, a warm smile lighting her face. "Show your guest away from the door. Underneath the chandelier is a better place to gather. Imagine if more arrivals were expected. You wouldn't want a crowd right on the threshold, making it difficult to enter."

The girls moved obediently en masse toward the center of the foyer, directly underneath a massive chandelier twinkling with crystals. When the older woman joined them, her student stepped forward.

"Miss Eulalie," she said. "I'd like you to meet my instructor, Mrs. Caroline Elmore, from Mountain Brook. Mrs. Elmore, this is our housemother, Miss Eulalie Carmichael."

When Caroline put out her hand, Miss Eulalie instantly grasped it with both of hers. The older woman held her hand warmly for several moments before giving it a few pats and gently releasing it. "I am so glad to meet you, my dear," she said. "How is your mother?"

Her mother? "Fine," she said haltingly, struck by the sudden awareness that she was woefully unprepared for the social occasion this was turning out to be. She should have known better: you didn't just show up at a sorority house. There was all sorts of preliminary and background work to be done ahead of time to ensure the success of the experience. She had done nothing. "My mother sends her regards," she said, not knowing if her mother knew this woman or had ever met her. Clearly, she should have found out earlier and procured her mother's own greetings.

Miss Eulalie nodded. "Please tell your mother how much we appreciate all the work she does as one of our most active Kappa alumnae. The letters of recommendation she writes every rush season are just *so* helpful. And her penmanship is beautiful. I pass her notes around to all the girls so they can see how it should be done." Miss Eulalie turned to her student. "Lydia, would you like to show our guest into the living room?"

Proudly Lydia led the group down the polished marble entranceway into a large room with shiny parquet wooden floors and a thick Oriental rug. The windows looked out on a lush side lawn bordered by rose bushes in bloom. In the corner was a grand piano set off by a stunning arrangement of fresh flowers in a tall crystal vase with a neck as long as that on a giraffe. It was almost exactly like one of the vases she'd received as a wedding gift. On a somewhat grander scale, the interior of this sorority house—just like the exterior—resembled any number of homes in Mountain Brook: the elegant marble foyer, the spacious formal living room. In flowing skirts, silk blouses, stockings and pumps, Miss Eulalie and the girls were all suitable grace notes to the elegance of their surroundings. Caroline was the only one without makeup, fingernail polish, and carefully curled or styled hair. Fortunately, she had put on a dress, but it was wrinkled from her suitcase and saturated with the strong odor of the Black Warrior River. Everyone else was attired as if for luncheon at the country club; in fact, the only time Caroline had ever dressed like that was for a debutante luncheon at the Mountain Brook Club. The girls also wore the same big smiles they'd had on since she walked through the door. She tried her best to return the cordiality, but she was afraid to smile that wide herself, for fear her teeth were neither white enough nor straight enough. The most amazing thing about the girls' smiles was they appeared to be genuine.

To her guest, Lydia indicated a chair next to the piano, and Caroline sat down first. The girls remained standing until Miss Eulalie selected her seat on the sofa next to the chair where the guest of honor sat. Then they settled themselves around the room, sitting with the same erect posture and crossed ankles as their housemother. But Caroline suddenly found herself unable to perceive the beautiful girls and elegant surroundings right in front of her. Instead, her imagination began to conjure what lay beneath the surface of the white marble foyer, the crystal chandelier, the magnificent floral arrangement on the grand piano. What she saw was the grinding of gears, the turning of wheels, the roll of the assembly line in a factory producing belles that would be released into society so they could preserve and perpetuate its culture, preside over homes that looked like sorority houses, and produce beautiful children who would in turn take their place in the sororities and fraternities their parents had come from. She'd had a similar revelation one night in the Eliot House dining hall at Harvard, when the senior tutor proudly disclosed to his tablemates that 88% of the Eliot House seniors had applied for jobs on Wall Street. Although he was clearly pleased with a statistic which to him signaled success, Caroline had been appalled. This news had crystallized all her disappointment with Harvard, which she believed was a place that should produce individuals, not company men for the establishment. Caroline had left the South to get away from the sororities and fraternities that supplied her society, only to find at Harvard a different kind of fraternity that supplied its own society.

And she had not even succeeded in getting away from the Southern sororities. Her own mother had come out of this same sorority house where Caroline now sat. She had been and to a large extent still was a girl such as those who sat chattering away happily in this formal living room. She was supposed to raise a daughter in the image of these sorority girls who would be a credit to the Kappa house and one day preside over her own house, preferably in Mountain Brook, that was a close replica of the sorority house she came from.

But something had gone wrong. The daughter had not been beautiful or even sociable. She preferred being alone, in her own room, with nothing but a book for company. The mother had branded this daughter a failure, and despaired of her future. Perhaps the mother feared the failure had been her own, that she would be blamed for breaking the cycle, and so cast the blame even more so on the daughter, who didn't understand what was wrong, because she did well in school, never got in trouble, and asked only to be left alone, in her room, with a book for company. As the daughter grew older it only got worse until open conflict erupted. Desperate, the mother tried to tell the daughter all the ways in which she was ruining her chances for a good life, all the ways she could still redeem herself and the opportunities available to a girl from a good family. Devastated by this criticism, the daughter shut her ears, shut her door, and resolved to go as far away as possible. Thus she escaped the crucible that was supposed to shape her into one of these pretty, smiling girls who now sat entertaining her. Somehow today she had come unexpectedly face to face with what she had run away from, what her mother had always expected her to be. She couldn't help but feel she owed the girls some explanation for why she failed to fit into their surroundings, but in deference to those surroundings, her words stayed politely on the surface.

"I'm afraid I just arrived back this morning from a weekend at the river." She indicated her crumpled dress.

"What a lovely place to spend Easter," Miss Eulalie observed.

"Miss Eulalie tells us to dress the best we can every day," one of the girls informed her brightly. "You never know who you will meet or what will happen. It could be a job opportunity or your future husband, and they are both more likely to come along if you always look your very best. Isn't that right, Miss Lalie?"

The suggestion of a frown put a brief crease in Miss Lalie's forehead. The girl realized then she'd said something not quite right, although she'd thought she was quoting her housemother verbatim. She'd find out later what she'd gotten wrong.

For now the older woman changed the subject. "I was so delighted to read in the paper of your wedding last summer. I enjoyed meeting your husband when he was a student here on campus."

"My husband?"

"Before he was your husband, of course. When he was in law school. You were in college. *Away*," she added apologetically, as if the University of Alabama were the only place to be, and any other place, even Harvard, was unfortunately *away*.

"Are you sure that was my husband you met?"

"Daniel Dobbs," Miss Eulalie affirmed, inclining her head majestically. "A very bright young man. He came around here on several occasions."

The sudden clanging of a bell in a distant room put an end to further conversation. Miss Eulalie rose from her chair, and after everyone had done the same, gestured to Lydia. "If you would show our guest the way," she said.

At the doorway to the dining room, a large black woman stood ringing an old-fashioned dinner bell. When she spied the group coming toward her, she broke into a wide smile and lowered the bell to her side.

"Miss Lydia," she said as they all approached. "Is this our guest today?"

"Yes, this is my instructor. Lottie is our head cook," Lydia explained.

"Pleased to meet you," said Lottie. "Y'all come in. Make yourselves at home."

Behind them a chorus of voices greeted Lottie, who stood at the threshold until everyone passed through. The clanging of the bell resumed to summon any remaining residents of the house into the dining room. At a given moment, the ringing ceased, the door closed, and Lottie disappeared into the kitchen.

The dining hall was the only room she had seen so far that looked at all institutional. It was filled with long rows of tables that today were mostly empty because of the spring vacation. In addition to the housemother and the half dozen girls she had previously met, there were about ten others all standing behind chairs at the one table that had been set for them at the front of the room. As if on cue, all pulled out their chairs at the same time. No sooner were they seated than three other black women emerged from the kitchen bearing platters of fried chicken, green beans, mashed potatoes and biscuits. Two busboys arrived, one with pitchers of iced tea, the other with a gravy boat and a bowl of whipped butter.

All sat with their backs straight and their hands in their laps. No one said a word until all the food had been placed on the table and the help had withdrawn. Then Miss Eulalie raised her hands, looked to her left and her right to clasp the hand of each girl sitting beside her. The others were quick to do the same until everyone was holding hands. Simultaneously, all heads bowed and the housemother asked the Lord's blessing upon this food and all these young women with her today. Amen murmured from around the table. After a decent interval, Miss Eulalie picked up the platter of fried chicken and turned with it to her left, where the girl seated next to her selected a drumstick.

"Thank you, Miss Lalie," said the girl. After placing the drumstick on her plate, she took the platter from the housemother and held it out for the girl on her own left.

Although Caroline was a guest here for the first time, there was no need to learn what to do. She simply needed to submit herself to the will of the group, to do what everyone else was doing, follow the manners and customs of everyone around her. No doubt this was the point of the sorority house, the way it readied the girls for the mission they would perform out in society.

This is not what she had expected when she'd accepted the invitation to be faculty guest at the Kappa luncheon for students staying on campus during spring break. Then she'd forgotten about the engagement altogether, as more pressing issues overwhelmed her thoughts. This morning she had just hung up with Mr. Laney's mother, who told her that he was indeed out of town—in New York, with her aunt and uncle, actually—when the phone rang again. It was Lydia, calling to remind her of the luncheon. Pleading exhaustion from a weekend away, she had tried to cancel. Lydia had protested so strenuously she'd reluctantly given in. But still it hadn't dawned on her that lunch at the sorority house would be anything other than the standard cafeteria meal in a dormitory. Although her own mother had been a Kappa, Caroline herself had never set foot inside this sorority house or any other.

It could not be said that it was like stepping into another era, since it was impossible to believe that people anywhere at any time had ever really lived like this or behaved this way. It was more like stepping into a fantasy world, where role players enacted an imaginary life bearing little relation to any reality of any time period, grounded only in the most exaggerated tropes about The South: the smiling black servant women, the dinner bell, the fried chicken. If the choreographed ritual and studied formality of the girls, with their elaborate manners and tireless smiles made her uncomfortable, she was the only one, and she tried her best to conceal this reaction. The girls were eating, drinking and chatting happily as their housemother looked on with approval. Everyone but herself was blissfully unaware that the tableau they were part of could be held up to outsiders for ridicule, condemnation or sociological observation. Another day, it might have all been a fascinating spectacle to witness. But she didn't have time for this now. She had her life to figure out. The conversation buzzed unintelligibly around her; she spoke and responded without knowing what she said.

When the table was cleared of the main course, a big bowl of banana pudding was placed in front of the housemother, who thanked the serving woman, waited until she had withdrawn, then held the dessert bowl while the girl to her left served herself. Miss Eulalie addressed Caroline from two places over. "Did you ever get the chance to meet Bethany Ball?" she asked.

"No. I'm afraid not. Who is she?" Caroline scooped out a small portion of pudding from the bowl now held out for her.

"She is one of our most distinguished recent graduates. A cheerleader, and then she went to law school."

"How interesting," she said politely, and turned to hold the bowl for the girl on her left.

"That's how I met your husband a few years ago," Miss Eulalie told her.

"I've met several of his law school classmates. I don't remember hearing about her." She nibbled a bite off her spoon.

"Bethany brought him by the house here when they were dating."

"Dating?" She looked up, puzzled.

"That's how he met your friend from the Brook-Haven School. Lily Templeton. She was a Kappa too, you know. He was smitten with her for a time."

She put down her spoon. "I don't understand," she said, thoroughly confused.

"When Bethany started dating someone else, he came back by here on several occasions to ask Lily for a date," the older woman explained patiently. "A very persistent young man, he is. He'll go far. I tried to tell Lily. It doesn't matter that he's from a small town. Went *away* to college. Didn't belong to a fraternity. That young man is going places. But." Miss Eulalie pursed her lips in displeasure. "Lily is one of those few girls I could never really reach. She wouldn't listen." The housemother's countenance brightened again. "You are lucky that you're the one he married in the end."

Sudden enlightenment clobbered her senses like the onset of influenza. Blows she hadn't seen coming, to the back of her head and the back of her knees, felled her instantaneously and left her so weak she could hardly sit straight in her chair. Her muscles turned to liquid, her mind was hazed with pain. Heat scoured her insides at the same time a chill spread across her skin like a cube of ice. She trembled as if with fever. Voices asking if something was wrong sounded too far away to be meant for her ears, which were so plugged up as to render her nearly deaf. Her tongue was too thick and her mouth too dry to form any words or make any sounds of her own. Vaguely she was aware of a flurry of consternation that someone was going to faint, about to vomit, or having a spell of some sort. Her vision was so blurred she didn't notice the glass of water until it was thrust to her lips. A soft, kind hand supported the back of her head as the glass tilted forward. A little water dribbled down her chin.

The cook arrived and stood at the head of the table, next to the housemother. "I hope everything was satisfactory," she said to the table at large.

"Thank you, Lottie," a chorus of voices declared in unison. "It was wonderful."

Miss Eulalie crooked her finger ever so slightly at the cook, who bent down for Miss Eulalie to whisper something in her ear about coffee in her private quarters. It was the housemother who led the way there, up a curved stairway of wide heart pine planks. On the next floor she ushered Lydia, her guest and the rest of the original group into a suite of rooms resembling a luxury apartment. The former gaiety of the occasion had hushed into a respectful solemnity. The girls knew that something HAD HAPPENED. The smiles they had previously worn gave way to thoughtful expressions of concern, equally sincere. The chattering had ceased completely. They all waited quietly, hands clasped in their laps. Then came a muffled knock on the door, followed by the entrance of one of the black women from the kitchen bearing a silver tray, with a silver coffee pot and china teacups patterned with tiny, delicate pink rosebuds.

The servant left, Miss Eulalie poured the coffee and handed around the cups. It was when everyone was served that all eyes turned on Caroline briefly, then lowered to the teacups. This was her cue, she realized.

"I'm sorry," was all she could think to say.

"Nonsense, my dear," said the housemother kindly. "We can tell you have received a shock. Let us help you. We are as used to that as to blown fuses."

"Blown fuses?" She looked around in bafflement.

"On Friday and Saturday nights," Miss Eulalie explained. "When all the girls are getting ready to go out at the same time. Hair dryers going full blast. A fuse blows every Friday and Saturday night."

The girls all nodded in solemn corroboration.

"People blow fuses too," Miss Eulalie said gently. "Our circuits overload and we burst into tears. Over a bad grade. A phone call from home. A break-up with a boyfriend. We have heard it all. Why don't you tell us? That's what sisters are for."

She looked from one face of kind concern to another.

"Yes! Tell us," Lydia urged.

She swallowed and put down her cup on the coffee table. "I didn't know that my husband had . . . dated . . . in law school," she explained in a weak voice that was barely above a whisper.

"But my dear," said Miss Eulalie, uncomprehending. "You were in college then. *Away.*"

"We were engaged!" she blurted.

"Ah," said the housemother. "I had not realized." She placed her own cup on the table. "Still," she said. "Engaged is one thing; married is another. Especially if the engagement is long distance. And of long duration. How long was it?"

"Three years." Her hands clutched at each other in her lap, in unintentional parody of the hand clasp perfected by the girls.

Miss Eulalie absorbed this information in silence. As ever, the girls took their cue from her and said not a word. "My dear," the housemother said finally. "Three years is *a long time*. You cannot expect a young man to go *all that time*. Alone. To the parties and football games. Besides," she shook her head. "That isn't what's done here. People don't go to social occasions *alone*. So Bethany Ball may have been your husband's date on one or two occasions. But that does not mean they were *dating* as we all thought."

The girls shook their heads in unison.

"On a campus as social as this one," the housemother continued, "it is common to arrange for an *escort* to a football game or a fraternity party if a girlfriend or boyfriend is unavailable or *away*. It doesn't mean anything. Escorting someone is quite different from dating. Bethany has very strong morals, and she would never accept a date from a man who was *committed*. Now, there are girls who believe that behavior is acceptable, and I'm afraid your friend Lily is one of them." Again the older woman pursed her lips in displeasure. "But Lily never agreed to a date with your husband, and I'm sure Bethany only agreed to go out as his escort. No doubt we all misunderstood the situation. What do you think girls?"

Given the floor, the girls broke out in a torrent of excited testimonials to Bethany Ball's character, along with elaborations on the differences between an escort and a date. Dating was for finding Mr. Right, and acting accordingly if he was found. Escorting was simply for not going alone to a party or football game.

Biting her lip, Caroline nodded as if these explanations soothed all her concerns.

"I understand your concern is that your fiancé may still have been playing the field during your engagement," the housemother went on. "Now, some young men will do that," Miss Eulalie acknowledged. "Especially if the girl in question is *away*. Sad to say, it can sometimes result in broken engagements. But my dear," the housemother broke into her warm smile. "That did not happen in your case. He married *you*. You are the chosen one. I fail to see that there is a real problem here. Just a cultural difference. Perhaps the college you attended was not so social."

True, she reflected. The college she attended was not much given either to dating or escorting. Fucking was more like it. Apparently, that was not a practice her erstwhile fiancé had left behind with his girlfriend—her—in the Northeast, although it was difficult to determine what role, if any, sexual intercourse played in this imaginary universe she had temporarily entered. Neither the housemother nor any of the girls had indicated the slightest awareness of the potential for sexual relations among unmarried young people.

Dazed, she walked down the block to her car. Twice on the sidewalk she encountered a group of girls who greeted her so enthusiastically—smiling and waving—that she was afraid these were students from her classes she was supposed to know. She did not feel capable of either summoning their names or conducting a polite conversation, but she stopped dutifully to exchange pleasantries, preparing to bluff her way through. But after the second group breezed right by with a chorus of "Have a nice day!," she realized that these were not students she was supposed to know; these were Southern sorority girls showering their smiles and good cheer on everyone they passed by, not only because everyone was a potential friend, an actual friend, a friend of a friend, a prospective husband or a job opportunity. They did it because they could. They were young and beautiful and filled with the sense that the world was theirs. They had so much of their own God-given bounty it was fun to spread some of it around in the form of smiles and greetings to perfect strangers. In its own way, however, it could be just as unsettling as the opposite behavior she was used to on the campus where she had attended college—*away.* There people often refrained from eye contact even with acquaintances and sometimes friends. It wasn't always rudeness, either, or lack of manners. Sometimes it was delicacy, a reluctance to intrude on someone's private thoughts or cross someone's individual boundaries without invitation. Truthfully, this is what she would have preferred today. Although the sorority girls were simply being friendly in the tradition of Southern hospitality in which they were raised, at this particular moment, their high spirits, their happiness, their youth and beauty were almost unbearable. It seemed an affront, to have all that gorgeous, happy girlhood thrust in her face while she felt so miserably the opposite of everything they represented. She would rather they ignore her so she could ignore them. And she was certainly in no condition to have a nice day.

~ 19 ~

He had the book lying on the console between them in the front seat of the car. Caroline did not have her copy with her, nor did she have the desire to make this particular journey today. She had just needed to get away, go anywhere. When she'd agreed to go last night, she'd been desperate for any escape. But it wasn't fair to Nick or to the book which had played such a vital role in her coming to consciousness. Long before she'd actually been able to leave home, this book had given her a life-changing glimpse of the outside Alabama world from which Mountain Brook kept her sequestered. This journey was one she had always wanted to take, but not in her current distressed and distracted state of mind. It should be a pilgrimage in which she paid homage, not a temporary diversion from her troubles.

"I think I made a mistake," she told him. "Maybe you better take me back. I'm really not in the mood to do justice to this today."

The light changed and he turned onto Lurleen Wallace Boulevard as if he hadn't heard her.

"See that sack on the floor at your feet?" he said. "Pick it up for me, will you?"

Leaning down, she said, "Please. I wish you'd turn around." Then she watched helplessly as he followed the signs for AL Hwy 69 S.

"Now open that sack," he said. "I've already had mine. These are for you."

She peered inside. There were two fresh croissants, one covered in almonds, the other oozing chocolate out the sides. Her stomach growled.

"You haven't eaten," he observed.

In fact, she had not eaten since lunch at the sorority house yesterday. She'd had neither dinner last night nor breakfast this morning. She began plucking pieces of pastry from out of the bag, with her head turned toward the window so he couldn't see her face, which was puffy and distorted from a sleepless night spent crying. He turned onto 69 S.

"How far is it?"

"About forty-five minutes to Greensboro."

"Greensboro?"

"Centerboro in the book. Why don't you take a look at it while I'm driving?"

She glanced at the book out of respect, but made no move to pick it up. "I'm really not up to this," she told him.

"It will take your mind off things," he said.

She could feel her eyes fill with hot tears, threatening to spill over, and turned back toward the window. On the floorboard, her purse held a pair of sunglasses, which would help if she dared to reach down. But if he noticed her tears or commented on her crying, she was afraid she'd lose it.

"You want to tell me what happened?" he said.

She shook her head fiercely and turned completely toward the window, as if she were fascinated by the passing landscape, so that all he could see was the back of her head.

"Eat some more," he urged.

The sack rustled in her lap as her hand felt blindly for another piece of the pastry. If she looked down at all, the tears she was holding in check might begin to fall. Perhaps if she focused on eating, the tears would recede enough so she could reach down for the sunglasses.

"You were very upset last night when I called."

"Please," she begged. "I don't think I can talk about it."

"Just tell me if something new has happened."

Instead of answering, she leaned forward and thrust her hand down toward her purse and came up with the sunglasses. Then she resumed eating until there was nothing but crumbs and a few almond slivers in the bakery bag.

"Thank you," she said, crumpling the bag into a ball on her lap.

He said nothing. The Alabama highway was becoming little more than a narrow, two-lane road, with blind curves and sudden dips. Without warning, her tears started spilling over, past the rim of her sunglasses, down her cheeks. Clutching the crumpled bag in her lap, she kept her head trained out the window so he couldn't see her profile. He reached into the glove compartment and pulled out a travel-sized pack of tissues, which he placed on her lap without taking his eyes off the road. She cried harder. Fortunately, he said nothing, even as she removed the dark glasses to press a tissue to her swollen eyes.

"I had lunch with one of my students yesterday," she managed finally, her voice almost choked off by a sob rising in her throat.

He nodded.

"She had invited me to her sorority house." The sobs came forth, one after another, overcoming her defenses and dissolving her in a fit of weeping. "I found out—" she tried to tell him. "I found out—" A sob seized her throat every time she tried to tell him.

He leaned down and pulled a thermos from underneath his seat. "Have a sip of this. It's just iced tea."

She didn't particularly want the taste of iced tea after the chocolate and almond croissants, but welcomed the cool liquid on her raw throat. It was strong tea, and the caffeine seemed to help. She'd had no coffee that morning.

"The housemother at this sorority house had met my husband," she was able to tell him. "When he was in law school. While I was still up there in school."

He nodded, his eyes on the road which was getting more and more tricky as it went deeper and deeper into rural Alabama. Even without other vehicles, it would have been a difficult road, but what made it potentially dangerous were the log trucks, the occasional tractor going five miles an hour, or a sputtering pickup pulling onto the road out of nowhere. "Go on," he said. "I'm listening."

"The Kappa housemother had met him," she repeated. "While he was in law school. How did she meet him? *He dated a law school classmate who had been a Kappa and a cheerleader for the football team!*" Her voice rose into a wail. "*Dated her,* I tell you. While he was *engaged* to me! Engaged *to be married!* Then." She caught her breath. "When that was over, there was another Kappa he wanted to go out with. Can you guess who that was?"

He said nothing. For some reason, this infuriated her. "Lily," she told him. "Lily Templeton. He wanted to go out with Lily Templeton when he was engaged to me. *To be married,*" she added furiously.

Still he said nothing. She couldn't understand why he didn't share her level of shock and outrage.

"Don't you see?" she cried, her voice hoarse. "He always wanted her. This goes back *years.* It's not a sudden whim. He's probably wanted her more than he's ever wanted me. And if she *had* gone out with him then, who knows? We might never have gotten married at all."

"Drink some more tea," he told her.

"Is that all you can *say?*" she wailed, her voice approaching hysteria. "Don't you *see?* What is *wrong* with you?"

She knew what was wrong: He had wanted Lily Templeton too. He had slept with her. Her shoulders began shaking. Her eyes ran; her nose ran. She felt like the ugliest, most undesirable woman in the world.

She whipped her head around to confront him with an angry snarl. "Is she just so beautiful?"

He didn't answer or look over at her.

"Tell me," she insisted fiercely. "Do you think she's beautiful? Tell me!" she commanded.

"Yes," he said quietly. "She's beautiful."

She bit her lip so hard she split the skin. He looked over, started to say something, stopped.

"But what?" she said sharply.

"I don't think that's why your husband has fallen for her," he said.

"Then why did he fall for her? Why did you fall for her?"

"I didn't fall for her."

"What do you mean you didn't fall for her? You think she's *beautiful!* You *slept* with her!"

He said nothing. She turned back toward the window so he couldn't see the tears running down her face.

"Is she so good in bed or something?" She hurled the question toward the window.

"Not really."

"*Not really?*"

"No."

"Why does my husband want her? Why did you want her?"

He didn't answer.

"Is she just so beautiful that every man wants her?" Her voice was a strange combination of a shout and a sob.

"I never wanted her," he said.

"You never wanted her," she repeated with disgust. "Is that why you *slept* with her?" she screamed at him. *"Because you didn't want her?"*

He chanced a quick glance at her distraught countenance. "I just wanted sex with her for reasons that weren't good enough," he said. "And I'm sorry I acted on it."

"Why?" she said. "What was the reason? Why did you want to have sex with her? Because she's so beautiful?"

"No. That wasn't the reason."

"What then? What was the reason?"

"I'd rather not discuss it," he said mildly.

"I'm sorry," she sobbed. "I'm sorry. It's none of my business. I'm sorry." She put her face in her hands and wept openly without restraint.

"There are some wet wipes in the glove box," he told her. "Why don't you wash your face? You'll feel better."

She was beyond feeling better, but owed it to him to comply, to make a pretense of making an effort to pull herself together.

"We're not too far away," he told her. "Would you look at this?"

He slowed the car and pulled off on the grass by the side of the road, where an old barn stood next to what had once been a pasture, or perhaps a field. Now it was empty except for weeds, old tires, a few rusted auto parts. In the distance they could see a smaller structure, just as weathered as the barn. He reached around in the back seat for his camera bag.

"I think people still live in that house," she told him. "Isn't that a clothesline they've got strung up between the trees? See?" She pointed toward what could have been shirts, or sheets, flapping on a line.

"I won't go over there," he said. "I'll just take a picture of the barn, with the house in the background." He opened his door.

"There's not much room here," she said. "If a log truck comes around this bend . . ."

"I'll be quick."

As she waited in the car, she picked up the well-worn copy of *Let Us Now Praise Famous Men* and thumbed through the photographs at the front. There was a close-up taken almost fifty years ago of a barn that could have been the one right in front of them. Then again, it could have been any barn in Alabama. That was the point of the photograph. The picture being taken today, she realized, would show how little had changed in almost half a century. Or had it? Fifty years ago, that piece of overgrown land would probably have been filled with at least a few grazing animals, or a crop of some kind. The barn, which looked empty and abandoned to the elements, would have contained some equipment, tools, feed or supplies. Was this progress they were looking at today? Or had life gotten even worse, even harder in this part of Alabama? As she was closing the book, she noticed familiar handwriting in the front. *To Nick*, it was inscribed. *Merry Christmas!* Underneath: *Love, Caroline.* She'd completely forgotten that she'd been the one to give him this copy of the book. What had he given her for Christmas that year? She couldn't remember.

He hopped back in the car and handed her the camera, which she placed behind her in the backseat.

"Take a look at this." She lifted the book up so he could see the photograph she'd found.

He nodded at it as he buckled his seatbelt. "That's why I wanted to get this picture." Glancing over his shoulder, he steered the car off the grass and back on the road. "Flip through those photographs until you find the one he took of Main Street in Greensboro. Remember they called it Centerboro in the book."

Carefully she turned the glossy pages. "Is this the one you mean?"

He looked over quickly. "That's the one. Keep it open to that page. We're almost there."

They passed newly planted fields with men in tractors going up and down neat rows of a young crop she couldn't identify. There were pastures with horses or cows, modest brick houses, wooden churches. A short while later, the highway took them right into the heart of Greensboro.

"Main Street," he said. "Look around you. See if you recognize anything." He grinned at her.

Openmouthed, she stared from the page of the book to the little town outside her window. "We've just landed in a Walker Evans image captured half a century ago."

He shouted with laughter. "It's amazing, isn't it?"

"Almost as if he did something to freeze it when he snapped the picture." She looked back down at the photograph. "Honestly, the only difference is the make of the automobiles. Otherwise, it looks exactly the same." Even some of the stores were still the same: C.A. Johnson & Son, a clothing goods store, appeared to have the exact same sign, although the awning below it was different. It gave her chills.

He pulled into one of the slanted parking slots in front of a sleepy sidewalk, mostly deserted except for an old dog lying in the sun in front of one of the shops. She put on her dark glasses and got out of the car with the book. He started across the street.

"Come with me," he said. "I want to show you something."

"Wait!" she cried. "Let's walk down the sidewalk. I want to look in these windows and see what's here."

"We will," he said. "Later. There's something you need to see first."

Reluctantly she followed. He led her across the street, down the block a short distance and pointed. "There's the courthouse."

"This is the county seat?"

"Don't you remember? It's in the book."

"You've been here before," she realized.

"A few times."

Without me, she thought with a pang, although there was no reason he shouldn't have come without her. He gestured forward and they walked over to a small square in front of the courthouse, where a statue of a man on a horse rose up before them.

"You know what that is?" he asked.

She squinted at it. "I guess that's supposed to be a Confederate soldier."

He led her to a bench facing the statue and took his camera out of its case as they sat down. "This is where James Agee met them," he said. "Right here, where we are today." He grinned at her.

"Them?" she said, astonished. "The families? Right here?"

"The men. What did he call them? Gudger is one of the names, I recall."

She thumbed through the book in her lap. "Woods and Ricketts are the other names."

He adjusted the lens and looked through the viewer at the statue. "They had all three come into town that day to see if they could get government relief money. Or work. Government work. But were told at the courthouse they didn't qualify because they were already employed."

"Employed?"

"As tenant farmers."

She shook her head and looked through the book for photographs of the three men.

"They were standing around talking, trying to figure something to do, when James Agee came up to them. 1936. Right where we are today. This very statue."

"The rest is history," she mused, flipping back and forth between the pages, staring at the images of the men. Her mind went back fifty years as she tried to imagine what would have gone through the minds of those men— poor, desperate, struggling through the Depression, with wives and children to support on what little they made as tenant farmers, raising a little cotton, a little corn. Suddenly she felt mortally ashamed of herself. Her own petty, self-inflicted problems were nothing compared to the life and death struggles these people had waged against the land and the times that had been set against them.

He stopped fiddling with the knobs on his camera and regarded her.

"It's rather awe-inspiring, isn't it?" she said. "To think this is where the book started."

"He went back with them that same day," he said, rising. "To where they lived. Now go over and stand next to the statue."

"No. Please. Not today."

"Keep your sunglasses on if you're feeling shy," he said, pulling her up. "But I'm going to take this picture."

He took at least two dozen, from different positions around the monument. For the first time she noticed what a beautiful spring day it was, a vast blue sky with a brilliant sun tempered by a perfect breeze.

"Great," he said, placing the cap over the camera lens. "Now let's go down Main Street."

"No," she said. "Let me take one of you. Pick the best position with the sun and show me what button to push."

"I don't want one of me."

"But I do. You've never given me any of your prints, and I'd like one of this. It's only fair."

"Okay." He ran his hands through his hair and took the camera strap from around his neck.

"Focus it for me. I'm hopeless at that."

He bent to one knee, trained the camera on the statue, looked up at the sky. "Let's move around here." After finding the place he wanted, he put the strap around her neck and got into position next to the statue. Then casually, over his shoulder, he made an obscene gesture at the Confederate soldier.

"No," she protested. "Don't ruin my shot."

"How do you want me then?"

"Just be yourself."

"That *was* me."

"You know what I mean."

"Give me something to think about."

"Imagine you're James Agee," she told him. "And you've finally found the white tenant farmers you were assigned to write about for *Fortune* magazine. You've finally found what you've been searching for, and you know it's going to work."

It was perfect; just what she wanted. She clicked several times, just in case.

"Done?" he said, shading his eyes.

"Done."

She took the strap from around her neck and handed him the camera. They walked back across Main Street, down the sidewalk of shops, looking from the photograph in the book to each place they passed, noting what had changed, marveling at what had remained the same. At the end of the block they found a diner. Without consulting her he pushed open the door and ushered her inside.

"Let's sit down for a bit, maybe get a cup of coffee," he suggested.

At this in-between hour, after breakfast but before lunch, it was empty inside except for a few booths filled with older men sipping coffee. Some looked up at the sound of the bell tinkling from its rope on the door, but quickly looked away, seeing no one but strangers they didn't want to be caught staring at rudely. The smell and feel of grease hung heavy in the air. She told him to pick a table while she went to the restroom.

Under the fluorescent lights in a cinderblock bathroom with whitewashed walls, she looked even worse than she'd feared. There wasn't enough makeup in her possession to conceal the red blotches on her cheeks, the mottled skin beneath her eyes, the patch of chafe under her nose, where she'd rubbed it raw from wiping it. Her hair was an unwashed mess. Her eyes were bloodshot. And the only thing in her purse was a bright pink lipstick. It certainly wouldn't help to paint a bright pink pair of lips onto her ruined face, especially because her lower lip had a crust of blood from where she'd bit it. She wasn't worried about the opinion of Nick, who never noticed her looks, but she suspected if she didn't know she looked so dreadful, maybe she wouldn't feel so dreadful. She sighed and leaned over the sink to splash cold water on her hopeless face, then dabbed gently with rough brown towels at the tender flesh.

The waitress was depositing two mugs of coffee and Nick was frowning at a carton of nondairy creamer when she slid into the booth opposite him.

"I'd like a glass of milk too, please," he told the waitress.

"Buttermilk or homogenized?" she asked.

"Not buttermilk," he grinned.

When she came back with the milk, they both poured some into the steaming cups of coffee.

"Are you feeling better?" he asked, looking down at his coffee while he stirred it slowly with his spoon.

She nodded, not wanting to re-open the subject with even a single syllable. Intent on his coffee, he didn't see her. When he looked up, she changed the subject quickly.

"You've been here before, you said."

"Yes," he nodded, sipping his coffee. "I learned the Scullys are originally from around here."

"You're kidding. I don't think you told me that."

"I've only recently become interested in this part of my family history."

"I didn't know you were interested in any part of your family history. Any more than you're interested in the family business."

Just then the waitress arrived with two huge platters of food. She placed an omelet in front of him and pancakes, hash browns and smoked sausage in front of her. She stared down at it.

"I didn't order this," she said when the waitress left.

"I did. Eat it. It'll be good for you."

"I'm not hungry."

"Yes you are."

"I do like smoked sausage," she conceded.

"I remember."

"From when?"

"Those times we went to Bogue's. We got a kick out of eating breakfast for lunch."

She sliced into the sausage with her knife. "So what did you learn about your family's connection to this area?"

"What you would expect," he said, swallowing and wiping his mouth. "They were planters. Cotton."

"How did they get from that to the business in Birmingham?"

"It happened right before the turn of the century, about twenty years after the Civil War," he explained. "Some entrepreneur who had a textile business up north—Pennsylvania—wanted to expand into the South. Birmingham made perfect sense because it was an industrial city close to where a lot of cotton was produced. So he looked for a Southern planter to go into partnership with him, and that was my great great-grandfather. Eventually he did so well that he bought out the Northern businessman and the family got out of cotton farming. Out of the country altogether and into the city."

"Which is why you didn't know about this growing up."

"All I knew is we had some antiques and heirlooms from a plantation in the Black Belt that was once in the family."

"I remember seeing that china in your mother's cabinet. And the silver—" she stopped, struck by the image of the Scully's antebellum family heirlooms, which reminded her of her neighbor, Ken Newsome. Or had he reminded her of the Scullys? She was confused, but couldn't puzzle it out now. "What got you interested in your family's past?"

He finished the last bite of his omelet. "You, actually."

"Me?"

"That box of stuff your aunt gave you. Remember? We went through it and you talked about making something out of it one day. Have you ever tried to?" He peered at her.

She blushed and began shredding the paper napkin in her lap.

"What's wrong?"

She didn't feel much like answering. Instead, she took a bite of hash browns, which she didn't feel much like eating, either. He reached over his empty plate with a fork and lifted one of her silver dollar pancakes.

"Do you still have that box? With those articles? I remember there was a letter from a Confederate general. I know you haven't forgotten."

"No."

"What's the matter?"

"I tried to make a novel out of it," she confessed. "I couldn't. I can't. I think my failure is one reason my life began to unravel. Another reason I grabbed the teaching job. So I wouldn't feel like such a complete failure."

"Failure?" he said, amused. "You tried for how long?"

She toyed with her fork. "Not long. Three months, four months."

"That's not failure. That's called just getting started. Take it from me. I'm the King of Failure. I know what failure is."

"No," she shook her head, started to say that he couldn't know failure if he'd never really tried anything seriously. But this would have been unkind, and besides, she was beginning to get a strange feeling that she didn't know him quite as well as she'd thought. For one thing, if he'd succeeded in kicking a drug habit, or problem, or whatever he wanted to call it, that was not failure.

"Anyway, your idea all those years ago made me start thinking of trying to do my own book," he said. "Not a novel, though. Nonfiction. About my family, going from cotton plantation owners to textile mill owners. It could be the story of the South, to some extent, not just my own family. The move from rural and agricultural before the war, to industrial cities and businesses after the war. Not just for wealthy white people either, but white tenant farmers and former slaves moved to cities to work in the mills. My father has a file cabinet full of documents, account ledgers, record books, and receipts that go all the way back to the beginning, to the founding of the business. Some of the stuff is even from the plantation."

She stared at him, her face breaking into a smile. As much as she loved his idea for a book, she loved his enthusiasm even more. "Have you done anything to get started?"

He thrust his hands through his hair. "There's a lot more research I need to do. But I have shown some of the family material to Stan Ellerby. You know who that is?"

She shook her head. "The name is familiar, but I don't think so."

He reached over and speared another silver dollar pancake. "He's a professor of Southern history at the University of Alabama. He wrote that book about the steel mills in Birmingham."

"Oh, yes. He's a famous scholar. Didn't that book win some kind of award?"

"The National Book Award. Anyway, I made an appointment with him at his campus office in Tuscaloosa one day about a year ago. He was very encouraging. Said he'd rarely seen such a private collection of 'primary source material'—is what he called it—and told me the way the journey from country to city was contained all in one family would make this a great book."

"Nick!"

"He suggested I take some of his classes. He teaches a couple of graduate seminars that he said would help me learn the history and get me going on the research."

"Why don't you? Why haven't you?"

"He's been on sabbatical this year. I'd have to start next fall."

"I'll be in the graduate program in English then," she said. "I'll take three graduate courses and teach one undergraduate class."

He raised his eyebrows. "I didn't realize you'd made any decisions yet."

"I planned to do this eventually, regardless. Anyway, I'm so happy about your book. It's wonderful to have a solid project."

"I don't know about solid, but it *is* fun. I've been photographing at the mills, even the one in Sylacauga I was supposed to manage. Going through all the documents. Many of them are handwritten, and the not-so-fun part is typing them up. I thought about hiring someone to do this, but somehow it helps me learn the material, trying to decipher the faded handwriting from another era."

"Sounds like a lot of work."

The bell on the front door tinkled as a group of customers walked in. They greeted some of the men who were just rising from one of the booths. Nick looked at his watch. "I've got to find a payphone and call my accountant," he said. "The tax man cometh and there are one or two items we've got to discuss today. Would you believe I actually have a talent for making my money grow?" He grinned and began sliding toward the edge of the booth.

She shook her head, smiling. "What was your major in college? Remind me."

"Art history," he laughed, running his hands through his hair before taking out his wallet. "But I always liked *Monopoly* as a kid. I usually won; I made the right investments. Same thing seems to be happening now, with the *Monopoly* money I got from my family."

"I'm impressed."

"Don't be. Any fool can make money out of money. And anybody who started life with as much money as I did has no excuse not to have made a whole lot more. It's actually kind of fun to play with it, even if it's not a particularly profound occupation. But I've got to find a phone. You want to stay here or walk around?"

"I'd like to go in some of these little shops and poke around."

"Okay. I'll find you."

He didn't wait for a check, just left two twenties and got up from the booth. She looked at the money, more than twice what was necessary.

"*Monopoly* money," he said, and winked.

* * *

She was in the hardware store when he found her, purchasing potholders decorated with the name of the shop in big block letters, followed by the name of the town in smaller print below.

"I bought two for each of us." She held his out for him.

"The perfect souvenir," he said. "Thank you."

"Now that I know you can cook."

The cashier offered a bag with the change and the receipt.

"Two bags if you don't mind," she said.

They walked back to his car.

"Do you want to go straight back, or would you like to see where they lived?" He unlocked her door and opened it.

"Where they lived?" She stared at him.

"The three families."

He pushed her gently toward her seat, but she couldn't budge. *"You know where they lived?"*

He nodded. "I've been there."

"You've been there?" She sat down in a daze as he closed the door.

"You know we always talked about visiting Hale County," he said when he got in beside her. "We never did, so I came here a couple of times on my own. I went to the courthouse once, and they gave me the name of a guy who could take me there." Looking in the rearview mirror, he eased out of the parking slot.

"Where is it?"

"Back the way we came. Back up 69 about fifteen miles, then take a right on some road. I've got the name in the glove compartment."

"I can't believe this."

"You want to go then?"

"Are you kidding? Of course I want to go! Are the houses still there?"

He shook his head. "There was a pile of pine boards used to be one of the shacks, so I was told. But maybe my guide just wanted a bigger tip."

She had a hundred questions, but suddenly he wasn't listening. On the edge of the town, he veered over into the gas station.

"I'm sorry," he said. "I just thought of something else I need to tell my accountant. Will you be okay in here while I make a call?"

He was in the phone booth for a good half hour. She leafed through the book, reading passages at random, wishing now she'd brought her own copy, which had markings and underlinings indicating her favorite parts.

"I'm sorry," he apologized when he got back in. "Are you terribly fed up with me?"

"Don't worry; I had Agee." She tapped on the book, smiling. "Did you get your tax matters straightened out?"

He frowned as he pulled the seatbelt strap across his chest. "I think so. For today."

"I didn't realize you were so busy with so many things."

"What things?" He cranked up the car and pulled out of the station.

"Your investments. Your book project. Tennis. Someone told me not long ago that you won the men's singles in the BCC tournament last month."

He shrugged. "My days are full. But my life is still empty."

"Empty? In what way?"

"How is any life empty? At least one important piece is missing without which life is empty."

"The book is an important piece if you do it."

He nodded. "A project about my family's history pleases me. I think because it connects me to significant elements in my past. Makes me feel like I'm putting myself together somehow."

"Does your family realize you finally took an interest in the business, so to speak?" She smiled over at him.

"Oh, this wouldn't matter to them. Just another one of my useless hobbies, they'd say." He reached under his seat, produced the thermos of tea and offered it to her. She opened it and passed it back to him. "You don't want any?" he asked.

She shook her head. "Does your family know about your investment success?"

He shrugged, handed the thermos back to her.

"Why don't you tell them?" She screwed the cap back on and placed the thermos on the floorboard. "I'm sure they'd like to know. They're probably afraid you're just running through your money. I bet they have no idea how well you're managing it and making it grow. They all have the wrong impression of you."

"I'd rather they base their impression of me on something other than money or success in business. That's part of the whole problem."

"But this isn't just about money. This is a character issue."

"Tell me how money is a character issue."

She gave him a look of exasperation. "You know exactly what I mean. You said it yourself earlier, about there being no excuse not to have made more money considering what you were given. It's about not wasting what life gave you. About taking what you started with and making something out of it instead of throwing it away or not making use of it. And you *are* making something out of it—your money, your life. But your family doesn't know this about you. They think you're just wasting your life like they probably think you've wasted your money. They don't know who you really are."

"Well, if they knew about my investments, they would just tell me to go into business as a financial consultant or something. What my father wants is for me to be respectable in a way he respects. Have a job he can mention to his golfing buddies at the country club. A job they'll understand. But I'm not interested in making a *career* out of moving money around. My God! I'd rather be a drug addict." He pushed his hair off his forehead. "Would you look in the glove box and find that piece of paper with the name of the road?"

Tucked between the owner's manual and his car registration packet she found a tattered envelope. "Gabriel Creek Road?"

"That's it. Help me look for it. We take a right."

For several slow, winding miles they said little as they looked for the turn. They found it not too far from where they had spotted the old barn on the other side of the road on their way down earlier that morning. Soon after taking this right turn off 69, the road began to climb. They passed a few trailers with neatly kept yards.

"What do you imagine they do for a living?"

"Catfish farming is the main industry here now. I'd guess they work for one of those companies. But that's just a guess."

"You'd have to find out. For your book."

"Why do you say that?"

"Because that's part of the story. What happened here, when cotton left but the people stayed."

"The catfish came."

They laughed. The road continued at an incline. Pavement gave way to gravel, the trailers with yards out front gave way to pine woods on either side. Then the gravel became a dirt road.

"Nick, are you sure about this?"

He grinned. "Did you really think asphalt would lead us into Agee territory?"

"What's the name of it? Where we're going?"

"Look on the envelope. Didn't I write it down?"

She looked at the paper in her lap. "Mills Hill?"

"That rings a bell. It was called something else in the book."

"It really is a hill, isn't it?"

When they reached what seemed to be the top, where the hill plateaued, the pine trees thinned suddenly and the road came to an end at a clearing.

"This is it," he announced.

For a moment she sat there in reverie, unable to move from the car, as the knowledge of what James Agee and Walker Evans had found in this spot half a century ago came over her. Through the windshield she could see a tumbledown shack up ahead.

"That's not one of the houses, then?" she pointed.

"No." He shook his head. "That's much more recent. Come on, I'll take you to the place I was shown."

Slowly she got out of the car and followed him through broken glass, rusted cans, thorny weeds which scratched her ankles. It was hard to look around because she had to watch every step so carefully. He led her near the edge of the hill, if that's what it was, and indicated a heap of old boards she was about to walk on as if it were just more debris.

"This is what I was told was one of the houses." He squatted down.

"This?" She knelt beside him. "You're sure?"

"I'm sure this is what I was told."

"Did you take a picture?" She brushed her hand softly along one of the boards as if it were an expensive piece of lumber in a showroom.

"I did take a photograph. Should I take another?"

"I'd actually like to be in one with this. If you don't mind."

"I'm going to get the tripod for this." He turned and started running back to his car.

"Be careful!" she called out after him.

When he returned, she was sitting cross-legged on the ground, reading from the book, and didn't look up as he set up his equipment. She had found one of her favorite passages, which Agee had written in verse.

> How were we caught?
> What, what is it has happened?
> What is it has been happening that we are living the way we are?
> How was it we were caught?

She was murmuring the lines to herself, unaware that he'd begun snapping pictures until he asked her to look up for the next one. She did so, holding the book in her lap with its cover facing the camera.

"Do you want to explore some?"

"Yes." She rose and cast a last glance at the boards she'd been sitting next to. "Let's go take a look at that place."

Leaving the tripod where it was, they picked their way slowly through vines, brambles and litter over toward the collapsing wooden shack. He tested the boards of the steps; some were sagging, others looked rotten. He stood on the open threshold that lacked a door and told her where to put her feet. The floor of the house didn't seem any more sound, and they tread gingerly with each step. If the house had ever contained any fixtures, those had been stripped. But it was filled with junk: milk jugs, plastic bottles, rusted mattress springs, broken chair legs. One of the rooms in the rear was piled so high with trash it seemed to have been used as a dump. Her eyes glazed with dismay. This wasn't history; this was now.

"Don't take a picture of this," she told him when she emerged from the room.

"What are you thinking?" He regarded her with curiosity.

"What Agee thought. I feel like a snoop, a privileged intruder into someone else's misery. The worst kind of voyeur."

"It *is* hard to take. We can leave. There's something else I want to show you anyway. We need to get back in the car."

But on her way out, she stopped by a window with no panes of glass, and stood staring through the empty frame at the pines and kudzu beyond, rooted to the spot. He waited for her at the threshold which had no door.

"Come on," he said. "What's wrong?"

For a moment she didn't answer, just stood staring out the window as if she hadn't heard. Then she sighed and began tiptoeing across the creaking planks. Most of these were warped, with cracks between them.

"It just occurred to me how close we are to Tuscaloosa and even Birmingham. But this feels like a different universe, a different time period. Yet we're not even sixty miles away from Tuscaloosa. Not even an hour away."

Distrusting the steps, he jumped down from the porch and held out a hand to help her do the same. "Thanks," she said, letting go of his hand. She turned around to look back at the house. "Actually," she said. "I've changed my mind. I think I *would* like you to photograph this place."

He was amused, but began unzipping the camera case.

"Do you mind?"

"Of course not. Just curious."

She shook her head. "Yesterday," she began. "Not an hour away from here, I was in a sorority house that had a white marble floor in the foyer and a crystal chandelier. It's almost inconceivable that just a few miles away, people are still living in shacks. One place is filled with elegance and refinement and beautiful girls; another has only the ruins of a miserable existence."

"The South has always been like that," he said, his face obscured by the camera. "The slave cabins were never too far away from the plantation manor." The camera clicked and he looked at her. "Do you want to be in this photograph?"

"No. I just wanted a reminder of what we saw."

They began walking back to the tripod and then the car. The sun blazed through rows of pine trees in the distance. It must have been around two o'clock.

"But we didn't see it, did we?" she asked him.

"See what?"

"Growing up in Mountain Brook, everybody was all alike."

"That's the whole point of Mountain Brook," he laughed.

"That's one reason I never particularly wanted to move back."

"But we did," he said. "We came back into the crucible that formed us."

"Why did we do that to ourselves?"

"Maybe because we're not yet fully formed? I've been told that about myself by many different people in my life." He laughed.

Back in the car, he let it coast slowly on the way down, his foot on the brake.

"Look for another dirt road to the right," he told her.

"You're kidding."

When he found what he thought he was looking for, he had to come to a complete stop and carefully maneuver from one narrow dirt road onto one even more narrow, squeezed on both sides by pine trees. This involved reversing, turning, and inching forward slowly several times. The road seemed little more than a trail.

"Nick, are you sure this is right?"

"No," he laughed.

"I feel like we're going into the heart of Alabama darkness," she said. "This can't be good for your car."

"Just red clay. Nothing that won't wash off."

Finally they arrived at another smaller clearing, where they saw a weather-beaten and collapsing shack much like the one they'd just left behind.

"This is the place where Agee lived with the family."

"The house?"

"No," he said, shaking his head. "Not the same house. Although the same little girl lived in this house when she was older. That's what I was told."

"Which little girl?"

He took the book from her and found the photograph, one of the most famous, of a ten year-old girl with wide-set eyes wearing a homemade straw sunhat.

He pointed. "Maggie Louise, he called her."

She peered over at the portrait of the child. "I remember. He loved that little girl. Thought she was so smart, had so much potential. He encouraged her to get an education, told her she didn't have to stay in Alabama the rest of her life and pick cotton."

"You know what happened to her?" He looked over.

She shook her head.

"About three years ago," he said, drumming his fingers on the steering wheel. "Four years ago now. She killed herself with rat poison."

Thunderstruck, she grabbed the book from his lap and stared hard at the photograph of the ten-year-old girl as her eyes blurred. "Why?" she cried stupidly. "Why? Why?"

"The right question is 'Why not?'" he said, getting out of the car.

Dazed, she got out of the car and walked with him over to the house. "She didn't get her education," she said. "She didn't get out."

"Does that surprise you?"

"It's just such a terrible, tragic irony. The University of Alabama is less than an hour away, yet this girl had no chance for an education."

"Well, you yourself know how hard it is to get out of your allotted place in Southern society. I don't think this girl got out of picking cotton until her twenties. Then I believe she worked at a truck stop."

He took photographs, but she was adamant in her refusal to go inside the house. An odd sense of delicacy prevented her from invading the privacy of a dead woman, the girl whose spirit and promise had died somewhere in a cotton field nearby.

"What's wrong?" he asked her.

As she struggled to formulate her response, her mind was grasping at all those fragments of family history she had grappled with for her novel. The shock of learning what had happened to Maggie Louise had catalyzed her consciousness and forced all those pieces to start falling into place.

"We are implicated in her death," she told Nick as they walked back to the car. "We're accessories to her suicide."

"My family could not have been their landlord," he told her. "They were out of cotton by the 1930s."

"You know what I mean." She lifted her door handle, but didn't get in and stood there staring intently at him on the other side of the car. "Both our families have been landlords—and much worse—in the past. Basically, most families who made it to Mountain Brook did so from the labor of people they exploited. Ten-year-old girls! Who didn't go to school because they were out in the fields picking cotton! Cotton that probably went to your family's mill in Birmingham."

"I know what you mean," he said quietly. "You think I haven't thought all this through before for myself? Why do you think I can't stand the idea of those textile mills? They used to use child labor too, you know." Abruptly he got in the car and slammed the door.

Chastened, she got in beside him. "I'm sorry, Nick," she said softly. "I was not just referring to you. I was talking about all of the families who prospered in Alabama. Who made it big in Mountain Brook. I didn't mean to say it was your own personal responsibility."

He put the keys in the ignition but didn't crank the car. "But it's hard to figure out just what my personal responsibility is," he said. "That's part of my whole problem in life. And by the way, from what I can tell, my great great-grandfather certainly did bring his plantation mentality to managing the mill's workforce, most of whom had been sharecroppers or tenant farmers on someone else's land. Many of them descended from slaves."

"That was a long time ago. I'm sure it's changed a lot in a hundred years," she said, as he released the emergency break and started the engine.

"Yes, but you can see why I've never felt like being a part of it," he said. "Not to mention the godawful boredom of managing a mill."

"I do see. I understand."

They said little as the car made its precarious way from one dirt road to another and then coasted slowly down the hill back onto Hwy 69. In some ways, Caroline reflected, her own quandary was a lot like Nick's. Although she had not inherited a personal fortune, she had inherited a life of privilege and affluence that had been built at the expense of others whose humbled lives occupied most of the rest of her state outside the bubble of Mountain Brook. She didn't know exactly what she owed back, but she did know she owed something. Perhaps this was why she had returned: there was a debt she had to pay. Perhaps this was why she had been attracted to a political animal like her husband. Politics offered a much more immediate and concrete form of reparation than literature. But education was probably the best remedy of all, and the classes she had taught at the University of Alabama had contained girls like Maggie Louise as well as sorority girls like the ones in the Kappa house. Although black students made up less than ten percent of the campus population, even twenty-three years after its integration, Caroline had taught a few of these students, at least one of whom was descended from slaves.

"What I can't get over," she said suddenly, tapping the photograph of the ten-year-old Maggie Louise. "This girl tells one truth about Alabama. Then those beautiful girls I saw yesterday in the sorority house tell another truth about Alabama."

"Beautiful sorority girls end up drinking rat poison too," he said. "Just like sons of mill owners put poison in their veins."

For something to do, she retrieved the thermos of tea from the floorboard, unscrewed the cap and took several sips although she wasn't particularly thirsty. She handed him the thermos and he took several long swallows. "The two different truths are still so difficult to reconcile," she said. "You know my husband's grandparents on both sides . . ."

He wiped his mouth with the back of his hand and gave her back the thermos. "Yes? I'm listening."

"They all went through the Depression as sharecroppers." She screwed the thermos cap back on. "They would have been like the kids in the families Agee wrote about. My husband's granny on his father's side lived in a shack like something right out of this book. I've seen it for myself."

"Where?"

"South Alabama."

"But they made it," he said, looking over at her. "They didn't kill themselves with rat poison. Their children don't pick cotton. And their grandson graduated from Harvard."

"It's remarkable, isn't it?"

"Is that why you fell in love with him?"

The question startled her. She hadn't really thought of it that way. "It's part of what I respect," she said. "That his family came from nothing except themselves. That he had nothing going for him except himself, and was determined to make something out of his life. And he is succeeding. You know . . . I think . . ." She turned her head and stared out the window, struck by a thought which had just occurred to her.

"What?"

"I remember him telling me, when we first met in college, that he used to dream about dating a girl from Mountain Brook."

"Aha!" he grinned at her. "The ultimate symbol of success, that you have made it in Alabama, if you got that Mountain Brook girl on your arm."

"It's not a joke," she said, irritated. "This is my marriage. Which has turned into a joke. Because I was probably more of a symbol to him than an individual woman. Now he's found a woman who's an even better symbol than I am. A sorority girl. A Kappa. A Southern belle. A beauty. I may come from Mountain Brook society, but I'm not really a society girl, and that's what he wants, to go in that Mountain Brook house he's going to buy. Then he will have completed his own family's journey from country to city."

She bit her lip and reopened the split where blood had crusted over. With one of the tissues she dabbed gently and then licked the sore spot. For a mile or two they were silent.

"You know it's not going to last," he said quietly.

"What's not going to last?"

"This craziness between the two of them."

"Maybe," she shrugged. "Maybe not. It doesn't matter now."

"Why do you say that? He'll probably come to his senses in a few months or even a few weeks. You could work this out. End up with a stronger relationship."

"I called him this morning before you came to get me, and told him he could go forward with his divorce proceedings."

"What?!" he cried, looking over so abruptly that the car swerved across the center line. Regaining control, he shoved his hand through his hair and then gripped the steering wheel. "Why didn't you tell me?" Then the car swerved again as he pulled unexpectedly into the parking lot of a Jitney Junior, where he came to a stop in a far corner, near the air pump. Unbuckling his seat belt, he leaned back against his door, folded his arms across his chest and regarded her with piercing intensity. "Now tell me what this is all about young lady," he said. "No beating around the bush. Talk to me and tell it straight."

"I *have* been talking to you," she protested, almost laughing. "For days."

"But this decision?" He seemed to be only half joking as he assumed the stern, inquisitive manner of a schoolteacher, shaking his head in consternation.

"It's simple, really," she said. "After I got back from that lunch at the sorority house yesterday, I understood that he didn't love me. Even more, I understood that I didn't love him either."

"This is too sudden," he said, shaking his head again. "You've been together over three years."

"Would those be the same three years when he dated a cheerleader? Tried to date Lily Templeton? And who knows how many others?" When he didn't speak, she went on. "You know, when he started law school here and I went back for my sophomore year, he said to me 'Let's just see what happens.' I was devastated. To me that meant breaking up. He said it just meant 'seeing what happens.' But when I pointed out, somewhat hysterically, that there was no middle ground—we were either committed or broken up—he proposed the next day. Obviously I should have realized that he wanted more women to 'happen' than just me. Only I'm just now finding out what 'happened' behind my back. When we were engaged."

"Pass me some of that iced tea, would you?" He reached for the thermos, took off the cap and drank the rest of the tea in three long gulps. "What do you mean you realized you didn't love him?"

"I'm afraid what I loved was having someone who loved me. I loved the feeling that someone out there loved me, and he gave me that feeling. When I realized he didn't love me . . . well, it's remarkable how little I actually miss *him*. I mean his presence, his company. When I first met him, in college, we seemed to have everything in common. And up there, we did. We were two people from Alabama at Harvard. Alabama is a lot to have in common at Harvard. You should know this from going to school up north yourself."

He nodded but said nothing.

She gave a rueful laugh. "But now that the two of us are back in Alabama, we seem to have nothing in common. So my pain is not from losing this person, but from losing the love I thought I had. But he doesn't love me. And it's not *him* I loved. My stupid infatuation with the neighbor was probably my first clue, although I didn't recognize it at the time."

There was a long silence after she put all that out there for both of them to hear. Somehow it made her feelings official and irrevocable, to put them into words.

"So," he said.

"So," she looked at her lap. "I'm going to let this happen. He's sending the documents by overnight delivery. They'll arrive tomorrow. I think she must be withholding some of her charms, because he's prepaying overnight return delivery." He smirked at that, but she pretended not to notice.

"Can it really be that quick?" he said, dubious.

"Three days after he files the divorce petition. He said it again: three days."

"No, I mean the money, the property . . ."

"There are no assets," she said. "He comes from sharecroppers, remember? He's only got debt. And I don't have a trust fund like you, so there's no money involved, no property. Just the cars, the wedding gifts, some furniture. We're each keeping what's ours, except I get his old car that I've been driving."

"That car is a piece of shit," he said. "First thing you do: get rid of that fucking car." He felt beside him for the door handle, pulled on it and hopped out. Leaning back in, with his hands on the hood, he asked if she wanted anything from the convenience store.

"I'll go use the restroom," she said.

When she returned he was already back with a half-eaten Hershey bar in one hand. He held up a yellow bag of peanut M&Ms. She shook her head. "No thanks." They didn't speak as he pulled out of the lot and finished the rest of his chocolate bar.

"Are you okay with all this?" he said, handing her the empty candy wrapper.

"How do I seem?"

"Not so good this morning," he told her.

"How do I seem now?"

"Better," he grinned.

She smiled back. "Today helped a lot. It was like old times, like what we used to do together. It was a good idea to come here."

"I thought so. But where should I take you now? How about I drive you back to Birmingham, so you can discuss all this with your husband in person?"

"No," she shook her head. "He's hell-bent on divorce. And it's for the best, really. Even if he changed his mind, it wouldn't give us the love I thought we had."

"So back to your apartment?"

She hesitated, shuddering at the memory of her sleepless, sorrow-filled night. "I guess that's the only place I have now." She tried to sound cheerful about it.

"You could come to the river."

"Oh, no. I know you need to get back to Birmingham. Deal with your taxes. Your *Monopoly* money."

"Actually, I was planning to go back to the river myself and spend the rest of the week there. I've got everything I need in the trunk. Why don't you come with me?"

The prospect was tempting. She could use some distance between herself, the dreary apartment and the dismal truths she'd arrived at there in the dead of a terrible night.

"Come on," he urged. "It will do you good. It will do me good too, to have company. *Please.*"

"Okay." She stifled a yawn, which she tried to transform into a smile. "If you're sure."

"I'm sure. But what about let's stop talking and you take a nap the rest of the way back?"

"I'm not that tired," she lied.

"Yes you are," he grinned.

"We never did talk about that missing piece."

"Missing piece? What do you mean?"

"In your life. That makes it empty."

"Oh, that. I'll tell you later. Get some rest now."

As she drifted into sleep, she suddenly recalled what he'd given her that Christmas. It was one of his jokes: a box filled with hastily assembled home-made coupons, obviously cobbled together at the last minute after she'd mentioned she had a Christmas present she was bringing for him that day. **This coupon is good for** *One Movie of your Choice;* **This coupon is good for** *One lunch at the place of your choosing;* **This coupon is good for** *One souvenir at the next gift shop;* **This coupon is good for** *One pizza of your design.* It was just like Nick: silly and sweet and good for a laugh. She'd put the box away in a drawer and never thought of it again, until now. Probably that box was still in her old bedroom, at her parents' house. As her thoughts turned into dreams, she was transported back to her old room, where she went rummaging through the clothes bureau until she found the box full of unredeemed coupons. Clutching it, she ran back downstairs and outside, into the orange Karmann Ghia shuddering at the top of the driveway. Gleefully she made her selection from the box and handed it over to him. **This coupon is good for . . .**

~ 20 ~

On the day that Daniel learned his wife was agreeing to divorce, Lily had plans that evening with her family to celebrate her father's birthday. In a year's time, Daniel realized, he could be included in those plans. But tonight it would have been inappropriate. Lily congratulated him on his news, but she didn't offer and he didn't ask to join her family later on. Needing to celebrate just a little himself, Daniel knocked on his neighbor's door, although he wasn't sure if Ken was back. He'd been gone for over a week on an assignment, and Daniel had not seen his car in the lot when he'd pulled in tonight after work. But to his delight, Ken came padding to the door in his sock feet and appeared glad to see Daniel.

"I just got home an hour ago," said Ken, gesturing for Daniel to enter the apartment. "I'm afraid I'm not up to going out tonight."

"Me either," he said. "I've got to get up early and drive to Montgomery tomorrow for a deposition."

"Beer?" offered his neighbor.

"Sure," he said.

In the last several months, Daniel had come to really like his neighbor and enjoy his company. Although Ken's family was much more well-to-do than his own, they had both grown up in small towns in Alabama, which gave them an instant bond. Ken was quiet and thoughtful, an excellent listener, which is exactly what Daniel had needed recently. Tonight he just needed to share his news and drink a beer with a friend. The only thing he was a little worried about was the timing. Today was Tuesday; he had sent the documents express mail for delivery in Tuscaloosa tomorrow, Wednesday. If she signed and sent them back the same day as she had promised, he would have them in hand Thursday. Friday he could file them officially at the courthouse. According to what he'd been told, the divorce petition should be granted by the following Wednesday. The closing on the sale of the house was set for

Thursday of the following week, eight days later. So there should be plenty of time for the divorce to go through before the closing took place. But what if there was a glitch of some kind? What if the petition was rejected for an unforeseen reason and had to be resubmitted? Would there be time before the act of sale on the house?

Ken rose from his chair and left the room to get fresh beers. Handing Daniel a bottle, he sat down in the other corner of the settee and regarded Daniel carefully. This is what Daniel really appreciated about his neighbor. So far Ken had not said a word. He had taken in everything Daniel had said, treated it with utmost seriousness and was now thoughtfully formulating his response. It would not be the kind of glib reassurance that was more dismissal of the subject than anything else, and usually made Daniel feel worse rather than better.

"Didn't you tell me an attorney in your firm prepared the document?" Ken asked.

Daniel nodded.

"What did he say about it?"

"That it's perfectly straightforward. If both parties agree, the judge isn't likely to raise objections. There are enough contested divorces to deal with that the court isn't going to turn an uncontested one into a problem."

Ken smiled. "What are you worried about then?"

Daniel gnawed the inside of his cheek. What was he worried about? Something, for sure, but he couldn't put his finger on what. Mainly, it all seemed too good to be true. With disgust, he realized he had the same problem as his parents: he couldn't trust good news. When Caroline had called this morning to tell him she was ready to sign his papers, he'd had a moment of pure exhilaration. Then the fear that something would go wrong had begun to creep in and slowly suffocate his happiness. But what could go wrong?

"Sounds to me," Ken was saying, "the only hitch could be some minor mistake in the preparation of the document. Which I doubt. But say the judge finds something. What then?"

Daniel had asked this very question of the attorney who'd prepared the divorce petition. He took a nervous sip of beer. What had the guy told him? Daniel nearly choked as the words came back to him. Coughing, he put his beer down on the tray-table in front of him.

"All we have to do is *amend* the document," he said. "Not resubmit. It can even be done the same day."

Joy surged through his body and he practically jumped up from the sofa in his rekindled excitement. Ken seemed to rise along with him. Daniel was prepared for a high-five; instead, Ken kissed him. Absorbed in his own swirling emotions, Daniel's first thought was that this wasn't what he'd expected. Then the reality of it dawned as Ken sat there looking at him searchingly. Daniel had been through this exact scenario in college with his minister, who was still a good friend. It didn't bother him; he just felt sorry he wouldn't be able to give Ken what he wanted. His neighbor was a good friend too.

Before either of them could say anything, the telephone from his apartment started ringing. Daniel had put the volume on high so he could hear the phone in case Lily called. Jumping up from his seat, he quickly thanked Ken for the beer, apologized for needing to answer the call, and rushed into his apartment to reach the phone in time.

Unfortunately, it wasn't Lily calling but his best friend Will Hill in Mobile, where he was a labor lawyer and his wife was in her pediatric residency. Daniel had left a message on Will's machine earlier that day. After Caroline called, Daniel thought he owed it to his friend to be among the first to hear the news straight from him.

But Daniel had forgotten that Will wouldn't know enough to be happy about this news, and in fact, his friend was somber and sad, going on and on about how sorry he and Rhea were for what had happened, couldn't believe it, didn't understand it, would never have predicted divorce. "Do you have time to talk? Tell me what happened?" Will asked. "I'm here for you, buddy."

Technically, Daniel did have time to talk, but did not want to tie up the line in case Lily tried to reach him. He needed to make this short with Will tonight, and fill him in fully another time.

"Everything's fine, Will," he told his friend. "It's good, really. This is what I want. I'm happy."

Will was silent. Then he said, "But what *happened*?"

Will could be so *inquisitive,* and Daniel was in no mood to be cross-examined.

"I'm glad you're okay," Will went on mournfully. "When Rhea and I heard your message, we figured . . . well . . . this is awkward, buddy . . . but we guessed Caroline must have had an affair or something."

"No, no," Daniel said with impatience. "Nothing like that. No one's having an affair," he said, before stopping to consider whether blow jobs constituted an affair. He didn't think so. And he didn't think sleeping with someone not his wife just one time amounted to an affair either.

"Daniel, I don't understand," Will said. "What is going on?"

Will could be so tiresome. Daniel said, "Look, I don't have time to go into this tonight. Just know that I'm happy about it."

"Now I'm really worried, Daniel," Will said seriously, with no intention of getting off the phone anytime soon. He seemed to be digging in for a lengthy interrogation. "Happiness is not the usual response to divorce."

"Trust me," Daniel said. "It's all for the best. It just didn't work out."

"Daniel," Will said. "You two made it through *three years* apart. If your relationship wasn't solid, it would never have survived that separation. There's something you're not telling me."

Ignoring this last statement, Daniel focused on the first. "Actually, Will, I think we *grew apart* more than we were aware during those *three years* apart. So once we got married, we realized we didn't have the relationship we thought we had. Simple as that." Daniel was rather proud of coming up with this explanation on short notice. It might even have been true.

"So this is entirely mutual, then? Caroline is in complete agreement?"

Much as he wanted to lay the issue to rest and put this conversation to bed, Daniel hesitated. It would be entirely like Will to call his mother, with whom he was close, and give her the third degree. As a Southern Baptist who lived in constant fear of the wrath of an angry God, his mother would strictly adhere to the commandment Thou Shalt Not Lie. If Will asked about Caroline, his mother would tell him the truth and nothing but the truth.

"Caroline suggested marital counseling," he admitted to Will. "At first. But now she's agreed to sign the papers. So all is well."

His friend was silent for so long that Daniel knew he should have risked a lie. Glancing at his watch, he wondered if he could plead fatigue. But it was only eight-thirty.

"Why didn't *you* want counseling, buddy?"

"No point. When you know, you know."

"What is it you know, Daniel?"

"That it's over. Listen"—

"No, you listen. When Rhea and I heard your message tonight—we played it over and over and talked about it—we both reached the same conclusion. Caroline must be having an affair with someone in Tuscaloosa. A colleague, a professor in the department or something. She told you about it, or you found out. Whatever, we assumed she had done something; you said she was *estranged*. But that's not what I've been hearing from you, and now you're telling me that she wanted counseling but you didn't. What in the hell is going on?"

"Can I call you tomorrow?" Daniel asked.

Will drew a deep breath. "Daniel?" he said, and paused to take another deep breath. "Do you realize this is the first time we've spoken in *months*? I have called you repeatedly to no avail, and left dozens of messages on your answering machine that have never been returned. Now I'm beginning to suspect that you've been avoiding me, and I'm really beginning to be afraid of the reason why."

"Can I call you tomorrow?" Daniel asked again.

"What I propose, Daniel, is that I come up there this weekend. To Birmingham. Rhea will be in rotation, so it's not a problem for me. I can even pick up Caroline and bring her over, so the three of us can sit down and try to figure this out before a horrible mistake is made."

"Will"— Daniel tried to object.

"Hear me out," his friend insisted. "You've always been very impulsive in your personal life, Daniel. I saw this over and over when we were in college. I'm afraid you're rushing into something you'll soon regret. Let me come up this weekend to help you sort it out."

"No!" Daniel told him emphatically.

"What is it you're not telling me, Daniel?"

"Nothing. Only I won't be in town this weekend," Daniel lied.

"Okay, Daniel," agreed Will, sounding fed up. "Call me tomorrow then. In the meantime, I want you to know that Rhea and I are very concerned. And I know there's something you're not telling me. Tomorrow night when you call, I want to hear what it is."

With relief Daniel hung up and looked at his watch. Ten till nine, not too late to call. But Lily wasn't home. What a dutiful daughter, Daniel reflected, to give up her entire evening to celebrate her father's birthday.

Then Daniel was struck by a terrible thought: What if Caroline changed her mind? What if she decided she couldn't go through with it and didn't sign the document or send it back when she said she would? *What if Will Hill called her and asked her to wait?* Any delay of more than a few days could complicate his plans entirely.

Daniel became so filled with alarm that he rushed into the hallway to knock on his neighbor's door. At the last minute he refrained, remembering there was a reason he shouldn't be doing this. He looked at his watch. Nine o'clock. That must be the reason his instincts had prevented him from knocking: it was too late. His neighbor had recently returned from out of town, and would be tired. Vaguely Daniel thought there might be another reason, but at the moment he couldn't recall what it was.

~ 21 ~

"Have you ever thought about living out here?" She turned to see Nick's reply as they leaned against the railing of the deck, where they'd been gazing at the water after clearing the remains of dinner from the patio table.

"I always imagine I want to live out here," he told her. "I love it on the river. It's so beautiful, and I get so much work done whenever I come."

"Have you ever tried moving out here?"

"I've never made it more than a long weekend by myself."

"Really?" She was surprised. "Why is that?"

"It's just so isolated out here. It's not that I need much in the way of human society, but I need more than what's available here, which is zero. After about two days alone, I'm so starved for companionship that I go scampering back to Birmingham with my tail between my legs." He looked at her with amusement. "That's why I'm so glad you agreed to come back with me. I'll be able to stay out here and finish all the work on my taxes."

She considered this for a moment in all seriousness. "I see what you mean," she said. "I've loved being out here alone during the day, but then again, I knew you were coming back in the evening."

"That makes all the difference, doesn't it? To have somebody you can be with in the evening?"

"Yes," she agreed, smiling. "I suppose that's why I got married so young. I don't have many people in my life, and I do need at least that one other person to be with in the evening." Struck by a thought, she turned toward him again. "That's your missing piece, isn't it?"

Instead of replying, he only laughed, tugged on the sleeve of her sweater, and said, "Let's go downstairs. I'll build a fire."

* * *

Tired after the day's excursion into Hale County, they were both content just to lean back against the cushions and gaze at the flickering firelight without speaking. There was only one thing she wanted to say now anyway, which was thanks. Without his help, she would have been mired in confusion over what had happened to her marriage as well as indecision over how to handle it, for months or possibly years. How could she properly thank someone for that kind of help, which normally required a paid professional who couldn't do nearly as much in such a short period of time? She struggled to rise from the soft depths of the sofa as her mind scrambled to put the right words together. He leaned forward and peered at her closely in the dim light, no doubt wondering if she was on the verge of another outburst of emotion or grief. She tried without success to say what was on her mind.

"Are you all right?" he said.

She nodded, started to speak, but still couldn't find the appropriate language. It all seemed inadequate. Instead, she just looked at him, and was startled to notice how handsome he was. Actually, she'd always known this, but had succeeded in closing her mind to it because she and Nick were just friends. They weren't interested in each other as anything more, she had assured her father years ago, when trying to persuade him to continue allowing Nick to take her out, just during the day, for hikes at Oak Mountain or a visit to the statue of Vulcan. Nick didn't want her as a girlfriend; he already had a girlfriend, plenty of them, one after another in regular succession.

"What are you thinking?" he said, leaning closer, as if to catch the merest whisper.

His lips formed half a grin, through which she could see his slightly crooked front teeth, one of them chipped. She'd always loved this part of his smile, for no other reason than that it was pure Nick Scully. A smile came to her own lips, as she now knew what to tell him, and she leaned forward with the words on the tip of her tongue. But instead of saying anything, she pressed her mouth gently on his.

They both recoiled a little in shock. This was not what she'd intended to do, and clearly, he had not been expecting it. Stunned with disbelief, she simply stared at him.

"Did you just *kiss* me?" he said in mock outrage, exaggerated by the full-fledged grin spreading across his face.

She felt herself grinning back at him. "I didn't mean to," she said, studying that face which pulled hers toward it like a magnet. "What I did was this." Again she pressed her lips to his.

"There," she said. "Was that a kiss?"

When she leaned back to look at him, his grin had disappeared, replaced by a serious expression she couldn't interpret. Was he sorry she had done this? Merely surprised? Conflicted? She couldn't tell.

"That was a kiss," he said finally, his voice husky, his grin slowly return-ing. "So is this." Then he leaned forward to press his lips on hers. "And this." Again his lips met hers. Tilting his head to one side, he surveyed her counte-nance as if trying to read her mind, see into her heart. Embarrassed by such a searching gaze, she looked down at her lap to avoid it. When she looked back up and smiled at him, he reached out with one hand to clasp the back of her neck. With the other he clasped her by the shoulder and pulled her into an embrace. Suddenly his mouth was not just on hers but inside hers, scooping out her soft flesh and devouring it as if his life depended on it.

They fell back into the cushions, where he continued to kiss not just her mouth, but her throat, her eyes, her earlobes and again her mouth, where his tongue joined hers with a moan of contentment, then reached all the way into the inner recesses of her being, where it took possession of her insides. She felt a revolution occur within, as something old, tired, worn-out and *wrong* was being cast off and replaced by something wonderful, new and *right*. She hadn't felt something this right in a long time; the rightness of what was happening delighted her. It was as if a thousand dormant cocoons had hatched a thousand butterflies in the depths of her being, or a thousand bubbles had been released. Just for a moment, she wanted to stop the kissing, to laugh out all the bubbles, or butterflies, rising up within.

He pulled back and regarded her, the beginnings of a grin playing across his lips. "You know the best thing about kissing you?"

His hair was an unruly tangle on his forehead. She reached up not so much to smooth it as simply to touch it.

"The way you kiss back," he said.

"Is that so," she said absently, pulling him toward her to kiss him back some more, if he liked it so much. Now it was she who kissed the grin on his face, the tousle of hair on his forehead, the soft lobe of his ear.

It could have been hours they lay there kissing; it could have been a matter of minutes.

"I've been wanting to kiss you like this forever," he told her, fingering the soft brown mole beneath her ear, right at the jaw line. "Will you let me make love to you?"

She had no words for reply, only kisses. But she wanted everything about him, everything he could do to keep this wonderful new feeling going inside her. Taking her by the hand, he must have known this.

"Let me get you upstairs," he whispered.

But on the way, something went wrong. As they left the warmth of the heaters and the fire, she shivered and grew cold. Her thoughts rose up against her. She was still *married*. Nick was a *friend*. If she went through with what she was doing, it would be *adultery*. A large red A, the logo of the Alabama Crimson Tide, flashed into mind like a warning. By the time they reached the bedroom, she felt completely frozen, not only from the chill of the night air but from the fright and doubt that had overtaken her.

"What's wrong?" he murmured, running his hands lightly over her body. "You're so tense all of a sudden."

"Nothing's wrong," she lied, even as her body stiffened further when his hands moved around her waist. But so much was wrong; it was called adultery. As if that weren't enough, she was also nervous, shy, completely unsure of herself and what she was doing.

"You want this?" he whispered.

His body pressed against hers, which had turned to granite. Something within wanted him badly and was struggling to meet him but couldn't break through the hardened outer shell her body had become. She nodded mutely.

Like the other night, he began to undress her while she stood as paralyzed as a stroke victim in the hospital, unable to move or do anything for herself. Only this time he went much more slowly, with an inquiring look after removing each garment, to see if she had changed her mind. Even naked, her face was immobile and her arms hung limply by her side. Again he put his hands around her waist to draw her toward him. Clothes had not been the problem. She was as rigid as before. His lips sought hers, but her mouth was dry and couldn't respond.

"Tell me what's wrong."

"I'm scared," she admitted.

"Of me?"

"No."

"What then?"

She stood there, her thoughts revolving wildly as he waited, his hands around her waist. What was she afraid of? Surely the decision to divorce released her from marriage vows. And she obviously wanted Nick as more than a friend or she would not be standing there naked in his arms. What was holding her back, then? Why was she suddenly so nervous and reluctant, as if on the verge of disaster? She couldn't destroy her marriage; that was already destroyed. But she could destroy what she had with Nick. Maybe that's what she was afraid of. She had just gotten him back, finally realized what he meant to her, and she didn't want to lose him ever again. If she got into bed with him, perhaps it would lead only to another loss. What if she wasn't good at this? What if she was a disappointment to him? What if she didn't mean to him all he meant to her? If this was a mistake, she had everything to lose. And yet, precisely because of what he meant to her, she had to take this risk.

"I feel like I don't know what I'm doing," she confessed finally in a whisper. "Almost as if I've never done this before."

"You haven't done this before. I haven't either." He pressed his fingers to her lips to stifle her protest. "Not with each other."

Taking her by the hand, he led her to the bed. He turned his back as she climbed in, and when he turned back around, he was as naked as she was. She lay prone and still, like a corpse on a marble slab, grateful for the pitch black which cloaked her fear and trembling. He leaned down to press his lips against hers, but it was still no good. Her lips felt numb; her mouth wouldn't open. It occurred to her that if there were such a thing as being "good in bed," then surely she was the opposite. Absurdly, that image of the large red A, the logo of the Crimson Tide, ubiquitous in Tuscaloosa, on every billboard, storefront and automobile, on every sweatshirt, backpack and ball cap, pulsed in her brain as her heart hammered in her throat. When she tried to banish the large red A from her mind, she succeeded only in replacing it with a parade of Miss Alabama faces from women she'd seen him out with before.

His hand stroked her face, traveled down her jaw, traced her lips with the merest touch, a brush of a butterfly's wing. "I'm just going to learn your body," he murmured. He explored the hollow of her neck, the jut of her collarbone, the curve of her shoulder, as if these were the most fascinating and desirable parts of a woman's body. The back of his hand brushed against one of her breasts as if by accident. He could explore that too, she realized, and tried to tell him, but only the smallest sound emerged from her constricted lungs. He seemed to understand nevertheless; his hand came back to her breasts with purpose this time, and at length. She began to relax. It didn't seem so much like adultery: it was just her breasts. She didn't realize how much the tension had eased until he told her, "I'm going to touch you down there." Muscles clenched again; her jaw tightened. He seemed to be moving away; the touch didn't come. When it did come, it was not what she expected, just a delicate fluttering of his fingertips on the inside of her thighs, like the tickling of a feather. Then his head was between her legs.

Anxious and embarrassed, she struggled to rise.

"*Please,*" he urged, the way he used to years ago when trying to coax her into his latest venture.

Once he had wanted to sneak a pizza from the Magic Mushroom through the exit door of a movie theater, so they could enjoy pizza instead of popcorn with the movie . . . *Please* . . . Another time he took her to the zoo, and insisted on riding the train, which was full of children and toddlers with their mothers . . . *Please* . . . That very first time he called her, when she said "I don't think I'll be allowed to go out with you," and he said, "Ask him again . . . *Please* . . ."

Desperately, her mind conjured these and other memories, one after another, and threw them up into a makeshift wall shielding her brain from what was happening to her body. Strangely, the stratagem seemed to work, and she ceased to mind so acutely the shock of an intimacy she was not prepared for. Now it felt almost like a drug had entered her bloodstream, tranquilizing the brain, relaxing the muscles. But instead of sinking into repose, she felt an odd pressure boiling up toward explosion. Suddenly pleasure took her body and tossed it about like a ragdoll. No sooner had this force spent itself than he slammed into her innermost being in a violent collision belied by the pleasure it gave her, again. And again and again and again until there was so much she couldn't contain it all. She cried out the surfeit as more crowded in on her. Afterwards, with ragdoll legs splayed beneath his weight, she lay lost in wonder as those bubbles of happiness rose to her lips. It felt like laughter when they finally escaped. She had no idea she was crying until he rolled away, gathered her in his arms, and wiped her tears with his finger.

"I wanted to put a smile on your face," he said.

"You did."

"Is this what you call a smile?" His finger traced the wet lines of her cheekbones.

"You must think I'm an idiot."

"No, I think you were still a virgin. That's all. No wonder your marriage didn't work."

In spite of herself, she laughed out loud.

"Now there's a smile," he grinned.

She loved this grin, the two crooked front teeth, the damp tousled blond hair tumbling down on his forehead. She started to reach for his face, but pulled back in another fit of shyness, unsure of herself.

"Now what?"

"I was going to touch your face."

"Why didn't you?"

"I wasn't sure you'd want me to."

"Now you *are* being an idiot. Of course I want you to touch me. I'm in bed with you."

She laughed again, ran her fingers through his hair, across his lips.

"Talk to me," he said. "Tell me why you were crying."

249

Her hands dropped from his face.

"Tell me," he urged.

"I was so happy. I thought I was laughing."

"Now that makes sense."

"I was overwhelmed. That's all."

"Overwhelmed?"

"So much pleasure," she said. "I didn't know."

"I was right. You *were* a virgin."

"Don't make fun of me. Please."

"I didn't mean to." He drew her closer. "Tell me what it felt like."

She studied his face, trying to decide if she could tell him the truth. "If felt like love," she said finally. "Exactly like love streaming all through my body."

"It *was* love," he told her. "It *is* love." He kissed her. "That's what I wanted: to make love to you."

"Thank you," she whispered.

"Why would you thank me?"

"For loving me so well."

"Don't thank me for that."

"I'm not just talking about being in bed together. I mean everything that led up to this moment. The way you came to get me. Brought me here. Helped me through what happened. But it's more than that too. It goes back years, to the beginning, when we first knew each other. The way we talked, and all those things we talked about. All those great times we had together. What we did today reminded me, brought it all back. I remembered . . . I realized . . . It's almost as if"— She stopped, not sure how to finish the sentence.

"As if I've loved you forever," he said.

She felt herself blushing. "I'm not saying you have. Just it feels that way."

"But I *have* loved you forever. I've never wanted another woman since I met you."

The absurdity of this made her laugh. "That's not exactly your reputation, you know."

"I didn't say I never wanted sex. I said I never wanted a woman—a particular woman—since I met you. Because I *have* loved you forever."

She saw the truth of this glistening in his eyes. "I didn't know," she said.

"Didn't you?"

"Well, yes," she admitted. "But it was more like brotherly love."

"Of course it was! It had to be! You were a baby. Sixteen! You're still a baby. But at least now you're *legal*."

"Why didn't you tell me?"

"Why?!" he cried. "What good would it have done to tell you? I was a mess. I had to straighten myself out. If possible. And you had to grow up, go to college. I didn't think it was fair for me to be your first, because I wanted to be your last. I hoped you'd have half a dozen boyfriends, and I'd have another chance with you someday. *If* I could straighten myself out. Which was a big if. Still, how was I to know some guy would get you all the way to the altar so soon? By the time I got home and read your letters after my first year in Switzerland, I heard you were already *engaged*."

"That's why you never wrote back?"

"That's why I never wrote back."

"I always wondered why. Then I told myself I had to put you out of my mind. In one way I did. On a deeper level, I guess I never did."

"I tried to put you out of my mind too. You see the results."

She laughed. "I like these results."

"Me too. But I should have waited after what just happened. I would have, you know. You needed more time. A lot more time to resolve this divorce business. But then you kissed me downstairs."

"Like this?" she said.

* * *

The next morning they woke late, lying entangled in a latticework of limbs under a bed sheet dappled by the sun. The beauty and wonder of it made her smile, until it occurred to her it was all too good to be true. But her smile had already told him what he wanted to know, and he was not to be denied. His touch banished all objections, and her body yielded to his insistence, which did not cease until every breath of pleasure had been exhausted.

Afterwards her doubts and fears returned a hundred-fold, compounded by regret and self-reproach. It wasn't just her father's apprehensions years ago that had caused her to shut her mind to Nick as anything more than a friend. It was her own qualms as well. There were all his women—those beautiful women—that he loved for a time as he had just loved her—and then left behind. She had not wanted to be left, discarded, forgotten. Better to remain his friend than become a rejected lover.

"You get a little fragile afterwards," he noted.

"Nick," she said, her eyes prickling with tears.

"Please don't try to tell me this is wrong."

"It's just—"

"What?"

"I know you don't stay with any woman for very long—"

"*That's* what's bothering you?" He sounded delighted. "Does this mean you want to keep me around?"

"I couldn't stand the pain of losing your friendship if—"

"Fuck friendship!" he said, amused. "I don't want to be your friend! I've always wanted to be more than your *friend*. I told you last night. I'll tell you again, as many times as you need to hear. I love you. I've always loved you. You're the only woman I've ever wanted. I'd marry you today if you'd have me. Oh—that is, if you weren't already married to someone else. But for once I'm in luck. Your husband is trying to get a three-day divorce. I'll marry you in three days. You have three days to decide."

"Be serious," she said, laughing.

"I am." But he was laughing too. He picked up a strand of hair off her shoulder and twirled it around his index finger.

"What about all those women in your past?"

"What women?" he said, wincing. "I told you. That was sex. And I'm sorry for it. I used sex like I used cocaine, to chase boredom. Which means I used women. And I hurt plenty of them, I'll admit, though I tried not to. I never lied about my intentions and I never once told any woman I loved her. But I knew I needed to quit using that as a diversion like I needed to get rid of the drugs. And for the most part, I did after I started that program in Switzerland. But speaking of which." Letting go of her hair, he propped himself up on his elbow and looked down at her. "If you want something to worry about, worry about the fact that I'm a recovering drug abuser, currently unemployed."

She laughed, but uncharacteristically, he was serious. "I mean it," he said.

"I don't think of you as unemployed. You may not have a conventional job, but you're not unemployed. And you need to start giving yourself some credit for what it is you do."

"Nobody else sees me that way."

"That's because you haven't let anyone else really see you."

"If I did, they still wouldn't see what you see. No one will ever understand what you see in me."

"Nick. People would think what I see is what any girl would see. Your family name and fortune."

"Like I said: No one would understand what it is you see in me."

"In time they would. We would turn out to be quite different from the typical Mountain Brook society couple."

"Former substance abuser with a trust fund marries former debutante. That's a very typical Mountain Brook couple. More or less."

"Who says we're getting married?"

"I do. You have three days to decide."

"We're only typical on the surface. And don't call yourself names."

"I was a user. Tell me what you think of that. You were way too polite the other night."

She reached up to stroke the blond hair that fell down on his forehead. Then she pulled him down on the pillow beside her. "The whole story shocked me," she admitted. "And it made me sad. Most of all, it scared me. For your sake. But . . ."

"But what?"

"Well, we all have *something*. I admire the way you wrestled with your problem and resolved it."

"Hopefully."

"It's the best anybody can say. But what about—?" She bit her lip, not wanting to name it.

"What? Now you've got me worried."

"Lily Templeton," she whispered.

"Your *friend?*" He chuckled.

She nodded.

Sighing, he rolled away from her onto his back and stared up at the ceiling for several long moments, as if the truth was written there. "I don't know if I can explain it," he said finally. "It's just—I didn't understand what it was going to do to me to see you get married to someone else. When I went to your wedding, I thought I had the situation in perspective. You were just one woman, ten years younger than me. I hadn't seen you in four years. There was a world of other women who could be the missing piece in my life. But when I saw you walking up the aisle, smiling and beautiful, I knew you were the only woman I'd ever be able to make my life with. Can you imagine how I felt?"

She swallowed hard.

"It's the closest I've come in a long time to thinking about going home and shooting up. Instead I grabbed your friend. I've lived to regret it."

"What about the woman who called here the other night?"

"Just a date," he yawned. "Not a girlfriend."

"There's really no woman in your life?"

"You," he said. "You. You are the woman in my life. Please don't tell me you're not. Nothing has ever made me happier than this. There's nothing I've ever wanted more than this."

"Is it supposed to be this easy for me to move on from a failed marriage?"

"No! It's not. You're supposed to suffer terribly, for years, because you married a jackass who didn't know how to appreciate you. You're supposed to go through a miserable period of mourning, where you do nothing but mope and walk the earth like a tortured lost soul. And I'd gladly wait as you worked your way through a decade of torment, except the last time I waited, you ended up married to someone else. This time, I'm not waiting."

She laughed.

"Seriously," he said. "It's not as if what we have here between the two of us is something that's just happened. Now is it, young lady?"

Smiling, she shook her head. "No," she agreed. "This is something that happened a long time ago. I'm only just now recognizing it for what it is."

"Give me some credit for recognizing it right away," he said. "Because I chose you a long time ago. But. I had to go through rehab. Then I had to wait and hope that you would choose me. Not until then, I told myself, not until she gives me some *sign,* will I ever offer my unworthy self. Not surprisingly, you chose someone else. Then, no sooner do you realize it's the wrong guy, but you give me my *sign.* You'll have to forgive me for acting on it at once."

"When I kissed you?"

"And how."

"But why me? Why I am the one you chose? I've seen some of the other women you were with. They're all so beautiful."

"You're beautiful, sweetie."

"Not like some of those girls I saw you with. They could win pageants."

"You've always been beautiful to me. Even when you still had those glasses, and that haircut."

"I don't believe you. How?"

"Because of who you are. I don't know if you have this problem, but my problem is, being with most other people—not just women—but being with just about anybody makes me more bored than when I'm alone."

She nodded.

"You have that problem?"

"Yes."

"You are the one and only person who can fill my mind better than I can fill it myself. The books you read, the things you say, the stories you tell, the thoughts you have—even when you were still a baby—I couldn't wait for the next time we were together. And you like having experiences. Not just going to a party or restaurant so you can be *seen.* Remember that time I took you to the *zoo?*"

"We rode the train with a bunch of two year-olds. How could I forget that?"

He was seized by a yawn. "I need some coffee," he said. "Have I told you what you needed to know?"

She nodded.

"You have three days to tell me what I need to know," he laughed. "Or you can tell me now."

"Actually, there's something I should have told you last night."

"What's that?"

"I love you."

~ 22 ~

After the rental furniture company loaded their items on the truck, there wasn't much left in the apartment besides some clothes, books and kitchenware. Nick had just taken the last of the books to his car when Daniel drove up. From the window in her basement living room, she saw the two of them nod to each other as Daniel got out of his car. She couldn't remember if her ex-husband knew who Nick was, but Nick recognized his future bride's first husband, and discreetly disappeared into the old lady's house for the glass of iced tea she had offered earlier. Daniel came around the back and into the apartment with no fear of being uninvited or unannounced.

"Who was that guy I saw in the driveway?" he asked her.

"What are you doing here?"

"I need to talk to you. Who was that?"

Folding her arms across her chest, she simply stood there in the middle of the empty room, frowning at him. He looked around.

"Where are you going?"

Still she remained silent. Despite the divorce—or because of its haste—she had known this confrontation was coming, perhaps was even necessary. But now that it was about to happen, her first instinct was to avert it. "You shouldn't be here," she told him. "I want you to leave."

"I need to talk to you," he repeated.

She couldn't stop herself now. "I don't know who you think you are," she said, "but you're acting like you have every right to come barging in, demanding answers, insisting that we talk. But we are no longer married and there's nothing to talk about. You have no business being here. Please leave."

His shoulders collapsed and the demanding demeanor gave way to tearful pleading. "I'm sorry," he said. "I really need to talk to you. Is there somewhere we can sit down in here?"

She made no reply as she considered how she wanted to handle the situation. On the one hand, he no longer had any claim on her, and his conduct laid no claim on her sympathies either. Had he always behaved this way? she wondered. So blind to anything but himself and his own needs? If so, the divorce was no wonder; the marriage itself was the mystery, the idea that she could have fallen in love in the first place. But on the other hand, the divorce had been so hurried it had hardly felt like divorce. Something told her this divorce would truly be finalized if she heard what he had to say.

Silently she led the way into the bedroom, where she indicated the bare mattress on the bed belonging to her landlady. It was awkward, but it was the only piece of furniture remaining in the apartment, the only place to sit. Heartened by the intimacy as they sat down together, he reached over to take hold of her hand. As she pulled away with a frown, she noticed his lip was trembling.

"I've been such a fool," he whispered.

She waited.

The divorce was all a mistake," he went on. "I'd like to forget the whole thing. I hope you'll forgive me and take me back."

She simply shook her head.

"It can be as if it never happened," he said, inching closer to her. "In Alabama, you can reverse a divorce within thirty days of getting one. Did you know that? We wouldn't even need to get married again. There's a paper we can file. To cancel the original divorce petition."

"Why do you think I'd want to do that?"

"Well, we could get married again if you want. But there's no need to legally. A lot of people don't even know we're divorced yet. Have you told your parents?"

He waited for her to reply and then took her stony silence as the answer he wanted to hear.

"See?" he said. "Your own parents don't even know. If we undo this mistake right away, it can be as if we never were divorced at all."

"Why would you think I'd want to be married to you now, after what you've done?"

This question hit him like a body blow which caused him to double over in pain. She saw the tears he was fighting to hide and control as he looked down at the mattress.

"Please let me explain," he pleaded, trying again for her hand.

She moved further away from him on the mattress. "Go ahead," she said. "Explain."

Unbeknownst to him, the story that tumbled forth was entirely familiar to her, if not the entire story. The name of Lily Templeton or the extent of their relationship was never specified.

"My parents think it's your fault for leaving," he concluded. "They say you're to blame for putting our marriage at risk. But I want you to know I blame only myself. I was so bored and lonely after you left. I can't explain it—you just felt so *gone*. Then this other woman led me on and I made a complete and utter ass of myself. Please give me another chance."

"I *am* to blame for putting our marriage at risk," she said quietly.

"No!" he cried, even as his face was transformed by joyful relief. "You had every right to pursue your career. My parents are so old-fashioned, Southern Baptist. The whole mess is my fault; I just want a second chance." He moved over next to her and tried to pull her into an embrace.

Shrinking back against the headboard, she kept her voice calm. "What happened to . . . this other woman?"

His hands dropped away. Nervously he moved to the edge of the mattress. They could hear footsteps in the room directly above them, along with muffled voices.

"Does that guy I saw in the driveway live here?" he said. "Is this his house? He's helping you move out?"

"What happened with the other woman?"

"She was just using me," he said. "To get to someone else. That's all it was."

"That's all it was?"

"Yeah," he said, nodding. "It was all nothing. She was just trying to make some guy jealous. Somebody named Nick Scully."

"Nick Scully?!"

"I think that's the name. Do you know who he is?"

"She told you all this?"

He shook his head. "I've barely even seen her since I closed on the house. She went out of town the next day. One of her friends told me. But I'm telling you: it's over."

"But that's only because she didn't really want you like you thought. If she had, where would the situation stand now?"

"Look. I'm so lucky I found out in time. She is not the person I thought she was."

"You know what? She's not even the issue. It's our relationship that isn't what we thought it was. That's why we're divorced. I don't think there's anything more to be said." She made a move to rise from the bed.

"Wait!" he cried, desperately grabbing her arm. "Don't you see? I lost my head! You weren't there . . . and this girl . . . well . . . she put the moves on me . . . and I just behaved like a stupid guy."

She stood up from the bed and glared at him. "And you think I want to be married to a stupid guy?"

He sprang up from the mattress. "You said yourself it was your fault for putting our marriage at risk!"

"Yes, that *was* my fault. But it was your fault for being so . . . unfaithful . . . when I was gone. I may have put the marriage at risk, but you took the opportunity to destroy it."

"So can't we talk about this? Try to work things out? I know that's what you wanted. We can do that now."

She stood there and looked at him so long without speaking that hope began to dawn in his eyes. Then she said quietly, "There was a time for talking about it. Trying to work things out. *Before we got divorced.* I begged you to. I went through hell when you refused and insisted on divorce. Well, now we *are divorced.* So the time for talking is over."

"But I told you! We have thirty days!"

"Thirty days," she echoed, shaking her head in disbelief.

"Of course at this point, we have less than the full thirty days," he admitted.

Shaking her head again, she left the room as he followed anxiously behind, grabbing at her arm, trying to stop her momentum and turn her around. She shrugged him off and continued to the door of the basement apartment. Pushing it open, she gestured wordlessly for him to leave. He stood rooted on the threshold.

"Please," he said, with tears in his eyes. "Let's undo the mistake. Don't you know what you mean to me?"

"I do know what I mean to you," she told him. "I'm someone you can forget about or cast off when I'm not around or something better comes along. I'm someone you think will just be there waiting with nothing better to do myself if your something better doesn't work out. That's why the divorce is no mistake. I remember trying to tell you years ago that you can't treat anybody like your Plan B. *You do not use people as a Plan B. I am not your Plan B.* Now please leave."

Without waiting to see whether he would do so, she turned her back on him and returned to the bedroom, where she closed the door emphatically behind her. With relief she finally heard his car pull out of the driveway. A few minutes later, Nick came downstairs and found her sitting on the bare mattress, staring out the window at the stump of the old magnolia tree. He stood in the doorway, leaning against the jamb. "Well?" he said finally, when she failed to turn around.

"Well," she said, turning and giving him a faint smile. "You were right. It didn't last. Over in a matter of weeks, just like you predicted."

He moved slowly into the room and sat down tentatively on the mattress. "And?" He raised his eyebrows.

"He wants to reverse the divorce. In Alabama, apparently, you have thirty days to file something that cancels the divorce decree. You don't even have to get remarried."

"You're kidding." He let out a weak shout of laughter that was more nervous than wild in his usual way. "Our native state provides so many ingenious ways for us to act like fools."

"Yes, but who would believe two people with degrees from Harvard could be such fools?"

"What are you trying to tell me, sweetie?"

"I'm trying to tell you I was a fool for not knowing all those years how much I loved you. And I didn't even recognize your love for me because it was so . . . so . . . *selfless*. Are you sure you want to spend your life with such a fool?"

In reply, he moved over and took her in his arms.

"There's something else," she said.

"What?" he said absently, as he stroked her hair and kissed the top of her head.

She pulled away from his embrace and looked at him. "She only went after him in the first place because she was trying to make someone else jealous."

Gathering her back in his arms, he didn't seem interested in hearing any more. "Guess who it was?" she breathed into his ear as he cradled her head on his shoulder.

"Who?" He smiled at her.

"You." She smiled back.

"Me?!" he cried, looking up at the ceiling and shouting with laughter in his usual way.

~ 23 ~

It had been only a few months since Evelyn Scully had last played tennis with her son. It was inconceivable that he had improved so dramatically, or that she had forgotten how good he was after watching him win the men's singles in March. The unavoidable explanation was that she herself was getting worse.

As if to corroborate her fears, Nick called out: "Mom! Normally you make that shot!"

Suddenly Evelyn did not feel like playing tennis anymore; she only felt like crying. Aware of something wrong, her son came up to the net.

"Are you all right?" he said, panting.

Wordlessly, Evelyn shook her head, tried to stem the flow of tears. "I think I'm ready to sit down and have some lunch." She managed a weak smile.

Surprised, Nick looked at his watch and frowned. They had barely played for half an hour; it was early for lunch, she knew. "Okay," he agreed anyway, without further comment.

He gathered their things from the bench and they walked to the club-house in silence. Not trusting herself to look at him, she kept her face trained straight ahead, although she noticed he cast several sidelong glances of concern, hoping to catch her eye.

Finally he said, "Mom, are you all right?"

Evelyn only bit her lip and nodded rapidly, blinking back tears.

Despite the early hour, the dining room was already becoming occupied with older ladies who would move to one of the other rooms for their bridge game after lunch.

"Should we sit out on the terrace?" Nick asked her. "Or would that be too hot for you?"

It was only the first of May, but Evelyn was feeling the heat much more than she used to. She would have preferred the air-conditioning indoors, but privacy was more important today. Nick had asked her here for a reason, and she knew he would not speak as freely around prying eyes and tongues eager to report the tiniest tidbit of gossip.

"The terrace is fine," she told him.

Taking her by the elbow, he steered her outside to a table by the railing and under a fan. They were the only ones on the terrace; she knew he liked it that way. With the fan and the breeze blowing from the golf course beyond the pool, it wasn't as hot as she'd feared, and as her son chatted easily about this and that, she began to relax. She almost began to feel normal. But after the waitress brought their iced tea and took their order, he leaned across the table.

"Now tell me what's wrong, Mom," he said.

Evelyn burst into tears, thankful that he had seated her with her back to the dining room. There was no one to notice but her son, who waited calmly for her to gain control and dry her eyes.

"Just tell me if you're sick, Mom," he said. "You could barely hold your racket up on the court."

"That bad?" She tried for a smile.

He nodded. "That bad."

She hesitated, not knowing how to tell her son this particular news. She'd hoped she wouldn't have to tell anyone, but the tennis courts had betrayed her, and Nick was undoubtedly the most sensitive and perceptive of her children, or of anyone she knew. Even as a child, his powers of observation and his aptitude for spotting the telling detail made him sharper than most adults, although he could not always, as a child, comprehend what he perceived. Driven by curiosity, he was forever asking questions and forcing discussions about the most delicate subjects, and she never succeeded in getting either the boy or the adolescent to accept that some topics were off-limits. When Nick came back after college, she finally began to relish having one other person with whom she could talk about anything under the sun without restraint or embarrassment. This was the essence of their special bond; not that he was her "favorite" or looked like a carbon copy of herself. Painful as the current subject was, she figured she might as well tell him as anybody, and besides, he would know right away if she lied, and wouldn't let her get away with it.

"It's menopause," she said in a whisper.

"Menopause!" he exclaimed, as if elated by this news.

"Sh!" she admonished him irritably. "Do you think I want the world to know?"

"I thought you were going to tell me cancer." He leaned back in relief and squeezed lemon in his tea. "How old are you anyway? Forty-five?" He grinned.

She couldn't help smiling. "Fifty-five, you charmer. So it came late for me. But still." She shook her head and looked away.

"Well, it had to happen," he said. "So what? It's not like you want more children," he grinned. "And you can't tell me you'll miss all that bleeding."

"Oh, Nick." She looked back at him sadly. "It's so much more than that."

"Is it?" he said. "So tell me. I don't know any women in menopause."

She almost choked on a sip of tea as a bitter laugh rose in her throat. "Of course you do. You know plenty of women in menopause." She whispered this last word as if it were unspeakable.

"Well, not to talk to about it," he laughed. "So tell me."

Evelyn studied her son as the waitress arrived with two club sandwiches and a pitcher of tea to refill their glasses. This was the extraordinary thing about Nick. He really did want her to tell him; he would listen carefully; he would ask good questions and he would have something helpful to say. No one else she knew would be this good to talk to, not her own daughter or even her women friends who had gone through the same thing themselves. Like the way he referred to a woman's bleeding, he didn't shy away from unpleasant or difficult subjects, or treat a woman's issues with the ridicule and dismissiveness so many other men would have. Her own husband would have been useless to talk to; he didn't have time for things like menopause, and she hadn't even told him. She felt her eyes fill with tears as she watched her son devour one quarter of his club sandwich. This was why she loved him so, and refused to despair over him like everyone else did. Her only concern was why no one else could see in him what she did. He was so much more than the careless escape artist everyone thought he was. Okay, so he couldn't face Palmdale Mills. But he could face menstruation and menopause. So she told him.

Just as she had known, he asked her one question after another, especially about her last doctor's visit, and before she knew it, she had recounted virtually the entire conversation, sometimes word for word. In the process, she stumbled across important details, facts and information that the doctor had clearly relayed but which had become lost in the fog of her brain and the devastating impact of this midlife phenomenon on every aspect of her being.

"So what he prescribed takes about two weeks to start working then?" said her son, casting an eye on her plate, where two quarters of a club sandwich remained untouched.

"Go ahead," she nodded at her plate, almost laughing and feeling strangely giddy.

Reaching over, he grabbed one of the quarters, plucked out the toothpick and took a hungry bite as if it were his first. "Two weeks?" he repeated, mouth full.

She nodded and wondered why she felt almost dizzy with a happiness she couldn't explain.

"How long has it been then? Since you started taking the stuff?" He looked at her over the rim of his tea glass.

"A little over a week," she told him.

He took another bite of the sandwich and chewed thoughtfully. "So you ought to start feeling better soon," he said, more to himself than to her. "And then you feel better and better as the stuff gets into your system?" He looked at her.

"That's what he said." Evelyn smiled, realizing why she'd suddenly become happy. She should start to feel better soon, and then better and better after that. It had just been so hard to believe, since she still felt so bad, that she'd almost forgotten there was supposed to be light at the end of this tunnel. She felt like she'd entered a terminal tunnel, such as the grave, from which there was no emerging ever again.

Nick ate the last of the club sandwich quarter and wiped his mouth with the blue cloth napkin. "Is your doctor a specialist in this?" he asked.

The question caught Evelyn off guard. She hadn't even thought about that. "I don't know," she said slowly. "I don't think so."

"Listen, Mom," he said, reaching for the last quarter on her plate. "If this prescription doesn't do what it's supposed to, you let me know. I will *find* you a specialist. Hear?" He paused to take a bite and for her to nod acknowledgement. When she did, he went on. "I don't care where we have to go: Atlanta, Dallas, New York, Boston. We will go there. What is our money for if not for something like this? I don't want you suffering like you are. And *I* will take you myself if you need me to. If Dad can't go, or you don't want anybody to know. Okay?" He dropped the remnant of the sandwich and pushed his plate away. "Okay?"

"Okay," she managed, with a catch in her throat, overcome by relief, along with gratitude and love for her son. He had such a good *heart*. Why couldn't people see that? Well, she knew why, but it didn't make sense to her. It wasn't that Nick did anything wrong, particularly, it was just that he didn't have a job, didn't take his place in the family business, didn't have a wife, didn't have a house, didn't have children, didn't have a very settled existence.

And for these reasons everyone was prepared to think the very worst of him, even his own father, his brother and sister. The slightest rumor about him always took on the most perverse implications simply because his life didn't have any of the usual trappings which thwarted idle gossip and speculation. Meanwhile, everyone but herself overlooked the most obvious and important part of him, which was the kindness of his heart. Wasn't that more important than anything? What kind of world were they living in where the goodness and sweetness of someone's heart was of so little significance that it wasn't even noticed? Fortunately, Nick had never been bothered by whatever people thought or said about him. She only wished. . . . She wished. . . .

Smiling, she reached her hand across the table to give his a squeeze. "Thank you," she whispered.

"Oh, Mom," he grinned, waving her emotion away.

"Now I want you to take a lesson from all I've told you," she said, striving for a lighthearted tone. "Your youth, your looks, your vigor—it doesn't last forever. We always think it will, don't see how things will ever change or be different, until suddenly, everything has changed, everything is different, and we haven't done a speck of preparing. So don't waste it all, don't wait too long . . ." Her voice trailed off, unsure where to go from here.

To her surprise, Nick's face got red and he stumbled on his words, none of which she could understand, none of which was like him. "Actually," he said, and then faltered, seeming embarrassed to say more.

"Yes?" she prodded, curious. She'd forgotten that *he* had asked *her* to lunch today. Then again, she forgot everything these days. But clearly something was on his mind.

"There is a reason I asked you to lunch. Something I wanted to tell you." But he couldn't bring himself to say more.

"Well, go on," she said, with mounting curiosity.

Although the terrace had remained empty of any other diners, he looked around carefully anyway. Just then their waitress emerged from one of the card rooms where the older ladies had begun playing bridge. She carried a pitcher of watery tea in which all the ice had melted. Both declined a refill or dessert.

"Just the check," Nick told her, holding out his hand. "We'll take it in when we leave, so you don't need to come back out."

"Let me," said Evelyn, even as she watched with secret pride as her son scrawled his own name and club number on the tab. Her two older children, even the oldest son Tom, were always happy to let her, as the matriarch, pick up the tab, even when they came with their families and she accompanied them alone. The point wasn't money, of which they all had plenty. The point was character, and she thought Nick's was made of finer stuff than just about anybody's, while everyone else thought he was such a reprobate. And yes, he had cut up in high school, experimented with drugs, dallied with too many girls. She knew all this. But this had not come from the core of his being, nor had it destroyed it. His soul was sound; it was intact. She knew it.

"You were about to tell me something." She had to nudge him along; he was getting lost in thought.

"Well," he started, ran his hands through his hair, looked at the pool, looked at her. "There is a girl. A woman. Someone I"— Again he ran his hands through his hair.

"Nick." She breathed his name with pure joy. "Tell me everything."

It came out in a rush: How this was the only woman he'd ever wanted to settle down with; she was starting a graduate program in the fall at the University of Alabama; he was going to take graduate classes himself; they wanted to live at the river house, so close to Tuscaloosa; he would take over all the expenses, the taxes, and the association fees; or he would buy the house outright from the family, whatever they all preferred; he was going to write a book; she was going to help him; she was going to write a book; he was going to help her.

Laughing, Evelyn held up her hands. "Wait!" she cried. It was too much, all at once. She couldn't take it all in and was getting confused. Which of them was writing a book? Who was she? "What is her *name*?" Evelyn cried.

Nick colored and didn't answer. Immediately Evelyn sensed trouble and feared the worst. She wanted this so badly for him. She hadn't even realized how badly she'd wanted this for him until he'd given her this glimpse of his possible happiness in a settled existence. With a mother's instincts, she knew she was going to have to help him. Of course, that's why he'd invited her to lunch. He needed her. First, she had to get it out of him. She took a long sip of her own watery tea. "Do I know her?" she asked deliberately.

He nodded, still unable to speak.

"Okay," she said evenly. "Who is she? What is her *name*?"

Nick started to say something, then couldn't. She waited, as her heart began beating erratically, which was part of her new affliction as well as a response to the conversation with her son. Finally, he told her, "She just got divorced."

Evelyn's thoughts raced too rapidly for her to choose her words with care. "Not that woman from the gala last month? The date you stood up?" There was nothing wrong with her that Evelyn could tell, only that there

266

was nothing special either. She just couldn't figure Nick with that particular woman. Plus, someone had mentioned the other day that Natalie Messer was dating the Keller boy, the one just back from Hong Kong.

He shook his head. "No, no," he said, staring out over the golf course. "It's not Natalie."

She leaned across the table to put him on the spot. "Tell me who it is, sweetie," she said gently.

"Caroline Elmore," he said, so quietly she could barely hear.

But she heard, and the shock sent her reeling to the back of her chair. She felt weak with dread. For a moment she couldn't bring herself to speak, then roused herself to say as normally as possible: "Someone was telling me a rumor about her getting divorced just the other day. I didn't believe it. I *can't* believe it."

She waited fearfully for some explanation from Nick. As if he hadn't heard, Nick glanced away and fiddled absently with the blue curly-topped toothpick from a club sandwich quarter.

"So you're telling me it's true, then?" Evelyn ventured bravely. "Caroline Elmore is really divorced?" Full of misgivings, she could hardly look at him.

He gave a curt, barely perceptible nod.

"Her wedding reception was going on right here where we're sitting not even a year ago," she observed. When Nick said nothing, she continued nervously. "I've always heard about marriages that didn't even last a year, but I never personally *knew* anyone who turned around and got divorced right after getting married. I just can't fathom it."

Still Nick said nothing. She had to know.

"Did you have anything to do with that divorce?" she asked him.

"I swear to you I did not," he said firmly, clearly prepared for just that question. "But Mom." His voice faltered. "It's complicated. It's"— He wavered and then couldn't say any more.

Evelyn couldn't stop herself. Shaking her head, she said, "Your fingerprints are going to be all over this, Nick. You know the things people say about you. What they think of you. It doesn't matter what the truth is or the facts are, but people are going to say you broke up that marriage."

"I didn't do it, Mom," he said.

To Evelyn, there was something primal about her son's declaration of innocence, and the way he looked at her as the only one whose opinion mattered, the only one who could give him absolution from the guilt everyone else would automatically project onto him. She had to make a split second decision. Actually, there was no decision.

"I believe you, sweetie," she said, forcing a smile.

No words came back from him, just a long, slow sigh of relief, as if he'd been holding his breath. Then she heard a sharp intake, as if he were holding his breath again, bracing himself for an onslaught of uncomfortable questions.

Evelyn decided not to ask any of these. Instead, she said softly, "You've always loved her, haven't you?"

This bowled him over; he was speechless. "Yes," he admitted. "But how did you know?"

"I remember that time you brought her up to the house," she told him.

Evelyn thought back to that day a few years ago, when she'd just arrived home from a long Saturday on the tennis courts. She'd been irritated to see Nick's car drive up with no warning and one of his endless girls. It was four-thirty, and she had one hour to get ready for a party she and her husband were going to that night. She wasn't fit to be seen, meet anyone new, or be polite to the latest girlfriend. Nick had assured her they were only staying a moment; he had to get Caroline back home before her six o'clock curfew; but he wanted to show her something first. What that was Evelyn couldn't imagine; she was flabbergasted to see Nick lead this girl into the dining room, open the china cabinet and pull out one of those dinner plates that had been in the Scully family for generations. Nick Scully interested in china?

She could tell this girl was different, and not just because she was so much younger. All the women she'd seen with Nick before were beautiful, fun-loving, lighthearted girls full of gaiety and laughter, like Nick seemed to be, on the surface. Evelyn alone realized that Nick had a deeply serious side he didn't know what to do with or how to handle except to keep hidden away beneath juvenile misbehavior.

As she stood there in the kitchen, drinking her iced tea and covertly observing the pair in the dining room, she knew something special was happening for her son. The girl was quiet and serious, with glasses and a severe haircut. They were poring over the back of the dinner plate, which was distinguished by two backstamps, one with the name of the famous manufacturer in England, and the other with the name of the importers in Mobile. From where she stood, Evelyn could not hear what they said, but it was clear the girl was every bit as smart as Nick. The intimacy of the scene startled her; she felt almost like she was watching them in a bedroom instead of a dining room. That's when she understood that this girl had reached that part of Nick he didn't know what to do with or how to handle, except now, when he was with her. And she knew he loved her precisely because he did not touch her. When they made their good-byes and were walking out the door, he ushered her through with his hand at the small of her back. At the last minute, he stopped himself from putting that hand on her, although he kept it level with her waist. Clearly, the girl was precious to him, and he did not want to risk the slightest damage to her or what she had to offer him.

She had never spoken to her son about this, but she had changed her mind about donating the china collection to a museum. A few weeks later, Nick had asked if he could have just one small piece from the pattern. He didn't tell her why or what it was for, but she knew, just as she knew that he would take good care of it and keep it safe. And she didn't tell him that she had decided the china would go to him one day.

Since then, she had always wondered why the connection between Nick and this girl had come to nothing. From what she had observed, the girl cherished Nick just as he did her. But then she went to college and Nick disappeared to go traipsing through Europe. Evelyn heard nothing more of it and saw little of Nick himself for several years. She assumed she must have imagined something when she saw them together that day, or misinterpreted what she saw. But now the image of the two of them together came sweeping back over her, along with the powerful conviction that she had been so completely right. Their connection may have been interrupted by separation, but it had not been forgotten or lost. They had found each other again; what they had was still there, strong, true and deep. Yes, the girl was young, but somehow, with her seriousness and intellect, she seemed older than those giddy girls Nick's own age. It was perfect. This was it. Evelyn knew it.

"I'm so happy for you," she told her son.

This bowled him over even more. Again his face got red and he couldn't speak for a moment. "Just like that?" he said, regaining his composure, along with his grin. "I was going to tell you the whole sordid saga of what happened to her marriage. I thought I'd have to defend my honor, explain my actions, vouch for my intentions in the whole matter before anyone would even think of being happy for me."

Evelyn shook her head, smiling. "I knew from that day you showed her the old china how you felt about her."

"How could you possibly?"

Evelyn shook her head again. She didn't know how to express it, didn't have her son's facility with language. "I could just tell what she meant to you," she said as her son peered at her curiously. "Remember how Norman Laney wanted me to donate that china collection?" When he nodded, she told him, "After that day, I changed my mind, decided I wanted you to have that china."

"Mom!" he said, then looked quickly away over toward the pool, as if taking a keen interest in one of the kids splashing there.

"When you get married," she added. "You *do* plan to marry her, I take it? I trust that's what this is about? You wouldn't have made a lunch and tennis date with your old mom just to tell me about a temporary girlfriend?"

"She insists on waiting a decent interval," he said quietly. "Otherwise, I'd marry her tomorrow."

This declaration gave Evelyn goose bumps. Nick was notorious for talking about what he could do, what he might do, what he thought about doing or what he wanted to do, and then never doing much of anything at all that anyone could tell. The determination in his voice pleased her very much.

"So tell me about your plans then," she smiled. "I don't need to hear about the past, but I would like to hear about the future."

Truthfully, Evelyn did need to hear about the past, not so much for her own peace of mind but so she could defend him against a world which would only accuse him of wrongdoing instead of rejoicing in his happiness. But at this moment, her highest calling was to enter into that happiness. So she sat back while he prattled on about their plans and dreams. She heard something about Europe this summer before she stopped listening and gave in to the pleasure of simply observing his eagerness and excitement.

"I always knew she was right for me," he concluded. "But I didn't realize just how much the right person could help my whole life come together. Or how ready I was for that to happen. If only. . . ."

"If only what?" She leaned forward anxiously when she noticed a shadow descend on his countenance.

"I would just prefer to be married," he said. For some reason, this admission made him uncomfortable.

Evelyn didn't know what to say, any more than she knew how she felt. It wasn't like her son to be worried about convention. So what *was* he worried about? Did he doubt the girl's commitment? Did he doubt his own ability to stay committed? If so, perhaps she'd taken the wrong tack. Maybe she needed to curb her own enthusiasm and help him put the brakes on his before he rushed headlong into unnecessary entanglement. She needed some answers, but she also needed to phrase her questions with care so as not to spoil this moment for him.

"Are you so sure about *marriage?*" She tried her best to sound like she was teasing. "I never thought any one woman would ever satisfy you for long."

"Oh, Mom." He ran his hands through his hair impatiently. "All those others . . . It was so stupid . . . Afterwards . . . I didn't even want to look at them, didn't know what to say to them, didn't want them around, didn't want to see them again . . . It was nothing . . . It was just sex."

"That's a shock, to hear you say that." She forced a smile. "Sex is nothing to you?"

"No, it's just . . ." Again his hands rifled through his hair.

"You're not having sex with this girl yet? Is that why you're so anxious to get married? If so . . ." She shook her head, suddenly alarmed.

He muttered something she didn't catch.

"What was that?" she said.

Unexpectedly, he grinned, and her heart leapt back to life. Then he said, "No! I don't have sex with her!" He laughed wildly in a way she hated to hear at this moment. She was getting exasperated, afraid, thoroughly confused. Why couldn't he give her a straight story? Why was he putting her on a roller coaster? She couldn't take this sort of stress right now. Nick could be so *trying*.

"I make love to her," he said. "It's totally different."

She stared at him, relief draining through her limbs, pride, joy and admiration surging upward until it erupted in a big smile.

"I love everything about being with her," he was saying. "Sleeping beside her, cooking dinner, watching movies, reading in bed . . . Everything! I want to be her *husband*!" Again the hands went through his hair. "As it is . . . well . . . for example, she won't let me get her a decent car. You should see this piece of shit she drives. I'm terrified it will break down in the middle of an intersection."

Remembering her son's old Karmann Ghia, which actually *had* broken down in the middle of an intersection on one or two occasions, Evelyn burst out laughing. Nick had grown up. It had finally happened. Just like that psychiatrist had predicted. Nick was even the exact age the doctor had mentioned to her and her husband. Thirty-two. It was something called prolonged adolescence, the doctor had said. Not uncommon in wealthy families, especially in younger sons, when there was no external need for them to take on adult responsibility. He might continue to behave like an adolescent throughout his twenties, the doctor explained, and then when his own need to take on responsibility became strong enough, he would begin to mature, probably by age thirty-two. Her husband had scoffed; she herself was skeptical. But here he was, her thirty-two-year-old boy, her beloved son, finally becoming a man. He had grown up late; this girl he loved, ten years younger, had grown up early. It all made sense. Evelyn was so happy she shook with laughter.

"Mom, it's not funny." He looked seriously offended.

"I'm just so happy for you. That's all," she said.

He looked away, over toward the pool, unappeased.

Evelyn quickly pulled herself together and tried to focus her thoughts on what she could possibly say or do that would help her son. This was a somewhat new Nick in front of her, and he called for a somewhat different approach.

"Okay," she said soberly, businesslike, as if signaling the start of serious discussion. "Surely you understand why she might hesitate to get married again so soon . . ."

"*Marriage* isn't the issue. She wants to be married as much as I do."

"I don't understand. What's the problem then?"

"The whole bride business. The idea of another wedding, so soon after . . ."

Evelyn was silent as she studied her son. "Are you saying this is what *you* want? A public engagement? Parties? A big wedding? Gifts?"

"No, no," Nick said with impatience. "You know I couldn't care less about all that society stuff. I just want her. As my *wife*."

"Heavens!" Evelyn threw up her hands. "Then who needs a wedding? Just get a marriage certificate! Do it at the courthouse!"

Amazed, he stared at her, and she was thrilled to see his grin return.

"You would be okay with that?" Nervously he ran his hands through his hair. "I mean . . . I *would* want you to be there."

"I would be ecstatic," she said firmly. "And of course I'll be there! As one of your witnesses. I'll be honored. Just tell me when."

Were those tears she saw in his eyes? No! Evelyn turned away, with tears in her own eyes, unable to face his. Nowadays she cried at the slightest provocation, and if she thought those were really tears in his eyes she knew she'd collapse in a fit of weeping. He swallowed what seemed to be a lump in his throat, but it couldn't be, she told herself. He couldn't have changed that much.

"Will Dad be okay with it? Tom? Paula?"

"Of course," she asserted, brazenly sweeping past any doubts. "After all," she said, her eyes twinkling. "What good is a social position if we don't use it when we really need it most to get away with something?" He loved this, she could tell. His grin was bigger than ever. But there was something she thought she should add, something else he needed to hear. He was ready for it too, or he wouldn't have even concerned himself with his family's reaction. And he would soon have a wife, maybe children someday. She hoped.

Having a family would entrench him in some society somewhere, whether he wanted it or not. So she told him: "That's the main reason to maintain your social position in the first place. So you can get away with something when you really need to."

~ 24 ~

When Caroline arrived at her parents' house, she realized it was almost a year ago that the household was consumed by the preparations for her wedding, and filling up with wedding gifts that arrived daily by the dozens. As was customary, the dining room had been converted into a showroom for displaying all the presents. The table had been laid with six place settings of her own china and crystal patterns: three of "Autumn" by Lenox, paired with an assortment of Baccarat goblets and wine glasses, and three of the everyday "Blue Mist" by Dansk, along with three settings of her everyday flatware, and three of the sterling silver flatware that was an inheritance from her great-grandmother. Stacks of napkins and placemats, numerous serving dishes, three decanters, condiment bowls, meat platters, cruet sets, salt and pepper shakers, five different sets of candlesticks, one silver epergne centerpiece and another Italian majolica centerpiece occupied every remaining inch of space on the dining room table. The sideboard and buffet tables had both been cleared of their usual items to make for more display room. On the sideboard went the trays, the barware, the wine openers and cocktail shakers. Vases, knickknacks, a soup tureen, a Tiffany's punch bowl set and the odd assorted "accent pieces" went on the buffet table. All the dining room chairs had been placed against the wall and stacked with boxes containing toaster ovens, crock pots, can openers, coffee grinders and blenders. Her mother had required the assistance of Mr. Laney to place gifts like the fern stand and the antique library ladder in strategic spots around the room that would show them to best advantage and not impede the flow of traffic viewing the gifts. When her mother had remarked that they really needed more than one room to display all the gifts, Mr. Laney had put his foot down.

"Your house would look like a department store, Midge," he told her. "Anything more than one room, and we're talking tacky. Maybe they do that in small South Alabama towns, but this is Mountain Brook. The dining room is all you get. Leave it to me. I'll make it work."

Mr. Laney had also insisted that each and every gift received *had* to be displayed, no matter how hideous or ridiculous, even the fake fruit and the plaster garden gnome.

"Mark my words, Midge," he had warned. "The people who give the worst gifts are the very ones who come by to make sure they're displayed. I have seen this time and again. If you don't put that artificial fruit in the silver epergne, you will live to regret it."

For the most part, however, Caroline had received lovely and expensive gifts whose only flaw was their uselessness. Even when she was embarking with such happiness on her marriage, very few of these gifts had really been needed. The waste of it all made her cringe with shame. Ice buckets? Tongs? She and her husband didn't drink cocktails, nor did any of their friends. They all drank beer—from the bottle. Although she was grateful for the gestures of giving, most of the gifts themselves were irrelevant to her existence. They were accoutrements for the lifestyle of her grandmother's day and earlier eras, when ladies were occupied with hosting other ladies during the day, for bridge games and Garden Club meetings, and entertaining their husbands' clients and colleagues at night. All these fine furnishings had been essentials and necessities to ensure a married couple's social and professional success. Since then, the world had changed, but the customs of the South, as usual, had not. The wedding presents she had received were for a Southern lady who didn't exist anymore, much as some people wanted to ignore or deny that fact, or turn back the clock. But even her grandmother, once a famous hostess, was no longer that kind of Southern lady. Nowadays, all that giftware was valuable primarily to the shops that specialized in selling it to wedding guests who purchased these goods as tokens of esteem and affection for their friends whose children were getting married. She would gladly have walked away from it all if it wouldn't have been an insult to abandon everyone's offerings as if they meant nothing. But for now, what it meant to her was movers and a storage unit; all that stuff was more of a ball and chain than even a marriage certificate itself. Perhaps this, too, was part of its purpose. At any rate, claiming and storing it was the least she could do to give her mother one less reason to be angry and humiliated over what had happened. And at least she had finally finished all those thank-you notes before news of her divorce went public.

Having heard the door, her mother now came downstairs to see who it was, and encountered her daughter in the dining room, gazing around the four walls as if seeing the place for the first time. Clearly her mother had just risen from a nap, as one side of her bouffant hair was flattened next to her head, while the other side sprang intact in its buoyance. Coming by at four, which was the middle of her mother's naptime, Caroline knew she was taking a risk that her mother would be as cross and fretful as a toddler whose afternoon nap had been interrupted. But there was at least an equal chance that her mother would still be so fogged with sleep that her reaction to Caroline's news would be delayed until after the hasty departure she planned to make once she'd dropped her bomb.

Her mother appeared surprised but pleased to see her. It wasn't like Caroline to drop by. But the first thing she said was: "Where is Daniel?" which caused a flood of adrenaline to begin streaming through her daughter's insides. Women of her mother's generation believed that men were the better half, the most important half, because they were the ones who made the money that made life possible.

Sighing, Caroline said, "I came to talk to you about Daniel."

"What's wrong?" her mother said quickly, her alarm system instantly triggered.

"This is hard, Mom. I don't know what to say, except I—we—"

"What happened? Is it true what I heard? Did he find someone else?"

Caroline stared at her mother in disbelief and couldn't find words for several moments. "As a matter of fact, he did," she admitted finally. "But . . ."

Her mother gripped the back of the dining room chair in a cold fury which drained her lips of color and contorted her features into an almost grotesque visage. Caroline could have been a child again, a girl or teenager facing her mother's ugly wrath. Throughout her childhood, whenever she presented anything less than perfection in her life or appearance, she had always been blamed for what went "wrong," regardless of how little control or responsibility she'd had in the matter. A mother's sympathy or compassion was unknown to her; still, she never ceased to be frightened to the core by the murderous rage directed at her by her mother's blazing eyes.

"I knew this would happen!" her mother said through gritted teeth. "You have only yourself to blame, you know. It's all your fault. You just *had* to go back to school, didn't you?" she sneered. "A college degree wasn't good enough for you. You had to leave your husband so you could go get another degree. You don't need another degree. You needed to make your husband happy. Who is she?"

Dazed, Caroline said, "Who is who?"

"The other woman, Caroline! The woman who came in after you left! I don't blame her and I don't blame him either! She saw an opportunity and she took it. That's what she should have done. That's what women are supposed to do! And he wanted a wife, not a bookworm! Not someone who wasn't even there. WHO IS SHE?" her mother shouted.

Caroline could hear the footsteps of her little sister Laura running out of her bedroom and coming down the stairs to investigate the raised voice of her mother, this petite woman whose beauty parlor hair, smashed flat on one side and triumphantly teased on the other, disguised the hellcat that terrorized their lives and frightened them all into passive compliance with her despotic dominion. It might have been funny, if it hadn't been so terribly real.

"Mom," she said as calmly as she could. "It doesn't matter who it is."

"Tell me who it is," her mother insisted grimly.

Spying her sister on the threshold of the dining room, Caroline gave a barely perceptible shake of her head which caused Laura to stop in her tracks and shrink against the wall, eyes wide. Unfortunately, her mother may have thought the shake of the head was aimed at her.

"You have got to tell me who it is!" her mother yelled. "Do you want me to find out at the *grocery store*? Do you realize I was at the *beauty parlor* when *Richard,* my *hairdresser,* told me the gossip about you?" Putting her head in her hands, she cried out as if in unbearable agony. "Do you want me to be the last to know who the other woman is too?" she shouted, looking back up. "Is that it? You want me to find out *in public*? Do you want to put me through that embarrassment as well? TELL ME WHO IT IS!"

"Lily Templeton."

"Your friend?" Her mother was aghast.

"I wouldn't call Lily a friend. Simply a classmate who treats everybody like a friend just in case."

"Well, she's as close to a friend as *you've* ever come. Oh good God!" her mother shrieked, putting her face in her hands again. "How could you do this to me?" She wailed so desperately that Pearl came running from the kitchen to see what was wrong. By now her mother was sobbing uncontrollably. "WHY HAVE YOU DONE THIS TO ME?" she screamed at her daughter.

Pearl looked from one to the other. "What's happened?" she said.

Mrs. Elmore pointed at her daughter. "Caroline has ruined this family!" she said. "She insisted on running off to Tuscaloosa and abandoning her husband. It's no surprise he found someone else! We will never get over the embarrassment of this! It didn't even last a year! And that big, beautiful wedding we were all so proud of! You've made a mockery of that as well as your family. You've made a shambles out of everything! Even your own friend turned on you. And who could blame her? You had a good man. Even if he *is* from a small town, it's the best you could have hoped for. Far better than I ever dreamed you'd get. With a Harvard degree and a law degree and a good job at an important firm. *Your* job was to be a good wife. To make him happy. Why was that so hard for you? He can provide everything—he's even trying to buy a house already. The only thing he might have needed from you was to join the Junior League. Instead, you bolted off to Tuscaloosa. Leaving your husband ALONE. UNATTENDED! What did you think was going to happen? WHY CAN'T YOU EVER DO WHAT YOU'RE SUPPOSED TO? YOU'VE NEVER BEEN ABLE TO DO ANYTHING! AND NOW YOU HAVE NOTHING!"

"I have a Harvard degree too."

"A lot of good it's done you! Do you think men care about that? If you do, you're a bigger fool than even I realized. Men want a girl who's fun, who knows how to have a good time. Who fixes herself up and is ready to go out. But all you care about is books! You do nothing but read all day long. What man would ever want to be with someone who has her head stuck in a book all day? You haven't even had your hair done since it finally grew out from that horrible haircut."

"Now Mrs. Elmore," Pearl interjected. "This is our Caroline. If this man she got is fool enough to walk off and leave, they'll be others."

"That's just it, Pearl," wailed Mrs. Elmore. "What makes you think there *will* be others? She didn't have *one single date* in high school."

"Now wait a minute, Mrs. Elmore," said Pearl. "There sure was somebody. Only I can't think of his name." She looked over to Caroline for help, but Caroline's lips were pressed together firmly in an effort to hold her face together and staunch the flow of tears coursing down her cheeks. "I'll never forget that car of his," Pearl went on. "*Orange.* And him so tall. Fine looking young man. He took Caroline out all the time in that orange car of his," Pearl concluded proudly.

"Nick Scully," said Mrs. Elmore, looking pointedly at her daughter. "Who only took you out because he felt sorry for you! Otherwise, he wouldn't have given you a thought!"

"Mom, Caroline is only twenty-two." Laura edged her way into the room.

"What does that have to do with anything?" She glared at her younger daughter. "She's ruined herself for life! All her chances. She'll never recover from the shame of this. None of us will!"

"Mom, please," Caroline managed. "Let me explain. Let's try to discuss this instead of just yelling."

"No!" yelled her mother. "I've heard all I need to know. You've lost your husband. That's all that matters. And you won't be finding a new one anytime soon! If ever!"

"Mom—"

"GET OUT!" her mother shouted, and stomped her feet in frustration. "Get out of my house! If you're so wild about Tuscaloosa and graduate school, then go back there! This instant. I don't even want to look at your face and I certainly don't want to see you in this house. Whatever's happened, you've brought it on yourself, so don't come back here looking for money or a place to live or anything. Do you hear me? Now go! Leave! Get out of my sight! If I never see you again, I won't be sorry!"

* * *

Her granddaughter was sobbing so hard that neither Mrs. Lambert nor her daughter Shirley could make out all she told them. This was just like what had happened when her granddaughter was in high school and had come over to the Lambert's house seeking solace after a fight with her mother. Back then, Mrs. Lambert had soothed her by saying that everything would change and work itself out when Caroline went off to college. She had been right. Her granddaughter had met this boy at the end of her first year. He had been a boyfriend, then a serious boyfriend, then a fiancé, then her husband. With a man by her side, Caroline had finally made her mother happy. But when the man left, Caroline lost both her protection and her validation. Midge had obviously torn into her daughter all over again.

"He wasn't right for you, honey," Mrs. Lambert said.

"He was just a small-town boy from nowhere, *on the make,*" Shirley added.

"He didn't want you for yourself," Mrs. Lambert went on. "He wanted you for himself. Marriages like that never work out."

This was the distilled wisdom from Mrs. Lambert's own married life, whose unhappiness had not been wasted now that she could share its hard-earned lessons with her granddaughter. In fact, her words proved so comforting to Caroline that she didn't even have to explain how she had arrived at her understanding of ill-fated marriages. But Mrs. Lambert had reached the age when she could look back and see the pattern. She, her daughter, and then her granddaughter had all made the same error. They had not chosen wisely in marriage; they had not chosen at all. They had allowed themselves to be chosen by men who never once thought what they could do for these pretty girls they were marrying. They thought only of what these pretty girls would do for them. It had taken Mrs. Lambert years to understand her mistake, and there was nothing she could do about it. Midge still didn't see her own mistake, although her husband didn't treat her right and never had. Her granddaughter had seen the problem and gotten out before her life was ruined. Mrs. Lambert was glad. She went into her bedroom to write a check for as much as she could afford. It wasn't nearly what she wished she could give, and her granddaughter tried to refuse it, protesting that she had not come for money, but for a different kind of help. Nevertheless, Mrs. Lambert thought that even as little money as she had to offer was the best kind of help she could give at the moment. It was also the best way to start reversing the role she had played in the mistake committed in her own life and then perpetrated on her daughter and granddaughter. Although they had all been raised with the idea that a woman needed to "get" a man, what this really boiled down to was making themselves attractive and available to men with looks, name and money, and taking the best offer that came their way according to these measures of a man. They were not taught to be free agents of their own lives; they had all been taught *to be chosen*. They had been taught *how to be chosen*. By a sorority, by a debutante society, by an eligible suitor. They had not been taught to choose anything for themselves, nor had they been given all the means necessary to make their own good choices about anything in life. Barbara Lambert had been told that she "got" the "best" man of her year, and he was sure to make a wonderful husband. They couldn't have been more wrong. And when her marriage proved a bitter disappointment, she had nothing to fall back on, no education, no college degree. As she stuffed the check in her granddaughter's handbag, Mrs. Lambert wanted to believe that she was making a start at putting a stop to all that nonsense.

* * *

The next time Caroline came over, Mrs. Lambert and Shirley were ensconced in the den as usual at two o'clock, watching *General Hospital.* When they heard the car drive up in the driveway, their first reaction was of contempt for Jim, who should have known better than to return from his errands so early, while they were still watching their programs.

Mrs. Lambert stubbed out her cigarette with disgust. "He probably forgot his wallet," she muttered, shaking her head in disbelief at his utter incompetence.

Shirley had gone to the window, parted the curtains they closed for their programs, and peered out. "No, Mama!" she said. "It's not Daddy. It's Caroline!"

"Oh, my lands," said Mrs. Lambert, clicking off *General Hospital.* She pushed against the sofa with both hands in an attempt to rise. "Help me get up."

Shirley had just stubbed out her own cigarette and pulled her mother off the couch when they heard the doorbell. Caroline seemed better this time, not nearly so upset, but still overwrought as she sat down in the den. Last time she'd been sobbing and pouring out an incoherent account of the divorce and her mother's reaction. This time, she didn't seem to know what to say, and just kept twisting her hands in her lap.

"Tell us what it is, honey," Mrs. Lambert said finally.

Then the words came pouring out again in another incoherent account that neither Mrs. Lambert nor Shirley could follow. "Remarriage" was the only word they could pick up on to make sense of what she was saying. It was not what Mrs. Lambert wanted to hear. She shook her head.

"You're just lonely, darling," she said. "He wasn't the one for you before. I don't think he'll be the one a second time around."

Then Caroline shook her head. Another torrent of words rushed out.

"It's somebody else!" Shirley explained to her mother.

"Who? Who is it?" Mrs. Lambert looked at her daughter, because Caroline was still so unintelligible to her.

"The Scully boy, Mama," Shirley said, before turning to her niece. "Is he the one who used to take you around all those years ago?"

Caroline nodded and looked at them nervously. They looked at each other.

"The Scully family"—Shirley started to say.

"Hush," Mrs. Lambert told her.

For a moment the three generations of women sat in silence in the den.

"He must have waited for you, didn't he?" Mrs. Lambert said.

Her granddaughter nodded. "Yes."

"Then he's the one," Mrs. Lambert said.

Shirley clapped her hands. "How romantic!" she said. "And another wedding! Just think, Mama."

Caroline's face clouded.

"Hush!" Mrs. Lambert told her daughter again. "Don't you remember what her father said about the fifty thousand dollar mistake?"

"The Scully family could pay for this one," Shirley pointed out. "They could put on the biggest wedding Birmingham has ever seen, and it would be pennies to them."

"No," Caroline said emphatically, shaking her head. "No wedding."

It was going to be at the courthouse, she explained. Downtown Birmingham. The following Friday. They would leave for Europe the next day. She wanted at least one of them to be there, at least one member from her own family as a witness. His mother would be the other witness. She knew they never went downtown, didn't like going there, but—

"We will both be there," Shirley told her immediately. "Mama and me. We will be there. Now. Where will you stay, the night before, since you can't stay at your mother's . . ." Shirley stopped as Caroline blushed, afraid she'd said the wrong thing, as usual.

"She can stay where she wants," said Mrs. Lambert, who interpreted her granddaughter's embarrassment to mean that she planned to stay with him. Mrs. Lambert did not want to get into this with Shirley right now. Living together was unheard of in her day; a girl ruined her life that way. This is what Mrs. Lambert was taught, and she had taught both her daughters this same lesson. But everybody had also said that divorce would ruin you for life, and they'd been wrong. Mrs. Lambert had ruined her life through marriage. Marriage was supposed to be her crowning achievement, the one that secured her happiness for the rest of her life. She had done everything "they" had told her to do in order to have the happy and successful life she was supposed to have. After more than four decades of unhappiness following her marriage at age nineteen, she could only conclude that "they" had been wrong. If they could be wrong about one thing, like marriage, then they could be wrong about others, like living together and divorce. She could only wish that divorce had come along when she was young. That she could have had a second chance instead of being stuck with her own foolish mistake.

"Stay here," Shirley said. "With us. We'll take you down to the courthouse. After all, the groom shouldn't see his bride until she arrives to get married. Even though there won't be a wedding, it will still be your wedding day."

* * *

The following Friday, Nick Scully was at the courthouse in downtown Birmingham a little early. It might have been the first time he'd been early for anything in his entire life. But his apartment was on the Southside, he told himself. The others were all coming from Mountain Brook, which was further away from downtown. Still. He looked at his watch. They were late. He ran his hands through his hair. He looked at his watch again. They were definitely late. No matter the heat, or his navy blue suit, he decided to go back outside to the courthouse steps and look for their arrival.

Halfway down the steps, he spotted a familiar car pulling up. His mother got out of the passenger side and came running up to greet him with a hug. But who had parked the car and followed behind her? He peered over her shoulder.

"Dad!" he exclaimed, shocked.

His father stuck his hand out and smiled. "Congratulations, son," he said.

When Nick grasped the outstretched hand, his father pulled him into an awkward embrace and patted him on the back. His mother looked away, fished a tissue from her purse, and wiped her eyes.

"Where is she?" His father looked around on the steps.

"Her grandmother is bringing her," Nick said. "Look." He pointed to another car just pulling up. "Maybe that's her now."

His father shook his head. "No," he said.

Nick watched in disbelief as his brother, sister-in-law, and their three children piled out of the car. Dressed in their country club best, the children came boiling up the steps. Their parents, equally well attired, followed at a more sedate pace, smiling and waving. No sooner had Nick fielded the pummeling from his nephews and the greetings from their parents, than he saw his sister and her family making their way toward them. Nick looked around in amazement at the group gathered together on the courthouse steps. Except for his mother's older sisters, it was his entire living family. He'd always thought he was the one who didn't matter, the unnecessary one, the useless one. It hadn't even occurred to him that anyone but his mother would want to be here on this day.

"The lunch!" he cried. "Let's go inside. "I've got to find a payphone and increase the reservation!"

As he ran up the steps, he could hear his brother and sister inquiring about the bride, who still had not arrived. He believed he heard the phrase "Just got divorced" from his sister, while his brother said something about "so young."

"Wait here!" he told them when they all entered the lobby.

Surely by the time he found a phone, called the restaurant and made it back to the lobby, she would be there. But she wasn't. His brother came up and took him aside.

"I can tell by the look on your face this isn't one of your pranks," he said. "To get us down here for no reason."

Nick shook his head. Just then the courthouse door opened. They all turned to see the new arrival, but it wasn't his bride. It was a handsome older woman with raven-black hair. She looked somewhat familiar, but was no one they knew. Unfortunately, instead of going about her business, she stood just inside the door. The situation in the lobby became even more tense, as Nick's family stood around silently, not wishing to speak in front of a stranger. Then to Nick's surprise, the older woman eventually turned to look right at him with a smile.

"You look like an anxious groom," she observed.

How had this woman—this total stranger—known anything about the situation? Was it that obvious? Nick nodded at her with a nervous grin and ran his hand through his hair. "She'll be here," he said, hoping to make light of awkward circumstances.

"She went down the block to get some flowers," the older woman said. "She realized she didn't have a bouquet."

It took Nick a moment to process what she was telling him. Then it him.

"You're the grandmother!" he cried, skidding across the slick floor in his rush to greet her.

Barbara Lambert had never in her life been so effusively welcomed by the cream of Mountain Brook society. In the middle of this throng surrounding Mrs. Lambert, Nick did not even see his bride when she entered the courthouse at last. One moment, he looked up, and there she was, waiting for him as he had waited for her.

He gasped when he saw her. She had always been beautiful to him, but today she was really beautiful. He'd forgotten she was going to the salon yesterday, and now her hair was all one length, swinging across her shoulders in a blonde swirl. It was absolutely . . . beautiful. And the dress was like something from the 1920s. Perhaps it actually *was* from the 1920s: a white flapper dress, with a dropped waist and a slightly ruffled hem falling just below the knees. It was amazing. After the ceremony, he would have to take her photograph getting into his Karmann Ghia in that dress.

He looked at the grandmother. "Your dress?" he asked her.

Surprised but pleased, she nodded happily. "It was my mother's," she explained.

The jewelry too, he guessed. Those drop pearl earrings and the three-stranded pearl bracelet he'd never seen her wear before. He hadn't thought of jewelry any more than he had thought of flowers for his bride. She had a lovely bunch of long-stemmed calla lilies in her arms that was exactly what he would have picked if he'd thought about it at all. He would have to do better than this from now on, as her husband. At least he had remembered the ring. He patted his breast pocket. It wasn't there. He looked up, his face frozen in panic. His brother offered some lame joke about cold feet. His family tittered nervously. Then Nick remembered he'd transferred the ring to an inside pocket. When he felt it there, he pushed free of the group and skidded over toward his bride.

"Let's do this!" he cried.

Smiling, she took one of the calla lilies, snapped off most of its long stem, and threaded the flower through the buttonhole of his jacket.

* * *

Caroline had not wanted to hold the lunch at either the Mountain Brook or the Birmingham country clubs. And for some reason, Nick did not want *The* Club, although he'd taken her there in the past and had a soft spot for the old place, with its famous neon sign and even more famous view of the city. She agreed to Highlands because she thought it would be empty of anyone they knew on a weekday at noon. But the first person she saw was Lily Templeton.

Fortunately, she and Nick were the last of the family group to enter the restaurant, because Nick had not trusted the valet with his Karmann Ghia. As soon as they arrived, the others waved merrily from a big round table in the far rear corner. It seemed easy to pretend she didn't notice Lily as she made her way over to her new in-laws. It also seemed likely that Lily would welcome the chance to go unnoticed for once in her life. But Lily hopped up eagerly to greet them as if there were no reason for either one of them to be anything less than delighted to see her. She certainly appeared delighted to see them, as if they were dearest friends she loved with all her heart.

"Nick Scully!" she cried. "Caroline! You two sure didn't waste any time! Are you dating now?"

Before they knew what she was doing, she was hugging them both with all her might.

"No, we're not dating," Nick told her, grinning as he peeled Lily's hands from where they lingered on his shoulders. "We're married."

"Married!" Lily clapped a hand on her mouth. "How romantic!"

"It is," Nick agreed. "But if you'll excuse us, we need to join the family."

As they made their way over, he murmured, "It had to happen some time. Be glad it's over."

But it wasn't quite over. Later, when Caroline went to the restroom, Lily followed right behind as if she'd watched and waited for this opportunity. The sumptuously appointed ladies room was filled with a soft ambient glow that came from no discernible light source, and the same festive jazz that played in the outer rooms was piped in at a faint volume. As Billie Holliday crooned *Stars Fell on Alabama*, Caroline braced herself for a confrontation.

She was taken completely aback when Lily threw her arms around her neck and hugged her tightly. "You owe me!" Lily cried happily. "You absolutely owe me! Now tell me *everything*. How did you get him?"

Caroline stared at her, dumbfounded that Lily expected thanks for betraying bonds of both friendship and marriage. Was it truly possible that some Southern girls were still raised to be these exquisitely beautiful and feminine creatures of the jungle, out to "get" the best man they could, any way they could? Lily apparently believed that all women operated by this primitive code, so that ties between friends could be a help but need not be a hindrance. Likewise, marriages and relationships already formed by others could be as fertile hunting ground as any in the jungle, if the best mates were those already claimed. Caroline struggled for a response to all this from the depths of her dismay.

"I *owe* you?" she said. "How could you say such a thing? After what you did with . . . Daniel?"

"Oh, honey," Lily giggled, moving over to the large square mirror framed in copper. "No offense. But I was never interested in your husband." She turned back toward her friend. "Your *first* husband, that is."

Caroline remained rooted to her spot, unable to move toward the facilities. "You sure gave a lot of people a different impression," she said.

Lily brushed that idea aside with a wave of her hand before digging in her purse for a lipstick. "I swear to you, I didn't do a thing with your husband that I don't do with every other man."

"But he was a *married* man," Caroline protested.

"It's up to him to remember that and behave like one, isn't it?" Lily said, leaning across the sink toward the mirror as she applied lipstick. "But he was all too ready to forget his marriage vows. I did you a favor. His true colors came out and you saw them for the first time when he went after me. Now be honest." Lily surveyed the results of her lipstick application. "Aren't you glad you're no longer with him?" Lily leaned back and dropped the lipstick in her handbag.

"Yes," Caroline admitted slowly. "But still. What you did . . ."

"That was nothing." Lily said, pulling out a tissue from the lacquered tray and blotting her lips. "Once in college? I was interested in this guy? So I made friends with his ex-girlfriend, who was still friends with his sister, who introduced me to her ex-boyfriend, who I went out with for *months* because he was best friends with the guy I was interested in. I had to go through *three people* to get to the guy I was after, and he wasn't nearly as much of a prize as

Nick Scully." Tearing her eyes away from the mirror, Lily looked at her friend and wagged her finger in a playfully scolding manner. "I tried to tell you that you had *dated* him way back when, but you were too . . ." Lily giggled. "You were too *stupid* to see it. So you should be glad I helped you see what you needed to see. Don't you agree?"

"Yes," Caroline said quietly. "I agree I was . . . stupid. But I can't say I owe you anything."

Lily gave a dramatic sigh. "I guess not," she conceded. "Not after what your wedding last year did for me."

"What did my wedding do for you?"

Lily moved closer and clutched her friend's arm. "Honey," she said. "That guy who lives in New York? Who bugged me to pieces for months? *Do you know who he is?*"

Caroline nodded. In spite of herself, the beginnings of a smile twitched at the corners of her mouth.

"Honey," said Lily, her nails digging into Caroline's arms. "He is a *Du-Pont*. There is no bigger prize than that. It may be time for me to quit all my fun and games and settle down."

Shaking her head, Caroline moved finally into one of the little rooms within the room housing the actual plumbing works. "I don't see Hunter DuPont moving to Alabama," she called from inside.

"Who said anything about living in Alabama? Why would you want to live in Alabama when you can live in New York?"

"I thought you said New York was more trouble than it's worth."

"It is if you don't have the money. But if you have the money, there is no place on earth more fun than New York City. And let me tell you: *He has got the money.* I will never do better than this. Why didn't you *tell* me?"

"I think I tried to." Caroline smiled outright as she emerged from her little room. "Only you were too . . . stupid? . . . to see it?" Rinsing her hands at the hammered copper sink, she looked up at the matching mirror above it to see Lily's reaction.

Lily nodded emphatically. "I sure was, honey. Can you *imagine*? If I had let a chance like that go by? I didn't even have to *work* for it. How do you think I'll do in New York?"

"You are perfect for New York."

Giggling with happy pride, Lily concurred that she thought so too.

"Wait a minute," she said, reaching out to restrain her friend from leaving. "You're not going to get away that easily. I have *got* to know."

"What?" said Caroline, turning back around with annoyance. Truly, she'd had enough of Lily. As comfortable as this ladies room was, it was too close quarters to linger for long with a girl who'd been to bed with both her husbands.

"How in the world did you get him? What did you *doooooo*?"

Caroline found herself stifling unexpected giggles, which piqued Lily's curiosity all the more.

"I need to *knoooooow*," Lily wailed in mock anguish. "For future reference. Please tell me."

"Okay," said Caroline, feigning seriousness. "You want to know? Here's what I did."

As she paused dramatically, Lily's eyes grew wide with anticipation.

"I did nothing to get him," Caroline stated flatly, almost in anger. "Absolutely nothing."

"Oh," said Lily, bored and disappointed with this answer. "That's exactly how I got Hunter too." She began prodding Caroline toward the door, eager now to exit. "But don't forget," she warned. "Guys like a challenge. Hunter will to have to win me all over again every day of his life. And that's how I'll keep us both going."

As they reached the door, Caroline was shaking her head.

"Don't try to tell me Nick Scully doesn't like a challenge," Lily admonished. "Because I know he does."

"You're right," Caroline agreed, opening the door. "He likes a challenge."

Lily narrowed her eyes suddenly at her friend as they reentered the dining area. "You're keeping your secrets," she accused. "Aren't you? You don't want me to know what you did to get him. Do you?"

Laughing, Caroline moved away toward her table.

"I don't blame you a bit," Lily whispered when she caught up. "You *shouldn't* give away your secrets. Nick Scully is just about the best-looking guy I have ever seen in my life. Not as rich as Hunter DuPont, maybe, but *rich enough*."

EPILOGUE
The Second Honeymoon

Norman Laney was sitting at a tiny outdoor table in the Campo Santo Stefano, not too far from his hotel in Venice. He liked the Italian custom of a glass of prosecco in the late afternoon, and it gave him something to do while his old ladies rose from their naps and dressed for dinner. He enjoyed watching the children kick a soccer ball around the square while the mothers chattered amongst themselves on the steps of surrounding buildings. His colleague, Elizabeth Elder, had accompanied him on this summer's trip to Europe, and she was sitting with him at his usual table that afternoon, also sipping a glass of prosecco, when a familiar-looking young man came running up with a camera around his neck. Bending to one knee, he quickly set about taking photographs of the children as the slowly setting sun enveloped them in a golden aura and gave them the appearance of angels frolicking in heaven.

"He looks like Nick Scully," Norman Laney observed.

"He is Nick Scully," said Elizabeth Elder.

"Did I hear someone call my name?" said the familiar-looking young man. Rising from his crouch, he turned toward their table and pushed his hair off his forehead. "Don't get up!" he cried, as they prepared to greet him. "Stay just like you are! It's a perfect photograph. Let me get this."

Elizabeth was charmed; Norman did his best to pretend to be.

"Sit down," said Norman afterward, doing his best to pretend to be cordial. "Tell us what brings you to Italy."

Nick grinned and ran a hand through his hair, but did not sit down. "I guess you could say I'm on my honeymoon," he told them.

"Honeymoon!" exclaimed Norman and Elizabeth, looking at each other in disbelief.

"Dear boy," said Norman. "I had no idea. Who is she? Where is she?"

As Nick whipped his head around, Norman and Elizabeth craned their necks to peer beyond him toward the narrow alley from which he'd emerged earlier. They saw no one coming.

"She should be on her way," said Nick, hastily putting his camera in his case. "Let me go get her."

"Wait a minute!" said Norman, reaching out to delay his departure. "Tell us who it is first. Is it someone from home? Someone we know?"

"You know her all right," Nick grinned. "But I'll let you see for yourself. Let me go find her, before she gets lost. I've lost her before." Dashing off, he called over his shoulder. "Not only in Venice! I'm not going to lose her again."

A few moments later, Nick re-emerged from the alleyway holding the hand of a young woman whose face they couldn't see as it was bathed in the light of the summer sun. Only when she was almost upon their table did they recognize who she was.

"Darling!" Norman exclaimed, delighted. "How lovely to see you. But what are you doing here?" He turned to Nick. "I thought you said you were going to get . . ." Norman's voice ceased abruptly in midsentence.

"My . . ." Nick gave a shy grin and held up a hand which had hers in its grasp. "Bride," he finished.

"I wanted to tell you, Mr. Laney," she said.

The welcome Norman had readied for Nick Scully's bride froze on his face. If he had been a character in a cartoon, which is how he felt at the moment, his frozen face would have broken off into fragments and rained down on the paving stones of the Campo Santo Stefano. The fragmentation of his face would have been followed by the splintering of every other frost-bitten particle of his body, until he was nothing more than a heap of rubble to be swept up and carted off by the street sweepers of Venice.

"Darling," was all he could say, sitting heavily back down and mopping his face with the handkerchief he managed to produce from the depths of his pants pocket. "So soon," he murmured, more to himself than anyone else.

Dropping Nick's hand, she moved closer to the table. "Nick is the right person for me, Mr. Laney," she told him. Turning around, she reached for Nick's hand to pull him closer to the table. "The only person."

"What on earth gives you that idea?" Norman Laney pierced them both with icy eyes glaring from his frigid face.

Caroline stole a glance at Nick and then looked back at Mr. Laney. "I don't know how to explain it," she said softly. "Except to say, he helps me be who I am, because . . . because . . ."

"Because I love her and want nothing more than to devote myself to her happiness!" declared Nick, winking at Norman Laney. "Because her happiness is my happiness! Because she brings out the best in me! You'll be amazed by what she does for me!"

"It's . . . it's always been this way, Mr. Laney. This is what we've always meant to each other . . . only . . . I didn't see it. . . ."

"Why don't you join us," suggested Elizabeth Elder. "Sit down. Norman, let's find the waiter so we can toast the happy couple."

Nick looked over his shoulder at the sun. He was grinning when he turned back around. "This time of day," he said. "When the sun is setting, it shines right into our bedroom"—

"Nick!" His bride blushed.

"I mean our hotel room." Nick ran a hand through his hair. "We have a window with a balcony on a little side canal, and this one gondolier comes down every afternoon. He stops right under our window and serenades his passengers during the sunset. If we don't hurry, we'll miss him today." He grabbed his bride's hand and pulled her away. "Tomorrow!" he called. "An hour before now! We'll be here!"

For a long while after they disappeared, Norman said nothing and refused to look at Elizabeth.

"What is it you think he does?" he said finally, staring straight ahead as the mothers attempted to round up their children amidst vociferous protests. "Why do all women fall for him so hard? What does he *do* to them? Is it something . . . Do you suppose it's something . . . *Sexual?*" He whispered this last word as he looked at Elizabeth.

"Of course it is, Norman," said Elizabeth.

"I knew it!" he said, banging his fist so hard on the table their glasses jumped. "What is it you think he does to get them under his spell? I'll bet it's not even *legal* in the state of Alabama!"

"Norman," said Elizabeth, shaking her head as her body shook with laughter. "I didn't mean to suggest that he does anything unheard of. Or *illegal.* For heaven's sake. All I meant to say is that most of what happens between young men and young women is sexual in one way or another."

"I am going to *kill* Julian," said Norman through gritted teeth. "When I get back home, the first thing I will do is kill Julian Petsinger."

"Julian?" said Elizabeth, surprised. "What does he have to do with this?"

"He swore to me," Norman said. "Four years ago, five years ago. When I learned Nick Scully had been taking her out. When she was still at Brook-Haven. *In high school.* Sixteen! Seventeen years-old! Julian swore to me that

Nick never once laid a hand on her in that way. Didn't even kiss her. And I was fool enough to believe it! Trust me, if I'd known the truth I would have found a way to put a stop to it!"

"What makes you think Julian wasn't telling the truth?"

Norman gaped at her. "You saw them together!" he cried. "You heard what he said! The setting sun shining into the bedroom! The gondolier serenading outside the window! You can't tell me you don't know what's happening in that hotel room!"

"Calm down, Norman." She laid a restraining hand on his arm. "I'm not talking about what's happening now. I thought we were discussing what happened back then. And I think Julian was telling you the truth."

"Oh, what does it matter?" he muttered.

"Well, think about it, Norman. I believe it does matter. It means a great deal."

"What?" He turned on her fiercely. "What does it mean?"

"It means his love for her is true. He wants what's right for her. What's best for her."

"Are you calling him the best?" Norman sneered at the thought.

"I mean he let her go free. Left it to her to find her way back to him if that's what she wanted."

Norman was silent as he considered this. When the waiter appeared, he asked for the tab. It was getting late, time for them to head back to the hotel and get ready for dinner.

"What do you have against him anyway?" said Elizabeth, as they rose from the table.

Norman turned to stare at her. "Elizabeth," he said. "Nick Scully doesn't even have a *job*."

"He does now," she said, proceeding ahead into the campo.

"What?" Norman stood still, temporarily stricken. He always hated being the last to learn an important piece of gossip. "I haven't heard of anything." He moved swiftly to catch up to her. "This is news to me. What job?"

"He's a husband now."

"A husband." Norman looked at her in disgust. "You call that a job?" A flock of pigeons took sudden, shrill flight in front of them, as if sharing in Norman Laney's outrage.

"I do call that a job," said Elizabeth, unruffled by either Norman or the pigeons. "To be a good husband requires hard work. That makes it a job. Same as being a good wife, a good mother, or a good father."

"It may be the only job he'll ever have," said Norman grimly, as they entered the narrow alleyway leading from the Campo Santo Stefano to their hotel.

"It may be the only job he needs."

"Considering he hasn't the slightest scrap of ambition!" Norman barked with contemptuous laughter, causing a couple heading in the opposite direction to give him curious looks and as wide a berth as the alley would allow.

"Maybe his ambition was to be with her. To be her husband."

"You call that ambition?" Norman scoffed. "And what about her? Let's say I don't give a damn about him. What about her?"

"Norman, you know very well you do give a damn about him. This could be perfect for both of them. Don't you see?"

"How could this possibly be perfect for her?"

"Remember what she said to you just now. He helps her be who she is. And you know how ambitious *she* is."

"I know how ambitious she *was*," said Norman bitterly.

"What makes you think she's lost her ambition?"

"I think she's lost her *mind*!"

At that point the alleyway narrowed further, so that the obese Norman Laney and the stout Elizabeth Elder were squeezed in by the walls on either side.

"Calm yourself, Norman," said Elizabeth, stepping back so Norman could proceed ahead single file. "She hasn't lost anything. She has *found* the right person. To help her be who she is, and achieve what she wants. And you heard what he said, about devoting himself to her happiness."

Norman stopped in his tracks and turned to confront her furiously. "He was *joking*, Elizabeth! Didn't you see the way he was winking at me?"

Elizabeth shook her head. "He wasn't joking. Underneath all his flippancy, he's every bit as serious as he is intelligent. I believe we *will* be impressed by what he becomes as her husband."

Norman made no reply as they continued to walk single file. Elizabeth waited for the alleyway to broaden so they could walk abreast before she continued. "They will do for each other exactly what we do in our jobs."

Norman said nothing until they emerged from the alley and headed for the door of their hotel. "What?" he asked with deliberate obtuseness. "What is it we do in our jobs that could possibly be like what they do to each other?"

Ignoring his tone along with his slight twisting of her words, she paused on the threshold of the hotel. "We help young people be who they are.

Accomplish their goals. You've said that to me many a time, when you've defined our mission as teachers."

"Well, so what?" said Norman, pulling open the front door with a vengeance.

"Nobody stops needing that kind of help. That's one thing marriage is for."

Elizabeth nodded politely to the hotel staff as they made their way to the elevator. Norman ignored them completely and jabbed angrily at the elevator button. "Well, I don't know about you," he said as they waited. "But I'm not going to be at my usual table drinking my usual glass of prosecco tomorrow afternoon."

"Norman Laney," said Elizabeth, as the elevator doors opened and they stepped in. She waited for the doors to close in front of them, grateful they were the only occupants. "You will be there at your usual table tomorrow afternoon. You will have a smile on your face. You will order a *bottle* of prosecco. And you will have a wedding gift waiting for them."

"A wedding gift?!"

"You will find it tomorrow in the shops of Venice. I'll help you."

"How about a plague doctor's mask?"

"Perfect."

"Perfect?"

The elevator stopped and they stepped into the hotel corridor leading to their rooms.

"Exactly what Nick Scully would love," she told him. "You know, Norman, the two of you have a lot in common. You love so many of the same things, including Caroline. So give this a chance. For her sake at least."

They arrived at their adjacent hotel rooms.

"If you make me go," said Norman, putting his key in the lock. "I'll be *wearing* the plague doctor's mask when they arrive!" He pushed open the door and closed it emphatically behind him.

Elizabeth remained in the hallway, trying to restrain her mirth. She thought of how Nick Scully would love nothing better than arriving at the table in the Campo Santo Stefano to find Norman Laney sitting at his usual table while wearing a plague doctor's mask. She could already see his grin and hear his wild shouts of laughter. Before sitting down, he would unzip his camera and start taking photographs.

* * *

In another Venetian hotel not far away, the newlyweds were lying in bed as dusk overtook the ancient city.

"We got back just in the nick of time," he said. "To hear the gondolier."

"That's how you are with everything," she murmured. "Just in the nick of time. I remember we smuggled a pizza through the exit door of the cinema just in the nick of time for the movie. We grabbed Chinese take-out and raced all the way out to Pell City and got there just in time for the last showing at the drive-in. The last showing *ever*, before it closed down. With everything you do, somehow you're always just in the nick of time."

"Does that bother you about me?"

"I love that about you. You found me again just in the nick of time. It's who you are. It's Nick. My Nick."

"And what are you?" he grinned. "Not my Mountain Brook girl. Unlike the first man who tried to be your husband, I never wanted a Mountain Brook girl. When I was at Princeton, I always wanted one of those really smart Harvard girls. That's what you are. You're my Harvard bride."

Laughing, she bobbed up from where she lay on the bed and seized her pillow. "I'm done with being a bride!" she cried. As usual, he was too quick, way ahead of her. Before she could smack him, he had snatched the pillow out of her hands and pulled her down on top of him, so it was only the pillow of her breasts which ambushed that antic grin on his joyful face.

* * *

In the other Venetian hotel, the phone rang in Norman Laney's room with an overseas call. The news could not wait for his return; Virginia knew he'd want to hear right away.

"Hear what?" he said gruffly. He was running late; his old ladies would be downstairs in the lobby waiting for him to take them to dinner. And besides, he was starving. He didn't have time for a phone call.

"Are you ready? Brace yourself, Norman."

"What is it?"

"It's about Caroline Elmore's divorce."

"What about it?"

"We know what happened now."

"What happened?"

"Nick Scully broke up her marriage and eloped with her before the month was out."

The long distance line crackled with static as Virginia waited eagerly for the explosion after dropping her bombshell.

"Who told you that?" he asked sharply.

"Everybody," she said. "Everybody is talking about it. That's what everybody is saying."

"Well, everybody is wrong!" Norman boomed.

His declaration startled himself even more than Virginia. He had not known he was going to say that. Suddenly Virginia understood.

"I'm afraid it's true, Norman. Nobody here can believe it either. But the Scullys themselves went to the courthouse and watched the marriage take place. The Elmores got a letter from Caroline. The only good thing anybody can say about it is it won't last."

"Oh, but it will," said Norman, more to himself than her. "It has."

This was lost on Virginia, who hadn't heard him and was much more interested in what she herself had to say. "Everybody is saying that Nick Scully did it just for kicks. To see if he could. Wreck a marriage one minute and get the girl to run off with him the next. But we all know, as soon as the thrill of that conquest is gone and Nick gets bored with his latest escapade, it will all be over. There's nothing in that relationship. It will never last."

"It already has lasted," Norman informed her.

"What are you talking about?"

"He's always loved her and she's always loved him, and that love has lasted through a lot of trial and error already. If it can survive the worst, it will positively flourish now." Norman twirled the phone cord as if to demonstrate the flourishing of this union.

"Are you trying to tell me this is true love?" Virginia scoffed.

"I didn't see it myself at first," he conceded magnanimously. "It's not always easy to recognize. Now you need to go tell everyone you know. Say you heard it from me. Nick Scully is not the villain. He's the hero. Okay? He didn't break up a marriage; he rescued the girl he's always loved from the depths of despair. Got that? I'm counting on you to spread the word and get the true story out."

If there was anything Norman loved better than hearing the gossip, it was *making* the gossip, especially because that was the only way to beat it. Tom and Evelyn Scully were going to love him for this: their no-good son transformed into the hero. Such was the power of good storytelling to make truth out of fiction. Norman had finally found the way to help this young man, and get back in the Scully's good graces for once and for all. Not to mention that if Caroline *had* to be married—and apparently, she did—he far preferred a husband prepared to put himself at her service rather than one who required hers to obtain objectives that had never been that important to her, namely money and position. That this new husband had those things already anyway was a delightful bonus that made every cell in Norman Laney's massive body hum with satisfaction.

"How do you know all this?" Virginia said crossly. Just when she finally thought she had a solid-gold piece of gossip Norman had not yet heard, he'd not only heard it already, he even knew the *true story*. It was infuriating.

"I've seen them. I've talked to them," Norman replied coolly.

"You've seen them?!" she cried. "Why didn't you tell me? Where?"

"Here in Venice. On their honeymoon. They told me the whole story."

This would only be a lie for twenty-four hours, because he *would* hear the whole story tomorrow, when he met them at his usual table for his usual glass of prosecco in the afternoon. And if necessary, he would gently advise them on which details to emphasize and which ones to leave out when telling their story to others. Even relationships that didn't have dubious origins needed a strong narrative to support them, as well as a strong supporting cast. Norman decided he would take the lead in supplying both, as his contribution to the health of a marriage that could help fix its society like it was going to fix the two of them, if only that society could be prevented from trying to tear it down. Alone, Caroline and Nick had both been failures—as man and woman—in the eyes of Mountain Brook. Married, they would make each other man and woman, which is often as far as success went in Mountain Brook. But together, these two could help change their world. He just knew it. Thanks to Elizabeth Elder, he could see it now. And thanks to Midge Elmore, who had been the very first to see it, years ago. Until now, no one had equaled Norman when it came to matchmaking, because you had to know more than just the two people. You had to have a *vision* of the future. But in this case, he had to hand it to Midge. She had seen what nobody else had. As soon as he got back home, he'd take her to lunch to celebrate. Highlands Bar and Grill.

After he hung up on Virginia, he reflected that the plague doctor's mask was probably not the best choice he could make for a wedding gift. Instead, he would get them a Harlequin mask. Harlequin had always been Norman's favorite commedia dell'arte character, and sometimes, against the odds and out of keeping with the traditional plot, it was Arlecchino who got the girl and lived happily ever after.

AUTHOR'S NOTE AND ACKNOWLEDGMENTS

In addition to one of my all-time favorite books, the classic *Let Us Now Praise Famous Men,* by James Agee and Walker Evans, I am indebted to the follow-up book, *And Their Children After Them,* by the reporter/photographer team of Dale Maharidge and Michael Williamson. Published in 1989, this book retraces the journey that Agee and Evans undertook through the sharecropping, tenant-farming country of Hale County, Alabama in 1936. Maharidge and Williamson interviewed and photographed many of those who, as children and young adults, had been the subjects of Agee's notes and Evans' photographs fifty years earlier. They also tracked down many of the descendants of the original subjects. The results of their research and documentation are fascinating, if at times painful to read. From their pages I learned of the tragic fate of the girl James Agee called Maggie Louise, who was ten at the time their paths crossed in Alabama. I saw a photograph of the flattened remains of a house belonging to one of the families. Over the years, I have taken several of my own personal journeys through Hale County, Alabama, especially during the time I taught at the University of Alabama in Tuscaloosa, which isn't far away. I am grateful to Dale Maharidge and Michael Williamson for enhancing my knowledge of the history and geography of this part of my native state.

I am always grateful to Tom Uskali, my dear friend and first reader, but this time I am all the more appreciative because this novel has been the hardest to get right. Without his insights and guidance, I could not have done it. My two peer reviewers, John Sledge and Lanier Scott Isom, both produced the excellent suggestions I've come to count on from them. Sean Smith, who at heart is still a History and Literature major, came through as always with multiple readings of multiple drafts. Jonathan Haupt is the kind of editor and publisher they supposedly don't make anymore. They don't, but somehow he's here, and it is my great good luck to be one of his authors.

Pat Conroy was the kind of mentor they never made, especially out of writers. His generosity to new authors was as heroic as it was unique. I have never encountered or even heard of another famous, best selling author who did what he did for fellow writers. He loved to discover literary potential in others and then encourage it to fulfillment. In his last years, he founded Story River Books so he could have a way to offer publication to those authors he discovered. In a publishing climate that has become almost impossible for all but the most commercially successful authors, this was a godsend to all of us who had a home with his imprint. And after he was a mentor, editor, publisher, and writer of forewords for us, he then became our champion promoter. Knowing that his name and fame would always draw a crowd, he put that at our service by accompanying us to book signings, literary festivals, panel discussions, and any event that would help bring attention to a new book by an unknown author. What is truly remarkable is how much he enjoyed doing all that he did for others. His death is a body blow to all the writers who were part of his mission. And for me, it is an irreplaceable loss of his unconditional love, unstinting support, and ceaseless cheering, not to mention the sheer joy of his company and the great gift of his conversation. The world won't be the same without him in it, and my life won't be either.

Finally, I would like to thank Brandon, who leaves the house before I get out of bed, examines complicated patients with rare and terrible diseases for at least eight hours a day, comes home with a smile for the children, waters the plants, and lights the grill to cook dinner while I'm in the study hunched over the computer trying to decide whether to use a comma or semicolon in that sentence, as if the fate of the world depends on my decision. Without him, I couldn't do that.